Fertility Pirates

I0633919

LYNN DONOVAN

ISBN: 0692573852
ISBN-13: 978-0692573853

A humanitarian project six hundred lightyears from home, how could they know it was a corrupt mission?

Fertility Pirates

The Abraham Project Series - Book v 1

© 2015 Lynn Donovan

Cover Design Copyright © 2015 Cora Graphics

Acknowledgements

As always, I thank God, first and foremost, for His unconditional love, mercy, and grace. Without whom I would not be able to write, or live, or breathe. You amaze me every day and I thank you from the bottom of my heart. May this book be for your glory and bless those whom you would bless.

Second, I thank all those who have been there for me during this writing. Beta readers, critique group members, and proofreaders. Among them, especially, I thank Aaron DeMott, Kessie Carrol, Emerald Barnes, Jeanette Mbewe, and my wonderful friend and grammarian, Cyndi Rule. You all rock and I could not do this without you!

Third, thank you, William (my youngest son) for staging and choreographing the martial arts scene. Play acting with you was fun and SO VERY helpful. Your knowledge is invaluable to me, I couldn't have done it without you.

Fourth, I thank **you, the reader**, without you, I would not be able to continue to do this thing called writing and publishing. You make me what I am, a published author, and I thank you! Although I write for an audience of one (God), I pray I continue to please your reading palates and you will continue to be blessed and entertained by what comes out of my feeble little brain.

Last, (but, as they say, not least) I thank my wonderful, faithful husband. All I need is the air that I breathe...to quote a really accurate song... and to love you. Your love sustains me and I can't imagine life without you. You are my number-one fan and I appreciate all your feedback, brain-blocking discussions, and wonderful suggestions that make my stories better than they would have been. I appreciate you so much.

'For I know the plans I have for you,' declares the Lord, 'plans to prosper you and not to harm you, plans to give you hope and a future.' Jeremiah 29:11

PROLOGUE

Zulu Date, 16.08.2211
Sector: Deneb of Cygnus, Planet-Omicron

This was unprecedented. Not one single person had been allowed to return to Earth, until today. Kita Jacobsen chewed at her index-finger cuticle as she swung her right leg violently. A dozen most uncomfortable metal chairs without arm rests, hardly suitable for a mother cradling a baby, provided the only seating around the perimeter of the cryogenic-hibernation pods. Ignoring the increasing ache in her right arm, she focused on the automated attendants' preparations. They seemed much more hurried then last time.

Pastor Oliver Pugh, a young man in his thirties who looked older by his refusal to receive hair treatments, had promised her she and the baby would be safe.

"It's what's best for everybody, I assure you," he had said with such confidence she believed him, but something deep in her gut told her he meant something else.

The baby, to be christened Michael Levi Jacobson, fought sleep while sucking on a make-do pacifier, which was nothing more than the top of a baby bottle, stuffed with soft fabric bandages and secured with lab tape. She had had no opportunity to grab the baby's supplies when Pastor Oliver tapped just his fingernails against her door late last night. Michael wouldn't need anything for the next three years while in his cryogenic stasis, so, instead of being difficult with Pastor O, she resolved to simply start over when she got home.

Tender words, which usually soothed his fretting, had no effect to calm him now. Anxious tears muddled her gentle cooing. Did he sense her anguish? A mere two weeks after his birth, this was the first time he had been denied a feeding, but the cryogenic procedure required his system be void of any foods, liquid or solid, just like his mother. So nursing was out of the question.

Pastor O paced at a distance, outside of the pod chamber, giving her privacy with her son, or was he keeping watch for those who might realize she was leaving? He smiled at her often through the transparent partition, but his eyes and crinkled brow exposed a different emotion. The knotting in her stomach confirmed his deception, or was it the cleansing procedure she had endured. Even his close-held thumbs-up gesture did little to comfort her.

A shrill bolt of fear shot through her nerves. Swallowing and closing her eyes, she turned her head toward the cryo-pods. Pastor O knows what he's doing, sending her home. Keeping Michael would upset the order of things. She wouldn't be the cause of such upheaval in the system. If only this part was finished and she was resting peacefully in her cryogenic capsule with Michael.

What if she was caught leaving? Would she be sent back to the planet? Would Michael be lost to her, forever? Then what—the colonies? A shiver

3

rippled down her spine. Shaking her head as if she were telling the shivering sensation, "Go away," she forced herself to not think about that. She trusted Pastor O. She trusted God. She and her baby would be fine.

In a very short time, she would sleep for what would seem like seconds, and then she'd open her eyes on her home planet and be surrounded by Mom, and Dad, and Molly.

Kita crossed her right arm over Michael and gnawed at another fingernail. This action served two purposes. It shielded him from the frenzied activity going on around them, and it availed her already raw cuticle to be further chewed, a nervous habit she had never out grown.

Eighteen of the twenty cryogenic hibernation pods, lining the circular room like dominos set ready to be toppled in a concentric design, were frosted over, already occupied, headed for other planets along the way. One was open, waiting for the emergency-scheduled passenger heading to Earth, Kita and child.

Glancing at her baby's sweet, velvety face, she reached for another of the tissues supplied for her needs and blew her nose. She had to be strong, for Michael's sake. Pulling another tissue, she swabbed her wounded finger and wrapped a make-shift bandage around each of the offended fingers.

She smiled as she smoothed down a tuft of silver hair which poked out from her baby's swaddled wrap. The soft rose-petal feel of him stirred a maternal consciousness so strong, it still amazed her today. Was she doing the right thing taking him home? Would he be accepted on Earth?

Here on Omicron his wolfish appearance was widely accepted as normal. The Omicronians who were half human, half silver wolf carried this genetic appearance. All of the fertility-assisted children bore half of the Earth donors' DNA, which increased their human aspects, but they all retained the dominant silver wolf mane and a short, velvety layer of light grey fur. It served them well as a sunscreen under the harsh dual suns. The only variation from a human face otherwise, was noticeable once they were older, a year or so, when they opened their mouths and a wide canine maw and sharp teeth were exposed.

Michael was no exception, but Kita loved him with every fiber of her being. From the moment she felt him flutter in her abdomen, she knew she loved him with all her heart. She also knew the surrogate pregnancy was a mistake. At least, it was a mistake for her. Giving this child up would not be a viable option. Her heart couldn't let go. Even when he was born, and she took in his canine resemblance with his blue-like-hers eyes, it had little deterrence on her emotional link to the baby, her son. She loved him so much.

She prayed her family would help her protect him from any inappropriate attitudes. Surely, by now people on Earth had become accustomed to intergalactic differences. It had been made law more than a century back to accept all peoples' differences, be it appearances or preferences. Everyone was entitled to fair and equal treatment.

So many questions still rattled around in her head, but Michael's safety was her utmost priority. If Pastor Oliver couldn't have guaranteed his safety, she would have stayed. Knowing it meant she would have to give him to the waiting surrogate parents. Her love for him was so great, she'd sacrifice raising him if it ensured his safety.

The leaders of the project were adamant, surrogates were not allowed to renege. It was the "supreme sacrifice" of the mission and nothing could *disrupt the continuity of The Abraham Project.* Austin Abraham had made that very clear. Perhaps she wasn't cut out to fulfill that supreme missionary attitude after all.

Thank God for Pastor Oliver's silent disagreement. He felt Kita had the right to refuse and it was he who had contacted Gordon, an IT guy, who sympathized with the pastor and had access to the communication system to secretly hail the intergalactic ship back to Omicron. All she had to do was keep hidden for a few weeks after Michael's birth.

Last night, Pastor Oliver whisked her and Michael to the shuttle and escorted her to the waiting spaceship hidden behind the third moon.

A mechanical attendant pressed in close to her face, drawing her out of the reverie, and swiped her forehead. Instinctively, she tightened her hold on Michael. Her heart pounded against her eardrums, distorting the almost human voice. It was the same attendant who had instructed her to release Michael while she underwent the cleansing.

"Yes, yes, I understand," she had snapped in response to the insistent machine with a human-like appearance. "I will not let go of my baby. You can perform the procedure while I hold him."

She remained defiant with obstinate glares. "He stays with me," she had said through clinched teeth.

The attendant clicked and squawked, apparently addressing another machine, and then turned back to her. "You may keep the child with you, Kita Jacobsen."

Michael had received the same cleansing, though scaled back. His liquid diet of mother's milk did not leave much waste in his digestive tract to purge. She understood the vital importance to be free of any solids in their systems, still, it was not a pleasant experience.

Finally, she, with her baby in her arms, was escorted by the mechanical assistant to the open pod. Pastor Oliver rushed in and offered his left hand, a gallant gesture of assistance, or was he hurrying her along? She accepted the steadying proffer as she stepped up on the lip of the vertical egg-like structure, and leaned back against the cushioned padding. Michael snuggled into her warmth at her right side.

"You're absolutely sure?" She held the pastor's gaze with concerned focus. "Michael will be all right?"

"Miss Jacobsen, I'm so sorry—" He cleared his throat, his tone hurried. He glanced over his shoulder, fear tightened his face as he drew in a deep, resolute breath. A large hand gripped his shoulder and the pastor stepped back.

Dr. Stork's neglected teeth, exposed by a broad, exaggerated smile gave his over-indulgent face an ominous appearance, as Pastor Oliver receded behind his superior.

"I assure you," Dr. Stork continued his mottled Cheshire-cat grin as he twisted a valve on her IV line. "You and the child will be fine. You'll arrive perfectly preserved as you are now. We anticipate no complications." The Doctor glanced at the retreating pastor and continued. "I have seen to your medical file myself and promise you the healers on Earth will know *exactly* what to do for you when you arrive."

Was this reality, or were the pre-hibernation drugs causing hallucinations? A pins-and-needles sensation radiated through her limbs. She tightened her hold on Michael. "Um, thank you, Doctor."

New tears sprang to her eyes. Could she trust what she was hearing and seeing?

"And..." He turned away, but she shoved a dead arm toward him to draw him back. "Thank you...for helping me." Her words seemed slurred. She turned her head to try to focus her vision from the corner of her eye. "...helpin' me keeb Mighel... and fur ledding us...gaw home."

He tenderly patted her left forearm. "Of course, my dear. Your return will be best for everybody concerned."

Why did everybody keep saying that? She tried to smile, but wasn't sure her face responded, as she watched the attendant administer a syringe into her IV tube. A soft hum grew to a loud buzz in her ears. Perhaps she had mistaken Dr. Stork's true intentions with the project. Perhaps, he wasn't such a tyrant to the cause, after all. Before she could allow these new thoughts a place to settle somewhere in her mind, she heard a distant mechanical voice.

"Just relax, Kita Jacobsen," the attendant coaxed. It paused over Michael's IV tube, and leaned in close to her face, obstructing her peripheral view of her baby. "Count backwards, Kita Jacobsen, from one-hundred. You will go to sleep, now, Kita Jacobsen."

Concern filled her heart. Dr. Stork had promised Michael'd be all right. She was beyond the point of return. She had to trust God, Pastor Oliver, and Dr. Stork. Her eyelids, too heavy to remain open, drew closed. She pulled Michael in close to her side, at least, she hoped that was what she did, her arms were so numb now. She could feel the sedation's pull on her conscience.

The attendants continued to work like hummingbirds around her pod, flitting from one task to another.

She swallowed hard, licked at her drying lips, and considered asking for some lip balm. She couldn't move her head to look at Michael, but trusted he was still safely tucked at her side. "One-hunred…" Her tongue felt numb. "Niney-nine…" Her body seemed to float above the cushioned padding. Each blink required great effort to force her eyes open again, still she glanced over at the Doctor and Pastor. "Niney-eh…"

Wait! Was that Michael in Dr. Stork's arms?

All went black.

CHAPTER ONE

Earth - Three years later…

Molly Jacobsen's sister wasn't supposed to come back to Earth—ever.

Yet, here Molly was, rushing through the crowded Denver Region Interplanetary Transportation Station to bring her sister home. Her parents and several friends waited at home for the two of them to arrive. Mom had planned the party for weeks, a party to beat all celebrations in the Jacobsen home—to date.

The telecom, sent to Earth once the interplanetary ship was within satellite range, had said Kita would need help when she arrived. But why? Authored by Pastor Oliver Pugh, who served as the Site Pastor on Omicron, it could be trusted. But why had he been so cryptic.

When Kita left, seven years ago, she had been a strong, vibrant woman of twenty. Finishing two marathons that year, nothing was beyond her abilities, and her spirituality exceeded most people her age. It certainly exceeded Molly's. A second cryogenic transportation was unheard of, at least local medical knowledge had deemed it dangerous after so short an interval. Was that why Kita would need help? How much damage would the second three-year stasis cause? What was so much more important six-hundred lightyears from Earth to risk her sister's well-being like this? That project leader, Mr. Austin Abraham, had a lot of explaining.

"Molly Jacobsen," her name squawked across the mass communication system. Every person in the T-station heard it through overhead iComm speakers in their individual language. The linguistic software technology at the intergalactic station was quite impressive, even to an experienced law enforcer who has witnessed all types of modern technology. Yet, the quality of the speaker still sounded like a damaged subwoofer. "Report to…gabardine info_mation kiosk."

Molly reached up behind her right ear to press an implanted iComm device. The message linked and repeated in her hearing. Chewing on the inside of her cheek, she pondered, *Gabardine information kiosk?* She looked around for something—anything, that had any resemblance to what gabardine might be. Frustration and fear roiled in her gut. The iComm-translation software missed the mark for the word, "information." Perhaps it missed translating the color by calling it *gabardine*. Was that green? Grey? Greenish-brown? Who knew? It made no sense. She did not need this. She needed clear instructions, "Your sister is located here, come get her."

Molly half ran, half walked through the T-Station, although running in public was considered improper social etiquette, like elbows on the table while eating, and as a law enforcer, social etiquette was mandatory.

Fear for what she would find when she got to her sister lingered in her thoughts. The math hardly added up. Kita had been gone seven years, that meant she was on the planet ten months, maybe eleven, before the decision had been made to send her back. Nobody ever returned from these things. It was a life-long commitment from the beginning. So, why Kita? What went wrong? Molly swallowed the bitter bile edging onto the back of her tongue. This had to be bad, really, really bad.

Kita was their parents' blond-haired girly-girl, Molly, the red-haired tom-boy. But, deep down, Kita had always been the braver of the two. Still. Molly swallowed, even though her mouth had become too dry to produce saliva. She pushed herself to walk faster. Was it possible Kita had simply changed her mind? Molly rolled her shoulders and neck while trying to keep her eyes on the crowd she maneuvered through. Should she flash her legal-enforcer badge to assume Priority Passage? No, that would get her nothing but back in the boss's office—Priority Suspended.

Anger, fear, and frustration stewed in her gut. This pilgrimage had made her mad from the get-go. She knew her sister would leave the minute she started talking about it, regardless of how the rest of her family felt. It was so like her.

Molly was all for helping the underdog, the helpless innocents, the oppressed. That's why she had joined law enforcement. And, sure, Jesus said, "Go and deliver the good news," but to trek across the universe, for people who needed help with *fertility* at the expense of her own family, no way! Not to mention forever leaving her twin—

Kita! Be all right! Molly stretched out her twin-senses but detected nothing. Her stomach knotted as her eyes darted from machine to machine, nothing resembled a gabardine kiosk. She stopped.

People rushed past her. Someone accidentally clipped her shoulder, causing her to stumble forward. Reaching up to touch her iComm link, a woman with bright blue hair and orange vertically dilated goat-like eyes, who had been walking toward Molly, collided into her extended elbow. A soul-signature surge of silver, unlike any human, pulsed around the woman's body.

"Uhhh!" Molly staggered backward and closed her eyes. She turned to apologize, but the woman flashed an angry orange look, moving quickly on her way. Like most travelers, she was in too big of a hurry to be cordial.

Molly reached up to touch the iComm link again. "Locate Map, Denver Region Interplanetary T-Station."

A map of the entire station appeared in her private visual range. All five levels were visible in touchable layers. "Locate—Gabardine Information Kiosk." The layers shuffled, a green light glowed on level one. Molly's eyes swept the map for her red mark. It was a personal, "You are here," that appeared on any locator accessed through the iImplant software. She was on level three.

"Show. Shortest—Undo, fastest route." A blue line appeared as if it were being projected on the floor, but only she could see it, leading her to a transfer lift to her right. She hurried and stood before the arch.

"Level one," she announced. A thin, red beam swept down her face, and then a green light flashed at the apex of the arch. She stepped through the lift and emerged on level one. Glancing around to get her bearings, she followed the blue line, constantly stretching out her senses for her twin. Why couldn't she *feel* her? As soon as they revived Kita from the stasis, Molly should have been able to sense her presence. What was wrong?

Mom and Dad had maximumly supported Kita's decision to take the pilgrimage. Of course they would. A pastor and his wife always support a missionary spirit. But this initiative was different. The entire family had to endure a six-month therapy regimen. Regardless of your certitude, it wasn't easy to let go of a family member—forever. The distance and hibernation cryogenics simply did not allow for return visits. Their only hope lay in future improvements to communications between interplanetary regions and-or improved transportation methods. But for now, it was a one-way trip—supposedly.

Since word came of Kita's return, Mom hadn't stopped crying "happy tears." She began immediately planning the homecoming party. For Molly, an array of emotions between joy and terror filled her heart and hadn't left. Something had to be wrong. Seriously wrong. That much she could *feel*. Now, whether it was what her mother called her gift of discernment, gut instincts, or twin senses, she couldn't decide.

Stepping in front of the dirty green-grey kiosk, she panted, "I'm…Molly…Jacobsen."

The black screen crackled and lit up. A simulated headshot filled the screen of an ancient computer pioneer, Steven Jobs, in a dark, high collar modern-day suit. His eyes seemed to find Molly's before he spoke.

"Molly Jacobsen?" The simulated Mr. Jobs smiled as if he recognized her.

"Y-yes," she said, trying not to blink against the Identification Recognition Scan sweeping her face. The results scrolled across the bottom of the screen, including her social identification and employment, "IRS-Confirmed, SID 932 27 T562 . Molly Nicole Jacobsen . CS-4 Legal Enforcer"

"Your presence is required at docking station J-two-nine-eleven. Please wait while I generate your Entrance Permission," simulated Mr. Jobs said.

Right. While the machine whirled and churned, Molly stared at the placard bearing the name sake, "Steven Jobs Memorial Information System." Chewing on the inside of her cheek and shifting her weight. There was nothing else to do but wait and read the front of the kiosk. Her eyes almost involuntarily roved over the biography of Mr. Jobs.

"Steven Jobs experimented with different pursuits before starting Apple Computers with Steve Wozniak in cir. 1976. Apple's revolutionary products, which include the iPod, iPhone, iPad, iWatch, and iComm are now seen as dictating the evolution of modern technology…"

Molly snorted a chuckle. Revolutionary products? The Apple iProducts were so antiquated, children studied about them in World History. Nowadays, technology was integrated into a person's physiology, not in a device. Still it did bear the iconic name iComm to this day.

At last, a red, rigid film squeezed out a slot below the SJM placard. Molly held it up to read. A poorly etched picture of her as she had stood before the kiosk being scanned for the ID confirmation, and the words, *Entrance Permission,* was printed in black. Below that, were fourteen numbers, *24.08.2214 11:23:17*—today's date and time.

Simulated Mr. Jobs continued, "Directions have been transmitted to your locator for your convenience. May I be of further assistance, Molly Jacobsen?"

A red blinking pin-point of light in her right peripheral indicated she had received the transmission. She tucked a thick strand of auburn hair behind her right ear and activated the locator. The blue line appeared, guiding her to the designated location. She took a step away, but then turned back to the Kiosk and leaned in toward the screen, as if she were speaking through a partially opened window. "No—um, thank you."

"Thank you for using the SJM Information System." It responded with too much exuberance.

Adrenaline surged through her arteries. Her heart doubled its pace. She scurried as quickly as she could maneuver between the mass of travelers. Docking station J-two-nine-eleven wasn't far from the Jobs' kiosk, but she had to pass through two security stations and one decontamination booth.

As she approached the first station, she groaned. People were woven back and forth through a system of polls and scratchy jute rope to efficiently move them forward without causing long, unmanageable lines down the corridor. This line moved continuously, as the security clerks merely verified each one possessed an Entrance Permission, but the line was longer than Disney Planet's latest, most favored amusement ride ever.

The second station was a whole other matter. Because she had no luggage, briefcase, or handbag, and was obviously not a traveler, plus, the Entrance Permission had been printed moments before, her pass was scrutinized as a potential forgery and she as a potential terrorist.

Pulling her out of line, they processed all the other people. Finally, they demanded she empty her pockets, which included her Enforcer Badge, so she paused slightly, making sure the front of the badge was visible, before placing it in the security tub. The badge did not impress any of the mechanical attendants, in fact it was regarded with indignation. "Your legal status cannot assist you in this matter, Molly Jacobsen."

The mechanical clerk pushed her hand holding the badge down toward the tub. Who knew these automated clerks were programed to be snarky?

Besides, she didn't intend to use her law enforcer badge to hurry the process along. After all, it was *they* who insisted she empty her pockets. Was it truly *her fault* the badge was among the items contained in her clothing? She never wore a purse, or a shoulder bag. Her pockets housed all the things she needed to carry, even while on duty. It was more convenient and easier to maneuver when spontaneity was required without having a purse to throw down, or strap down, or whatever. Besides, if her enforcer status would have been helpful to hurry things along, it would have been activated when the iComm link scan indicated she was a level CS-4 legal enforcer.

She then was subjected to two, not one, but two body scans. After the electronic sweep, which produced no hits, a manual inspection, from head to toe, was performed much rougher than necessary. The pat-down was just rude and invasive. She shifted her weight from one foot to the other. This was harassment. She considered a defensive protest as she crammed her belongings back into her pockets.

Finally, she was allowed to move forward to the next checkpoint. Lord only knew what she'd have to endure there. Her imagination churned up images of herself standing, arms and legs spread wide, disrobed, and being scrubbed down by robots in pale-green haz-mat jumpsuits and dark lensed goggles with long-handled wire brushes and anti-everything soap.

As it was, the soft spoken, third station's attendant asked her to step into a four foot by four foot vestibule where a white mist passed down over her, like a thick fog coming from the mountain tops. A green illumination in the mist indicated she was cleared to exit the opposite side. The haze puffed out with her when the door opened, as if she were escorted by an apparition. This was the decontamination process? Nothing like she anticipated. She wanted to apologize to this third station attendant for being so agitated, but once on the other side, all she could do was stare at the attendant through the glass enclosure. She held up her hand, and gave a slight wave, to say thank you. The mechanical being nodded slightly. Perhaps communication had been achieved after all.

Now, she could go to the docking station and find her sister. She skipped sideways as she pulled her gaze from the attendant and faced the corridor.

"Tack protocol," she cursed. Let them try and stop her from running now. It would get her a reprimand from the chief. Conduct Unbecoming an Enforcer. But who cared! Her sister needed her, and she needed to find out what was wrong! She sprinted to Docking Station J-two-nine-eleven.

A uniformed attendant of nondescript gender stood behind a metal and glass pedestal. Molly rushed to the *WAIT HERE* line and shifted her weight as if she were needing a relief station. A green light appeared in her right peripheral. The attendant lifted its face toward her. Molly blinked against the quick ID Recog Scan.

"Molly Jacobsen?" the attendant confirmed.

"Yes." Impatience crawled all over her, like a cluster of spiders running from smoke, but she had to keep calm.

Fluid down, Mol! A slight smile tugged her mouth as she thought of her grandmother. She would have said, "Cool it, girl!"

"Oh Grams, nobody says 'cool it' any more, it's 'fluid down' now." Molly fondly remembered correcting her ancient grandmother.

Molly's eyes darted from the attendant to the heavy metal doors to her right. Kita should come through those doors any minute in a wheel chair, or walking on her own. Molly wasn't sure what she'd see. She still couldn't sense her twin?

"Can you tell me anything about my sister?" she asked just for good measure.

The attendant touched the air. It was accessing its own information screen.

"Kita Jacobsen…is in route."

Every fiber in Molly's being jumped when the heavy metal doors broke open. She closed her eyes for a second to steady her nerves. An older man, a grandfatherly type, in a white lab coat stepped through. What hair he had on his head was mottled grey and white. He scanned the waiting area, touched behind his ear, and zeroed in on her.

Molly swallowed and watched the man approach. She was frozen in place.

"Officer Jacobsen," he confirmed.

"Yes." She squeezed the word out of her constricting throat. Suddenly, tears stung her eyes. Fear, relief, anxiety—all three fought for their place in her conscious mind.

"Can we sit?" The man gently guided her elbow.

Molly nodded. Not so gracefully, she collapsed in the chair. Her nerves were shot.

"Miss Jacobsen, we think your sister has suffered a...cognitive cessation."

Molly tilted her head as her right eyebrow shot up. "A what?"

"Well, we're not sure, yet. We don't know exactly what has happened. Your sister arrived here in cyber-hibernation, as you know. When we reversed the stasis, she—" he looked down as if he were searching for something on the floor "—became hysterical."

"Hysterical?" Molly struggled to understand. Why was everybody being so cryptic?

"Yes, she's conscious, but heavily sedated. I—I wanted you to know before we transfer her to the healing facility."

"Healing facility!" Molly repeated, dumbfounded. She sent out a quick twin-search. Nothing. "But our mother..."

The healer's attention suddenly focused on Molly's face. "Are-are you all right, Miss Jacobsen? You look pale."

"Um, yes, I—it's just that, she's my twin. But I can't *feel* her." Could he possibly understand?

"Ah, yes, well she's heavily sedated, as I said. We hope to learn more when we get her to the healing facility."

"Will you be attending her...healing?"

"Yes, forgive me, I'm Dr. Polaris." He bowed his head slightly. The ancient ritual of shaking hands had long since been discouraged. It had simply gone out of style. It still felt awkward to Molly not to shake a person's hand. Her grandmother was a stickler for manners. Dogmatically, she had taken this ritual to her grave.

"Dr. Polaris? Well—thank you, Doctor," she stammered.

"There—there's one other thing." The doctor ran his hand through his hair on the back of his head like he was trying to rub something irritating his scalp.

Molly stared at him until he looked back into her eyes.

"She—your sister has attached herself to—I don't know how to explain this…"

"Just say it, Doctor," Molly snarled.

"Well," he continued to worry the spot on his head, "she clings…to a—" he swallowed hard and lifted a cold, hard stare directly into her eyes "—a doll."

"What?"

"A doll, Miss Jacobsen, your sister clings to a child's doll—insists it's her…her son."

CHAPTER TWO

Molly stared at the shiny circle of pink scalp skirted by soft white and grey hair as Dr. Polaris walked toward the metal doors from which he had entered her confused and frustrated world. Who is this man? She shoved an aggressive strand of auburn hair behind her ear and touched the iComm link to mentally access the Legal Enforcer's Civilian database, *Search, Doctor Polaris*.

Information scrolled in green letters at her lower visual range. "Dr. Norton S. Polaris, PhD, Psy. SID 874 57 T974..." She gasped when she saw the "T" in his social identification number.

"Doctor!" She walked quickly to catch up with him. "You're a...a twin?"

"Yes, I was. Let's hope *your* connection will help bring yours back." Sadness permeated his eyes.

"But—she's already back."

"Not entirely." He slipped through the metal barriers and was gone.

Molly stared at the cold, impersonal doors. "… PhD, Psy," she re-read his credentials. He's a Psychologist. Not a medical doctor. Molly slumped into a seat.

"What's wrong with my sister?" She reached out with her "gift," against her own moral code, and searched deep into his emotions.

Isolation. Twins don't feel isolation, unless—his twin was not—what—alive?

She reached out again, but not as deep. *Concern. Confusion. Kita.* He was worried about Kita and he acknowledged the twin connection, but… something else. She couldn't quite distinguish—

Agitation forced her up. She shook out her limbs as if she were about to run, but paced instead. The uniformed attendant's eyes followed her, even though its head never rose from the standby posture. It was unusual for anyone to physically exhibit such impatience. The bot stood ready to make a security alert if she should become too animated.

Glancing to her right lower peripheral, light green numbers perpetually glowed the twenty-four hour time, 13:47.

It's been an hour. Geez!

Interplanetary travel had begun over the last decade, to the degree that it was common now. Passengers of different cosmic origins along with Earth ethnicities shuffled past her sister's empty arrival station. Molly still found the differences fascinating. Some were tall and slender. Others were short and broad. Some were multi-colored, while others were mono-hued. Some had markings like cheetah spots, others had stripes. They all moved as one herd toward their departure station. Their general emotion was so strongly unified, she sensed one large numb reprise.

These were business assignees, not one of them traveled for fun. Apparently, the thrill of traveling had been lost long ago by repetitious blasting into Faster-Than-Light travel to peddle their wares, attend their meetings, gather information, and appease the bosses.

The room swirled and tilted, and Molly staggered to a stop. *Kita!* Her knees weakened, and she fought to stay upright. She collapsed into a chair. A buzzing sound filled her ears, drowning out the travelers.

She pushed out to sense her sister. The spinning reversed directions then tilted and reversed again. It was like being on the Twirling-Tilt at the fair. Nausea swept over her, and bitter fluid touched the back of her tongue. Her arms drew up across each other as if she were desperately holding on to…something. She glanced down at her empty embrace. Tears pooled in her eyes and threatened to spill. She swiped at them with vehement desperation.

Shaking her head, she closed her eyes, reeling backward, mentally, to separate from the twin connection. Something solid banged against the heavy doors, bursting them open, and causing her body to jerk. A sheeted gurney shot through the gap. Two medical attendants guided the mobile stretcher into the waiting area. They were dressed identical to each other, white, high collar shirts, black belts, white slacks, and black, rubber soled shoes. Their uniform had an oriental combat look about it, although such practices had been outlawed decades ago. The only remnant of the ancient practice was its Korean Region dobok style and only in public service uniforms.

Molly eased herself up to stand. The swirling sensations nearly set her back down. Inwardly, she had to pull back further and completely cease her connection with Kita.

Once stabilized, Molly took a deep breath and stepped over to the gurney. Kita's sunny highlights had faded to dull, ash-brown, damp lumps that clung to her like leeches strung across her pale face. Her eyes rolled around under heavy lids. Shiny tracks dampened her cheeks. Was it tears or residual chemicals from the Cryogenics? Even her once brilliant freckles were bleached out in her pallor condition.

A lump under her sister's sheet did not escape Molly's sharp, ever-monitoring eyes. The doll? Molly's heart broke as she wrapped her arms around herself, clinging to the imaginary something her twin-symbiotic conduit had seemingly placed in her grasp and watched her sister's gurney float by. How broken was Kita's mind?

"Maulry," Kita mumbled.

Molly's senses returned to her twin. Could she filter the confusion and help bring her sister back, like Dr. Polaris had suggested? Something like a duo-psychological crutch? Kita was physically here, but her mind was far, far away. So, why did she need such heavy sedation?

Glancing up at the corpsmen, she explained her presence. "I'm her sister, Molly Jacobsen."

The Malibu-blond attendant nodded. He stood as tall as Molly, five foot, ten inches but more broad in the shoulders. Either he had spent a lot of intimate time with free weights or he was a more realistic replica of a body builder. Probably the latter, most subservient positions were bots. Only Legal Enforcers were one-hundred percent humans. Even today, artificial intelligence technology couldn't fully integrate the cognitive differentials necessary to appropriately handle a potentially illegal situation.

Bot or human, it was strangely onerous to distinguish the difference these days. Soon, it would be impossible. But, these corpsmen had to be bots, they were too similar in stature, like someone had picked all the five-foot-ten body builder models for this service, although they represented the typical diverse ethnicities of Earth humans.

Molly accepted the blond's nod as permission to follow.

Kita absently cooed toward the lump under her pristine sheet. Even in her heavily sedated sojourn, her focus was on comforting the doll. Molly blinked quickly and drew in a sharp breath. She would not allow tears. Not now. Not here.

Following the two corpsmen and the gurney to the transfer lift, she waited a step or two behind. The dark-haired, Asian-looking attendant announced, "Service Garage, Level one. Personnel, two—and..." The bot glanced at Molly. "Correction, Personnel, three—and patient." The four passed through to a cool, dim-lit garage. An emergency transportation vehicle hovered near the garage lift. A third coffee-brown skinned attendant jumped out of the driver's seat and sprinted toward the back of the vessel. He quickly opened the rear doors while the two guided the gurney into the vehicle and hopped in on either side.

"Okay. We will see you at Hope Memorial Healing Station," the driver said as he secured the doors, without actually looking at her.

"Wait!" Molly grabbed his sleeve before he rounded the vessel. "I can't ride with you?"

"No! You must secure your own transportation." He pulled himself out of her grasp as if he had been contaminated and hurried to the driver's seat.

"What? You're kidding! But, that's my—" she hollered at the departing vehicle "—sister!"

Slapping her pocket, her trembling fingers fumbled to grab her badge and waved it over her head. "I'm a legal enforcer…!"

The emergency vessel decreased in size and sound as it sped away. Eventually, she turned with an exasperated sigh. She'd never been in this underground garage. Nothing looked familiar. Activating the iComm device she requested, "Locate, Mass Trans Platform." The map glowed before her. She pinpointed the MTP, found her "You Are Here" red marker, refocused past the readout to the transfer lift, adjusted myopically back to the illuminated map, and bit her lip. It was a thirty-minute walk to the MTP. Running would get her in even more trouble, but at this point, what could it matter. She touched the virtual glowing MTP and called out, "Status." Red letters crawled along the bottom of her peripheral, "MASS TRANS SYSTEM OFFLINE – APPROXIMATE WAIT TIME, unknown."

Molly adjusted her vision back to the transfer lift. She fingered her LEP badge in her palm. Tentatively, stepped in front of the arch, squared her shoulders, and cleared her throat. She held up her badge to the laser scanner and announced, "Officer Molly Jacobsen, Emergency Transfer Protocol, ETP-57-562, Hope Memorial Healing Station, Urgent Care entrance."

She drew in air and held it while she waited. The moment that passed spanned time like a documentary about the planet's origins voiced over by a monotonous whispering Welch-region accent. At last, the green light illuminated, and she

jumped through the transfer lift before it, or she, or anybody else changed their minds.

Molly looked around and saw an Emergency Vehicle gliding through a portal. She ran through a set of automated doors and located the information desk. Panting, she tried to speak with calm reserve. "I'm Molly Jacobsen...my sister...Kita Jacobsen...is in that—" she pointed toward the vehicle bay "—emergency vessel."

The female admin's eyes met Molly's. A serene look of concern washed over its face. Molly blinked once, as the ID Recog Scan passed over her, and focused on settling her lungs.

"Yes, Molly Jacobsen, please have a seat in the waiting area, and the doctor will be with you after your sister's condition has been assessed." The admin bot smiled warmly.

"But, wait, I've already talked to the doctor. He-he knows who I am." She patted her chest as if that identified her connection and relieved the admin bot's concern for protocol. Molly leaned over the counter. "I *need* to be with my sister!"

She spoke too loud, another social faux pas, but it was beyond her control. Efforts to fluid down had failed. Her adrenaline had taken over.

Warmth left the attendant's face, but the curved, smiling lips remained in place. "Molly Jacobsen, please have a seat. The patient has to be registered and assessed before she can receive visitors. Surely you are aware of the protocol."

Heat flushed Molly's face. She broke eye contact first and looked over at the sterile, multi-chaired room. Tucking her lips in on themselves, she slowly walked over to the designated area, took a deep breath, and flopped down, hard. A quick twin search brought back swirling, sleepy sensations. She instantly blocked them and folded her arms across her stomach. An involuntary huff escaped her lips as her eyes fixated on the now inactive admin. Angry glares left unfulfilled satisfaction when the receiver remained dormant.

A trilling, familiar ring sounded in her iComm link. At her peripheral, the word *Mom* glowed in blue letters. She touched the device. "Hello, Mother."

Molly explained why she and Kita were not at their house yet and updated her with what little she knew, sans the doll detail, quickly assuring her mom she would let her know when Kita could be seen.

"No reason to come up here 'til then, Momma. Really." The last thing she wanted or needed was her mother's additional high-strung emotions.

An average built man in dark dress pants, a soft green button-down shirt, and a long white lab coat approached Molly. His grey eyes were anything but average—serious, yet seductive. Did this man have any idea how gorgeous he was? Molly stood almost at attention.

"Mom, I've gotta go," she said without taking her eyes off the approaching Adonis.

An expression washed over his face, a scowl of sorts. Did he disapprove her phone conversation, or was it what he had found when he examined her sister?

"I'll let you know the minute I know something, okay?" She disconnected before her mother could protest.

"Miss Jacobsen?" the man stated. The name tag above his pocket read, "Dr. A. Abraham, MD."

"Yes." Her eyes dropped to the name tag a second time, as one eyebrow shot up. *Abraham?*

His scowl was replaced by a placid professional demeanor. "I'm Dr. Abraham. I'll be attending your sister's healing." A routine statement for a routine greeting, but this would not be a routine encounter.

Molly cut to the chase. "You're not related to Mr. Austin Abraham of The Abraham Project on Omicron, are you?"

His chin rose slightly. A pronounced bulge in his jaw tightened as he appeared to be considering her question. "Well, yes—" his voice deepened "—he's my father. But about your sister—"

"That's interesting..." Molly folded her arms across her chest and glared at him. "What happened to Dr. Polaris, he said he would be my sister's healer?"

"Yes, well, I—" his eyebrows pressed together just before a facade, almost like a costume ball mask, transformed his face into a practiced, doctorly semblance of compassion "—is there a problem, Miss Jacobsen?"

"A problem?" Molly forced her back teeth apart. Was he serious? "Are you Austin Abraham's son?"

"Yes."

"Yeah," Molly paused, utilizing her interrogative skills to decipher his body language. "Have you read my sister's medical file?"

"Yes, of course, and I—"

"And you know that she is returning from *your father's* program. Like this. She's seriously messed uh—something went horribly wrong out there, Dr. Abraham. And now, here you are, her healer?"

A frown cracked his facade. "Miss Jacobsen, I assure you, I—"

"You assure me what, Dr. Abraham? That I can trust you?" Her eyes bore into his. "*Your* father assured us Kita would be safe. *Your* father assured us nothing bad would happen to her. Now, you want to *assure me* that you, of all people, will help with her...'cognitive cessation'...?" Molly scraped her teeth across her bottom lip to draw back the spit she had sprayed.

Abraham glanced over his shoulder. "Miss, I must ask you to calm down or—"

"Or what?" Molly quipped.

"Or, I may have to order you sedated as well."

Molly glared at him. Anger burned in her face and her gut. She drew in a long composing breath, and then slowly exhaled. Her behavior was far outside the realm of socially accepted behavior. This was going to get back to her Chief, and she was already in enough trouble. She had to fluid down.

Unclenching her fists, she stepped back one step, and relaxed her posture. A sigh escaped her lips along with the surrendering affirmation, "Okay."

Dr. Abraham's jaw went smooth and his voice softened into almost a confidential whisper, "Actually, my father and I are..." He looked away as his hand reached for his dark-brunette mane. His fingers disappeared into the mass of waves and then emerged as his hand reached the back of his head. Something permeated his grey eyes. Molly observed the transformation through a glaring squint. Was it utter sadness?

He cleared his throat. "I haven't interacted with my father for a very long time. We are not, shall I say, close, and to further answer your question, no, I haven't been involved with my father's project. I am the healer on duty here and have been assigned to Kita's case. Dr. Polaris and I will be closely monitoring your sister's recovery."

Molly stared at the doctor. Did she dare? She pushed her senses—*pain, neatly masked, but deeply felt.* What had happened between this man and his father? She also sensed, *loss.* He had lost someone close.

Molly pulled back. Naked exposure of a person's inner feelings was not always a *gift* in Molly's opinion. That was why she had made it her moral code not to *sense* anybody without their permission. And hardly anyone ever gave permission. Today, she'd broken that code, twice. Heat swept over her face. She looked away first.

Silence filled the void between them.

"Now," Abraham continued as he cleared his throat. "If you have a problem with that, then—"

The ER doors broke open with a sudden and loud banging sound as a nurse in maroon scrubs peeked through the opening. "Doctor? She's ready for transfer."

Dr. Abraham glanced at Molly and turned to address the nurse. "I'll be right there, Roxy." He turned back to Molly. "You want to accompany your sister to her room?"

"Of course." She shoved her animosity aside—for now. Should she call her mother? Biting her lip, she watched Kita's gurney, guided by the maroon clad nurse, float by.

Dr. Abraham gestured his consent for Molly to walk ahead of him. Her eyes trailed over his stature as she walked around him and followed Roxy and her heavily sedated sister.

Mom could wait a little bit longer.

CHAPTER THREE

Kita hummed a lullaby as she slowly rocked her baby. His soft, silver-haired crown brushed against the underside of her chin. With each rocking motion, she inhaled and exhaled, drawing in the scent of her baby, absorbing the full-sensory of this moment. A smile lifted the edges of her lips. This was even more wonderful than she ever imagined. Did Mom feel this way with us girls? *His silky soft silver-white hair, or was it fur, felt so soft to her touch. She couldn't get enough of him. Sleep gently beckoned her rest-deprived mind.*

Beep...beep...beep.

What is that? Kita tried to open her eyelids. They were too heavy. She listened closely. Beep... beep...beep.

What...is that? It was irritating. *That's going to wake my baby. Somebody make it stop!*

Beep…beep…beep.

Stop! Please stop making that noise!

"M'baby!" Kita mumbled.

"Kita, it's Molly."

"Maulry, makit stop."

"Honey, make what stop?"

"Thanoise, makit stop. It'll wake da baby."

"Oh, Kita—"

Was Molly crying? Kita slowly forced her eyelids apart. Tubes rose from her body. Rails framed her bed. She reached up to wipe her eyes, but her wrists were held down. Someone was holding her left hand. Fear surged from her gut and into her chest, like a tidal wave swamping a lifeboat. "Don't touch me!"

Someone stood over her. No, wait! She squinted and forced her eyes to focus. It looked like —

"Molly?" How could Molly be here?

"Kita. it's all right. You're in the healing station —" Molly squeezed her hand "—on Earth."

Kita's eyes darted from IV machine, to ceiling lights, to Molly's face and back again. She looked down the length of her body. She was…on Earth. Her baby was—

"My baby!" Kita fought against the restraints.

"Oh, honey, your baby isn't here." Molly gently pushed Kita's shoulders against the pillow.

"Isn't…here?" Kita collapsed under Molly's gentle press. "They promised!"

"No, he—he isn't here."

"Where is he? Molly, where is he?"

"Just rest."

Mom walked up to the bed. "Baby," she spoke softly, "it's going to be all right. You get some rest now. We're all here—with you. And…" Her tears spilled over her apple-red cheeks. She turned away and dabbed her face with an over-used tissue.

Kita watched her father gather her mother in his arms and guide her to the chair. Her mom whimpered, "Oh Levi, this is so—"

Dad patted her back. "Sarah, honey, I know. I know."

Molly's face hovered above Kita's. The twin beacon engulfed them both as Molly spoke softly. Warm sensations washed over Kita's body, releasing the anxiety. Her eyelids became heavy again. She resisted the sinking pull, but sleep had other ideas. Or was it the medications? She let Molly's voice lift her spirit and gently rock it into slumber. It felt good to *feel* Molly again. "Maulry," Kita mumbled.

"Shhh. Rest now," Molly soothed. "I'm not going anywhere."

Kita's consciousness floated down, down, down into a world of peace, happiness, and her baby's warmth. She inhaled deeply as the scent of Michael filled her senses once again. A lullaby gently escaped her lips, the rocking chair her metronome.

***

Dr. Abraham topped off his tepid coffee with steaming black brew, folded down into the break-room chair, and touched his iComm device. "Access patient file, number six, five, seven, three, eight." The file appeared virtually before him. He touched the air which caused layers to move only he could see. Squinting and turning his head to peer at the information from the corner of his eye, he sighed. Either the Healing Facility on Omicron had an odd way of recording patient data, or something wasn't right. He shook his head as he re-read the physician's remarks for who-only-knew how many times. The words, 'Baby Condition: Data Not Known,' chilled him to the bone. Yet, there was a Certificate of Death for a Baby Jacobsen. He shoved those documents aside and pulled up the recent information on his patient. Something was definitely wrong. Flipping back to the referring physician's files, he viewed a video.

"This can't be right!" he mumbled and slapped the transmission closed. Activating his iComm link, he commanded, "Call, Dwayne Friedman."

Tones and clicks sounded before his call was answered. "Deuce! How's it hang—"

"Dee Wayne, old pal," Deuce interrupted. The metal chair squeaked as he leaned back and crossed his legs.

"Oooo, that sounds like trouble. What's up?" Dwayne chuckled.

"Listen, I need your help."

"Uh, sure. What kinda help?"

"*Your* kinda help, buddy."

Dwayne drew a long slow breath and let it out just as slowly. "Okay, who you wanna hack into?"

"No hacking—exactly." Abraham walked to the panel of flat-screen computers, pulled a flash film from a drawer box, and inserted it in a slot on the side of the wafer thin machine. "Listen, this is important and confidential. Can you come to the Healing Station for coffee? I'm buying."

"Uh, sure, when?"

"Now?" Abraham's fingers tapped the virtual keyboard.

Dwayne paused, "Yeah, sure. Not like I got anything important—"

"You know, I wouldn't ask if it weren't—"

"I know, Deuce. I'll be there shortly," Dwayne sighed.

The film squeezed out from its slot. Abraham held it up to the light. "Thanks Dee. I'll owe you one."

"You already do my friend."

CHAPTER FOUR

"Two coffees, please," Dwayne said with a wink. The black-haired, black nailed teenager popped her gum, rolled her unnaturally vibrant aqua-blue eyes beneath black dusted eyelids, and stepped away to fill his order. Dwayne turned to scan the Healing Station's coffee shop. No Dr. Deuce. He reached for his iComm, "Message, Deuce, I'm here, big guy. Coffee's getting cold. Falling in love with gothic barista."

Ms. Gothic placed the two heat-preserving cups on the counter and popped her gum. "That'll be twenty credits, ...*sir*."

She had been taught the proper protocol of polite interaction, well at least she uttered the words. Dwayne leaned on one elbow across the counter. "It's on Doctor Austin Abraham's credit."

She popped her gum and lifted the scanner.

He blinked as the light flash over his eyeball.

"You fly, you buy," she said with an ornery grin that revealed a missing cuspid.

"Hey!" Dwayne frowned and lifted the two steaming cups.

"Dee!" Abraham patted his shoulder.

"Dr. Deuce!" Dwayne walked with Deuce to a table and chairs against the wall.

"How ya been?" Deuce took one of the cups and gingerly sipped its black liquid.

"Good, good. You?"

"Yeah, I've been okay."

"Hey, listen, I heard about your mom. I'm sorry man." Dwayne glanced at the barista. Eye contact with Deuce was too awkward.

"Yeah, it wasn't sudden though, she was ready to go. Really looked amazingly peaceful when she passed, so..." Abraham shrugged and watched the feet of a male nurse walk past their table. The mint green scrubs indicated cardiology. Awkward silence lingered between them. They sipped and watched people move around.

"So, what's it you need *my kinda help* with?" Dwayne cut the silence, curling his fingers in the air for quote marks.

Deuce pushed Dwayne's hands down and glanced around without moving his head. "Oh, nothing really, I just missed seeing ya, buddy. Hey, you want some gum?"

Deuce reached into his shirt pocket under his lab coat and pulled out a package of wintergreen chewing gum, handing a strip to Dwayne.

Dwayne looked at the gum and glanced up at Deuce. Deuce's left eyebrow rose. He'd seen that look before. The hair on Dwayne's neck rose slightly as he reached for the proffered gum. "Thanks, but I think I'll save it for later."

Deuce shrugged. "Suit yourself. Listen, it was great to see ya, but I've gotta get back to the ward. Got a reeeally interesting case." His eyes bulged slightly as he stood up. "You take care and"—he tapped behind his ear—"there, that should reimburse you for the coffees."

Deuce pressed his lips together in a straight line smile, but humor was not prevalent in his eyes.

Dwayne watched the doctor walk away. He patted his pocket with the chewing gum. What was Deuce up to?

***

Dwayne locked his garage-apartment door, sat in front of his personal external communication device, a flat black tablet, and pulled the gum wrapper from his shirt pocket. He gently removed the wrappings. "What have we here?"

He inserted the film from Deuce's gum wrapper into the input slot. Squinting to focus on the data glowing before him, he tapped his virtual key board. "Hmm."

Activating another program, he set it to run. Meanwhile, he rummaged through his films and pressed one into an additional input slot. *Tap tap tap.* He ran the program. His computer hummed as he stared at the virtual screen, clicked the keyboard, hit enter, and waited for the program to complete. The results glowed on his virtual screen.

"Oh, wow! Deuce, what have you gotten into now?"

***

Molly lifted her head and winced. *These chairs!* She rolled her head around from left shoulder to back, right shoulder to front, and straightened her back. Vertebrae after vertebrae cracked running up her spine, like the chasing lights of a theatre marquee.

"Michael…" Kita muttered.

Molly slid over to her sister's bedside. "Kita. It's Mol—"

Kita gasped as she tried to sit up straight in bed. The restraints tugged at her wrists and held her in the horizontal position. Molly reached out with her twin beacon to sooth her sister.

"Oh Molly!" Kita whined. Tears spilled down her temples, into her hair.

"What happened?" Molly pulled her chair closer to Kita's bed.

"I don't know, Mol." Kita swallowed. She seemed to struggle to put her thoughts together. Molly waited patiently. "I was so excited about this pilgrimage. I was determined to help those poor people. They were beautiful, too, Molly. It's as if they were a cross breed of human and silver wolf. Everybody on that planet looked like that. I can't imagine how or why.

"They have long silver fur on their head and a fine pelt on their face and body, otherwise, they look just like you or me." Kita's breath came quick as she spoke. "We were given options, we could donate our eggs, we could surrogate a baby, or we could do both. I thought I wanted to do both...it was encouraged to do both. It was a beautiful exchange."

Molly swallowed. "So, what happened?"

"I couldn't do it, Mol. When the baby I carried started moving inside me"—Kita hiccuped and swallowed agonizing tears—"I realized, this stuff is real, you know? I just couldn't do it."

She grabbed at Molly's wrist as best she could with the restraints holding her back. "I prayed with Pastor Oliver, from the moment I knew I couldn't go through with the surrogacy exchange. He told me it was all right. I had the right to...change my mind. He said he understood, and—Molly, he protected me. He and Lucy took me into their home after the baby was born. They took care of me until the transport arrived—"

Kita's words were drowned out by her tears. Molly held her hand, and her conscience, and let her cry. Finally, Kita continued. "They said Michael and I—that's his name, Molly, Michael Levi Jacobsen."

"After dad?" Molly ignored the hitch in her own voice.

"Yes." Kita's face brightened through her tear soaked smile.

"Anyway," Kita looked at the ceiling as if she were watching a video-stream. "Pastor Oliver said Michael and I would be perfectly fine, you know, traveling back to Earth. They said the cryo-suspension was safe, it would prevent him from growing so that when we got here, he'd still be two weeks old and I'd be like…the age I was when I left Omicron. How old are we now? I'm so confused."

"We're twenty-seven." Molly sniffed. "But, I guess you're still twenty-one. I don't know how that works."

"Twenty. Seven…" Kita repeated the number as if it were completely foreign to her thinking.

"So…" Molly prompted her sister.

"So, I got into the hibernation chamber with Michael and…" Kita's tears chased the other down the sides of her temples. "Dr. Stork pulled Pastor O away from me. I was so scared. I just knew he was going to send me back to the planet and force me to give Michael to the surrogate family. But he said any fertility program had to allow a birth mother to…to have a change of heart. And then I went to sleep. When I woke up, my baby was gone, and… and a doll was in his place. Oh Molly! What happened to my baby?" Kita sobbed without abandon.

Molly's twin beacon held Kita's emotions, and, although it hurt so deeply, the two cried as one.

"I love you, Mol—"

"I love you, Kiters."

Molly pressed her forehead against her twin's. She smelled something unfamiliar to Kita's usual musk, it was sweeter. Molly opened her eyes. Kita's gown was soaked with a creamy liquid. "Kita! What's—?"

Kita looked down, "Oh! My milk. I-I'm still lactating. I need to feed Mich—" Tears poured down the side of her eyes re-saturating the hair at her temples. Her whole body cried for her baby.

Molly stared at the growing wet circles on Kita's gown. How could this be Kita's imagination? Could she be having all these physical signs and *not* have a baby? If she could find Dr. Polaris, maybe he could explain. But not Abraham! She would need to get him reassigned. Her jaw bulged as her back teeth pressed together. No Austin Abraham would ever come near her sister again, if she had anything to do with it.

Molly touched the nurse's call button. Her sister's anguish was almost too much to bear, but she stood near and held Kita's hand. Molly knew Kita was not crazy. She had not had a mental breakdown. She was telling the truth. Something had happened to her nephew. She needed to find out what. She touched the button again.

CHAPTER FIVE

Molly sensed more than heard someone enter Kita's room. She lifted her head to see the two doctors draped in white lab coats, standing just inside the door. Neither one wore an expression Molly liked. She drew in a breath, wiped drool off the side of her chin, and straightened her achy back. Dr. Polaris' eyes stayed on Kita, but his hand gestured for Molly to come with them. She rose, glanced over at her mother sleeping on the little sofa and mouthed, "Her, too?"

Dr. Abraham nodded.

"Mom." Molly gently touched her mother's shoulder.

She jerked awake. "Is Kita all right?"

"Yes, the doctors want to see us." Molly glanced back at the door. They had already stepped out.

"Oh, okay." Her mother slipped on her canvas loafers, grated her fingers through limp blond hair, and followed Molly.

"Mrs. Jacobsen, Miss Jacobsen," Dr. Polaris began. "Let's go where we can sit down."

The two doctors guided them to an overflow room. Molly and her mother sat on one couch, the two doctors on the adjacent one. The benign walls were bare except for an iComm screen with local news and a running ticker of global news. The grey-green herringbone patterned couches were utilitarian, comfortable enough, but nothing you'd want in your own home. Molly thought of the gabardine information kiosk, it had been a similar hue. This seemed to be a standard color these days.

"We have examined your daughter," Dr. Polaris continued. "And we have read the medical report that accompanied her from Omicron."

Molly observed Dr. Abraham's stoic expression. She sensed something—*incongruence*.

She hated him for who he was, who his father was, what the project had done to Kita.

Dr. Polaris' voice commanded Molly's attention, "As you know, Kita was involved in a Fertility Assistance Project on a distant planet called Omicron. Apparently, this project included surrogacy pregnancies, of which your daughter agreed to participate. The medical report thoroughly documents the process, prenatal care, delivery, and there is a signed Affidavit of Agreement from Kita. Further, it states that Kita delivered a baby, but the child was, regretfully, still-born."

He drew in a deep breath, as if this statement took all the wind from his lungs and he was required to replenish them with one huge inhale. His wet, red-rimmed eyes met her mom's, who, in turn, smiled. Molly gritted her teeth. How could her mother buy any of this crap? Dr. Abraham never lowered his eyes and yet didn't exactly meet Molly's glare either. She sensed he was uncomfortable. Good!

"It states further that she suffered psychologically from the—" Dr. Polaris pushed out his lips. He chose his words carefully —"unexpected outcome, and…" He glanced at Dr. Abraham. "Well, we believe her level of disappointment affected her deeply. She developed an attachment to a child's doll in order to cope. The medical staff on Omicron did not have the expertise necessary to treat her, so, in her best interests, they opted to send her home."

Molly paid close attention to what he said, how he chose his words, somewhere in between was the whole truth. The elder doctor continued to disclose his diagnosis while Molly's skepticism continued to build. His eyes moved to Molly's, then returned to her mom's. Was he looking for understanding or agreement…or compliance? Molly felt none of these, except growing anger. It was not like Kita to be so weak minded. This was something entirely different.

Her mother laid a gentle hand on Molly's vibrating leg. A dull ache knotted in Molly's calf muscle. How long had she been bouncing her leg? She stretched out and crossed her ankles and arms. If she was interrogating herself right now, she'd note that she was closed off from accepting of Dr. Polaris's discussion. Surely he wasn't fooled either.

Ignoring the taste of blood in her mouth, she gnawed on the inside of her left cheek. It helped her keep her trap shut while she listened to this bogus report. At least gnawing on her cheek didn't agitate her mother.

"Now, Dr. Abraham and I have examined Kita. We've run a complete lab profile on her, and we find that she does, indeed exhibit physical evidence of being pregnant and delivering. There are some discrepancies in the lab reports, but we feel, in time, this too will be explained." He glanced at Abraham.

Molly noted Abraham's expression did not alter when Polaris glanced at him. If the psychologist was soliciting confirmation, he was getting neither yea nor nay. Anger percolated in Molly's gut. She sat up straight and leaned with her elbows on her knees. Her fingers intertwined as if she were praying. This was nonsense. A frozen cave man on the other side of the planet was discovered centuries ago, and his DNA was recovered and exploited for decades afterward.

Kita was cryogenically suspended with all the knowledge of modern medicine. There was no way her lab work here, on Earth, would render inaccurate results.

Would it?

Molly stared at Abraham, willing him to look at her. His eyes quickly glanced at her but just as quickly settled back in his neutral space in which he had been focused during this conference. Did his opinion differ? Why didn't he say anything?

"All we can do at this point," Dr. Polaris continued, "is help Kita through this grieving process. Physically, she's fine. Since she was suspended, her body still needs to heal from the birthing experience. But it shouldn't take more than four to six weeks for that process to be complete." He paused again.

"The other healing process may take longer"— he looked straight at Molly—"I'm counting on your twin connection to be a guide for her recovery, Molly." His smile was weak and waned quickly.

"All right?" Polaris patted her mother's hand. She touched tissue to tears and forced an appreciative smile for the doctor.

Molly seethed. She hated her mother's compliant attitude. Heat rose in her face. Her lips pressed down into a frown. She turned all her rage on the younger doctor. "And what do you say, Dr. Abraham?"

He turned a cool glare toward Molly. "I—I concur with Dr. Polaris." He looked down at the razor-sharp edge of his pressed pants and picked at a nonexistent speck on the crease.

Molly jumped to her feet. "This is waste-material, and you both know it! What really happened to my sister?"

"Molly, please!" Her mother reached for her arm but missed.

"Mom, this is a line of...crap." Molly softened her tone toward her mother.

"Officer. Jacobsen." Dr. Polaris stood. Dr. Abraham followed his lead. "Please settle down! I told you earlier at the transportation station. Your sister is going to need your connection. I meant that sincerely."

"Because you don't mean any of *this*, sincerely. Do you, Dr. Polaris?" Molly retorted.

"No, that's not what I'm saying." He swallowed and looked down as if he were searching the ground for something. His hand worried that spot on the back of his head. "The medical files are very thoroughly documented—"

"But you said yourself that the lab work here was inconsistent!" Molly pointed toward Kita's room without taking her eyes off Dr. Abraham. "She's still lactating for goodness sakes!"

She knew she was shouting. Her mother shivered. Security would probably be called in to corral the crazy woman in the over-flow room.

"...And I explained how that could be," Dr. Polaris said with a much calmer voice.

"You're telling me that a woman can lactate two weeks after a still-born birth? Seriously?" She stared at the inexpressive junior doctor. Why didn't he say anything?

"Mrs. Jacobsen, please." Dr. Polaris sought her mother's assistance.

"Molly!" Her mom whispered through clinched teeth. Her eyes bulged.

A lifetime of silent discipline by the pastor's wife curbed Molly's behavior, but then she shoved the child-within aside and continued her quest for the truth. "That—that's not good enough, Doctors!"

Molly searched Dr. Polaris's eyes for some level of realism. He knew this was a cover up, professional courtesy to the doctors on Omicron, something, but it was not the truth. She rubbed her left temple and sat back down next to her anxious mother. She had to remain fluid. Neither of them would get anywhere if she didn't get a hold of her own emotions and speak logically, not hysterically.

Professional protocol demanded professional respect, but this was her sister. Somebody had packed Kita's medical file with obscurity, and these healers were accepting it, which only added to Molly's resolve that these doctors were either stupid or covering something up. This younger doctor, with his sultry good looks and silent personae, muddled Molly's sensory perceptions, but she knew what she knew. This information was veiled and inaccurate.

She cleared her throat. If she was going to get any information out of these two, she would have to play a compliant, over-protective sister, rather than an enraged psychopathic officer. "I'm sorry. I'm…just worried about my sister."

"Of course," Dr. Polaris responded with a half-smile.

Molly felt her mother relax a little.

"There…" Dr. Abraham exchanged a weary look with Dr. Polaris, "is one other thing worth mentioning. You need to be aware the PASS, um, Physical Assessment Status Scan, rendered some results pertaining to your sister. The, uh, medical file from the Project's clinic confirms our results. It appears her ability to"—he swallowed—"have children on her own would have been impossible."

"What!" Molly nearly stood up. "What are you saying?"

"According to the medical file from Omicron, Kita was sterile on initial assessment, but was deemed adequate to surrogate with artificial conception, uh, a donor's fetus."

"Well," Dr. Polaris pushed his hand out in front of Abraham, as if he were holding a child back in his seat. "As I said…"

Was that a glaring glance to the younger healer? Molly's fingernails gouged her palms.

"We are continuing to review Kita's condition —"

"You mean to tell me that my sister is—what, went on this mission, a mission to help with infertility and was found to be sterile?" Molly knew her voice was too loud, but this was quickly becoming more than she could tolerate. Molly glared at the young doctor. "Does that even make sense to you, Dr. Abraham!"

"Molly!" Her mother reached to touch her, but she jerked away and paced the room.

"Miss Jacobsen, please settle down." Dr. Polaris glared at Dr. Abraham. "Our diagnosis is not complete, these are our preliminary findings and we really are not sure what is and what is not. Please, we should not jump to any conclusions at this time."

"Jump to any conclusions! Are you saying your scanners are inaccurate? Are you saying your lab technicians have messed up? Are you saying—"

"Miss Jacobsen—Molly, please settle yourself." Dr. Polaris tried again, "Let's focus on what we do know, and that is, Kita needs your love and support. She has a long way to go with this cognitive cessation. You've got to be strong and *settled* for her sake."

Molly stopped pacing and stared at the elder healer. His words slowly soaked into her mind. She softened her tone. "Can—can we take off the restraints, let her move around?"

"Yes, I think we can do that," Dr. Abraham spoke for the third time.

Molly exhaled heavily and sat back down. Her mother did the same.

"Now, help me understand this—" Molly worked toward that state of fluid. "—You say Kita's physical examination indicated she *did* give birth, but her lab work is inconsistent with a—with the baby being"—she swallowed and rubbed her left temple—"all right?"

Her mother sniffed and wiped her eyes.

"That's correct." Dr. Polaris nodded. He reached over to a corner table and pulled out another tissue, gently handing it to her mother.

Molly stared at her and then lifted her glare to Dr. Abraham. "What are the inconsistencies?"

The doctors exchanged a look.

What did that mean? Her eyes darted between the two. "Doctors, what are the inconsistencies?"

Dr. Polaris opened his mouth and paused, and then he blurted, "I'm sure it's nothing, just a pathological discrepancy due to the effects of the cryogenic stasis."

The speed at which he threw that out there was unsettling. Molly switched into an investigative mode. At least in this frame of mind, she could control her emotions. Polaris was the mouthpiece, Abraham had subtle tells. She kept an eye on the younger healer's reactions. His unconscious body language was better than a false-words reader.

Dr. Abraham's eyes never dropped, yet his focus was somewhere between her and her mom. It was as if he were staring at…her ear. Like one does at a podium lecture when one focuses their sight just above the audiences' heads. It appears the speaker is looking directly at the audience, but in reality he is not. Was that what Abraham was doing? Performing an ancient internal technique to control his emotions?

"Yes, you've blamed the hibernation before." Officer Jacobsen pressed on. "But, what I want to know, Doctors, is, what are the discrepancies?"

"Right now, it's not important." Dr. Polaris stated as he stood.

"Not impor—" Molly's temple pounded.

"What is important is that we do everything we can to help your sister return to reality." Dr. Polaris gestured for Molly and her mom to exit the room.

"Of course, Doctor," her mother said and shot Molly a look she knew all too well. *Shut up and behave.*

Molly pressed her lips together and let her shoulders roll forward. Her mother's looks still affected her, same as they did when she was a child. She would shut up, for now. Maybe she could get this information out of the younger healer. If she could speak to him alone. Corner her prey. He certainly did *not* agree with everything Dr.

Polaris said, she sensed that without really trying. But how far could she trust the son of the man who probably caused this problem in the first place?

"Dr. Abraham," Molly tried to sound kinder. "Surely you have information about your father's project that could help us determine what happened?"

"Actually, Miss Jacobsen, I..." a crimson flush washed over his face, "I haven't been in contact with my father in quite some time. But I assure you we will do everything possible to help your sister."

"Of course." Molly pulled her eyebrows together and stared at the young healer.

"Miss Jacobsen," the younger doctor began. "We are still developing your sister's diagnosis. As long as Kita continues to give us approval to disseminate her medical information, we will keep you informed. Now, Dr. Polaris is right, we must work together in order to help Kita. *Something* happened to her out there that affected her deeply. We—we've got to do everything we can to help her deal with it and move forward in a healthy manner."

Molly held her eye contact with Abraham, but he looked away first. Molly rubbed her tongue across the front of her teeth and let her glare linger.

"Well, we will keep you informed." Dr. Polaris stepped toward the door. Dr. Abraham, again, followed his lead. The two doctors dipped their heads and walked out of the room.

CHAPTER SIX

Molly sat down in Kita's room, drummed her fingers on the arm rest, stood again to pace the room, and then sat down, again. Blood oozed from her inside cheek. Her eyes swept the room. Mom was occupied. Kita was sleeping. Both looked quite peaceful. With all the sedation and anti-depressants, Kita'd be asleep for quite some time. Molly glanced at the clock in her peripheral. She glanced at her mom resting on the couch, shoved unruly hair behind her ear, and reached for her iComm link as she walked out to the hall.

"Call. Sal."

His ringtone—Beethoven's Fifth—resonated in her hearing. "This is Officer Joseph Salazar. I'm not available at this time, but you know the drill... BEEP."

"Sal!" Molly almost hissed from forcing herself to whisper. "This is Mol. Listen, call me back—I need—I—just call me back." Molly disconnected. It was very seldom she could not reach her enforcer partner. A nurse scurried past and entered her sister's room. Molly sighed. The restraints were coming off, that, in itself, had to help Kita on many levels. Anticipating Sal would call back, she observed the movement in Kita's room from the hall.

Marti and Steve Tyris, missionary coordinator's at Dad's church, approached, gently hugging her before going into Kita's room and doing the same with her mom.

She was right, her iComm link tinkled an ascending tune. "Sal!"

"What's up, Mol? How's Kita?"

Turning her back on the room, she lowered her voice. "Yeah, she's okay, I guess. Listen, I need your help, I-I need ta—I need relief."

A long sigh, he wasn't pleased. "Sure, when?"

"Now! Where can I meet ya?"

"Come to the garage."

"Okay, twenty minutes?"

"That's fine." Sal didn't push for an explanation. She was grateful for that.

Molly stepped back into Kita's room. Her sister was free of restraints and sleeping soundly. Her mother knelt in prayer at the little couch with Marti and Steve. Molly allowed herself an expressive eye roll, since her mom couldn't see the rebellious action. "Mom, I've gotta...go do something. I'll be back later."

Her mother glared over her shoulder with drawn eyebrows, twisted around to sit on the couch, and exhaled an expressive sigh. She shrugged quasi-approval, and settled back on the couch with a distant gaze in her eyes. Marti sat beside her and Steve stood near his wife. They continued to talk in quiet tones.

Molly walked faster than she intended. Sal had what she needed. Maybe he'd help her investigate this Dr. Austin Abraham when they were done. There had to be more to his connection with this mysterious father than he was revealing. Polaris had lied. She knew it with every fiber of her being. But why? To think, they called themselves healers. Who were they protecting?

An image of the younger doctor approaching her in the entrance waiting area, before she knew who he was, filled her mind. Her initial reaction to his extreme good looks only fueled her anger. Question was, who was she angry at, herself or him?

He was probably very accustomed to women succumbing to anything he said like hormone saturated school girls. Well, Molly was not, nor ever would be, such a disgusting thing. She hurried even faster to the Transit.

***

Molly hopped off the mass transit vessel and nearly jogged past three additional houses before arriving at Sal's apartment-garage. She avoided the main house and slipped quietly past the parking platform to Sal's garage apartment. Sal yanked the door open before she could knock.

She sucked in a quick breath, "Sal."

"Come on in," he said more as an exhale than an invitation, as he stepped aside. Before closing the door, he scanned the path to the street, and then turned a disappointed glare toward her.

"Look, I'm sorry!" she blurted. "You don't know what I've been through."

She suppressed a grin. He enjoyed this as much as she did, but he had to act like it tacked him off.

"Just come on." He walked to the back of the garage, unlocked a two-door cabinet, pulled out two identical sets of foam forms, one blue and one red, and handed her the red set.

Molly was already jogging in place and winding her arms around like a double windmill. She nodded her appreciation and pulled the forms onto her hands and head. Sal did the same and turned to face her. Molly reached out and smashed her padded fist into his left cheek.

"Ow! Molly! I wasn't ready!" He handed her an opaque case.

She responded by opening her mouth.

He placed the mouth guard between her teeth, and she clamped down, just missing his bare fingers. He jerked back and glared at her once more.

"Well, get ready," she mumbled past the guard.

Placing her left hand over her right padded fist, she bowed deeply from her waist. Her eyes never left her opponent. Sal did the same and stepped back into a proper stance.

Molly stepped back as a mirror image of him and stared over her padded fists. She flung at him with a melee of venomous strikes. Her right and left jabs pushed him backward. He recovered his balance and threw a left hook. She recoiled and staggered backward. He lunged forward with a set of empty jabs but was met with a spinning round house to his right hip.

"Umpf!" escaped his lips. He walked it off. He'd taken that hit better than she expected. She was beating up the wrong person, but then again, she couldn't beat up the healers. A grin separated her lips and exposed the slobbery mouth piece as she stepped back to regain her balance. An image of the pretty healer's face replaced her partner's and her grin widened. She locked into the ready stance.

Sal reset his own position to reflect hers. His jaw muscles bulged. Molly knew that look. He was suppressing anger.

"What?" She egged him on.

"Okay." He nodded and lifted his right knee. His foot shot out for a horizontal extension kick to her left thigh, but he used the momentum to deliver a left hook kick to her right thigh. She bounced back on her left foot to absorb the dead-leg sensation. He lunged forward and flared a jab. She grabbed his shirt and rolled her weight back which propelled him over her body, crashing into two refuse receptacles sending the content down over his face. He jumped to his feet, shoving garbage off his forehead.

Molly raised an eyebrow. In partner lingo, it meant, "Want more?"

Steamy body heat blanketed the windows like a sheet of wet plastic wrap. The smell of sweat and guttural noises filled the garage. His insatiable pride held a stoic mask firmly in place with each of her ferocious strikes, but she knew her partner well enough to recognize his suffering.

Molly completed a roll and spun to stand over him. Black filled her brown eyes as her pupils dilated with excited fighter's lust. A wicked smile tugged at the corners of her mouth and a strand of saliva dripped from her mouth guard.

Sal rushed forward leaning his shoulder into her gut, wrapped his left arm around her right thigh, and pulled her leg up. Molly's balance went with the pull, and her bottom slammed into the floor. "Umpf!" The breath escaped her lungs. Sal pressed his forearm across her collar bone holding her against the floor. "Had enough?"

"Not a chance." Molly hooked her left foot over his right ankle and twisted him over. She threw a left hook to his face and jumped up, bouncing in place while he recovered his own dignity and stance. The smile never left her face. He hated that smile, it was as much of a weapon as the physical impacts from her fist and feet. Never losing eye contact, she turned her shoulders to deliver a reverse hook kick but met empty air. Sal had backed away. Was he giving up? Molly moved forward, but he put up his hands.

"I give," he panted. "You win. I'll tell you...
anything...you wanna know. Just don't kill me."

Heaving for air, she lowered her hands to her
sides. A deep cleansing breath helped slow her
breathing to a more normal rate.

"Geez, Mol, what crawled up your—?"

"Sorry." Molly jogged from side to side and hit
her foam covered fists together. The exertion felt
good as hot fatigue replaced stone-cold frustration.
"Really? You had enough?"

She knew he had, it was easy to sense that
without reaching out to connect.

Sal nodded, laboriously drawing breath, and
favoring his left rib cage. She had nearly beaten the
crud out of him, but she knew he'd never admit it.
She took off her foam helmet and slipped out of the
hand protectors. She felt better, but he looked
terrible. The grin never left her face.

At that moment, the door swung open, and
Molly spun around, startled. A man walked in. A
disapproving look etched his face. Sal yanked off
his gear and yanked Molly's out of her limp grasp.
He put them away and locked the cabinet. The
man stood still as Sal ignored him.

"So—" the man said, not looking at Molly, "LEPers can perform illegal physical contact, but us everyday, ordinary citizens cannot?"

Molly cringed. The referral never set right with her. The name Legal Enforcer Personnel, shortened to LEP, quickly became LEPers to the civilians. It always conjured images of white, flaky skinned, diseased people from the Bible. But the nickname was what it was and was widely used by the civilians.

"That's about it." Sal shrugged.

Molly stood statue still, watching their exchange. It seemed friendly enough. She tossed a glance at Sal. Apparently, the man wasn't as threatening as he tried to appear.

Sal stepped up next to Molly and lifted his left palm toward the intruder. "Molly, this is my step-brother and roommate, Dwayne Friedman. Dwayne, this is my partner, Molly Jacobsen."

"Pleasure." Dwayne nodded and walked toward the stairs leading to the apartment above the garage.

Molly nodded in response. With the exhaustion and dissipating concern, words would not form on her lips.

Half way up, Dwayne turned back to her. "Jacobsen? Any relation to Kita Jacobsen?"

Molly's brow knitted. "Yeah, how do you know Kita?"

"I don't really."

"What does that mean?" Molly looked over at Sal.

He shrugged. "How do you know Molly's sister, Dee?"

"I'm tellin' ya, I don't really." He continued up the stairs.

Sal caught up with his brother to grab his shoulder and turn him around. "What *do* you know, Dee?"

Dwayne tsked his tongue. "I was asked to look at some—information. That's all."

"If it involves my sister, I want to know what you know!" Molly butted in. Tension quickly replaced the workout's warming calmness.

LYNN DONOVAN

Dwayne looked back at the door he had entered, and then up at the door he wished to pass through. "Let's go up, okay?"

"Your *step*-brother?" Molly mouthed to Sal as they followed Dwayne to the shared apartment.

Sal nodded and shrugged at the same time.

"Look," Dwayne began, "I realize you're LEPers and all, but should you be doing this, here, where you could be...monitored?"

"Yeah, well, ya know." Molly dismissed his concern.

"Oh-kay." Dwayne drew out the word and sat down at his computer stand.

Sal walked straight to the food preserver and pulled out two waters. He handed one to Molly and wiped his dry lips with the back of his hand. He twisted the lid off and drew longingly at the cool liquid.

Molly hung back from Dwayne's computer station, fighting the urge to shove up against the back of his chair. She knew from experience that technical people needed their space, but the anxiety and fear she had endured since the telecom had arrived kept causing her to ignore social

90

etiquette. A cramping stitch in her side prompted her to drink deeply of her water container.

Dwayne accessed some files and moved a folder over on his visual screen. Sal drank from his bottle and eased himself against the back of an overstuffed and overused recliner. Molly leaned against a table with her arms cradling the bottle in her hand and tried to keep her foot from bouncing against the floor. Dwayne meticulously sorted through the applications.

"I—uh, I've been doing some research." He glanced up at Sal and back at his screen. "For a friend, and I've found some interesting inclusions on a data file." He paused.

"Look, what I've found here, the way this stuff was hidden, it could be corporate espionage. I mean, it's really encrypted. I just got lucky and found it. Whoever did this, they meant for it to stay hidden."

Rubbing his unshaven chin he continued, "I'm just saying, you two better watch yourselves. These people seem to be powerful."

"Yeah, how powerful?" Sal glanced at Molly.

This was all Molly needed to break her respectful distance. She rushed up behind him and grabbed his bicep, like an eagle snatches up a gopher. "Look, if you know something about my sister, you've gotta tell me. Nobody is working with me at the Healing Station…and I know the medical records are fictitious."

"How did you know that?" Dwayne winced under her grip.

"She's my twin." Molly held on, searching his face for comprehension. Did he understand a twin's connection? He struggled against her merciless grasp. Her glare lowered to her hand, and she released her prey.

She cleared the self-conscious disdain from her throat. "We have a connection. All twins have it. I guess."

Heat flushed her face as she looked away, and gulped her water. The cool liquid soothed the embarrassment. She didn't normally talk about her *gift*. But it was her proof Kita had been robbed. The medical files and healers were lying, or deceived. Michael had been kidnapped, or something. "Anyway, I know what she feels. There is nothing masking her *grip on reality*. Her child was born alive, and she was taking care of him up to the point she entered a hibernation chamber."

"Well." Dwayne tapped his laser-projected keyboard. "According to what I have been given, there is a stream recording of the child's birth—Are you sure you want to see this?"

"Dwayne," Molly growled, "Did you see me kick your brother's butt downstairs? Show me what you have!"

"Look. I'm all about finding a smoking laser, but this is really," he swallowed, "well-hidden encryptions, that usually means it's dangerous, and a nerdy-guy with computer savvy goes missing."

"What has well-hidden encryptions?" Molly reached to grab his arm again, but he pulled away. Sal placed a calming hand on Molly's shoulder.

"These medical files, the stream, there's a lot of, shall we call it 'editing,' you know, 'alternate ending' type stuff." Dwayne stared at her like a terrified rabbit trying to talk his way out of a coyote's trap.

"Show me!" Molly demanded.

Dwayne swiveled in his chair. Pleading eyes met his brother's. Sal shrugged and raised one eyebrow. Dwayne took a long breath but let it out briskly. "Okay, but what are you going to do with this information?"

Molly looked at Sal. She hadn't thought that far down this trek. "What can we do? Report our suspicions to the chief and get an investigation started on The Abraham Project?" Molly thought out loud.

Sal shrugged one shoulder and nodded. "Maybe."

"Oooh no!" Dwayne's voice cracked. "Then you'll have to reveal your source, and I'm in super-hot fluid! No way!"

"Look." Molly raked her fingers through her sweat moist hair. "I'll guarantee you anonymity, like a punk-snitch. Your name will never be revealed. I—I promise you that. Okay? Now, show me what you've got!"

Dwayne sat still for a moment staring at his glowing keyboard. He took another of his long breaths and touched the laser projected keypad. He reached up to the virtually lit screen to enlarge icons inside of icons. Finally, he had a stream window on the screen. "You're right, *something* did happen. I don't know what, but I know this video-stream is false."

He touched the Play icon. The three stood silent as they watched Kita give birth. The camera had been placed at an angle to allow privacy, so it was difficult to actually see the baby, but the room fell silent once he was delivered. The healer vigorously massaged the baby with a small blanket, although the baby was not actually visible on the recording. Just an arm here and a leg there could be seen. The nurse and healer spoke to each other, but their words could not be comprehended. Kita lay still, too still, on the delivery bed, but her voice could be heard. She cried, "What's wrong?"

No one answered. The healer wrapped the blanket around the baby and carried him out of the room. The stream continued to display Kita in the same motionless position, but she could be heard sobbing, "This can't be happening…"

A nurse administered some fluid into her IV, and Kita's head rolled to one side. The screen faded to black static.

Molly stared at the static. Tears filled her eyes.

Dwayne looked at Molly over his shoulder. "Now, let me show you this." His fingers flew over the virtual keyboard. A chart appeared on his screen, underneath the stream which was reset to the beginning. He hit play, and the scene repeated itself, except he had slowed it down and the chart at the bottom showed several different colored lines darting up and down as the stream played forward.

"There!" Dwayne ran his fingers across the keyboard. "See that?" He pointed at the line chart.

Molly saw nothing. Dwayne looked at her for confirmation. He huffed impatience, reached up to his virtual screen, placing two fingers on each side of the two corners of the line chart, and drug the chart out, enlarging it. "Now, do you see it?"

Molly leaned in. She saw where the chart did not line up with itself, and the lines changed colors. On another track, a solid line continued across the chart.

"That?" She pointed at the break.

"Yes, that," Dwayne said. "That's where alternate ending stream was spliced in. And this…"

he pointed at the solid line, "is where a frame was frozen and continued until the point where she is given an IV injection. It was really heavily encrypted. Nobody was supposed to find out. But, well, you know." Dwayne lifted his hand and examined his fingernails.

"Okay, you're good. What does this mean?" Molly said.

Dwayne shot a look at his brother and then at Molly. "It means, Miss Lady LEPer, you've got a case for an investigation. These medical records have been altered. Somebody doesn't want anybody to know what really happened in that birthing room."

Molly glared at Dwayne. "These are the files that were sent back with Kita?"

"I assume so." He shrugged.

"And you got them, how?"

Dwayne swung around in his chair. "Punk-snitch anonymity, remember?"

Molly sighed. "Okay. Punk-snitch anonymity."

Molly's iComm link signaled an incoming message. Sal jumped. He had received it, too.

"It's the chief," they said in unison and reached back to activate their communication. *Your presence is required immediately. My office. -OC.*

Dwayne's eyes darted between the two LEPers and a smile crinkled his eyes. "You two are so cute."

Sal slapped at the back of Dee's head, but Dwayne ducked.

"Yeah," Molly swallowed a dry knot. "And I think I'm in trouble."

Sal threw his water bottle in the plastic recycle bin. "What did you do?"

"Well, I might have used the transportation lift without valid cause."

"You what?"

"Look the Mass Transit was offline, and they had whisked Kita off to the Healing Station. What else was I supposed to do?"

"Molly!" Sal hurried toward the door. "Come on. I've got a squad bud, you can ride with me."

Molly rolled her eyes and followed Sal down the stairs.

CHAPTER SEVEN

"Chief, you wanted to see us?" Sal shoved Molly in front of him as they entered the office. Molly glared at her partner as she stumbled in and snapped to attention.

"Close the door." Chief Odeb Chisula already sounded tense. Postured behind his desk, with steepled fingers resting on the surface, as if he had been waiting for them with a cool, casual anticipation of a school principal, he appeared to be the icon of patience. Molly knew different. His dark, oily complexion revealed none of his agitation, but the red framed, brown and cream mottled eyes, with dilated black pupils lost in a dark-brown iris, exposed all she needed to know. She was in big trouble. Light reflected off his dome-smooth head, accentuating every tell-tale tendon bulging from his long, razor-rash, adult acned neck to the unique coning apex of his scalp.

Sal pushed the door closed and snapped back to attention. Molly swallowed hard. The chief made her nervous even when he wasn't angry, although she couldn't think of a time she had been in his office and he *wasn't* angry.

The chief touched a screen only he could see. "Let's look at what we have, shall we, 'Illegal and Unauthorized use of Transportation Lift,' 'Misuse of LEP badge for access through a security station,' 'Bribing security personnel at said security station.' Shall I continue, Officer Jacobsen?"

"Sir, I was trying to get to my sister, and I did not bribe anybody. I merely asked if there was any way to speed things along."

"Uh huh," Chief said without looking at her. "Says here you offered fifty credits."

"I was placing my credits chip in my pocket— they make you empty everything out, ya know. And I did not *use* my LEP badge. I was just trying to be sure they did not misplace it. They misconstrued—"

"Jacobsen!" The chief's veins bulged farther from his neck. Molly snapped to attention. She stared at the pulsing vein near his collar and chewed on the inside of her cheek.

"What gives you the right to misuse LEP privileges to transport yourself when you are not in the line of duty?"

"But, sir, my sister—"

"I know why you were there, Jacobsen. I'm the one who authorized you to have the leave, remember?"

"Yes sir, and I appreciate it, sir. But—"

"The Mayor has called my office twice today. The Legal Enforcer Board has called three times. They want to make an example of you and your shenanigans."

"My shenanigans! Sir, my sister was transported without me! The Mass Transit System was offline—"

"Shut up! Jacobsen, just—shut up!" He rubbed a large, dark, knobby knuckled hand down the front of his face. "Do you have any idea how much trouble you are in this time?"

Molly closed her mouth. Blood oozed from the raw spot on her cheek.

"Sir," Sal offered.

"And don't think you can explain her way out of this either, Salazar!" The chief's face turned darker, oilier, the pigment of an angry man with skin too opaque to reveal the flooded blood vessels.

"No sir." Sal wisely remained at attention. "But, sir, we have found anomalies in Molly's sister's records that merit...some attention."

The chief glared at the two officers. His eyes darted from Molly to Sal. "They want you suspended for misusing your credentials!"

"Sir, please. You can suspend me, whatever, but first hear what I have to say!" Molly spoke without breaking her posture of attention.

The muscles in the chief's jaw bulged and released. Oversized lips pressed into a tight, flat oval. Molly and Sal stood perfectly still, the less movement, the better. The chief closed his eyes, released an exasperated sigh, as he leaned his lanky frame back into his overused chair, and rocked thoughtfully back and forth. His fingers steepled above his chest, elbows at the arm rests.

He stared at the triangle formed by his fingertips. At last, he looked up. "What do you have?"

Molly told the chief what the healers had said and her own observations, leaving out the twin connection details. Then Sal told him about the findings with the medical records, without revealing the source. Molly concluded, "Chief Chisulo, if nothing else, my sister was robbed of any hope for future children."

The chief looked up sharply. This piece of information might be the dagger that penetrated his armor. His face contorted. "What do you mean?"

"Kita's doctor said the physical assessment scan indicated she is now sterile. She certainly was not sterile when she left, that was part of the qualifications to be accepted. They only want female candidates who can help by donating to the fertility cause. Chief! Now, she's sterile! Somebody or something made her that way and it happened on that planet. This Abraham Project is crooked and—and they need to be stopped."

Molly gnawed at the inside of her cheek desperately fighting traitorous tears, while the chief stared at his steepled fingers. Mentally she crossed hers. Closing her eyes, she focused her will toward him. He was impenetrable. Silence wedged between them like a concrete wall. Finally, he opened his mouth and shut it again. His eyes rose to meet hers, and he let out a long resolute sigh.

"All right," he began. "Write up your report, submit it to me by shift change."

Relief washed over her like a sudden rain shower in the Colorado desert plains. "Thank you —"

"Not so fast—" He held up his hand like a cross guard. "—For all practical purposes you're relieved of duty as of now and without pay—"

Molly opened her mouth to protest.

"Hold on." The chief sighed. "However, I'm placing you on a covert operation. Your pay will be channeled through a different funding so it will appear you are being reprimanded financially. Give me the name of your sister's missionary coordinators here on Earth, we'll go through those same channels to get you on the next pilgrimage —"

"I, sir, I didn't mean…" Her eyes bulged as she glared at Sal for help.

"Sal won't be able to provide you any backup, but I'll see to it, personally, he is kept informed. For appearances sake, he will be reassigned also. You'll be completely on your own, Jacobsen, for the most part. You go check out this Abraham Project and find out what happened to your sister. Report to me weekly." He touched the screen in his vision and typed something.

"What? But Chief, we couldn't communicate with Kita except through a trans-planetary telecom which took months to dispatch."

"There, I've transmitted two things, Information about Gordon, our inside infil and—"

"An inside infil?" Molly's eyes widened.

"He's on site, on Omicron—" the chief's eyebrows shot up toward his absent hair line "—as an IT programmer, and he's a good agent, dependable."

"On site? You mean there's already an investigation?"

"Yes, we've had him on site for years. He'll be able to get your reports to me, don't worry about how, he knows how. Just journal your activities and deliver them through Gordon." The chief's eyes met Molly's and for the first time they did not flare with anger. "Connect with him as soon as you can, and *be careful*."

"What's the second thing?"

The chief leaned his head to one side. "Beg pardon?"

"You said you were transmitting two things…" Molly stared at the blinking red light in her peripheral.

"Oh, yes, the confidential file on what we know so far."

A chill ran down Molly's spine as the chief glared at her. She dropped her eyes to the floor. "I —yes sir."

"This kills two gracks with one rock, so to speak. Assigning you to this gets *you* out of the immediate attention of the Board. And, we've been discussing sending an officer out there for some time." The chief stared at his desk. He opened his mouth, then closed it. Finally, he raised his eyes to hers.

"Your sister's case is not isolated, although she's the first we've seen returned to Earth. If it hadn't been for some guy, a uh, Pastor Oliver Pugh on the planet, we wouldn't have—Well, anyway, Gordon has transmitted some other interesting anomalies. There's more going on out there than what happened to your sister, Molly, for one thing, according to Gordon, this Pastor Pugh hasn't been seen since your sister's return trip. What's worse, we are suspecting a black market fertility exchange. We have coined the term, 'Fertility Pirates.' It's bigger than you realize. I want you to investigate beyond what happened to your sister, find out where this black market is sending frozen patho-specimens and to whom they are making their exchange. We suspect it is a far-reaching operation. And, Jacobsen…"

She hardened her stare.

His voice softened for the first time. "Be careful! Stay in contact. There's a lot of financial gain with this operation and that makes it dangerous, very dangerous."

"Yessir!"

"You're dismissed." The chief dropped his eyes to his desk. Sal and Molly exchanged a partner's knowing look and walked out.

"Well, that went well," Sal said as they reached the Trans lift. "Garage, two personnel."

They stepped through and walked to his squad bud in silence. Molly transmitted Marti and Steve Tyris' information to the chief as they glided toward her father's church. She'd dealt with Marti and Steve when Kita was preparing for her pilgrimage. Now, it was Molly who would prepare. She opened and scanned the confidential file. A knot twisted in her gut. All this needed a comfortable place to sit and process in her thinking cabinet. So far, it was still searching.

CHAPTER EIGHT

"Odeb, I don't like this—" Pastor Levi Jacobsen protested into his iComm link to the LEP Commander, nodding and shaking his head, until his tidy, more-salt-than-pepper hair fell across his greying brow, as if the caller could see his gestures. His squared off jaw, framed by distinguished laugh trenches, hung suspended, ready to counter when he could.

"I—I *realize* she is a trained offic— ...yes...of the LEP force, I—I understand...I get that—" A fatigued muscle clamped down on his neck from continuous nodding. He massaged the bulging ligature and continued his defense.

"—Come on, Odeb, she's my daughter...We nearly lost her sister...I don't feel comfortable facing this risk again...Do you realize what her mother and I have been through?" Levi raked his fingers through his hair. A father's fears eroded his pastoral patience. He bulged his eyes, over finite wire-framed glasses, toward his missions coordinator and pursed his lips to convey his frustration, immediately regretting the emotional display.

Marti Tyris fingered the ribbons protruding from her Bible, her worried, watery eyes never leaving his. She bore far too much blame for Kita's current situation. He didn't blame Marti for what had happen to his daughter. No one was to blame, other than Austin Abraham, for the way The Abraham Project had been exploited. Still, the chiseled worry lines in Marti's round face grew deeper with every unsuccessful protest he presented to Chief Chisulo.

Without a cordial salutation, or any salutation at all, he disconnected and stared at Marti. There were no words.

"Well...?" The ribbons blurred under her worried fingers.

"The Commander and I go way back. College, you know? I thought I could have some leverage."

He drew in a long, slow breath and let it out just as slowly.

"They are sending Molly."

"I gathered that." Her voice barely above a whisper.

"Undercover."

Her eyes widened as did her mouth.

"This thing is big, really big, Marti. They've got one person on the inside and now they need an officer on site. She's their logical choice." He rubbed his hand down his face. "You know, I get that, but when it's your own daughter—"

"I know." Tears spilled from Marti's empathetic eyes as she met his moist, bloodshot gaze. A vacuum of silence hung between them.

"Okay." Marti swallowed. She was a quiet woman who worked diligently behind the scenes. The success rate of the missionary projects she and her husband coordinated was one-hundred-percent, with this one exception. But it was her husband, Steve, who had the sanguine personality to articulate what she masterminded.

"Oh, Pastor, how can we send anybody to that planet? We need to ensure Molly, and others, are safe and in one piece?" She startled and sat straight up. "Oh Pastor, I didn't mean it like that."

"I know you didn't, and you're right, if they're gonna knowingly send my only other daughter, and more recruits, into this marauders' den, we need to have a solid plan to get them there and back safely and—unharmed."

A simultaneous nod confirmed their resolution.

***

Molly led her partner into the simplistic, stagnate church office. "Hey Dad."

He glanced up, but it was Marti who responded. She rushed to her feet, tossing her Bible into the seat she'd vacated, her voice saturated with emotion. "Oh Molly!"

Rising on the balls of her arch-supporting shoes, she pulled Molly down into a guilt-laden hug. This wasn't helping Molly's nerves. Molly's eyes beseeched her partner as she endured the claustrophobic canoodle.

Sal dawdled two or three paces behind. His palatable unease did not escape her senses. Many long hours of surveillance, with nothing to do but talk, had revealed his painful history with a family church and the vehement break from it. Knowing what she did accentuated her appreciation for his continued participation. Soon, he would be reassigned. They both knew it was a matter of time. However, preparing for this extreme expedition was terrifying enough. Having her partner present, as he always had been, much like her dad's unchanging office, gave a comfortable familiarity to an otherwise overwhelming future.

Sal's eyes roved over her father's walls and paused on one spot. A half smile softened his otherwise stern face. She followed his gaze to the professionally framed grammar school artwork displayed as if it were a national treasure. Heat flushed her face.

"Let's sit down and discuss our plan." Her dad had stood at last, gesturing for them to come on in. His personae of coherent confidence, as if they were planning a quick trip to the eastern hemisphere, annoyed Molly, until her eyes leveled with his. They revealed exhaustion and weariness.

These same eyes she'd seen the months before Kita's departure. The Pastor, as she and Kita referred to him when they were irritated with him, was always strong and faithful on the surface, but she knew deeper down, exactly how he felt in this matter. She was fighting the same objections.

Glancing at Sal, she chuckled to herself. Want to compare painful histories? Try being the pastor's daughter. The one who didn't get it. All this supernatural hocus-pocus hadn't made sense to her for a long time. It was Kita who had absorbed these teachings like a sponge. She was the perfect pastor's daughter...and look where it got her.

But this came down to family. That bond had never been broken. Only her bond with the faith her father clung to so adamantly had crumbled from Molly's heart. What had happened to her twin was wrong from so many angles. Anger didn't begin to describe the cesspool of emotions churning inside her. This wasn't as simple as a playground bully. This was much more ominous.

Sal and Molly pulled in extra chairs as they eased down, favoring sore ribs and thigh muscles, for the briefing. A heaviness, like a fifth person, settled with them. Brainstorming and strategizing usually exhilarated Molly's senses. But this, this was so far out of her element. There were too many unknown variables, suspicions of powerful and underhanded counter strategies, and she would be all alone, no back up, no time-out, no King's Xs.

If there was a God, He, literally, would be the only one who knew what was going on in that organization so far from Earth. Was she truly strong enough to carry this through, alone? Her trained legal enforcer mind said, "Yes." Her gut screamed, "No!"

Still—this *was* for Kita...and Michael. Her nephew. Kita's son. The idea had not solidified in her thinking yet.

Her father laid out the plan he and Marti had etched out just moments before. Her chief hadn't given her much choice with this assignment, but who better to investigate Kita's case than her own twin sister. As terrifying as this assignment was, Molly knew it was right.

Augmented by her "gift," solving a crime was a slice of cake. She'd been on so many successful overt ops, her confidence was well established on solid precedence. This would be no different. In fact, it was because this trail was forged by Kita, Molly knew her probabilities were elevated. Put the three-year cryogenic hibernation aside, forget the six-hundred-lightyear distant, eliminate her personal and physical risks, this investigation had to be assigned to her. She was the only one who had all the advantages.

Yes, her thoughts settled, who better than Kita's twin to trace the tracks to where—she gritted her teeth and forced back tears—Kita lost everything.

From what she'd gathered while scanning the confidential file, this piracy, or whatever, was intricate, resembling Mafia-type activities here on Earth, and she knew how dangerous those types were. Her stomach knew it, too. Every time she thought it through, it protested with refluxed acid.

The Chief had said what happened to Kita was only a small part of what was going on with The Abraham Project. It was the hub of a bigger wheel of crimes that could only be imagined. People, embryos, and oocyte cryopreservation, aka frozen eggs, were being exploited, somehow. She had to find out what was going on, who was doing it, and figure out how to stop them.

Her father continued to lay out the plan. His voice hummed a lyrical white noise to her brain. She forced herself to focus on the details. The next transport for the pilgrimage was in three months. Molly had to be on that transport. The normal prep time was one year, minimum, but this couldn't wait that long. It would be three years before she reached Omicron, as it was. Who knew how much more corruption would be instigated by then? A niggle of concern for the Pastor who helped Kita escape bore a tiny hole in Molly's mental storage cabinet.

"Okay," her dad summarized. "Molly and I'll work on an intense crash course on Missionary Bible applications. We'll work on some one-liners you'll need to incorporate into your pattern of speech. You know, like responding with 'Praise the Lord,' and 'Amen to that,' maybe a 'God bless you,' once in a while will authenticate your role. That shouldn't be too difficult, you've heard them all your life, you just got out of the habit." He smiled a weary smile.

"Marti will integrate you into our current pilgrimage group. It'll be the perfect opportunity for you to practice using these phrases—" he glared over his glasses. "—You're already in good shape, Mol, so the physical training won't be a problem. We'll say…"

Marti lifted her round tipped nose into the air. "We'll say she has been preparing with another team that fell through, and I am moving her over to this team. They'll certainly accept that because these pilgrimages dismantle pretty easily when people get into the thick of the preparation process. No judgement, just facts, three months before departure is exactly when the deterioration of hearts and minds begins to happen. It's absolutely believable."

Marti knew what she was doing. Her usually introverted character took a back seat to a confident and determined strategist. The influence quickly saturated the briefing and Molly's apprehensions began to loosen their grip on her heart.

Her father nodded as he addressed Sal and Marti, "I'm confident she can slip into the missionary role. It was prophesied over her when she was…oh, eleven or so"—he faced Molly now —"remember?"

Molly suppressed an enormous eye roll and nodded. Heat flushed her face. That may very well have been what pushed her away from this religious entrapment. Why did her dad have to bring that up? Prophecy wasn't going to keep her alive and intact. It would be her skill and wit developed from LEP training. The challenge would be switching between missionary role and investigator role without stirring up suspicion or attention. This was the objective of any undercover operator, don't break cover.

"There's a meeting tonight." Marti's voice broke through Molly's thoughts. "I'll go with you and introduce you to the group. For now, let me send this."

She touched the air in front of her, slid a finger across her virtual screen, then touch, touch.

A red light blinked in Molly's peripheral. She nodded and accessed the file.

"This is a…cheat sheet, of sorts. It'll help with your crash course, and you'll be able to quote the

Bible like nobody's business. Just in case. Now, it works on an algorithm for cognitive thought. You'll see. So, you think, oh let's say, 'eye of a needle' and it brings up Mathew 19:23-24 'Then Jesus said to his disciples, "Truly I tell you, it is hard for someone who is rich to enter the kingdom of heaven. Again I tell you, it is easier for a camel to go through the *eye of a needle* than for someone who is rich to enter the kingdom of God."'

"Or you think, 'talents,' and it brings up Mathew 25:14-30, 'For the kingdom of heaven is like a man—"

"—traveling to a far country," Molly experimented with the cognitive algorithm. "who called his own servants and delivered his goods to them...And to one he gave five *talents*..."

Marti stared at Molly, her mouth still poised to speak. "Well," Marti smiled. "Those other missionary candidates will think you're a Bible scholar from Zion itself."

Marti looked down at her lap. A pink hue flushed her face. "I—I put it together for myself, but I'm sure it will serve you well."

Molly frowned at her father. Her ability to memorize Bible verses had been a delight to him when she was small, and she had enjoyed pleasing him with her accurate recall. But the thought of it now left a bitter taste in her mouth. It had been nothing more than a dog-and-pony show for his congregants. Until now, it seemed like useless trivia bouncing around in her head. This algorithm would be a handy tool for the façade in case her memory failed her.

"Thank you, Marti. Um-God bless you." Molly's eyelashes veiled her eyes from Sal's scrutiny. It was she who felt the heat of embarrassment this time.

Her dad's eyes exposed his increasing weariness. But there was something else. Molly reached out with her senses. Something she had not done with him since she made the decision to have her own independent thought about God and this religion stuff.

Warm, sparkling pastels showered down around her mind. She lingered in the mingling of his feelings and hers, like walking through a glitter-filled rainbow, holding his hand. He welcomed her presence. She sensed fear for her safety, he would miss her, too, but he trusted her and knew she'd resolve whatever had gone wrong. Molly pulled back. Tears stung her eyes. She had no idea he had so much confidence in her. Perhaps his delight in her had not been a dog-and-pony show after all.

CHAPTER NINE

"Everybody!" Marti clapped her hands. Men and women, talking in groups of threes and fours, turned to Marti when she spoke. A table had been set up with coffee and fruit juice. Marti and Molly eased over to it as Marti continued.

"Pilgrims—" Marti deepened her voice to project its volume "—I'd like you to meet Miss Molly Jacobsen."

"Hello, Molly Jacobsen," chanted the pilgrims. A giggle rippled through more than half the attendees. The pastor's daughters were well known.

"Hello," Molly waved. Her tone sounded mature and confident, completely hiding how stupid she felt. She shoved down the awkward feeling of anxiety. Marti prepared two coffees and handed one to her. These people had been working together for nine months and had become quite familiar with each other. The training they had been through formed this bond, which would sustain them while they were out there, essentially on their own.

All eyes were on her. Molly smiled and scanned the group. There were nine women and four men. Adding her made ten women, fourteen total. She sipped her cup of coffee in an effort to disguise her discomfort. It was the same ridiculous feeling she'd had in middle school when they'd moved, changing schools in the middle of the semester. Funny how little things like that resurface even when you're grown.

This was her first hurdle, being accepted into the group. A group of her peers, as it turned out. She knew half of them from her teen years. Marti's cognitive cheat sheet activated. *Jesus said to them, "A prophet is not without honor except in his own town, among his relatives and in his own home." Mark 6:4* Molly chuckled to herself, the last thing she needed was one of her team members suspecting her motives. Their expressions appeared to be happy and welcoming, but her senses returned territorial offense, especially from Davidette, Alyce, and Reah. Some people never change. She swallowed. An undercover cop had to be a chameleon.

Marti sharpened her glare at the gigglers and cleared her throat. "She will be joining you on your voyage in three months."

Eyebrows pulled together, curious gazes became cross glares, and all whispers ceased. The room stilled to an uncomfortable silence.

"The missionary group she *was* with will not be able to complete their training, and I suggested she come finish preparations with you. I know you will all welcome her with open arms and hearts."

The attendees shuffled toward her, extending their own personal greeting. Even the three former cheerleaders welcomed her to the mission, whether they meant a word they said or not, at least they were being civil.

That's when she saw him. He stood at the back of the group, but as the barrier of people dissolved, their eyes met.

He smiled.

She frowned.

Davidette, alert as usual, stepped between them. "Well, Molly Jacobsen, I thought you were a guest speaker, to show us self defense—"

"Yeah. Davidette, could you excuse me?" Molly shoved her aside and ignored the huff.

Her eyes pierced his.

"Hello, Molly."

"You! You're going to Omicron? As a missionary?"

"Well, yes."

"Really? So...why didn't you mention this when I asked you about your father's project, Dr. Abraham?"

"Call me 'Deuce,' please. Everybody does." He glanced at the onlookers.

"Deuce?" Her eyebrows drew tighter.

"Yeah." He looked down. "It's a gambling thing, really. I suppose my dad coined the nickname. Mom was his queen of hearts, and I was his...deuce." He looked back up into her eyes. "In Poker, a two is called a deuce, being a junior, the second Austin Abraham. Thus—Deuce. As I understand it, they were his signature cards. His wild cards. I don't know..."

He was rambling and cleared his throat. A pink hue surfaced through his rugged skin tone. "It's what I've been called all my life…" He ran his hand through his dark brown mane. The tendrils curled around his fingers. "Get it?"

"Yeah, I get it," Molly said, "What I don't get is why *you* are going to Omicron as a missionary. Your father runs the program. Why wouldn't you just…just go?"

"I know." Deuce stared at the floor. "It may not make sense to you, but it does to me. Why are *you* going? Your sister just got back from there and with not very good results, I might add."

Molly flinched. Had her covert mission already been blown? *Think fast!*

"I'm sorry." Deuce ducked his head to meet level with her eyes. "That was uncalled for. I—I didn't mean to be so harsh."

"No, no you make a valid point." Molly tried to stall. She had rehearsed several scenarios with her dad to prepare for the questions the other voyagers would ask. Too bad the Biblical cheat sheet didn't include those canned responses. This threw her off, she never dreamed she'd be having this conversation with her sister's healer.

"I do want to know what happened to my sister, but more importantly, I want to complete my...calling." Molly reverted to a modified version of the canned response. Still the words were dry in her mouth. "These plans have been in effect for a long time. Besides, Kita will be fine with Mom and Dad. I have a limited window to make the voyage. Communications are improving all the time. Soon we will be able to talk just like we do here on Earth, then it won't seem so far away. Will it?" She forced a pleasant smile, though it felt awkward.

Deuce returned an equally awkward smile. "That sounds reasonable."

Did it? Or was he just sizing her up? How could he be that naïve? Something about him heightened her senses. She did not trust him. Yet, she felt drawn to him like a bug to a night light. It was ridiculous. Her insides felt warm and her mind felt slushy.

Mentally shaking those thoughts from her head, she adjusted her thinking. If nothing else, maybe she could find out what he knew about her sister's case. Maybe that explained why he was going. Did he suspect foul play, too?

No, wait. He'd been part of this group for the past nine months. Before he accepted Kita's case. Why would he leave a successful career on Earth? He had said he and his dad were not close. This was something she needed to work out immediately or this whole plan could fall apart before she ever boarded the transportation vessel.

But then again, he was his father's son and was probably going to participate in the lion's share of the profits. Hadn't it been compared to the mafia? Didn't the mafia pass their businesses to their sons? Molly shook her head. Either way, she needed to know what this Dr. Abraham was up to. And the only way she knew to do that, as an undercover enforcer, was to stay close to him and find out what made him click.

"What's wrong?" Deuce pressed his head back on his shoulders like a rooster.

"I don't understand." Molly noted every physical movement. Eye dilation, jaw tension, hand and body movement, anything to indicate truth, or more importantly, lies.

"Why would a healer with an established practice pack up and go six hundred lightyears into outer space to be a missionary? Especially since his father is the one running the project."

"Well, that's half of it," Deuce began, "Sure, it's true my dad is the Project Lead, but I told you before, we haven't exactly been on the same plain in a while. My mother's gone." He looked directly into her eyes. A flash of pain washed over his face and then was gone. Ah, that was the loss she had sensed when she first met him.

"She passed last January. I figured since I'm finishing up with my residency, I'd take my medical bag and go rekindle a relationship with the old man. But, I want to go there with a purpose of my own."

His speech seemed well rehearsed, just like her bottled responses.

He leaned close to her right ear. His warm breath brushed her skin and goose bumps prickled across her scalp. "You know what I mean?"

Molly fought the shiver as the warmth cascaded down to her mid-section. The sensation was disturbing, although not unpleasant.

"Yes, I-I suppose I do," Molly spoke quieter than she had intended.

It was a good thing their plan was not in favor of her faking an identity. "Hide in the open," her dad had called it. She fought hard not to roll her eyes. Between half the recruits from her childhood and Dr. Abraham, her cover would have already been blown, and she hadn't even left Earth.

An updated training schedule transmitted to Molly's iComm link, along with everybody else's, at the evening's end. The next meeting would be Saturday at the secondary learning track field. It was the physical fitness part of the program required by most missionary initiatives. Like her dad had said, she was in good shape, thanks to her occupation, but she questioned some of the other pilgrims' physiques. Even with three months to go, they had a lot of work ahead of them to accomplish a level of "physically fit" by her standards. What had they been doing the previous nine months? She chuckled and then chastised herself for judging her fellow man. What if the physical fitness she observed at this meeting *exhibited* the result of nine months' work.

The smile stayed on her lips longer than she had intended.

CHAPTER TEN

A tray of food sat untouched in front of Kita on a hover table. It felt good to be free of restraints, but her engorged mammary glands emphasized the painful longing in her heart. She missed his presence, his smell, his soft skin, his cooing voice. Tears spilled, again. Would she ever stop crying? She reached for the cup of tea and saw Molly.

"Mol!"

"How ya doing, sis?"

Kita drew in a deep breath. "All right, I guess."

Her sister sat on the side of Kita's bed and picked up the fork. She scooped some mashed white vegetable and held it at Kita's mouth.

Submissively accepting the bite, she pushed the texture around before swallowing with disgust. "Oh, yuck!"

"I know, but you've gotta eat," Molly consoled.

Kita nodded and laid her head back against the stiff pillow. Another tear traced the already established track down her cheek.

Molly's lip quivered, but she held back the obvious emotions. She lifted another bite. "Kita, how would you feel about me going to Omicron?"

Kita's eyes flew open as she sat straight up, almost knocking the tray back. "What!"

"How would you feel—"

"I heard the question. Molly! Why would you do that?"

"They cannot get away with this. You've been robbed. The chief has agreed to an investigation and…" Molly stared at the heap of food on the fork. "I've been assigned."

"Oh, Molly!" Kita reached out, her elbow pressing into the mashed whatever, and pulled her sister into a hug. Molly couldn't hide anything from her twin, she was scared. Kita held her for a long moment, just like she did when they were little.

Kita's ragged breath followed another uncontrolled outpour of emotion. How much of this was hormones and how much was despair? The twin symbiosis encircled Kita's senses. Her throat squeezed tight, and she could barely swallow. There, with Molly's arms around her, the two cried as one. Michael's absence, the mysterious violation, broken dreams, and disappointment flowed in a stream of grief and misery.

Molly leaned back and wiped her eyes. "Okay, so tell me everything you know. I've got three months to prepare."

"Three months! Molly! That's not enough time."

"Well, it's what I've got, so it's what I've got." Molly shrugged.

"Okay," Kita repositioned herself and pushed away the tray. Over the next three hours, she told Molly everything she knew about The Abraham Project, who she had met, who the technicians were, the healers and other staff at the clinic, and the local people whom she *thought* they were helping. She told her about the housing and the work assignments. She told her sister everything she could think of, no matter how small. Every detail mattered and would help Molly find Michael and stop this horrible operation.

***

Molly jogged from the Mass Transit Vessel to the track field. The warm-up was enough for her, however, when she stepped onto the field, the other participants were lined up performing jumping aerobic exercises. She fell in and joined the warming up. *Birds of a feather*, she mused.

"Listen up," Coach Ramdha blew his whistle. His thighs and arms were thick, and his shorts and T-shirt were tight, grey and stretchy. He was shorter in build but perfectly suited for this position. At least he had been twenty years ago. He looked like a retired physical education gym teacher who had let his stomach muscles go.

"We are going to put you through an obstacle course today. You will not be buddied up, however, I want to remind you this is a team effort and how you respond to your struggling team member will be part of your score. The person who scores highest on this exercise *will* receive a prize." His eyebrows jumped up and down with an enticement that told Molly the prize had to be lame.

Competitions had been disapproved a century ago as unfair to the weaker athlete who might try just as hard but could never succeed in a brutally competitive environment. Why was he forcing them to strive for a winner?

"Line up over here, and get ready," the Coach instructed. Fourteen various physiques jogged to the place designated and continued in place. Molly resisted rolling her eyes. She'd never outgrown the gesture. This group certainly had a ways to go, but their attitude impressed her more than she would admit. To anybody.

"On your mark."

Fourteen figures stopped in place, like a game of freeze tag.

"Get Ready."

Fourteen casual starter positions were assumed.

"...Go!"

Molly jogged effortlessly to the first obstacle.

There were ten rows of ten foot long by six inch wide posts laid horizontal, ten inches off the ground and eighteen inches apart. The recruits tip-toed through the posts. Pam, short in stature and thirty pounds overweight—mostly in her hips and thighs—tripped and skinned her knee. Nonetheless, she gallantly recovered and rolled off the horizontal posts. She stepped back into the obstacle approximately where she'd fallen out. Each carefully placed step she took was accentuated by a whisper, syllable by syllable chanting, "Yea…though…I…walk…through… the…val…ley…of…death…"

Daniel and Julio jogged backward until they were sure she was moving forward.

The next obstacle was a vertical version of the first. They had to climb the posts and go over the top, then down the other side. Molly reached it first and scaled it with ease. She jogged in place next to the structure and observed her teammates with varying efforts to pull themselves up the posts, swing their legs over, and lower themselves down the other side.

At least four other members, Sonya, Daniel, Julio, and Deuce, were obviously in good physical shape. Sonya was some sort of athlete. Her lean, muscular body had her up and over with impressive agility. What sport did she play? Molly made a mental note to ask. Daniel was short for a guy but appeared to have been a regular in the gym. He pulled himself up and over mostly by his arms. Julio stood nearly six foot and worked construction. He too was muscular and strong. He climbed the tower like a rock climber. Deuce surprised Molly the most. Sure, he was lean *looking*, but his muscles were linear. Maybe he had been a swimmer? Molly wondered what their stories were prior to becoming pilgrims.

The other nine people made it over, while the five who got over with little effort stood around the obstacle and clapped and cheered. Pam took the longest, but she made it and everyone chanted her name to encourage her over. She half giggled and half cried when her feet touched the ground on the back side of the monster.

Molly patted her back and flashed an encouraging smile. This was an opportunity to practice her missionary spirit. "Praise the Lord. Good job."

Deuce shoved an elbow into Molly's side and ran to the next obstacle. Molly stared at his back for a moment. "Oh, no he didn't!" She ran to catch up.

The group followed their cue and ran to the balancing beams. There were two rows, each person stepped onto a beam and tried to maintain a reasonable distance. "The faster you take this, the easier it is to keep your balance," she instructed the others as Molly ran across.

The four made it with little problem. Alyce, Davidette, and Reah walked it with such grace and fluid movement. Apparently, they had maintained their dancer's elegance. One thirty-something year old woman, her name might have been Roma, took a step, stepped off, took a step and stepped off, but she made it down the length.

Molly shrugged and patted her back. "Hallelujah. Good job. "

Her dad was right, she was definitely out of practice speaking these spiritual accolades, but practice would make perfect, as they say.

Roma smiled weakly and leaned into her run to the next obstacle.

Fifteen feet of primate bars awaited them. The first five feet sloped down slightly, the second five feet sloped up at a fifteen percent grade and the last five feet were straight, parallel to the ground. Molly sighed. This should be interesting. She visualized carrying those lagging behind on her shoulders to get them across but suppressed the chuckle that followed the thought.

The up slope proved to be the most challenging to everyone except the five. However, those five stood at the side of the obstacle and cheered the others to the end. When one fell off, the stronger ones pushed them back up until they had ahold of the bars. Soon they were on their way again. It generally took two and sometimes three to lift the person, depending on weight. But they all made it down the line.

Next was a rope ladder. This one would be a killer. It was not tied at the bottom and only one could go over it at a time. Plus, it would swing and twist miserably if you did not use your legs and arms to stabilize it. Molly clapped her hands as she expressed these instructions. Hoping she sounded helpful and not insulting. They seemed to receive her information thankfully and watched her crawl up and down the wiggly thing. Their efforts were admirable but painful to watch. Deuce struggled here, too. Molly, again, suppressed a chuckle.

Hands flailed but recaptured the rope. Legs swung out and eventually reattached. Finally, everyone was up and down, and no one was seriously injured, yet.

Good thing there's a healer in the group. Molly smiled to herself and felt a sting of guilt for once again judging her fellow man. Another sensation shimmied up her spine. Her father's teachings resonated in her mind. *Your words are powerful. Be very protective of your thoughts and your tongue.* She regretted the thought all together. "Don't let anyone get hurt because of my careless words," she prayed. It felt weird, but it didn't hurt to throw that out there. After all, she was practicing to be a good Christian missionary.

The next obstacle looked gentle enough. It was a platform, three feet off the ground. It had a sixty degree ramp up to the landing and a ninety degree drop off on the other side. They were to run up the ramp, across the top and jump off.

Simple enough.

Molly took off. Julio and Daniel were at her side, they jumped in unison. Three quickly landed behind her. She ran forward to get out of the way, and then heard it.

Crack. "Ahhh!"

Molly looked back, every one gathered around the fallen. She leaned to see who was down. It looked like it was one of the men. She moved to see around the mass of bent-over bodies.

It was Deuce! An invisible fist slammed into her gut.

"No, no. It's okay, really," Deuce said. An embarrassed chuckle effervesced with his words. But his pale face told a different story. Two men took an arm and pulled him up on his good leg. He gingerly let down the injured ankle.

"Ahhh!" he hissed and lifted it back up. "Look, it's not broken. Just let me sit down for a while. It'll be all right, just a strain."

"Self-diagnosing, are we?" Molly cajoled and leaned closer to his ear, so only he could hear. "I heard the break, Doc."

Deuce's look tossed daggers. The coach ran over, first aid kit in hand. He pulled off Deuces shoe and sock and sucked in air. "Have mercy!"

The ankle was starting to swell and turn purple. He pulled out an ace bandage, a break-and-shake ice pack, and wrapped the ankle. He knew what he was doing.

"So, you okay for us to continue?" Molly asked Abraham.

"Yeah, sure. Go on," he said through his teeth.

"Come on, everybody, let's finish for Deuce!" She rallied the others. This was her best thespian act yet.

Two three-foot walls loomed at a short distance from the pack.

"For Deuce!" The chant began as thirteen ran, jogged, and walked over to the next challenge.

Warming rays augmented the physical challenge. Stamina waned. Sweat rings darkened T-shirts. Heavy breathing filled the air. Those who could not swing their leg over and land on the other side were helped with interlaced fingers for a step up. Over the two walls, the remaining thirteen went, continuing to chant, or more accurately pant, "For Deuce! For Deuce!"

They collectively moved toward the water jumps. Several shoes hit the water's edge, but the mass of legs moved forward. Last were the tires, and everyone meticulously stepped through them and ran back around to where Deuce was seated on the grass.

Adrenaline surged and shoved exhaustion aside. They jumped up and down and slapped each other on the back. Deuce was receiving shoulder slaps, too, and head rubs.

"Some people will do anything to get out of an obstacle course," Hayden teased the downed doctor.

"Thank you, Jesus." Resounded through the weary group. Hands slapped other hands in the air. They'd all finished but one. Hopefully he wasn't badly injured, but Molly had her doubts. Exhilaration gushed through her system. She laughed and rejoiced with the others.

The fist slammed into her gut again. She had allowed herself to be caught up in the activity and forgot her role. Her smile faded into a frown. She stepped away from the jovial mass. Hands on her hips, as if she had a stitch in her side. The alarm remained present. She could not slip up like that again. Not when she was six hundred lightyears from Earth. This training was more than physical strengthening. She had to hone her mind into the duality of her role.

Sirens sounded in the distance. The Emergency Vessel glided next to the group of people. Deuce was quickly loaded and whisked away. The missionary recruits clasped hands and began to pray.

Molly stood ten feet away from the group. The coach slapped a folded up package of Instant Pop, popcorn in her hands, "Congratulations, you're our winner!"

She stared at him a moment and then switched her gaze to the Emergency vessel as it grew smaller. The *near-miss* sensation still prickled. She could not allow that to happen again.

CHAPTER ELEVEN

Molly's iComm link sounded. Red letters displaying *Mom* scrolled across the bottom of her visual range. She touched behind her ear. "Hi, Mom."

"She's going home!"

"Kita? Already? Wonderful!"

"I know! She's doing so much better. I don't know what you said to her, but—"

"Mom…it's because I'm going after this guy!"

Silence.

"Mom."

"You're investigating this?"

"Yes ma'am."

"How far?"

"What do you mean?" Molly swallowed hard. She knew what her mom was asking, but had to stall.

"How far will you have to go? To—to investigate this?"

Molly squeezed her eyes closed. The words would not come.

"You—you're going to Omicron?" her mother said at last.

"Yes ma'am."

"Does your father know?" She sounded as if she were hissing.

"Yes ma'am." Molly cringed. Her mother's heavy breathing sent chills down her spine.

She finally said, "How—how can he guarantee this doesn't happen to *you*?"

"We're working on that, Mom." Molly tried to be the adult speaking to an adult. But the child within, the one who feared making her mother mad, wanted to go hide somewhere and wait for Daddy to come home. Why hadn't *he* talked to her about this? Why was she hung out in the wind like an old, dirty rug for her mother to beat the information out? Things never change.

"Working on that?" Her mother exhaled the words.

Okay. Molly took a deep breath. If this has been left to her, she would face it head on. What could her mother do, spank her? It was time to put old baggage aside. She glanced around. Could she call for back-up? "Mom, what else can we do? Somebody has to go after this man. He cannot continue to get away with this. It's immoral. It's piracy! And I think there's some kidnapping, too!"

"So—you believe Kita? Her baby is alive?" Molly heard the hitch. Her mother would need time before she could speak again.

"I—I'm a grandmother?" she squeaked at last.

"Yes, Mother, I believe everything Kita said."

"But, why you?"

"Why not me? I *am* a civil officer."

"Yes, but you're *our daughter,* and we nearly lost your sister. They cannot do this to us again!"

The prodigal son who had stayed behind. Marti's cheat sheet sprang to life in her virtual range, "Luke 15:25-31 '"The older brother became angry and refused to go in..."

Why did that come to mind? Molly shook her head. "Mom—"

"I won't stand for it! It nearly killed me when Kita left. I did everything I could to be strong, to be supportive. Look how that turned out. I can't go through this again, Molly! I just can't."

"Mom! Kita's son is still on that planet. And somebody stole her future ability to have children. They're pirating the Earth women's donations. They have to be stopped. And, I'm going to stop them. I'm going to recover what was stolen from Kita and the other women. I'm going—to bring Michael back."

Silence filled the air waves. Not the kind of silence that exudes peace. This silence made Molly's skin crawl. Like when a dog is barking and barking, but suddenly he hunkers down, shows his teeth, and growls a low, deep-in-the-chest growl. That's the sound which tells you to run. That's the stifling, thick silence Molly heard in her iComm link.

Finally, her mother snarled, "Then, you go after that bast—" Molly knew her mother was crossing herself. "You go bring my grandson home, and you put that man in the deepest, darkest hole of confinement you can find."

"I will, Momma." Molly pressed her teeth together. She refused to cry.

***

Three months later, Molly stood outside of the boarding lobby. Her parents and Kita stood with her. Tears streamed down their faces.

"Now, you communicate with us as much as you can, honey." Her mother touched Molly's hair for the ten thousandth time.

Molly let her mother fidget with her collar and arrange her hair. Her mother needed to touch her before she left for six or seven years.

"I want you to take this." Her father shoved a worn Bible into her hands. Tears glistened his eyes.

"Your Bible? Dad, I can't." Molly pushed it back toward him.

"No. I want you to have it. I—" He closed his eyes and swallowed. "Molly. I insist. I want you to take this, and in times of need, I know it will serve you as keenly as it has served me all these years.

Besides, I have made a lot of notes in here. Think of it as another cheat sheet!" He feigned a smile.

Molly cringed. Marti's cognitive cheat sheet had been more of a nuisance than an asset. "Okay."

She pulled the gift to her chest and glanced around, trying to control the rebellious tears.

Deuce stood alone. His crutches no longer looked out of place. Had he been anybody other than the head-of-the-project's son, he would have been removed from the missionary roster. But he was the son. His smile seemed plastic as he acknowledged introductions from other recruits.

The missionaries hugged and kissed their families.

Molly turned to go, also, but Kita grabbed her one more time and kissed her hard on the cheek, "That's for Michael." She let go of her twin, her tear-soaked eyes smiled.

Molly stumbled through the metal doors that led to the transportation vessel. She allowed herself one last fleeting glimpse over her shoulder before the doors closed. The three Jacobsen's held each other and stared at her. A vacuum seal sucked the doors locked and set the barrier. This was the proverbial point of no return. Molly swallowed and lifted her chin.

Deuce gracefully swung his crutches and his reinforced ankle down the corridor. Hayden's hover truck hummed louder than normal under the weight of his and Deuce's trunks. The two had had some sort of bro-bonding since Deuce's mishap.

Molly forced her eyes toward the end of the corridor and moved forward. Trunks, suitcases, and hover trucks clicked and hummed as the fourteen walked the long, lonely gangway.

Inside the shuttle, their carry-on luggage was stowed by the flight staff. As seating was established, their voices grew louder. Soon, laughter filled the cabin. Hayden stood in the aisle while bubbly Julie squeezed past him, jabbing him in the ribs for her efforts. Sonya stood at the entry and pretended to be giving a safety lecture. Davidette leaned over the back of her seat talking to Alyce and Reah. Pam leaned over Alyce's seat to join in on their conversation. Daniel and Julio jabbered in both Spanish and English. They appeared to be so excited, they didn't realize they were mixing the two languages. Usually soft spoken, Roma's and Miriam's voices carried over the pandemonium. It was as if they all were heading for a weekend of gambling in Neo Las Vegas.

Molly sat at the back and watched the celebration. She caught herself giggling at the antics of her fellow recruits but the jocularity was wasted on her. She sent a message to the chief and then considered writing a quick note to her family, kind of a "last will and salutations" sort of thing. She suppressed the urge. Still, the idea kept resurfacing in her thinking. She updated her investigative journal instead.

Miriam stood in the aisle and read the Bible, book of Exodus, the part where Moses led God's people out of Egypt. Molly couldn't control the smile on her face with the thought of Miriam in Moses' tunic and holding his staff. Miriam was a sweet early-thirties woman who had never married. Small and slender, but she could hold her own. Her hair presented her greatest challenge in life. Taming the long curly locks was an hour long ritual for her every morning. Probably why, today, she had it submitted into a single braid down her back, nearly reaching her waist. She sang beautifully and led every one, now, in a song written by a modern spiritual band, "Apple of His Eye," based on the words she had read moments ago.

Molly updated her journal entry and looked past her virtual screen. Deuce struggled down the aisle.

"Hey, loner!" He gathered his crutches into one hand and hopped sideways to sit down beside her.

Just invite your happy little self over, Dr. Abraham. Molly suppressed the indignant sensation rising in her chest.

He didn't notice. At least he didn't act like he noticed. He laid his crutches down along the frame of his seat and buckled his safety belt. Apparently, he was staying. Molly disconnected from her virtual screen, as if he could see what she had been typing, and laid her head back against the head rest. It felt good to close her eyes. They burned from crying. Leaving her family was the second hardest thing she'd ever done. The first was telling

Kita goodbye, a little over seven years ago. Visions of Michael, as she imagined him, flashed in her mind. A smile bowed her lips as she thought about him with Kita's blue eyes and her deep set dimples. Her nephew. He'd be six by the time she arrived. Molly shook her head with wonder.

"So," Deuce interrupted Molly's thoughts. "This is it, huh?"

"Yeah, I suppose it is."

"Look, it's not gonna be all that bad. Once you get in the hibernation pod, it'll feel like—"

"I know, Deuce. It'll feel like I woke up from surgery or a really hard sleep, only it'll be three years later and with a really funky hangover. Why you so concerned about me?" Molly rolled her eyes over to her intruder.

"Well, you seem to be the only one who's not celebrating." Deuce smiled but did not look directly at her. He watched the other twelve pilgrims' frolics.

Molly watched him. If only he wasn't Austin Abraham's son, she might let herself be attracted to him. But knowing his lineage, he *was* the enemy. No matter how good looking and compassionate he seemed, he knew something about Kita, and he had not shared that information with her. That, in itself, made him a suspicious person of interest. How much did he know about his father's operation? That was still a mystery, too. One that Molly would discover, or die trying. With that thought, she fought the urge to write that will and salutations again.

"Listen, if it would make you feel any better, I'm not going into hibernation right away."

Molly stared at him. "What do you mean?"

"The ankle is not completely healed. If I go into hibernation now, I'll still have to heal once we land. I'm going to stay awake, follow through with my physical therapy, read some books, do some star gazing, you know. And when my ankle is healed, then I'll go into stasis." His smile seemed warm, genuine.

"Really? I didn't know this. I—I'll stay awake, too. You'll need company. You shouldn't be the only human being awake for, what—?"

"Six weeks…to three months, actually." Deuce's smile faded. "But why would you want to stay awake. With me?"

"I'm not going into stasis until everybody's in. That's the fine print in my contract. Call it what you will, but I don't trust anybody, especially"— She swallowed—"well, I'll go under after you go."

Deuce smiled. "Actually, Molly, I'd appreciate the company."

Annoyance bubbled in her gut. Why did it aggravate her when he was being nice? "I'll help you with your physical therapy, and you can transmit some of your books to my iComm link. What did you bring any way?"

"Horror, Sci-Fi, Classics like Agatha Christie, Who-done-it-type stuff, Cops and Robbers." He chuckled. "I don't know if you'll like any of them, they're not romance novels."

Angry heat washed over her cheeks. "Seriously? That's where you want to go with this? Romance novels? I'm going to be the only person for you to talk to for three months, and you want to go there?"

Deuce just smiled and watched the pilgrims' guileless elations.

"Besides," Molly shrugged. "How dusty was that library if you dug out something as ancient as Agatha Christie?"

Deuce stared at his lap. A slight smile lifted the edges of his mouth. "My mom loved the classics from the twentieth century. It makes me feel closer to her to read them again."

Molly nodded and looked out the small window. Could she be anymore insensitive? She pressed the ridiculing feeling down where she could deal with it later. Maybe she would apologize at some point during the next three months. What else did she have to do but work on a little self-improvement? Mentally, she shrugged.

***

Davidette, of course, started a game of Bible Trivia during the relatively short trip to the interplanetary ship. Molly glanced at her Bible cheat sheet icon and couldn't help but smile. She resisted the urge to participate. Deuce slept. Was he still on pain meds? Molly shrugged and continued accessing her library database. If she was going to be active for three months with Deuce, she wanted her own reading material. She entered an update into her journal for the chief and sent a copy to Sal.

Note: I will postpone hibernation until Dr. Abraham has deemed his broken ankle healed and is placed in suspension. It may be as long as three months. This time may prove valuable for covert interrogation. What does he know about my sister's medical files? Hopefully, our seclusion will allow me to gain his trust and his knowledge.

The animated attendants passed out a meal which consisted of six butter crackers with matching disks of cold cut meat and cheese, a squeeze tube of mustard, and a one ounce package of dried fruit. Eight ounces of bottled water or juice was offered as well. Everyone accepted their meal with silent gratitude. Only crinkled wrappings could be heard in the stillness, crunching and sipping soon followed.

Then, Hayden hollered, "Hey, I can't finish this sandwich, anybody want my left overs?" The group erupted in laughter. The attendants seemed to be oblivious to the humor or the insult. Molly giggled, and Deuce opened one eye.

"What?" He sat up straighter, looking around.

"Nothing, eat your lunch." Molly pointed at the little box waiting on his lap tray.

***

Approaching the docking station, the attitudes sobered. Everyone strained to look out the tiny windows at the interplanetary ships that stood side by side in the transportation bays. Molly felt it too. That realism in her gut that said, *Wow, this really is it.* She took a deep breath and heard the same expressive sigh throughout the other twelve people. Deuce was craning to look out the window, too, but she sensed he had an uncanny calmness about him.

Molly pushed an elbow into his side. "A credit for your thoughts."

"Huh." He glanced at her. "Oh, I was just thinking—nothing really." He looked at his lap then out the small windows.

"What?" Molly chuckled. "Come on, we're gonna be alone for at least six weeks in one of those things, don't clam up on me now."

"I was just thinking how my mom would have loved an adventure like this. Not that she'd want to join up with Dad or anything. Just the whole, you know, let's go save a race of people sort of thing." Deuce slid another quick glance at Molly.

Molly's heart twinged. She sensed the depth of grief he still nurtured for his mother.

"She must have been a special woman," she whispered softly and placed her hand over his arm.

His eyes met hers, and for a moment, she felt something between them. But that couldn't be, he was the enemy. Kita lost too much for her to forget who he is.

A hush seemed to thicken the air as the attendants instructed everyone to stand and file out. They exited the craft and shuffled through a white and aluminum corridor. Signs hung on each joint, "Waiting Station Ahead."

Silent tension was palpable. Soon they would board the interplanetary ship and prepare for the twenty-four hour process of being nestled into their hibernation pods. They looked like holocaust victims walking into a gassing chamber rather than an interplanetary ship. Molly blocked their emotions. She was having her own tug-of-war.

Miriam suddenly broke rank and ran to a refuse receptacle. Julio rubbed her back and handed her a handkerchief he kept in his back pocket.

She wiped her mouth and handed it back. He shook his head. She dropped it in the receptacle and managed a watery smile. "Thanks."

Pam handed Miriam the last of her water bottle, and Miriam swished it in her mouth and spit the liquid into the canister.

Everyone waited until she was ready to move on. Then the group moved down the corridor. Molly smiled. The program had bonded them into a team.

Deuce winked at Miriam as he made his way past her. It wasn't a flirtatious wink, more like, *you're okay, come on let's go,* sort of thing. Molly noted the gesture. It was sweet. Besides, her lunch of crackers, cold cuts and cheese wasn't sitting too well in her stomach either.

Silence loomed over the group like a fog as they traversed the length of the corridor and trickled out into a plain-vanilla waiting station. Here they would sit and wait until they were instructed to board the Interplanetary Ship Canaan Land. The attendants stood in the customary "stand-by" posture.

A communication screen lit up with the words, "Welcome Interplanetary travelers. Please be seated while your ship is readied for your adventure." The screen went blank.

An older version of Deuce appeared on the screen, grinning broadly. "Welcome, pilgrims, Austin Abraham here." He wore a cream colored linen suit with a light blue shirt and matching tie.

Molly turned toward Deuce. He stared, slacked jaw, at the screen. How long had it been since he'd seen his dad?

"You are about to embark on a lifetime adventure that you will never forget. This decision has not been an easy one to make, I'm sure, so I want to take this opportunity to introduce you to the people you are coming to help."

The stream continued to play. Silver haired people, just like Kita had described, stood embracing Earth missionaries. Small wolf-like children played together and made faces at the camera. Mr. Abraham narrated the whole time. He expounded on the accomplishments made by the pilgrims' presence. He introduced childless families who looked sad. Then these same couples stood holding three or four children with the distinctive silver fur-like hair. The babies and parents nuzzled noses and waved at the camera. They mouthed the words, "Thank you."

Why was there no audio when the locals spoke, only Mr. Abraham's voice-over? Molly considered the oddness of that revelation.

Abruptly, that invisible fist slammed into Molly's gut. She stared at an image of Kita, a very pregnant Kita, embracing a native couple. The female touched Kita's swollen belly and spoke toward the camera.

Molly focused on Kita's expression. She smiled, but it was Kita's *performance* smile. Molly knew it well. All the while, Mr. Abraham's voice joyfully described the various programs available to the locals, including surrogacy.

It was Molly's turn at the receptacle. Deuce patted her shoulder, but she pulled away from his touch. Miriam held Molly's hair back, and Pam searched for tissue. Julie asked the attendant for water and was instructed toward a machine that dispensed cool drinks. Deuce faded back into the outer edge of the team.

Tears stung Molly's eyes. Anger burned with each convulsion. She squeezed her eyes tight, but could not purge the image of her sister. At last, Molly stood. Julie handed her the water bottle she had purchased. Molly uttered something like, "Thank you," and washed her mouth out with the cool fluid. Silently, the twelve stood with Molly.

"All right, passengers," the attendants came to life.

Fourteen heads turned in unison.

"It is time to board the Interplanetary Ship Canaan Land. Please move toward the boarding platform and be prepared for your boarding authorization scan."

A small blue box flashed a red-orange light at each individual as they stepped onto the platform and another identical attendant gestured toward another corridor. One by one they were approved for boarding. Again, the mass waited until everyone was ready to move forward. Finally, as one symbiosis, they walked down the corridor. Cumulus silence enveloped them as they made their way through the filter-lit passageway. A large wing-like door stood open at the end and grinning mechanized attendants emerged to greet the pilgrims.

It was like walking into a grandly decorated yet compact hotel. The Lobby was plush with carpets and velvet chairs. A smartly uniformed crew stood at attention, forming a line between which the fourteen were to advance onto the ship. Scans were performed and quarters were assigned. Everyone bovinely followed their attendant to their quarters. The instructions were to relax until departure and then meet in the dining hall for a specially prepared dinner. This last meal would be nothing more than broths and juices. Over the next twelve hours, they would undergo preparations for the hibernation suspension process.

Molly and Deuce would not be partaking of the fast and would eat a normal meal after they sat through the other's minimal dining experience. Until then, she sat on her small platform bed and thought about Miriam, who was probably reviewing her Bible lesson on fasting. Molly smiled and let out a long sigh. The image of Kita from the infomercial still painfully etched in her mind's eye. Would that image ever fade? Not likely.

Molly updated her investigative journal. She could not help but include the infomercial and its content. Could she get a copy of it? She'd let Sal know, perhaps he could work some of his charming magic and obtain a copy.

Tears threatened, she bit her lip, and forced her emotions back in their black box. She could not allow herself to cry. She had too much to do. She had a nephew to rescue and a race of people to save.

How she would save them, she still didn't know.

CHAPTER TWELVE

Awkward expressions of anguish and wretched glares for unshared misery donned the faces as the twelve passed in and out of the relief facilities, making their muted feelings known to Deuce and Molly. The waste-purging prescriptions had been dispensed six hours ago.

Davidette growled as she emerged from the facility, "I swear, if Miriam sings, 'I surrender all' one more time, I'm going to hurt her,"

All Molly could do was sympathize and comfort. "Just a few more hours and then you will sleep."

Molly forced a pleasant smile. To be honest, she looked forward to the next six hours being over and the twelve placed in their hibernation pods. They were not the best of patients. But then again, she was not the best of nurses. Deuce, on the other hand, was in his element. He was passing out cool, wet towels and speaking encouraging words to everybody. He was—a saint.

What was she thinking? Molly jerked her gaze back to Davidette who ran back into the facility.

The current topic of conversation was disgusting. Why couldn't they get through this phase without discussing it at such length? Bowel cleansing. Lovely! But, this was all they talked about at the moment, and she had to stay engaged with the other twelve pilgrims.

So, poop talk it was.

Julie smiled apologetically and pushed past Molly to dash inside the facilities. Thank who ever built this ship, the facilities were accommodating, and no one had to wait in line. That would be a whole other repulsive task if there were a limited number of stalls.

Slowly, the time and the bowel contents ran out. It was the hour for everyone to be suspended. Molly hugged and kissed each of them goodbye. She waved vigorously as she walked backward away from the hibernation pods and ducked into her quarters.

She sat on her bed as she reclined back on her pillow. Her stomach knotted fiercely. What was it about those pods that made her feel so—afraid? Other than the fact that her own twin sister might have had all her eggs stolen while she was suspended. But how? Was that even possible?

Molly sat straight up. She needed to witness the suspension process. Maybe the thievery happened before the stasis was fully activated. But that didn't make sense either. As much as she feared the process, she had to oversee it. She hurried to the pods.

Deuce was checking vitals and reassuring Pam. Faces were obscured by breathing masks. Worrisome eyes caught sight of Molly. She fought the urge to bite her lip. Hayden's breathing seemed erratic. His face was covered in sweat. Molly sensed pain, or was it fear? She walked over to his pod and touched his shoulder. She pushed calm, peace, and rest into his senses and felt him respond. He waned a smile and closed his eyes. His breathing slowed. Warm breath fogged his mask as a sincere, "Thank you," escaped his lips. Molly tilted her head. A satisfactory smile settled on her face.

She was needed here after all.

Deuce nodded toward the attendants. Anesthetizing medication released at once into the twelve intravenous tubes.

Molly watched the effects wash over her teammates. Worried faces melted into sleepy, eye batting yawns. Alyce jumped from one of those falling dreams and settled back into a pre-slumber state. She smacked her lips as her face softened. Robotic personnel darted from pod to pod checking iComm charts above the patients' heads and touching their own hand-held devices, confirming, status normal.

Everyone drifted to sleep just like they were about to go into surgery. Phase one was complete. Molly stared at the catatonic forms. Anything could happen at this point. Who would know...

Just then, Hayden's eyes popped open.

Deuce stepped up to his monitor. He gestured for an attendant to confirm the readings. It began leveling Hayden's pod to horizontal.

Deuce turned to Molly, alarm filled his eyes. "His appendix just ruptured!"

He yelled at the mechanical attendants, "I need a sterile field over here, stat!"

An anti-bacterial laser washed over Deuce's upper torso while another attendant pushed surgical scrubs over his hands and onto his shoulders. He let his crutches fall to the ground. Molly stepped forward to retrieve the crutches, but Deuce hollered, "No! Molly, this is a sterile field now."

A third attendant altered the fluids entering Hayden's IV. His eyes closed, and his face relaxed.

A vacuum of air pushed past Molly, lifting her bangs and hair. The room had been sterilized. She stood stunned, clutching the frame of Pam's pod.

The assistant wrapped a mask around Deuce's nose and mouth as a tray lowered from the ceiling next to Hayden's now horizontal pod. Deuce's back was turned toward Molly, but his arms moved quickly. Two mechanical attendants assisted.

Molly stared at his back, frozen by fear.

At last, Deuce pulled the sterile garb, letting it fall, hopped back, and picked up his crutches. A red line marked the incision on Hayden's abdomen. No stitches, the wound had been glued. The assistant ran another laser light over the wound and sprayed a sealant. No bandages.

The attendants confirmed everyone was ready for the next phase and began removing breathing masks, taping eyelids closed, and sealing other facial orifices with pathologically compatible gel and tape. Breathing machines were activated immediately upon the insertion of tubes.

"Wh—What happened?" Molly found her voice.

"I don't know. His appendix suddenly ruptured. Thank God he was on the monitors, or we wouldn't have known." Deuce glanced at her, his attempt to conceal a smile failed.

He'd enjoyed his last bout of hero healer. The satisfaction on his face stirred Molly's anger. "You mean to tell me, he could have died?"

"Well, yeah, if we hadn't caught that in time."

Molly stared at him. This sudden, impromptu surgery seared to her core. Her knees went weak.

She leaned against Pam's pod. Was this how they stole Kita's ovum after she was anesthetized and before the hibernation suspension? Who would have done it? Could the attendants perform such a delicate procedure? They were programed to do no harm, but what if…

Still that didn't make sense. Kita had been pregnant. She bore a child. But, if the insemination was in-vitro…

"It's all right, now." Concern filled his face.

She was too stunned to respond. Her body trembled with fear and rage.

He touched her shoulder.

She jerked away as if his hand were fire. "I—I need to lie down," she muttered.

The attendants continued to prepare the twelve for hibernation. The emotional interchange went unnoticed. Focused on their devices, transparent covers slowly moved into place, sealing the travelers inside. A clear green gel filled the pod as their bodies began to float. The attendants checked and confirmed the bodies were fully suspended, all vitals were normal, and then pressed another icon on their devices. The pods instantly frosted over.

"The cryogenic process takes six seconds, Dr. Abraham," an attendant reported to Deuce.

"Good, then, we'll leave them to sleep."

It ducked its head as if saluting him and returned to monitoring.

Molly's eyebrows pressed together. "They answer to you?"

"Well, I am a healer." He looked past her to the overhead monitors. Leaning on his crutches, he walked the length of the pods. Apparently satisfied with the individual readings, he turned. "What?"

Molly frowned. "Hayden won't heal until we get there and he is...thawed out?"

"Essentially." Deuce looked into her eyes. "Right."

"But...he'll be all right."

"Yes." He donned a reassuring, practiced smile.

"Were—were there healers present when the other pilgrims..."

"I have no idea." Deuce stared at her.

Could he possibly know what her mind was churning? Her mouth drew up on one side, and she walked away. She needed to think about this, alone, behind a locked door. Nausea plagued her again. Would she ever hold down a meal?

***

A few days had passed. The indistinguishable passing of time left daytime barely different from night. Without the Zulu clock and the ship's scheduled artificial lighting, Molly would be completely disoriented.

"What are you doing?" Deuce gingerly made his way to stand behind Molly. The large observation deck quickly became a common gathering place for them both.

"It's beautiful out there, you know," Molly stated without looking around.

"Yes it is, but…"

Molly looked at him for the first time since he'd entered the observatory. "But…" She frowned. How'd he know there was a but? "I miss the sunrise. I miss waking up to morning light. I miss seeing the sunlight fade and knowing it'll be time to go to bed. I miss my family. I miss my—normal life."

"There's a certain amount of depression that has to be dealt with when one is off planet, especially during the travel time. That's the main reason for the cryogenic stasis, not only does it prevent the space depression, it also suspends aging and other physical changes so that when you arri—"

"Deuce," Molly heard the sharpness of her voice and cringed. "I know all that. Okay? You asked, I told. I wasn't looking for a diagnosis."

Deuce looked down and pressed his lips together. "Sorry, just habit, I suppose."

"You're forgiven." Her gaze returned to the star-streaked pallet of FTL travel.

They stood silent. This could be a long three months.

***

Six weeks later, a cane had replaced his crutches. Their days became routine, breakfast, physical therapy for Deuce, exercise for Molly, shower, lunch, afternoon on the observation deck, thinking, journal writing, dinner, more physical therapy, and an evening on the observation deck. They had movies to watch, books to read, and time.

She knew little more about him now than she did the day they boarded the transport.

It was the evening hours. The celestial canvas changed little by their time-keeping devices yet held their gaze in a mesmerizing anticipation. It was like being in an art museum when a certain painting drew you in and your eyes could not get enough of every minute detail.

Molly gripped the railing and chewed the inside of her cheek. *Who are you?* She studied Deuce in her peripheral. Her mind and her gut quarreled over the question. She had witnessed nothing but kindness, compassion, and transparency. However, he was Austin Abraham's son.

Kita had been violated. Deeply. How could Molly possibly trust anybody within any approximation to The Abraham Project leader?

"Why are you going to Omicron?" She turned to observe his subtle reactions.

He stood statue still, staring at the star light streaks.

She stood still, too, as if any movement on her part might prevent him from answering this crucial question. One thing she had adapted to in these six weeks was silence between them.

He ran his fingers through his hair but did not turn his gaze from the star splattered scene. "I—I suppose you'd say I'm mending fences."

Then he glanced at her. "My father was hardly ever home. He—he was always off on business trips. 'Building nations,' Mom called it. She never spoke against him or his absence. Then one day, he just didn't come home. I don't know if she heard from him or not. I know I never talked to him again. He sent presents at Christmas and birthdays, you know, but I never *saw* him anymore."

He walked over to a chaise lounge but didn't sit. "Well, I must correct that statement. There were always presents at Christmas and my birthday with his name on them. I'm not sure if he sent them or if mom just made it look like he did. It would be like her…"

He swallowed and sat down hard. "She thought the best of people. She was amazing, really."

Molly pressed her senses toward him. He was guarded, uncomfortable, and straining to contain his emotions. She didn't want to empathize, yet she wanted to learn more about who he was. And he was finally opening up. Could she trust this story he was exposing? It could be part of the ruse. Wasn't she herself telling half-truths to disguise her true intent? Yet, she sensed sincerity. Guilt snagged her heart.

This man was not the one who hurt her sister. This was not the one who stole Kita's future. This man was hurt by the same person. Only maybe his pain ran more deeply, because this man had his past and his future stolen from him. Not by a mentor but by his own father.

She walked over to the lounger next to his and eased herself down. "So, why are you going to Omicron?"

Deuce glanced sideways at Molly. He chuckled and eased himself into the lounger, "Like I said, I'm mending fences, I suppose."

"Aren't—aren't you afraid?"

"No." He shook his head then paused. "Maybe. I don't know. I *am* worried *who* I will find. I really don't know my father. And what I've seen as a result of his program… I'm not sure I'm going to like the man I'm going to meet—"

He looked back at the star-streaked view. It was as if he were thinking out loud. "What do I do then?"

Molly nodded. She knew exactly what he was saying. She had the same concerns about her mission. The *real* mission. What was *she* going to do once she landed? How was she going to take this pirating operation down with one inside agent and a delayed link back to Earth?

Dinner sat like a rock in her gut. She rubbed her temple with two fingers. There was so much information she needed to gather. All she had so far was a twin connection. There was the physical evidence, the video-stream of her very pregnant twin, Kita's lactation, the healing station's PASS scans.

She glared at Deuce. How much did he know? "What were the discrepancies with my sister's lab work?"

Deuce cleared his throat. He returned to the rail and bumped his toe against the frame. His eyes searched the florescent-striped expanse.

Molly waited.

"There's DNA tracers whenever—" Deuce leaned back holding the railing with both hands. He blew out a long breath "—when anyone expires, there are DNA tracers that mark the time and cause of death."

He looked down at Molly. Empathetic pain filled his eyes. "If a fetus expires, there are these same tracers. We can analyze the tracers and determine exactly when and why the death occurred. Two weeks after an alleged still-birth, your sister was suspended cryogenically for three years. The tracers should have still been preserved, but—"

"But, they weren't." Molly finished his sentence.

He looked at her, and then looked past her like he was running something through his mind. At last he said, "Right."

"Because..." Molly stood. "Dr. Abraham, the fetus did not expire!"

Deuce's eyes darted back to meet Molly's. "I—I don't know that."

"Yes, you do! It's the only logical explanation."

Deuce shook his head and closed his eyes.

"Okay, what if—" Molly hesitated. Should she reveal what she had seen in Sal's apartment? She swallowed and pressed on "—What if I told you I know a person who has some information proving the medical files were altered."

Deuce's eyes flared. "How do you know that?"

"I'm a LEPer, Doc, I have sources," Molly defended.

"Who is this source?"

"That's confidential."

"So were those files!" Deuce spat.

"What files?" Molly felt her temper throbbing in her temples.

"The files *I gave* a confidential source to investigate their validity. The files that you apparently confiscated. How did you get those files?"

Molly had never heard Deuce sound so angry. A small part of her feared the tone she was now hearing. This was the Austin Abraham she feared.

"I told you, that's confidential."

Deuce lunged to grab her, she side stepped him and kicked his bad ankle. Deuce collapsed to the floor, wincing in pain. Molly stepped back, her own hot temper blocked her from sensing empathy or concern. She turned to walk away.

"Molly!" Deuce called through clinched teeth. "I—I'm sorry."

"Sorry? Sorry for what? That your father lied to my sister? Sorry that my nephew was stolen from her, or sorry that you accused me of doing something illegal when it's you and your father who is—" Tears and a constricted throat prevented her from continuing.

"It's not me! It may be him, but it's not me!" Deuce winced as he pulled himself up to his hands and knees. He steadied his cane and pulled himself up the length of the cane, dragging the wounded ankle. He quickly moved his right hand to the railing and pushed himself up to a full stand, greatly favoring the ankle. "Molly, please."

"Please. What?" Molly spoke through clinched teeth.

"Help me get back to my quarters." He pleaded in a softer tone while hopping on his good leg. "I can't make it by myself."

Molly stared at him. She couldn't move.

He struggled between the rail and his cane to remain upright. His body went off-balance in a head long plunge.

She scooped him under the left shoulder and draped his arm around her shoulder, pulling his waist into her side to support his weight. He hopped as she guided. Soon, he sat on his bed. She rushed to the infirmary and retrieved two cold packs, two small towels, and a package of inflammation reducing pain pills. Returning to his quarters, she wrapped the packs in the towels, and placed them on either side of his ankle. He closed his eyes. She handed him the pill package. He opened them and drank the pills down with the remains of a water bottle on his side table.

"Better?" Molly watched his reaction.

"Better," he stated through closed eyes.

Molly turned and left his quarters, turning off the light as she exited his room. She bit her lip. Why had she acted like a three year old? Maybe he wasn't the enemy after all. How *did* Dwayne get that file? Deuce had to have given it to him. Maybe she'd ask him tomorrow if he knew Dwayne Friedman. She didn't have to reveal who he was other than her partner's step brother. She entered her own quarters and spread out on her mattress.

She wouldn't sleep, but she would rest. Visions of a pregnant Kita embracing the Omicronian couple flashed before her mind's eye. Tears spilled and rolled down her temples. Deuce, lying helpless in the observatory, begging her to help him. Her own hot temper, feeling no empathy. What kind of a monster kicks a wounded man and then doesn't help him up? She closed her eyes and drifted into a fitful slumber.

CHAPTER THIRTEEN

Deuce handed Molly a cup of freshly brewed coffee as she entered the galley. Guilty eyes could not meet his.

"Good morning," he said with a casual shrug.

"Morning." She mumbled and dared a glance at him. "How's your ankle?"

"It may have set me back a few weeks recovery, but it's all right."

"I'm sorry."

"No, I'm sorry. I provoked you. I just didn't know you were skilled in physical combat." A half smile creased his face. "You learn that in LEP training? I thought that kind of defense was banned."

"Yeah, well, I might have picked it up somewhere else."

"Uh-huh." Deuce sipped his coffee, peering over his cup.

"Yeah, a friend of mine, Dwayne Friedman, taught it to me." Molly held his gaze at last.

His eyes widened. A huge grin split his lips apart. "Dee? Dwayne taught you that? Now I know you're lying!"

"How do you know Dwayne?"

"Dee and I go waaaay back, Miss Jacobsen. How do *you* know him?"

Molly looked into her cup of coffee. The black liquid swirled but gave no hint of how to answer his pointed question. She considered how far to take her charade. "Okay, he didn't teach me physical combat, but my partner, Sal, did. Dwayne is his step brother. That's how I know—what I know."

"I see." Deuce studied Molly's face.

Her full attention focused on sipping her coffee, avoiding his scrutiny. "So...now we know. What are *we* going to do about it?"

The investigator was back on track.

"Well, *I'm* going to work on getting my ankle healed completely. Then, *we* will go into our hibernation pods and wake up on Omicron. Then —"

"Then?"

"We will find out what my father is really up to," Deuce said as he limped out of the galley on one crutch and turned off the light.

Molly stood in the dark and watched him wobble down the narrow hall toward the observatory. Technically, her cover was blown. He knew she wasn't going to Omicron for the missionary experience. But, then again, neither was he. She sighed and set her coffee down. She would help him with his physical therapy. It was the least she could do since her outburst had set him back. But, she still did not trust him. She couldn't trust him. Not completely.

**

Molly entered a report in her Journal.

Zulu Date, 25.11.2214

Tonight Dr. Abraham will enter his hibernation pod. Once secured and at least six hours into his cryogenic stasis, I will enter mine. I do not want to leave anything to chance. Despite all I have been told, I fear for my own safety.

That entry gave her pause.

I have instructed the attendants to revive me first before all the others, further ensuring I am last to go under and first to revive. With these procedures in place, I feel confident my safety cannot be compromised. God help me if I'm wrong. It's the best I can do to ensure no harm. I am reminded of the prayer Kita and I recited when we were little, "I pray the Lord my soul to keep." Keep me, Lord, as I slip into unconscious vulnerability. Protect me from the evil one's hands.

SIDE NOTE: Sorry, Chief, I'm sure you don't want this in my report. Just understand that out here, alone with one person I gauge as my enemy, it's difficult not to include a prayer in my report. I am a pastor's daughter after all.

Dr. Abraham has divulged he is the one who made Kita's medical film available to the technical source. Apparently we have a mutual friend. That said, the information is known by both Dr. Abraham and myself. The medical file was altered, and the victim's lab reports clearly indicate the lie. There is no physical evidence that the victim delivered anything other than a live baby.

What is the senior Abraham really doing? How far reaching is his operation of piracy? I can only hope I find out. Soon, as far as my conscious mind is concerned, I will set foot on Omicron and begin my investigation. God help us all.

End report. Officer Molly Jacobsen, Send command 675342.J14.

Molly closed her iComm link and sat up. She accessed her biblical cheat-sheet app. The familiar passage was pinned for quick access. Psalms 138:7 "Though I walk in the midst of trouble, you preserve my life. You stretch out your hand against the anger of my foes, with your right hand you save me."

"Let it be so, dear Lord, Amen," Molly prayed. This had become routine, too.

Molly drew in a long slow breath. Today was the day. She swallowed the dry knot of fear in her throat. Deuce would be in the relief facility most of the day. Purge prep. She remembered the other twelve and their misery. Later would be her turn. Molly scrunched her nose and pressed her lips together at the thought. Her last few hours and she would be completely alone and miserable. That three year old within trembled. The adult turned a blind eye.

Molly met Deuce exiting the men's facilities.

"You look pale." She cringed at her own words. What a stupid thing to say!

A raised eyebrow was his only response. This was going to be a long twelve hours. Molly followed him into the Observatory.

"I think this is the worst part of this whole hibernation thing," Deuce finally said with a solemn smile.

"Yeah, I suppose so." She looked away. That and having your future children stolen, she couldn't help but think about her sister.

"So, your ankle's feeling good?" she asked for lack of anything else to say.

Deuce looked down at his foot and rotated the ankle. "Yeah, I'd say it's good as new. At least, it's good enough. I know these three months were, well, boring, but they were worth it to arrive in sound shape. And I appreciate you being awake with me. It would have been—"

"Yeah, sure." Molly waved a dismissive hand. "Besides, I got a lot of reading and journaling done, so it hasn't been all that bad." She forced a smile. Truth was, the time had allowed her to develop a habit of reading her dad's Bible and saying a prayer or two, for the legitimacy of her undercover, of course. It had been a long time since she had done either. If she was going to pull off this façade of a missionary pilgrim, she needed to look and sound the part.

The star-streaked observatory scene flashed in her mind. She would have missed seeing that, also, if she had gone into the hibernation pod with the others. A sigh escaped her lips. Not to mention, the time had been important to her investigation. Dr. Abraham was an enigma, but she had certainly determined he did not approve of his father's practices. There was an underlying sense of disgust, or something like that, when they talked about what had happened to Kita.

Still, Abraham, Senior was Deuce's father, and, as they say, blood is denser than water. No telling how that would play out once they arrived. She'd keep her eye on him and be wary all the same. *Sorry, but you're guilty until proven innocent, Dr. Abraham.*

Deuce rose quickly and dashed to the relief facilities, partially bent toward his left. Molly watched him go. An attendant approached her from the other direction.

"Molly Jacobsen, your meal is ready."

"Thank you. I'll be right there." Molly glanced one more time at the hall where Deuce had exited. Even though the food consisted of broth and juice, a liquid diet before the great purge, she decided to go enjoy her last meal for the next two years and nine months.

"Let Dr. Abraham know where I am, will you," she said to the attendant as kindly as she could manage.

"Of course." It answered with a slight bow of its head.

***

Molly watched while the attendants meticulously prepared Deuce. He seemed subdued. And why not? He didn't have to be concerned he might lose a part of his pathology.

She squelched that selfish thought and forced a smile. "Have a nice nap."

He leaned back and placed his breathing mask over his face. A rumble in her lower abdomen told her she needed to go, but she didn't want to miss one second of his suspension. Weighing the odds of how long it would take her and how long it would take the attendants to get him fully under, she decided to run for the facilities.

When she returned, he was still wearing the breathing mask. She had not missed much of the process. The attendant moved in close to his IV tube and held a hypodermic syringe. "Are you ready, Dr. Abraham?"

"Yes." Steam fogged his mask as the muffled word was spoken.

Molly waved goodbye. His hand rose and bent fingers waved back.

Tears stung her eyes. *This is ridiculous.* She clamped her jaw tight.

The attendant pressed the tip of the syringe into his IV shunt and slowly injected the anesthetizing fluid. Deuce winked at her before his eyes closed, and his breathing slowed. His mask continued to gather moisture until the attendant removed the mask and completed the tubing and gel process. Soon, Dr. Abraham was fully suspended behind a frost covered transparent cover.

Molly hurried to the relief facility. Now she was alone for another six hours, but she was safe. There was no one left to interfere with her suspension procedure. Her anatomy would be unharmed. So why were her senses tingling with apprehension?

She glared at the attendants. Once again reassuring herself, they were programed to do no harm. But what if—no, she wouldn't accept that thought. Not now. Not so close to going into suspension. She had to believe the plan was a solid and safe plan. Besides, she would *not* endure three years' solitude simply because she was terrified of the suspension. Every fail-safe process had been incorporated into her plan. She was safe! She had to believe that. She had to trust...God. Could she do that after all this time? What choice did she really have?

Another thought occurred to her. She'd insist someone at the healing station scan her immediately upon arrival to verify she had not been robbed of her fertility. In fact, she'd insist her team hold off on any donations until she had a better feel for what was going on. And she would *not* blow her cover. She nodded to herself. That was her plan.

A cramp bent her over. She dashed to the facilities.

CHAPTER FOURTEEN

"I'm still your older sister." The twinkle in Kita's eyes amused Molly.

"Yes, but I had cell division first!" Molly quoted her age-old come back and smiled brilliantly as her sister pushed her three-year-old in the swing. Molly twisted in a swing next to him. It was good to be with Kita and her son. She looked out across the play yard. A loud noise rumbled beyond the trees. Molly stood and shielded her eyes from the afternoon sun. Her gaze swept the tree line.

"What is that?" she said more to herself than to any one, stepping closer to listen. Cracking sounds carried on the breeze, and the ground rumbled. The tops of the boughs swayed at a distance toward the playground, heading straight for them. They parted as a deep-creviced, carved figure of a giant wooden woman, leaning at a sixty degree angle, led the bow of a huge ship onto the playground. The trees were crushed to the right and left of the ship's hull like small sticks.

"Pirates!" Molly screamed and turned to grab Michael, but the swing twisted and buckled in his absence. She swirled around desperately searching for Michael and Kita.

Kita stood alone on the lawn, tugging at her milk-soaked shirt. Her feral, tear saturated eyes stared at the threatening ship.

Molly fought a stifling sensation and looked over her shoulder. The ship gouged into the immaculate lawn as if it had run ashore at the playground's edge. Michael stood among several pirates on the bow of the ship. One draped his rotten-rag-covered arm around the boy's shoulder. Their evil grins bore decayed, brown stained teeth.

Cold fear washed over Molly like a spray of northern sea water. She shivered violently but kept her eyes locked on her nephew. Michael bounced up and down, laughing and waving.

"Michael!" she screamed with all her might, but stopped abruptly, feeling her throat shred by the effort.

***

A bone deep chill raked Molly's body, causing a convulsive shiver that painfully tightened her skin with enormous goose bumps. Her body wouldn't obey her desire to rub the limbs. Panic crawled all over her like a thousand spiders. She couldn't move. She couldn't breathe. Suddenly, a gagging sensation tugged at the back of her throat. Something passed over her tongue and a bitter taste lay in its wake.

"Molly Jacobsen," an unnatural voice called her name. "Molly Jacobsen, you are on the Interplanetary Ship Canaan Land. You have been revived from hibernation. You are all right, Molly Jacobsen. You will be cold, but we are warming you now. You will feel better soon, Molly Jacobsen."

She forced her eyes open. The view blurred by ointment was confusing. Tremors in her limbs had a mind of their own. Warmed blankets swaddled her trembling body. She closed her eyes and let the warmth seep in. Soon, the bone-deep cold penetrated the wrappings, and another blanket, freshly warmed, replaced the first.

She was waking from hibernation. Her eyes darted across the other pods. She blinked repeatedly to clear her vision. She was the first to be revived. She sighed in relief. That part of her plan had worked. Yet, her heart pounded. An unrelenting fear tormented her lethargic mind. She tried to relax, let the warmth ease her into wakefulness.

An attendant examined the IV tube running toward her wrist. "This is a warmed saline to help with your recovery. Try to relax, Molly Jacobsen," it said.

Her legs and arms felt disengaged from her body. She had to look down at them in order to lift them, and open and close her hands. So odd. Involuntarily, she placed her hand on her lower abdomen. Was she all right? No one had told her about the waking process. It was weird, disorienting, and—cold. She focused on breathing. In…out…in…out.

"Sit up, slowly," the attendant instructed her.

She complied. A nice hot shower would be wonderful right now. And—and some food.

"Let's swing our legs over the side," the attendant coaxed her.

It was a painfully arduous routine but proved to be necessary. When she stood, she collapsed, and fell back into the pod seat. "Whoa!" she croaked. Her throat burned with raw pain.

She rolled her eyes, grateful she was the first to be revived with no witnesses to observe her weakness. She let her eyes rove over the other thirteen pods. The pods were drained of the impact absorbing gel, but the breathing tubes were still in place, no longer popsicles but not fully awake either.

Molly stood again and held on to the padded platform. She fought the dizziness and forced her eyes to focus on one object, the pod next to hers. Deuce's pod. Deuce, asleep with a breathing tube protruding from his taped mouth. She focused on his closed eyes. The spinning in her head slowed. The nausea subsided. She took a deep breath and a step away from the pod.

Her knees buckled, but she stiffened her muscles. At last, they were holding. She took another step and pushed her palms into her lower back. Stretching felt remarkably good.

"I'm the first to revive, correct?" Molly whispered to the attendant at her side.

"Yes, Molly Jacobsen," it answered.

"No one…nothing interfered with the suspension during these—two years and nine months?"

"That is correct, Molly Jacobsen," the attendant assured.

She stared into the amazingly human-like eyes. They were incapable of lying. She knew that. Still, she felt a weird inkling that meant something was askew. Then again, she had just been revived from nearly three years hibernation. Could these sensations be trusted? And with that, she took another step. Eventually, she had made her way around her bed and felt confident enough to let go. She crept across the pod chamber and looked over her shoulder at the thirteen who emerged in various stages from their induced slumber.

She craved solitude. Perhaps she could update her investigative journal before she showered or ate. Assuming her fingers were working and she could type. She flexed her hands as she traversed the corridor.

***

"Good morning!" Miriam entered the dining hall. A bowl of something similar to cream of wheat sat out for each person, the fast break meal.

Molly smiled. "Good morning!"

Other's just nodded and ate their beige cereal. Miriam stopped in front of one bowl and stared at the content. Cheerfully she whined, "No coffee?"

Some giggled.

Like Molly, the first priority meant a shower and fresh clothes. Eventually, all fourteen recruits sat at the oval, under-lit table, an empty bowl shoved aside to be retrieved by the attendants.

Miriam nodded to Davidette.

Davidette cleared her throat and then cleared it again. Recovering from the long sleep was harder than anyone had anticipated. "We will have another seven hours before we embark on our pilgrimage. That will allow us to fully recover from our slumber. I hope."

Her own sluggish eyes looked into each of her fellow pilgrims'. Molly glanced at Deuce. They shared a humorous grin.

"We will meet with our fore-travelers and be assigned quarters. There will be a 'Dinner slash Introduction' this evening honoring us. Please hear me when I say this." She paused for effect. "Tonight's dinner should be amazing, but do not over eat. You must monitor your intake over the next twenty-four hours. Be polite and show your grateful spirit, but *take it easy*."

She looked at Hayden who sat in a hover chair. "I understand you endured an impromptu emergency appendectomy before you went into hibernation."

Hayden nodded.

She glanced at Deuce then back to Hayden. "You will need to allow yourself time to recover, obviously. Please visit with your physician regarding your limitations." She gestured toward Deuce. "And may I add on a personal note, thank

God you were here, Deuce. I understand we might have been reduced to thirteen had you not been present."

Deuce lowered his gaze and pursed his lips. Hayden nodded and glanced at Deuce. Molly rolled her eyes and looked off to her right. *Men!*

Davidette cleared her throat. Solemn intent returned to her countenance as she scanned each face. "Tomorrow we will receive our assignments and get started with the purpose for which we have traveled these many lightyears." A giggle escaped her lips. "I, for one, am anxious to get started, aren't you?"

Some nodded. Some giggled. Other's mumbled. Still others just sat and listened. The term, "not a morning person," had a whole new meaning when one came out of a three-year stasis.

Molly endured Davidette's self-appointed master of ceremonies. She had a different agenda to pursue. Curiosity fluttered in her gut. Her eyes met Deuce's. Wonder what activities he would seek once he embarked on this mysterious planet. She raised her hand. "If I may…"

Davidette acknowledged her with a nod.

"Let's not jump into anything too quickly when we get out there. Because of my sister, I obviously have some concerns, and I'm sure Dr. Abraham will be able to put my mind at ease, but until then, please promise me none of you will volunteer for any...pathological procedures." She scanned the women's faces. Each seemed to understand, and she sensed compliance.

"Quite right, Molly. Now," Davidette continued. "Let's all start walking and exercising—*gently*. We need to revive our muscles and our minds. In a few hours, I'd like for us to meet in the observatory and have a moment of prayer and thanksgiving." She glanced at the Zulu clock. "Let's say, oh eleven thousand."

A red flush filled her cheeks. "Did I say that right? I mean at eleven o'clock. Okay?"

Molly fought the urge to roll her eyes but noticed Deuce lost his battle with the same urge. *So much for his missionary spirit.* She lowered her head to hide her smile, while her eyes stayed on him, and fidgeted with her empty bowl.

What? He mouthed. She bulged her eyes and shoved her bowl away.

Miriam took a double take at the two of them and furrowed her brow. "In seven short hours we all need to be showered, packed, and dressed to exit this ship. Take all your belongings. As you know, this ship will be placed in service elsewhere."

A sigh escaped her mouth, her eyes focused on something high on the ceiling but far away. "It still amazes me that we are able to do this. The harvest is abundant, the harvesters so few."

Harvest. The word sent chills through Molly's midsection. The image of Kita flooded her mind. Michael! Would she see him soon? Among all the children she expected to see, would she know Kita's son? A daunting emotion washed over her. She dipped her head and focused, again, on her empty bowl. Something like agoraphobia filled her head. She needed to be alone. She pushed away from the community table and made her way toward her quarters.

"You all right?" Deuce's voice came from behind.

"Yeah," she answered automatically. "Just need some time. Don't seem to have my bearings yet."

"Understandable." He looked her over. Always the healer. She forced a smile and turned into her room. Her door hit something, and she turned to see why it wouldn't close. Deuce's foot blocked it. His face peered through the gap. "Meet me for a walk in a little bit?"

"Sure," she agreed mechanically.

"The observatory?"

"Right."

Deuce nodded and pulled back from her door.

Molly pressed her eyebrows together as she closed her door and turned the lock. She stared at the barrier between them.

Shrugging the odd behavior off, she sat down on the platform bed and activated her iComm link. The journal appeared before her eyes. She entered a supplemental report noting her curiosity about Deuce's intentions and sent the file. A red flashing beacon lit up on her virtual screen, she touched it. A message sprang up as if on a transparent film.

Molly, You made it. I'm Gordon. Your report is received and will be sent post-haste. Welcome. See you soon. –G.

Molly pushed out her lower lip. So the insider is alive and well. Good to know. Pushing off her bed, she strode toward the door. She would meet Deuce for a walk. *Keep your friends close, and your enemies even closer,* the thought filled her mind. She had a mission to fulfill, but first she needed to regain her strength, walking with the program director's son would accomplish that very duality.

Another red flash appeared. Gordon again? She tapped her iComm link.

You have a difficult task ahead of you. You have friends. Be careful. –AF.

CHAPTER FIFTEEN

"AF?" She paced her small room. Was Gordon playing a trick on her? An initiation, ha ha, we gotcha sort of thing? Molly puzzled over the message. A tap on her door broke into her thoughts. Deuce! She cracked open the door.

A sliver of Miriam's face peeked through. She spoke softly, "Molly? Care to join us?"

Molly glanced at the time. It had not been a full hour yet. She flashed a warm smile. "Sure. I'll be right there."

Thirteen pilgrims sat quietly, waiting for the fourteenth. Heat rose in Molly's face as she entered. Why did they need her present before they could begin? She sat. Deuce's eyes met hers.

"Sorry," she mouthed as she shrugged.

He returned the gesture.

Immediately, Miriam stood and cleared her throat. Her glare remained on Molly for a moment longer than necessary.

Always in trouble. Molly pushed the irritation aside. Hibernation lag.

"Well, Pilgrims, we made it!" Miriam clasped her hands in a single clap. The expanse of the Grand Canyon could not compare to the broad smile on her face. Her soul signature sparkled, and her words were carried by breathless effort. Definitely hibernation lag.

"We're starting a little sooner than we had said, but you'll understand why in a few minutes. Now, let's join in thanksgiving." Miriam bowed her head, and the other's followed. Miriam prayed, expressing thanks for safe travel and asked for blessings over the work they were about to do for the people of Omicron. Everyone echoed her final word, "Amen."

"As I said earlier, we will be dined tonight, so when we disembark, please be dressed in your Sunday best. We want to make a good impression, don't we?" Miriam giggled like a school girl. "Please remember your protocol lessons, but be yourself and have a good time." She swung her fist in the air before her torso.

Okay, now she was trying too hard. Molly sensed—nervousness. That was curious. Perhaps she would keep Miriam under surveillance as well as Deuce. One never knows. Moles could be anywhere, anybody, especially overly enthusiastic participants. Molly started. Technically, *she* was the mole.

Miriam looked up, from the corner of her eye, and paused. Molly, like everyone else, followed her gaze to look up in the same direction but saw nothing. Miriam waited. Her eyes darted from the ceiling to the recruits and back. A goofy smile slid from her face. Her forehead wrinkled down toward her brow.

The ship's iComm system crackled. "Is this on? *Tap tap tap*...Are you sure? Oh, oh, okay, *Ahem*, H-HELLLOOO Pilgrims from Earth!" A smooth deep voice spoke too loudly.

Deuce rolled his eyes and lowered his head. Apparently, he recognized the speaker's voice. Molly couldn't take her eyes off him. This could only be one person—

"This is Austin Abraham." His southern Earthly regions' accent rang through, elongating both names. "And I want to be the first to welcome you to Omicron." Again the planet's name was elongated in that southern drawl. "We are so happy to have you here, and we thank Gawd you have arrived safely with His grace and mercy."

Deuce's eyes shot up to meet Molly's. She lowered her chin and rolled her eyes up as if she were peering over reading glasses sitting low on the bridge of her nose. *Really?* Deuce shrugged and widened his eyes then rotated his eyes up and over. Molly suppressed a smile. She'd never seen him squirm like he did now.

"Okay," Mr. Abraham continued. "So we look forward to the hour you will disembark, and we get to welcome you properly! And I hope y'all are hungry 'cause there's a feast awaitin' ya."

Molly could hear the jovial smile in Mr. Abraham's voice. But an oily feeling slithered down her spine. She tightened her limbs to suppress the shiver. Deuce didn't appear to be happy by the greeting either. The others, however, exhibited elation. They cheered, girls hugged girls, and the men fist bumped and patted shoulders.

"Until then," Abraham spoke again. The recruits quieted. "Fare thee well sweet princes and princesses of Earth and Heavenly realms. Oh I probably shouldn't have said that. Huh?...What? Oh. Well...here, you turn it off." The ship's speaker squawked, clicked, and then went silent.

Deuce closed his eyes as he shook his head. Hayden shoved him over, and then grimaced and held his abdomen. Deuce glanced at Hayden with a crimson-stained face and a half smile. Hayden sat back in his hover chair with obvious discomfort. Of course, he would be excused from the cryogenic reviving exercise.

"Okay, well," Miriam drew everyone's attention. "We have hibernation fatigue to get over so let's walk around the ship and get our blood flowing again, shall we?" Ever the cheerleader, she coaxed the sluggish participants to their feet. "Attendants, if you please." A lively recording of spiritual music blasted throughout the ship. Its cadence was matched by Miriam's walking pace. She, of course, led the pack.

***

Everyone stood, as Miriam had requested, in their Sunday best, waiting to disembark. All except Hayden, of course. He sat in a hover chair, waiting for a medical attendant to transfer him to the infirmary. He looked exhausted. The wing-like airlock door creaked and snapped as the three-year-old seal broke open. The attendants stood at attention on both sides of the door, just as they had when the fourteen boarded. Deuce seemed to hang back, so Molly took her time and let everyone push ahead of her. Her senses tingled with something familiar yet out of place. It filled her mind like a lingering perfume. She stared at the growing gap of the rising door.

First feet, then legs, then torsos waited on the other side of the ever rising door. Strange sounding music, comparable to the Atlantic Island's with drums, flutes, and other string instruments unknown to the pilgrims, played on instruments fashioned from wood. Its rich, hollow reverberations bounced off the hard surfaces of the embarking station. Silver-haired children stood with many flower bouquets. As the pilgrims stepped out of the ship, the children stepped forward and handed over their bundles. Awkward kisses were laid on one cheek then the other as the pilgrims bent down to accept the vibrant colored plumage.

Silver-haired adults stood behind the flower-bearing children, proudly claiming their offspring by resting their hands on the child's shoulders. Wide canine grins were in full bloom as well.

"Where's Pastor Oliver Pugh?" Miriam asked, scanning the greeters. Molly scanned the faces as well. The Chief had said Oliver Pugh had not been seen since Kita's escape.

A tall slender man with Deuce's grey eyes stood to one side, acknowledging each person as they walked past the children greeters. His stark white suit reminded Molly of an island host in the Caribbean. He gleefully patted the shoulders, but his eyes roved over the disembarking travelers. He looked for one passenger only, his son. When at last he spotted Deuce, his smile widened even more than what seemed possible.

"Austin!" he shouted and threw open his arms. It was the same voice they had heard hours ago welcoming them.

Deuce slowly stepped into his father's embrace, said something against his ear, and buried his face into his dad's linen covered shoulder. When they finally broke from their hold, both wiped wet eyes. The other thirteen stood to the side and watched Abraham and son. A single clap resounded, then another. Soon, the whole crowd was clapping and cheering the Abraham reunion. Deuce flushed pink, but Mr. Abraham beamed with a father's pride and draped his long arm over his son's shoulders.

A stick-like object was handed to Mr. Abraham. He turned it over in his hand and scraped a thumb nail against the one end. He said something to the man who handed it to him and nodded. He held the stick up to his mouth and began to speak. It amplified his voice, like the iComm links back on Earth, and the crowd hushed.

"Welcome pilgrims! Friends, I'd like you to meet my son, Dr. Austin Abraham."

Cheers erupted all over again. Mr. Abraham shook his son, and Deuce tilted his face as flower pedals fell over their heads and shoulders. "Son, and pilgrims, I'd like you to meet His High Exalted, Argenteus Lupus and his wife Her High Exalted, Lily Lupus."

Cheers continued to resonate across the masses. The fourteen pilgrims stood generally together as Lupus and his wife walked over to them. One by one, each pilgrim introduced himself or herself.

Kita's description held true. Their silver fur-like hair, and short fur-covered faces were the only feature that distinguished them as different from Homo sapiens. Molly's heart ached for her sister. She sensed the familiar tangent waves of Kita's presence gently crossing the rhythm of the life energy. How could her essence be present? Kita left this planet over six years ago. Yet there it was, the familiar awareness of her twin sister as if she literally stood just a few feet from Molly.

Again, she hung back and observed. These leaders interacted with her fellow pilgrims with such ease. A child stood mid-section tall between the Lupuses. Each pilgrim was greeted the same. Mr. Lupus would kiss their cheeks, and introduce his wife. She would kiss their cheeks, and reach behind her to tug the lad forward for an introduction. He nodded his head in greeting as he quickly squeezed back behind his mother, too young for diplomatic protocol.

Kita inundated Molly's senses. She could almost smell her sister's organic scent. The closer to the honored recipients, the more she was consumed with her sister's signature. At last, it was her turn to be greeted. Mr. Lupus' voice was gravelly, but the kiss he placed on her cheeks was tender. His face felt like velvet. Mrs. Lupus gently kissed Molly's cheeks in turn. She smelled of a sweet bloom, similar to gardenia, and her skin was soft as a rose petal.

Molly uttered an awkward thank you. Lily Lupus, routinely now, reached between herself and her husband. "May I present our son, AJ?"

A low buzz filled Molly's ears. She could barely hear Mrs. Lupus' voice. Molly smiled and lowered her eyes to greet their son. The buzz exploded in her head. A white light flashed and filled her vision. Two blue eyes penetrated the vast whiteness. Kita's eyes timidly looked up at Molly as the whiteness evaporated like a warmed mist.

Her heart slammed against her chest, and her breath froze in her lungs. The boy bore the silver mane of his people, but the face was Kita's. Her soul signature was so strong with this child. He had to be Michael!

This was the twin connection she had felt. Kita's child had the same...frequency. Vertigo consumed her. She fought to stand firm, but her knees buckled.

Mrs. Lupus grabbed Molly's arm, and Deuce quickly took hold of her other.

"Are you ill, my dear?" Genuine concern gleamed in Mrs. Lupus' eyes.

"No. No, I—I," Molly's eyes still locked with Michael's. Even he remained in front of his parents this time, staring at Molly with great curiosity.

Deuce supported Molly fully now. "We're a little weak from our stasis. I'm sure we'll all be better after our meal and a good night's rest."

"Don't make excuses for me." Molly pushed Deuce away. He stumbled slightly, favoring his newly mended ankle. She wavered on unsteady legs before he regained his supportive grip on her arm.

Mr. Lupus cleared his throat. "Yes, yes of course—" He held a repugnant glare on Molly "—Well then, Austin, we need to get these fine people to the feast!"

"Indeed." Mr. Abraham clapped his hands twice. Two mass transit vessels pulled up behind him, and he grandly opened its doors. With a wave of his hand, he sunk into a deep bow. The pilgrims moved toward the two vessels.

"This will take you to our home." Mr. Lupus announced and swept his family off to their personal vessel. Mr. Abraham's eyes swept Molly's unsteady posture. She peeled out of Deuce's hold and stiffened to brace herself. Mr. Abraham returned his gaze to Deuce. "Son, you…and Miss Jacobsen are welcome to join our transport."

"No, you go with your father. I'm fine. Really." Molly swallowed hard. "I'm fine."

Wobbly legs betrayed her statement as she made her way to the transport vessel. Deuce waited until he saw her seated in the vessel before he returned to join his father.

The Abrahams bent at the waist and entered the Lupus' smaller vessel, and the procession lunged forward. The masses cheered and waved goodbye as the two vessels pulled away from the embarking station.

The wooden islander's music trailed behind them.

CHAPTER SIXTEEN

Omicronian scenery dashed past the observation windows of the mass transport vessel. The new pilgrims' eyes drank in the unique landscapes. It appeared to be tropical, almost New Caribbean-like, except there was a dry desert feel to the air. How could the plants look so tropical when the ground and the air seemed so dry? Molly stared with blind eyes toward the simple architecture of the city, and then the countryside patches of homes and crops. The magnificence of it all was lost on her.

She had just faced her biggest fear, and yet it had been her greatest hope, finding Michael. The audacity of that man flaunting her nephew right under her nose. Molly released clinched fists. Blood rushed back into her whitened knuckles as a tingly sensation replaced numbness. She shook off the feeling both in her hands and in her mind.

Solid up! This is why you're here. She released her lower lip from its assailant, her upper teeth. The metallic flavor of blood augmented the bitter taste already dominating her palate.

Molly closed her eyes and drew in a slow, steadying breath. *Fluid down, Mol.* Her sister's voice resonated in her mind. A slight smile tugged at the corners of her bruised lip. This new presence that matched Kita's settled into her aching bones. Solace accompanied its existence, and Molly allowed it to find a place in her heart.

This was good. Michael's link would guide her. Soon as this nausea goes away.

An unwanted sigh escaped with the breath Molly released from her lungs. Could she keep her emotions in check? This undercover stuff was harder than she imagined when her own flesh and blood was involved. She set her back teeth firmly together, and opened her eyes. The scene outside the windows stayed out of focus. She concentrated on her task at hand, tonight—this farce of a feast, tomorrow—Gordon. At some point she needed to find Pastor Oliver. Where could he be?

A bolt of fear shot through her. She sat up straighter. Was her own fertility intact? Item number three on tomorrow's agenda, get a PASS.

***

Sparkles danced across the surface of a long driveway as the vessels passed over the crushed purple-pink material. The Lupus' home, nestled against a wooded curtain of evergreen forestry, stretched beyond their visual range. Davidette's long slow whistle said it all. Nervous giggles rippled through the vehicle.

"Holy Moses!" Daniel spoke slowly, "I fully expected a castle."

Molly nodded. The sprawling adobe home sat at the apex of the driveway. It was not a castle. It didn't have turrets or stone, but it was huge and multi-storied. She counted three above ground. Wonder how many levels there are below ground? Perhaps on Omicron, this was indeed a castle, sans the moat and drawbridge. Attendants stood at the ready on the rounded steps leading to the entrance.

Mr. and Mrs. Lupus exited their vehicle followed closely by Michael. A warm smile brightened his face as he turned toward Mrs. Lupus. His mouth moved, and she bent to say something to him. He nodded, ran past the attendants, and into the house. Molly caught her breath as he disappeared into the shadows. The warm exchange lingered in Molly's senses.

The pilgrims continued to exit their vessels and stood next to the transport until everyone was ready to walk into the home. Molly's eyes returned to the entrance and the shadow through which Michael had slipped.

Mr. Abraham smiled and waved the pilgrims forward. Like one organism, they shuffled toward tonight's hosts. Mr. Lupus gestured with open arms and welcomed the newcomers to his home. With wide strides, he led the procession. The attendants stood statue still until the last human passed through the entry doors. Molly glanced back as she stepped over the threshold. The attendants were gone. She pursed her lips and followed her group to the feast.

Castle or not, the banquet hall was as majestic as any castle imagined. The food table stretched the length of one expansive wall. Attendants stood every three feet behind the food, ready to place any chosen selection on a plate. The meats were varied from roast to goodness-only-knew-what-it-was, vegetables and cheesy pastas covered a third of the table, breads filled another quarter, fruit pastries and individual cakes covered the last quarter of the spread. Fruit drinks, teas, coffee and water were brought to the tables after everyone was seated.

Molly's mouth watered from the aroma. Her fork stopped mid-way to her mouth when Michael ran in to join the Lupuses at the head table. The meat in Molly's mouth would not grind down small enough to swallow. Delicately, she spit the mass into her cloth napkin and tucked it back into her lap.

"You all right?" Pam leaned over to whisper.

Molly nodded. "Not sure what that was." They exchanged an understanding smile, giggled, and mirrored each other's shrug. Pam turned back to her own plate and lifted another forkful.

Molly's heart doubled its pace and her throat tightened. She pressed her lips together as she watched Michael interact with the couple he knew as his parents. She allowed her senses to reach out and mingle with his essence.

He looked up, his eyes met directly with hers. A warm smile lit up his face.

Whoa! Did Michael sense her touch? He turned to Lily and said something. She nodded and motioned toward his plate. He lowered his head and ate vigorously. His eyes peeked up at Molly as often as she dared to glance at him.

A crazy fantasy played out in her mind. *She'd jump up and run over to Michael, screaming about how he was her nephew, and she would take him home to his real mother.* Molly closed her eyes and pushed the hysterical scenario back into a subdued place in her mind. She pushed the food around on her plate but she couldn't eat another bite.

The plates were cleared, and three iComm screens lit up around the room. A stream began to play praising The Abraham Project and all that

Austin Abraham and his pilgrims had done for the people of Omicron. Oliver Pugh shook Mr. Abraham's hand and swept a gesture toward all the exuberant couples holding babies and toddlers in their arms. The recording device followed his gesture and scanned the many Omicronians. They articulated their joy and thankfulness for the families the pilgrims had helped create and the populace that was being restored to the people of the planet.

The stream ended, and Molly exhaled. Her lungs burned from the pressure. Kita had not appeared in any of the scenes. Apparently, it had been updated from the one that had been shown on Earth at the transportation station. However, Pastor Oliver was present at the recording

Sure, they would have new testimonies, more current interviews. It made sense, and yet Molly's heart ached for her sister and what she lost, rather than gained from The Abraham Project. Something began to gnaw at her gut. Did this mean Pastor O was near by?

She chanced a glance at Michael. His seat was empty as was Lily's. Perhaps he was being put to bed. Another pang ripped through Molly's heart. How she longed to read a bedtime story to her nephew, wish him good night, kiss his soft head, and pull his covers up to his chin.

"Molly?" Deuce stood in front of her table, gesturing for her to go with him. "I'd like to introduce you."

Molly's eyes darted over to Mr. Abraham and back to Deuce. A sigh escaped before she had a chance to curb the rudeness. She forced a smile. "Of course."

She took a sip from her glass and stood up. Deuce walked the length of the table and reached for her hand when she rounded the end. *What am I, a puppy?* She squeezed her eyes and shoved the thought back out of her way.

"Dad, this is Molly. The woman I told you about who was kind enough to stay up with me for nearly three months while my ankle healed." Deuce beamed.

"Well, Molly, I am indebted to you then. If there is anything you need or long for, you come directly to me, and I'll see that you get it." Mr. Abraham spoke louder than necessary.

As a matter of fact, sir, I'd like to know what in Hades' Half Acre you did to my sister and her baby! Molly swallowed those words back. "Well, it was my pleasure, sir. And I'll keep that in mind." She winked and turned to go back to her seat. Bitterness lapped at the back of her tongue. *Don't get sick now!* The room swayed as her chair seemed to telescope away from her. She forced one foot in front of the other to close the ever widening gap.

Miriam cleared her throat. "May I ask, where is Pastor Oliver? We were hoping to see him tonight."

Shuffling feet and hollow footsteps sparked a new level of chatter. Mr. Abraham and Mr. Lupus turned away from Miriam and her question to observe the two dozen silver-maned children filling three rows of the wooden risers. A woman knelt down in front of them, her wolf-mane flowing down her back. She raised her arms into the air, and poised with pointer fingers touching thumbs, like two "okay" gestures. All eyes in the choir were on her.

Miriam's eyes met Molly's and they exchanged a shrug. Anticipation of the first sound hung in the air. The woman's arms swiftly lifted higher and came down. The children took a quick breath and began to sing.

The song held everyone in awe.

Molly forced herself to return to her seat. She tripped and landed hard in the chair, but being seated helped settle the nauseating vertigo. She grabbed her water glass and gulped the cool liquid, while scanning the children. Kita's blue-eyed son stood on the top row, just past half way, and toward the right side.

Twenty-four children sang to the newcomers, but Molly's tunnel vision could only see one, Michael. His mouth opened wide with the long notes. He dipped his head forward with a running chorus. His chin rose with the high notes and tucked toward his chest with the low notes. The harmony was exquisite, far beyond anything Molly had heard by the children's choirs on Earth. Faces around Molly exhibited the same amazement and transfixed fascination, her own nausea and vertigo long forgotten in the angelic song.

When the voices and music faded, everyone jumped to their feet and applauded wildly. Molly's hands stung from her own over-zealous clapping. She whistled as if she were at a pep rally and ignored the disapproving glares from Miriam and Davidette. Pride pressed against her ribs like a balloon inflated inside a bird cage.

Suddenly, she stood stone-statue still, her hands frozen mid clap. What was she doing? For all anyone knew, this was a group of children, welcoming new pilgrims to their planet, not her nephew's performance. She had to get control over her heart and keep her place below the radar, undercover, and in character. Biting her lip, she sat down. Why hadn't she recorded the performance? She needed proof of Michael's existence. Activating her recording app, she'd get what she could as the children shuffled off the risers. Mentally, she kicked herself.

Pam leaned over. "You okay?"

Molly deactivated the recording. "Yeah."

She stared at the table. What excuse could she use? "I—I need some rest."

"Yeah, I hear ya." Pam leaned back in her seat.

Mr. Abraham stood and pumped flat palms to quiet the cheering. The ovation slowly waned to an attentive silence. "That was a stellar performance, Mrs. Canem. Let's hear it one more time for our grammar school choir." He led in another round of enthusiastic applause.

"Now..." he spoke before the applause faded. His voice drew everyone's attention. Seats were taken and all eyes were on him. "I know it's been a long and exciting day for you all."

Heads nodded as a soft buzz vibrated through the pilgrims. A sudden lethargic, weighted sensation pulled at Molly's limbs as if gravity had increased. She glared at Mr. Abraham.

"So, we will bid you adieu," Mr. Abraham's broad unsettling smile haunted Molly's senses. "And send you all to your assigned quarters for an evening's rest. You will find your belongings have already been placed in your rooms. Miss Miriam has—" he nodded toward her "—been given the assignments. It will make more sense to you once you are back at the Missionary Base. But Miriam will transmit the information to you as she sees fit. Thank you all once again for coming and serving these beautiful people of Omicron."

The Lupuses stood up, applauding the pilgrims. The pilgrims stood, applauding the Lupuses. Molly stood. Lead-laden arms could not rise to clap even if she felt compelled to do so. She stared at Mr. Abraham. He leaned over and spoke to Mr. Lupus who nodded in return. Abraham's eyes scanned the pilgrims and settled on Molly. A dark, brownish-black soul signature, an indication of dishonesty, flashed around him then vanished.

The room tilted again. Molly stepped to her left to maintain her balance and glared intensely at the senior Abraham. He was causing this. But how? Molly glanced right and left. Her comrades were engrossed in their exchanged accolades. Why was she the only one affected by him? Then again, she had the stupid *gift*.

The applause faded, and everyone began to shuffle toward the exits, yawning and blinking sleepily. Deuce and Mr. Abraham led the pack out to the waiting transportation vessels. The Lupuses stood on the large porch waving as the vehicles pulled away. Molly twisted in her seat to watch Michael, nestled between the two parental forms, happily waving until they were out of sight.

Molly's hand rested on her chest above her heart. The heartbreak beneath consumed her. She bit her lip to stay the tears and closed her eyes. For the first time in a long time, she earnestly prayed.

Lord, help me do this.

CHAPTER SEVENTEEN

Burrrpp, Burrrpp, Burrrpp

Molly's eyes shot open. *Whatsit?* Drool moistened her right jaw. She wiped it with clumsy fingertips.

Burrrpp, Burrrpp, Burrrpp, her wake-up alarm sounded.

A red light blinked at her right peripheral. *Oh.* Molly sat up, touched her iComm link. "Access message." The text illuminated before her.

Molly, you will be placed on Security detail today. Attached is your clearance code. It will transmit when you close this message, and will lodge in your personnel profile. Don't mention you already have it. Come find me as soon as possible. –G

"Save message." The image shifted like a piece of paper being blown by the wind and grew smaller until it disappeared. Immediately, another red light flashed. Molly swung her legs onto the floor. She thought the code transmitted automatically. "Download file." The red light continued to blink. Hmm. "Access, message."

You will find the attached file interesting in your quest. –AF

"Okay, open file." The simulated sheet blew away and drifted into an iconic file folder, and then it flipped over and enlarged. The image of an invoice settled in her visual range. Molly scanned the information. *Cryogenic Supplies, Canisters, multi-layered pallets, and tubing.* Her eyebrows shot up. *Delivered to AA@AP Ent.* The signature was illegible, just a scribble of initials. But, she interpreted the recipient—Austin Abraham at Abraham Project Enterprises.

Hmm. Okay, AF, whoever you are, you've got some interesting information. What does it mean, though? Maybe Gordon will know. Molly pulled her hair back and secured it with an elastic tie, ever present on her wrist. "First things first—Coffee!" She pulled on pants and a clean t-shirt, slipped on lace-up loafers and opened the door to her room.

The scent of coffee and sweet rolls filled the hall. She closed her eyes and drew deeply of its fragrance. This place can't be all bad with smells like that early in the morning. She followed the aroma as a smile lifted the corners of her mouth.

Miriam sat at a high table, nibbling on a muffin. Molly nodded as she entered the common kitchen. One by one, the new pilgrims gathered for a morning start of coffee, juice, cereal, an odd smelling milk, perhaps goat, muffins, cinnamon rolls, and fruit.

"Feels liked a hotel breakfast bar, doesn't it?" Pam smiled as she sniffed an orange. At least it looked like an orange. When she cut it open it was purple but smelled ripe and sweet. She shrugged and sunk her teeth into the pulp.

"Yum," she pulled the wedges apart and devoured the whole thing.

"Where's the bacon and eggs?" Deuce entered the kitchen. Giggles rippled among those seated. He pulled out a chair and positioned to sit down. A bell dinged, and a bread box-type door slid open. Everyone stared at the box door. A plate with four pieces of bacon and two over-easy eggs sat in the opening.

"By golly!" He lifted the plate to his nose to inhale the steam. "Smells like bacon and eggs." He shrugged, looked around, pulled out a fork from a basket, and sat down to eat.

Julio walked up behind Deuce and sniffed the air. "How'd you do that?"

"You got me." Deuce shrugged and shoved a forkful of eggs into his mouth.

"Hmm." Julio walked over to the box. "Two pieces of wheat toast, lightly browned, two poached eggs, and shredded potatoes, lightly crisped, please." After a moment's wait, the bell sounded, the box door slipped open, and there sat a steaming plate of the same.

"Peasy!" Julio took his plate, grabbed a fork, and joined Deuce at the table. The others looked at each other as if they had one thought between them, jumped up, and lined up in front of the magic food box. Nothing was impossible. Every food requested appeared in the door, Omelets, biscuits and cream gravy, granola bars, and even prunes in heavy cream. That one caused an uproar of laughter and a blush in Miriam's cheeks.

A man dressed in a light-blue barong button-down shirt, carpenter-style tan shorts, white socks and brown leather sandals stood in the door of the common kitchen. His eyes scanned a transparent magenta clipboard in his hands. "Miriam?"

The laughter faded as everyone turned toward the voice.

"I'm Miriam." She briskly wiped her hands on a napkin and swallowed.

"Ah, yes, well we need your group to gather outside, we will assign responsibilities and get everybody settled with their assignments."

Miriam's eyes swept the faces of her people around the table, "Of course, we'll be right there."

"Neat-o mosquito." Mr. Socks-and-Sandals slipped out of the kitchen.

"Ah man!" Pam shoved her elbows on the table and her chin into her hands.

Miriam tilted her head with concern. "What?"

"There're mosquitos on this planet?" Pam smiled wickedly.

Everyone laughed. Chairs rubbed on the tile floor as Miriam's group meandered toward the front door.

Mr. Socks-and-Sandals stood out on the lush lawn, a tall slender man stood at his side. He wore a black linen suit with a white half-collared shirt buttoned all the way up, but no tie. They solemnly watched as the pilgrims piled out onto the porch and crossed the lawn to join him. The two suns were already hot, and there was not a hint of a breeze.

"Why'd we have to come out here to get our assignments, the kitchen was just as good?" Julio whispered to Deuce.

Deuce shrugged and made his way across the lawn.

"Welcome!" the man said with a lilting French Region accent. "We are so honored to have you join us. I am Oliver Pugh's Associate, Jacques Breneé, and this is Benjamin Bordowski. He will give you your assignments and get you started. I only wanted to offer you welcome in Pastor O's stead and open with a word of prayer, shall we?" He bowed his head and began to pray.

The pilgrims lowered their heads but fidgeted under the warming suns. After they all said, "Amen," Jacques excused himself with a French salutation, "Bon jour," and walked toward one of the buildings.

Benjamin's eyes swept the clip board. "Dr. Austin Abraham…"

"Wait!" Miriam interrupted. "Where is Pastor Pugh?"

Jacques paused in his retreat and slowly turned to face the new pilgrims. A patient smile bowed his thin lips. "Pastor Oliver sends his apologies. He has been…unavoidably detained. Pas de soucis, um…no worries."

With that, he turned and continued his departure.

"But…" Miriam's eyes followed the odd man. Pam looped her arm into Miriam's and pulled her back into the group.

Deuce stepped forward, "Yes, um, here. I'm Dr. Abraham"

"Ah. Obviously, you are assigned to the infirmary," Benjamin ignored Miriam's question and continued, snorting a snicker, "It's not like we'd assign *you* to janitorial services."

"Obviously," Deuce responded with a polite smile. "And which way would that be?"

"Ah, that's what we like, Eager Beaverness." Benjamin's mouth split to expose oversized teeth and pushed his face toward the others.

"He looks a bit beaver-ish." Pam whispered more to herself but Miriam swatted at her arm. A soft giggle rippled through the pilgrims.

"Shush." Miriam's eyes bulged as she glared at anyone with whom she could catch eye contact.

An uneasy sensation settled in Molly's gut. Just where was Pastor Oliver? Chief Chisula had said he hadn't been seen since he helped Kita escape. Ben's voice broke into her thoughts. "Once everyone has received their responsibilities, we will take a walking tour of the community. After we have completed our tour, you will know where you need to go for your assignment."

Ben spoke slightly louder than conversational, as if he were projecting his words to be heard over a background noise. What background noise he thought he was talking over remained a mystery.

"Fair enough," Deuce stepped back with his comrades but tossed an eye-rolling glance at Molly. She suppressed a grin.

Ben called each name and told them where they were assigned. Molly focused her attention to memorize each, in case it was important later. She could investigate Pastor Oliver's whereabouts later.

Hayden's name was called but, naturally, would be assigned after he had recovered from his appendectomy. The rest of the assignments lined up as predicted, food preparation, gardening, and teaching. Julio received the expected assignment with the current construction project, an aquifer.

Molly received Security. She shifted from one foot to the other, suppressing her anxiety. Would this tedious process ever be done? She needed to talk to Gordon, the sooner, the better.

Finally, the names were called and assignments received. The thirteen followed Benjamin from building to building for a quick tour of the village, ending in the community cafeteria where they sat together for lunch, and then were released to go to their assignments.

"Well, people, this is it," Miriam said. "Feels kind of like graduation."

The pilgrims greeted one another with hugs, fist bumps, pats on the back, and wished each other luck and blessings, lingering as long as comfortably allowable before they left the cafeteria. Benjamin hung back and reiterated directions, but didn't hurry them to depart. Seems he knew how to handle new pilgrims. Deuce followed Molly through the cafeteria doors. "Shall we?"

She glanced over her shoulder as if she hadn't realized he was there. "Yeah, I guess I'll see you around."

"I'm sure you will." A nervous smile crinkled his eyes but quickly faded.

She stopped walking. Did he mean that? She longed to linger, even for a few more moments? "I'm surprised you're not assigned to the TAP offices." Internally, she cringed.

He opened his mouth with a sigh. "I meant what I said. I came here for a purpose, not as a tag along."

"So you did." Molly meant to utter that profound statement and gallantly walk away completely in control of her emotions, but she couldn't resume walking. Reluctance held his gaze a moment longer. Their bond, formed over the three months alone on the ship, was still part of her. She just wasn't ready to be autonomous. "Um, as soon as you get settled, could you do me a favor?"

Deuce didn't seem eager to leave either. "Of course."

"Would you schedule a PASS for all of us girls?"

He stared at her a moment. Then he nodded. "Sure."

She fought the sensations inkling in her heart, resisting an urge to hug him as a thank-you, as a good-bye, as an I-had-a-good-time. But, she had a duty to perform, this, whatever this was, stood in her way. And yet she lingered. There was nothing else to say although she wished there was. He knew her fears. He knew why she wanted the PASS. It was time to part. Why couldn't she take a step away? This was ridiculous. She had to be the first to leave. She broke eye contact and forced her body to walk away.

CHAPTER EIGHTEEN

"I'm not sure how much training you have in security, but by the looks of you—" Roger Dunn stated as his eyes shifted from Molly's head to her toes "—I'd say you'll do just fine. Besides, it's pretty quiet around here."

Molly's eyebrow rose. Quiet, huh? Her sister lost her child and left this planet sterile. You call that quiet? Not to mention that one other little thing, what was it, oh yeah! Pirating!

Roger had disproportionately short legs compared to his long torso, which made him seem short, although he stood nose to nose with Molly. His face was impeccably shaven and his eyebrows appeared to have been waxed and combed. His hair parted sharply on the far left side of his head and neatly followed the contour of his scalp, just past his right ear, and then swooped back to gently touch his collar. If Molly didn't know better, she'd swear he wore a toupee. But no one wore those things anymore. Modern medicine had overcome baldness. Perhaps things were different so far from Earth.

"I'll be fine," she responded.

"Okay, well, first you will need security clearance—"

Molly opened her mouth but closed it again.

"And, in order to get that, you need to view these orientation streams. So, if you'll have a seat —" He gestured toward a room full of chairs. It looked like the briefing room back on Earth. "We'll get you started."

He lifted a remote iComm device, pointed it at Molly's face, and pushed some buttons. A green light blinked to her left peripheral. She sat down and activated the demanding light.

A red light flashed in her right peripheral. A message. As Roger left the room she accessed it.

Reminder: Do not let Roger transmit clearance, it will over-write current clearance. Tell him the orientation program transmitted it at the conclusion. –G

She smiled. Save message.

Immediately, the red light flashed again. Of course. These messages must be piggybacked with Gordon's. Hmm. Another thing to talk to him about.

"Open Message."

Use extreme discretion when choosing allies. — AF

"Save message."

Including you, AF. Molly activated the security orientation stream as the clock crawled by like an arthritic snail.

***

"Okay," Roger stepped back into the room. "You ready to get your clearance and go on the real tour?"

"Well, I believe I already have the clearance."

"What?" Roger lifted his remote iComm devise and pointed it toward Molly's ear. "Hmm."

"The-the orientation stream said something about it being transmitted at the end of the file." Molly put it out there.

Roger pressed his lips together in a frown and nodded. "Wish IT'd let us know when they modify these things."

Molly blew out a breath as casually as possible. It worked.

"Well, then, let's go meet your fellow security staff and see what you will be securing." Roger smiled. A confused glint remained in his eyes, but he didn't say any more about the clearance transfer. Molly fell in step behind him as they left the briefing room.

Roger led her through the offices. "Here at SHQ, that's Security Headquarters, you'll find we are a friendly bunch."

Molly rolled her eyes as she followed him through the partitioned maze. She met her fellow officers, the dispatcher, an Omicron female named Lana, and the Head of Security, "Sarge," he insisted on being called. Sarge had been on the first pilgrimage with Mr. Abraham. He appeared to be Molly's dad's age. But who knew?

Roger pointed out the break room—Coffee!

Afterwards, they crossed the compound and entered a laboratory, or at least an outer glassed walkway. Four rows of tables stood in the middle of the room, covered in glass beakers and crates of test tubes. Six desks faced the three walls. A glass door opened into the lab, and another glass door exited on the opposite side into this same walkway. The entire laboratory could be visually scanned from here. Offices jutted from the glass passageway across from the lab. Beyond this appeared to be the entry to the infirmary. Molly strained to peek through the doors.

"This is—" Roger tapped her arm with the back of his hand. "Molly!" He drew her attention back to him. "This is Dr. Timothy Stork."

"I'm sorry." Molly suppressed the heat rising to her face. "Dr. Stork. Yes. It's nice to meet you. Wait. Dr. Stork? Seriously?" Her eyes darted from the doctor to Roger. He was nothing like she had imagined. A non-assuming sort of man, one would never mistake him for a healer or a scientist. With the exception of his mottled stained teeth, he looked more like an older version of a seasoned waiter, or a hotel concierge.

"Yeah, I get that a lot." Dr. Stork sighed as his passive eyes remained on hers. She sensed disdain.

"Geez, I'm sorry." The heat took control of her face. He had no idea she was not reacting to the irony of his name being the fertility specialist and having the name Stork. She had a whole different startling awareness. One her sister had conjured by her tale of escape. Would Molly ever learn to remain neutral in her reactions?

"No problem, really." Stork flippantly dismissed her perceived reaction. "This is where we process and maintain our fertility assistance." He gestured toward the lab. "We collect donated ovum from the pilgrims in the infirmary. We marry them to the designated father's cells and, voilà, we produce fetuses. We sustain the fetuses after division of eight to sixteen cells through cryopreservation.

"It's very exciting, what we've developed here, really." Dr. Stork beamed. "The human DNA is removed, and the native female's DNA is inserted, therefore the resultant child is genetically correct for the couple. Studies are being conducted as we gather more data, but so far, there have not been any difficulties."

His eyes darted from Roger to Molly. "Oh, but that's not to say we anticipate any problems. We are scientists, and we have a pathological need to document data." He chuckled.

"And how do you catch the fetus at that cell division?" Molly bent to look through the glass wall at the vials lining the large table.

"Good question." Dr. Stork glanced at Roger. "Well, it's an established procedure to ensure the fetus's integrity, but...I suppose in layman's terms you'd say, we freeze the fetus at the precise moment it reaches the eight to sixteen stage. We've had a high success rate with the Omicron subjects. Due in part, to the fact that in the natural, they have four to six babies in a single pregnancy. Much like their wolf ancestry."

"Oh." Molly nodded. If she understood the doctor correctly, any child from her sister's donated ovum would resemble the Omicron parents and not the donor. So how would he explain Michael's keen resemblance to Kita and her amazing blue eyes? She tucked this tidbit of information away for later thought. "And...what about the surrogates?"

A dark look washed over Dr. Stork's eyes but was gone just as quickly. Molly tilted her head and watched his soul signature flare brownish-black.

Dr. Stork cleared his throat and glanced at her escort. Roger's eyes went to the floor, but Dr. Stork maintained a pleasant façade with a patient smile as if he were answering juvenile questions from a primary school child.

Molly held her gaze.

"Well, we are always working to improve all of our programs. Our goal is to reach a one hundred percent success rate." Dr. Stork tapped his fingers on the lab table.

"Okay, and..." Molly resisted tapping her own fingers.

"And...we are exploring various options to reach that goal." The doctor shrugged.

"Uh-huh." Molly sensed deception but couldn't pinpoint whether the doctor completely lied or simply diverted from truth. Staring at Dr. Stork did not prompt him to continue. She struggled to stifle more questions. All in good time.

"Well, let's continue with our tour, shall we?" Roger prodded Molly to follow him through the infirmary door.

He introduced her to key personnel, paused to greet Hayden in his room, and crossed the compound to the Technology Center. Molly's heart sped up a beat. She looked forward to meeting Gordon.

The Technology Building was the smallest of all. Inside, five people sat at five iComm screens. Two women and three men intermittently stared at the transparent green-hued screens and typed on their virtual keyboards. All eyes looked through their screens when Molly and Roger entered the building.

A man at the far end jumped up. "Roger!"

"Hey, Gordon. This is Molly. She came in with the new pilgrims and is assigned to security. I'm just showing her around."

The investigator in Molly's head noted Gordon's blue eyes, contrasting his milk-chocolate skin. He had a young, energetic face. She would place him at about her age. Again, nothing like she had anticipated for an infil.

"Splendid." Gordon smiled warmly and reached to take Molly's hand.

She hesitated. Gordon took her hand into his and pumped it up and down. Her grandmother would be pleased to see the obsolete custom was practiced here. Perhaps without the germ-fear, it had never been lost. She gripped his hand firmly and shook it in response. Something smooth with sharp edges pressed into her palm. Her eyes searched his face, but he gave no reaction.

She maintained a neutral look. Pulling her hand back, she palmed the square, nonchalantly slipping her hands into her pockets and deposited the note. Hopefully she could get away from Roger and see what it contained.

"Great to have you here," Gordon continued. "If there's anything we can do for you from the Intelligent Technology Department, you just let us know."

Another man shook his head and stood next to Gordon. "That's *Information* Technology, ma'am. There's always a goof among the balls." He patted Gordon's shoulder and leaned into Molly with an open hand. "My name's Matthew."

She shook his hand, too.

Gordon frowned. "Nobody knows what IT stands for, I can call it what I want." He turned toward Molly. "We are always happy to serve security needs." His smile was too big. Did no one see his false bravado?

"Well—thank you."

Roger led Molly through the compound, introducing her to other personnel and showing her what security's responsibilities were in each area. She politely acknowledged everyone's introduction and committed to memory faces with names. Her trained investigative eye noted file storage, locked doors, and areas that Roger *did not* take her through, anything of interest to be explored at a later time.

At last, they circled back to the SHQ. Roger indicated a desk for Molly and a personal locker for storage. She opened the locker just because it seemed the thing to do and found five film-wrapped uniform shirts with her last name sewn across the pocket. "Oh, wow!"

She picked one up and ran her fingers across the stitching. Her eyes met Roger's. "Impressive."

A smile lit up his face, and he nodded. "Things get done quickly around here," he explained and turned to lead her back to the work room.

She mumbled her thanks and took a seat at the desk. Opening the drawers, she found them adequately supplied with writing styluses, film pads, and all the administrative needs to do her job.

"Okay, so, tomorrow at oh-seven-hundred hours everybody meets in the briefing room—the room you used today to view the orientation streams—where assignments and updates will be reported. Until then, I'd say you are free to do whatever you wish." He touched the back of her shoulder. "Report here at oh-seven-hundred, in your uniform."

"Well, thank you very much." Molly nodded. Roger returned the nod.

Molly took her uniform shirts and walked straight to her quarters, rubbing the stiff square in her pocket as she crossed the grassy compound.

In her room, she quickly retrieved the folded note. *Ever have trouble sleeping? The cafeteria has prime pie and a superior assortment of teas. Even at midnight, you can get an insomniac special. –G*

At last, she would get to talk to Gordon.

CHAPTER NINETEEN

No one was more surprised than Deuce when the plate of bacon and eggs materialized inside the food preparation box. It was pretty advanced technology for an outpost. Hopefully, he'd find the infirmary as advanced.

He sniffed the food. "Smells like bacon and eggs."

Scanning the counter, he found utensils, and sat down to enjoy his hot breakfast. He couldn't help but chuckle as the others ran to get their share of the hot food. Soon, Deuce's plate was clean. He had thought machine generated food would be flat, tasteless. This, however, was *exactly* as full of flavor, including the saltiness of the bacon, as the real thing.

A peculiar little man stood at the galley door. He looked like a badly dressed tourist, sans a fanny pouch and a map-of-the-stars guide. This odd little man waited in the courtyard where another man, dressed like a slick gentleman's gentleman, or a government official, introduced himself as Pastor O's associate and the odd man as Ben Bordowski.

Ben laboriously gave them their assignments, beginning with Deuce. The advantage of having a last name which began with A. Naturally, he was assigned to the infirmary and tried to escape the drawn-out process. He was eager to check on Hayden and see what shape the infirmary was in. But ol' Ben threw out the "Eager Beaverness" insult, halting Deuce making a hasty exit.

He was stuck. Should he claim a patient needed his attention? He glanced at Molly. Then again, this gave him a little more time with her. He wouldn't buck the system, not yet.

Molly was assigned to security, no surprise there. The tour ended in a cafeteria where they sat together for lunch until Beaver-face, that is, Ben Bordowski released everyone.

At last, Deuce had a moment alone with Molly. He wanted to tell her thank you. He wanted to express how much those three months had meant to him. How terrified he was to be here with his dad, but how she had made it all seem worthwhile. Instead he heard himself say, "Shall we?"

He cringed internally. Why didn't he say what he wanted to say? *Geez.*

Molly walked with him for a while. Deuce lingered as long as he could without being too obvious, but Molly seemed eager to get to her assignment. Maybe they could talk later. Then she was gone.

An odd feeling settled in his gut. He stopped and faced the direction she walked. Molly's figure grew smaller as she made her way across the courtyard. Why did he feel so—like something was now missing?

He rubbed his arm as he walked toward the infirmary. He needed to focus. He needed to see the facility and assess where he could be useful. Still, he would miss the day-long interactions with Miss Jacobsen.

For the next two hours he endured orientation streams and paperwork, so when a stack of patients' files were offered, he emphatically accepted. The infirmary was small, fifty beds in all, and linked by a single door to a laboratory whose primary focus encompassed the fertility issues. Most patients were obstetrics in one form or another. The rest were sick, injured, or recovering from surgery, Hayden being among the latter.

Aquifer construction proved to be a source for injuries, and that seemed odd. Five injuries were attributable to that undertaking, a twisted ankle, two significant contusions from falling stones, one sprained back, and a deep laceration from piping. Deuce made a mental note to look into the safety issues for that project.

He read through each patient's file and organized them by severity first and proximity of their room second. He made his rounds and spoke to each patient, checking their wounds, re-bandaging when necessary, and reassuring each they were recovering nicely. Hayden looked so good, Deuce promised to release him tomorrow. He made a note in his file to have home-health care, if available, to verify his continued recovery. It wasn't like he could go home and have his mother, sister, or girlfriend check on him from time to time.

Finally, he located the obstetric files and rifled through the current patients' information. The Omicronians had multi-gestation pregnancies—a litter, so to speak. The surrogate donors, six in all, were carrying single fetuses. Ah, five were singles, one had twins. *Nice.*

The films indicated all were progressing without concerns. He returned them to the document room, where they would be properly filed, and scanned the other cabinet fronts. A quick inhale caught in his chest when he located the inactive files. He pulled random sleeves before he found Kita Jacobsen's. His heart pounded against his chest as he pulled the film from its folder. A quick glance over his shoulder assured him no one was around. He slipped the document film into a blank sleeve and put Kita's now empty folder in among the current patients' files and lifted the stack to place them in the container marked, "To Be Filed." He placed the blank sleeve between his arm and ribs and headed to the infirmary cafeteria for coffee.

At a secluded table, Deuce sipped at a very hot coffee, using that physical gesture to glance around, reassuring himself he was alone. He laid the blank sleeve with Kita's film on the table and reached in with two fingers.

"Here you are," his father exclaimed.

Deuce pushed the film back into the sleeve and looked up. His heart throbbed in his throat, and his breath pounded his lungs. He felt like he'd been caught with his hand in the proverbial cookie jar.

"Hello." He cleared his throat and spoke as casually as he could. "How are you today, sir?"

"Good, good." Abraham eyed the unmarked sleeve beneath Deuce's hand. "I was hoping you could spare some time for your old man."

"Oh, I don't know. I'm on 'til seven, and then I'm on call 'til tomorrow morning." This was as reasonable an excuse as he could come up with.

"Well, son, surely you can squeeze me in? After all…"

"Of course." Deuce forced a smile. "I'll see what I can do."

"Sure, sure." Abraham's bushy eyebrows pushed down over his eyes as his scowling glance targeted the curious blank sleeve.

Deuce never could lie well as a boy. He intentionally leaned on the file and prayed he'd outgrown that deficiency as an adult.

"Well," Abraham clasped his hands. "You just drop by whenever you can or give me a call, and I'll come have"—he leaned over and looked into Deuce's cup—"coffee with you."

"That'd be great." Deuce lied again. "Well, I better get back." He stood placing the medical file under his arm.

"What's that, son?" Abraham stared at the brown folder.

"What? Oh, nothing. A patient's film I need to return to Filing. I forgot I had it actually." Deuce winced internally but maintained a perfect poker face, he hoped. Okay, maybe that deficiency was not completely conquered.

Deuce walked out of the cafeteria with his father and stayed by his side, escorting him as it were, to the exit doors. He held up his travel cup in salute to the man who glanced back to wave one last time. Probably should work the old man in, but not now, tomorrow, maybe. He slipped into a supply closet and pulled out the film. Kita's pregnancy was recorded as normal, no complications or concerns. "Surrogate Assigned" area had a number, 9979-18767P4. Was this to keep the surrogacy confidential? He'd check on that system when he could. "Baby Condition, Data Not Available."

Impossible.

Deuce read the entire medical file, fingering the attached film. Could it be the same as the video recording he had viewed on Earth? He needed to check, but where? Gingerly, he slipped the film back into the blank sleeve. The door knob clicked as it turned, and he startled.

"Doctor?" a human nurse said, curiosity written all over her face.

"Um, yes, nurse…" Deuce looked at her name tag, "Rebecca."

"Is…there something you need, Doctor?" She eyed the patient's sleeve in his hand.

Deuce picked up a box of gauze. "No, I found what I'm looking for." He held up the package, proving it was what he needed.

She nodded slowly, but her eyes never left his. When she stepped back and held the door open for him, he walked swiftly down the hall and turned into an empty patient's room. He waited what seemed like a reasonable amount of time and exited the room. Intent on returning to the document file room. Once safely in the room, he replaced Kita's film in her folder, returned it to its place in the inactive files, and blew out a stream of air and relief.

He had patients to see and procedures to learn. Soon, he'd have a better idea of where he could view Kita's video and possibly how to dig deeper into her medical records. Until then, he needed to get busy.

Maybe I should go see Dad when my shift is over. He let that idea settle in his thoughts as he muddled through his responsibilities. The doctoring he knew, it was the routine he was learning. The clock turned quickly, and in no time it was seven o'clock.

"Well, see you all tomorrow, I suppose," he said to the top of Nurse Rebecca's head. She was finalizing her data entry for a patient and handed the shift overview to the oncoming Omicron nurse. She glanced up and mumbled something. It sounded like, "Sure."

"Well, good night," Deuce said in spite of the awkwardness. He walked straight over to The Abraham Project's Headquarters. As he entered the empty building, he followed a distant illumination and found his father's office suite. The large double door groaned slightly as Deuce pushed it open. He stopped and stared at his father's form bent over his desk.

Abraham Senior looked up.

Deuce smiled warmly. "I figured you'd still be here."

"Austin! Come in, come in. I just ordered dinner, can I get you something?"

"Sure...and it's Deuce."

"Oh, right, right. What will you have?"

"Whatever you're having will be fine."

"All right." Abraham reached up to his iComm link. "Call, Marcos." He winked at his son. Deuce sat in an oversized chair in front of his father's desk and nodded.

"Marcos, my son will be joining me for dinner, will you double my order? Yes. Thank you." Abraham touched his iComm link again.

"So, how are you settling in, son?"

"Fine, the infirmary is just like any other Healing Station. Just need to learn where things are." Deuce crossed one leg over the other and turned slightly in his chair.

"Excellent." Abraham looked down at a document on his desk. He picked it up and placed it in a drawer at his belly.

"And how's your comrade—Hayden is it?"

Deuce stared at the space the document no longer occupied. What he wouldn't give to be able to glance at the contents of that lap drawer. "He's recovering nicely. I'll release him tomorrow. I'm hoping we have some sort of home-health care staff to look in on him. I hate for him to be alone in the quarters. Since, you know, everybody is on assignment during the day."

"Oh, I'm sure something can be arranged. You let me know if you have any trouble with that.

Whatever you need, son, I'm sure it can be arranged." A broad smile punctuated his statement.

Bitter bile churned in Deuce's throat. Something about the way his father said this made him feel like a kid who stole a piece of candy, because he could, because his dad owned the store. He could just walk in and take or do whatever he wanted, regardless of whether it was the norm or legal or what.

Keeping his independence from his dad's influence might be harder than he realized. That thought made him want to walk out, to get as far away from this man as humanly possible. What was he thinking? How could he possibly maintain autonomy with his father's influence saturating everything? How could he have been so naïve?

Abraham's eyes met Deuce's. "I'll just throw this out there, okay, don't get offended or anything…"

Here it comes. Deuce held his gaze.

"I could really use your help here, at headquarters." Abraham's creases deepened as his smile stretched across his face.

"Dad, I appreciate your offer. I'm needed at the infirmary. I'm sure I can serve you better in that area," Deuce stated calmly.

"Oh, sure. Of course, of course." Abraham rose from his chair and circled his desk. He threw out his arms and approached Deuce.

Deuce stood and embraced his father.

"It's so good to have you here, no matter where you work. You know that?" Abraham patted his back and stepped back. The groan of the doors announced the entrance of Marcos and a wheeled cart draped with a white cloth. Covered plates sat on top. Marcos was a tall Omicron, and his physique appeared to be well sculpted as if he worked out often. He could easily double as a body guard with that build.

He put the table against the wall and pulled two chairs to it. Abraham nodded approval. Marcos reached under the cloth and pulled out salt and pepper crystals, two crystal glasses, and a bucket of ice. He placed four pieces of ice in each glass, reached under the cart again for two bottled waters, and twisted their lids. He poured each one slowly. The bubbles foamed a slight head and settled quickly. Finally, Marcos lifted the plate covers and placed them under the cart.

"Will that be all, sir?" Marcos bowed his head and waited.

Abraham glanced over at him, "Yes, yes, thank you, Marcos."

"Yes sir." Marcos walked quickly from the room and closed the doors as he passed over the threshold.

Deuce whistled. "Pretty slick, Dad." He walked over to the cart and inspected the meal. The plates contained a one-pound lobster tail split down the middle, roasted asparagus with a square of butter slowly shifting over the side, and a dinner salad with a white creamy dressing speckled by green and red flakes. There were two small bowls of warm garlic butter, and a basket lined with a white linen cloth filled with four yeast rolls. Deuce drew the aroma into his lungs. "The rolls smell heavenly."

Abraham smiled. "Don't they though?"

He sat down and added butter to a roll. Silver utensils chinked against fine bone china as they cut and lifted the food off their plates.

"Mmmm," was the only utterance between them.

"That was amazing." Deuce wiped his butter saturated mouth and stacked his silverware in the middle of his plate. He took one more drink of the bubbly water. "This planet has lobster?"

"We have our ways." Abraham smiled and pushed his chest out slightly.

"Ways? What ways? How else would you get lobster six hundred lightyears from Earth? Was it imported with our transport?"

Abraham's smile faded. "Yeah, it's imported."

Deuce held eye contact with his father. Was that the truth?

Abraham broke eye contact first. "Well." He looked back up and smiled. "Tell me about your day?"

Deuce stared at his dad. A subject change, or did he really want to know how his day went? "Day was good. Doctoring is doctoring, just learning the routines of this facility, you know?"

"I imagine so. And, you like this"—Abraham's eyes fluttered slightly—"healing?"

"What are you asking me?"

"I'm just asking if you enjoy what you're doing."

"Uh-huh." Deuce searched his father's face.

"What?" A wrinkle formed between Abraham's eyebrows. He pulled at some remnant lobster meat and dipped it and his fingers into the frothy butter, then raised the whole to his mouth to suck the oily meat from his long fingers.

Deuce stared at the messy process. An edge of disgust formed in his gut. "I didn't come all this way to—to work in your shadow, Dad."

"Oh, of course, of course." Abraham rose from his chair, wiping his hands in his oversized linen napkin. He walked over to the side board, opened the cabinet, and poured himself a brandy. "May I pour you one?"

"No thank you, Dad. I need to go get some rest. I'm on call, and I'm still having some hib-lag." Deuce rose and walked toward the double doors, but glanced back at the table.

"Sure, I understand actually. That three-year hibernation does a number on your system." Abraham abandoned his brandy and walked to the doors with Deuce. "Well, we can talk more tomorrow. You wanna join me for dinner?"

"You know, I don't know how things will go, but—sure if possible, I'll try to join you. I'll let you know." Deuce leaned toward his father, as if to hug him, but then straightened, and shook his hand instead.

Deuce crossed the compound fully intending to go straight to his quarters, but he glanced at the infirmary. He'd check on Hayden one last time.

On his way toward Hayden's room, the document file room door caught his attention. It was slightly ajar. *Oh Geez, did I leave that open? Prime investigative skills there, Deuce!* He gently eased the door open. Molly spun around and sucked in air.

"Well, hi there." Deuce smiled at her expense.

Relief washed over her face. "Good grief, you scared me!"

"Yeah, sorry. So, what did you find?"

Molly stared at Deuce a moment. "Nothing. Yet."

"Well, let me show you what I found." He entered the small room and closed the door.

Turning to the file compartments to his left, he pulled out Kita's sleeve, then her film, and handed it to Molly.

Her eyes scanned the film.

"What am I reading here?"

"You're reading about an OB patient who had a completely normal and healthy pregnancy right up to the point that she delivered. Then, Data Not Available."

Molly's face drew up into a scowl.

"Molly, they have computers that prepare food with exact precision, better than anything I've ever seen on Earth. The iComm system is first class, high tech. The surgical procedures are beyond anything I've experienced back home. There's a man in the infirmary who had a twisted ankle, and he will walk out of the facility tomorrow, fully healed. There was a gal with a deep cut who went home today. The biggest complication for her injury will be infection management."

"What are you saying?"

"I'm saying, with all the technology, which is *obviously* more advanced than what we have on Earth, how could they lose a perfectly healthy fetus at birth when he had been progressing normally and without any complications?"

Molly nodded. "Good point." Her eyes scanned Kita's film again. "So, what's happening here, Deuce?"

"I don't know yet. But..." Deuce laid his hand over Molly's.

Her eyes darted up to his.

"I'm trying to figure it out."

Molly turned her head slightly to the right, but her eyes stayed on his.

"Molly, I know. But, please, you can trust me."

"I—I do, yet I don't. I don't know what I believe. I don't trust your dad. And blood is denser than—"

"I know. Believe me, I know. But think about it. Would I have pulled your sister's file first thing and showed it to you if I had another agenda?"

Molly's eyebrows shot up. "You have a point."

Deuce nodded. "Something's wrong here. I don't know what it is, but I do know this, lobster, in the shell, cannot be produced by a machine."

Molly's face tightened with confusion.

"I just had a lobster dinner with my dad that was amazing." Deuce explained. "The machines work on a more macro level, aligning proteins. Sure, the meat could be produced but not the whole tail. Yet we both had a one-pound lobster tail tonight for dinner. Not only that, but he ordered my plate and it was delivered in ten minutes."

Molly stared at him.

He shook his head. "It all adds up to something. I don't know what yet, but between you and me, we'll figure it out."

"Okay." Molly sounded sincere. Did she really trust him? He'd have to make sure she never had cause not to.

CHAPTER TWENTY

Molly put Kita's film back in the sleeve and re-filed it. Deuce cracked the door open and peeked out. No one walked the hall, so he slipped out and pulled Molly close behind him. They scurried out of the infirmary like mice. An uncontrollable giggle started low in Molly's gullet and bubbled out of her mouth. Deuce chuckled, escalating into a full laughing fit. They had to stop walking near the living quarters, Molly bent over and placed her hands on her knees, shaking with laughter. Deuce gently slapped her on the back. "Stop!"

"I—I can't." A familiar emotion settled in Molly's heart. It took her back to the three months alone with Deuce on the ship. She hadn't realized how much she missed his presence until just this minute. Her eyes rose to Deuce's face.

Laughter crinkled his eyes and creased his cheeks. She'd never seen him laugh like this before. She stood straight and faced him. Their laughter slowly ebbed to a chuckle. Their breath came in great gulps. Deuce's eyes penetrated hers. She stepped up close to him, and he touched her shoulders to pull her into an embrace. His lips covered hers. She wrapped her arms around him and kissed him back, deeply.

"Psst," Miriam whispered from a side door to the living quarters.

Deuce and Molly pulled away. Heat swept over Molly's face. Deuce wiped his lips with the back of his hand. They both gasped for air.

"You, idiots, get in here!" Miriam whispered as loudly as she could.

Molly glanced at Deuce and ran to the door being held open by Miriam whose eyebrows rose in disapproval. "Did we *not* cover this in our missionary training? No fraternizing with each other in plain view of the general public." She pushed her elbow into Molly and frowned.

"Yeah. Sorry." Molly kept her eyes toward the ground and ran down the hall. *What was I thinking?*

"Molly!" Deuce called after her.

She jumped when her door slammed, but she couldn't do anything about that now. She hadn't meant to slam it. Not really. She just wanted to get into her room and away from Deuce, and the glaring reprimand in Miriam's eyes. *Geez, I thought my mother was six-hundred lightyears away.*

Molly stood inside her room, her forehead pressed against the door, and her hand on the frame above her head. *How could I be so stupid?* Spinning around, she threw herself across her bed and bounced twice before settling into the mattress. The memory of his lips over hers caused a warm sensation to sweep over her. Squeezing her eyes closed couldn't force the feeling away. She sighed.

Shower! She pulled out pajamas, a robe, and her shower bag. Slowly she opened her door to peek out. Deuce was gone. A heavy feeling dropped down into her gut, and she stomped down the hall to the women's facilities.

***

Dingle, dingle, ding.

Molly's eyes flew open.

Dingle, dingle, ding.

She touched her iComm link. Red letters ran across her visual range. *Gordon at Midnight.* She forced herself up, swung her legs over the side of her bed, and glanced at the time. Green numbers, *23:45,* illuminated in her right peripheral.

"Okay." She rubbed her nose and took a deep breath. Smacking her lips, she stood and reached for her shorts and t-shirt. Was it as warm at night? She glanced at the pants hanging on her chair but decided to chance it with the shorts. She pulled on socks and lace-up shoes, opened the side table beside her bed, and pulled out the small square note. Tucking it into her pocket, she staggered to her door. A quick look down the hall and out she went.

Gordon sat with his back to the door of the community cafeteria. Molly crossed the expanse and pulled a tray from the stack, stepped up to the food bin, and announced, "Pie, apple." A moment passed as she glanced over her shoulder. Gordon was reading something and appeared to ignore her. The food bin sounded, and the door rose. She pulled the pie onto her tray. "Chamomile tea, a hundred and twenty degrees Fahrenheit."

Shifting from one foot to the other, she waited. Soon, the door opened again, and she slid the hot tea onto her tray. Casually glancing around the cafeteria, she saw two groups of people sitting together engrossed in conversation and eating with sticks from white boxes. Huh, Asian-Region food? Gordon sat alone.

"Well, hello," Molly said to Gordon, standing next to his table.

"Oh, hi. Molly is it?"

Had she misunderstood his note? But then he fluttered a wink.

"Yes. Mind if I sit down?

"Not at all. Having trouble sleeping?"

"Yeah. I heard they had amazing pie. I guess it haunted my dreams."

"I can understand that." Gordon smiled and watched her settle into a chair. "Go ahead, taste."

Molly cut the wedge with her fork and lifted it to her mouth. The smell of cinnamon and butter filled her nostrils. "Mmm."

She placed the bite in her mouth and closed her eyes. "Oh my gosh," she mumbled around the apple filling and crust. "This is amazing!"

"Uh-huh." Gordon nodded.

He placed some five inch by seven inch films he was holding in the middle of the table. Molly glanced up at him. He nodded his head slightly. She took another bite of pie and placed her other hand on the films. She moved her eyes only and glanced around the room. No one seemed to be paying any attention to them, so she pulled the films closer to her side of the table. She finished eating the pie and sipped at the tea.

"What is this?" she spoke softly.

"Take them with you. Study them. You decide what they are," Gordon said as he stood.

"Wait." Molly half stood. "Do you know AF?"

"AF? No, why?"

Molly let out a long sigh. "Well, every time you send me a message, he does too."

Gordon sat back down. "What do the messages say?"

"Like, be careful who you choose for allies—you have a friend—stuff like that. Oh and," she glanced around without moving her head, "an invoice."

"An invoice? For what."

"Well," Molly glanced around again, "I can't exactly slide it across the table!"

"Oh sure. Here, let me transmit a secure address. Send me a copy." He touched his iComm link and typed on a virtual keyboard only he could see. "You know, I've suspected something like this was happening. The messages always show a stowaway signature. I blew it off as a programing error."

A red light blinked in Molly's right peripheral. She accessed it and touched her own virtual keyboard.

Gordon's eyes moved to his right. "Good. I'll see what I can decipher with the protocol origin. But—"

"But what?" Molly glared at him with confusion.

"Well, if it was piggy-backed with my message, the original protocol may be hard to find. There's something else, too."

"What?"

"Molly, think about it. If your AF is piggy-backing with my transmissions that means we've got more than one...emissary, and he's in our system."

"So there's no way to discover who this is?" Molly's eyebrows creased deeply above the bridge of her nose.

"I didn't say that." A mischievous grin slipped across Gordon's mouth. "I'll see what I can find out about your friend."

"Yeah, *my* friend," Molly repeated, "An informative friend. A good friend. A. F." Her eyes widened.

"What!"

"A Friend, A.F., could it be that simple?" Molly shook her head, "Surely not."

"Look, there's no telling, I'll see what I can find out and let you know."

"Okay, sure." Molly wiped her hand over her left eye. A yawn forced itself upon her.

"You better get some rest." Gordon smiled and rose again.

Molly reached up to her iComm link, "Oh hey, here's my report for the chief."

"Okay—got it. I'll get it out first thing in the morning."

"Peasy." Molly yawned again. She watched him walk out of the cafeteria and looked down at the films under her hand. Finishing the tea, she took her tray to the dish depository, the films held between her arm and rib cage.

Molly returned to her room and sat cross-legged on her bed with the films spread out in front of her.

Records of other women whose babies were documented as "Data Not Available" lay across her bed covers. Just like Kita's file. Was this code for not a live birth? Tears blurred her vision. Molly blinked to clear her sight. Omicronians adoption records. "Hmm."

Her eyes swept the films. On her right were the nonviable birth records, on her left adoptions. "Wait a minute." She counted the births, then counted the adoptions. "Same number. Okay."

How can I match these up? Molly scanned for a pathological match, blood-type, identification number, something to link with these births and the babies adopted by the local couples. *There's gotta be a way. Gordon wouldn't give me these, an exact match in numbers if they did not correlate. But what is it?* She bit her lip and held up a film.

"Okay, dates line up within forty-eight hours." But is that enough? She opened a file in her data iComm and listed the birth mother's names. She'd interview these women once she located them.

Michael's smiling face filled her thoughts. Kita said she had him with her until she went into the hibernation pod. Molly shuffled through the surrogate films. None were for the Lupuses. *Hmm.* Something else to look into. She piled all the films together and placed them in the second drawer of her desk and crawled into bed, breathed a heavy sigh, and surprisingly drifted off to sleep.

***

Something was wrong. Molly made her way through the darkened compound with a sense of urgency gnawing at her gut, pushing her to move as quickly as possible, yet her eyes took in every detail. Hating this feeling, she hoped she'd know what it was that drove her on when she found it. Because, right now, nothing seemed out of place.

A swarm of bees whizzed past her. Their collective bodies formed a golden-black cloud. She stopped to watch them shrink with distance, then grow as they returned to encircle her. She stood still. Their eerie buzz seemed amplified as they swung around her. She could make out words. "Beeee cautious. You have friends." The sound faded as they disappeared into the woods behind the buildings. She stared at the spot in which they vanished.

A red light filled the compound. She held her hand up in front of her face. Her skin glowed with the crimson illumination. A sound drew her attention to the ground. A lobster waddled up to her foot and clicked its pinchers. Abruptly, it stiffened, frost covered its shell, and then it was completely frozen like it had been dipped in liquid nitrogen. A colony of ants swarmed the lobster and carried its exoskeleton away.

Molly stared at the spectacle as it trailed a path out of the compound. She looked to the right of the lobster's path. A muster of peacocks loitered about. They nervously glanced around before lowering their heads to search for food. "What are they doing out at night?"

A strange glow illuminated from the center of the birds, rising higher and higher. Various colors beamed toward the sky then bent into an arch and shined down over Molly, like a rainbow of energy. She smiled and lifted her hands in the multi hues, wiggling her fingers between the colors. Tears streamed down her face as she laughed through her sobs. She had felt this same sensation when she connected with her dad.

The cloud of bees darted back and spun around her again. They encircled her several times and flew straight up above her head. She looked up to see the golden cloud become a dot and blend with the dusky purple sky.

She lowered her eyes. Mr. Abraham's angry face was inches from her own. She jumped back, gasping for air.

***

Molly sat straight up in bed. Her heart pounded against her chest. Each breath came with great effort, as if she had been running. She pushed her fingers through her unruly auburn strands and licked dry lips while her eyes focused on the time.

05:30.

The spooked sensation lingered in every fiber of her being as she stared at her door.

"Coffee!"

CHAPTER TWENTY-ONE

Gordon sat at his work station, the only person in the IT office. He enjoyed his hour alone before the other's arrived. Without wasting the precious solitude, he transmitted the report from Molly to Chief Chisula. The Secured Satellite Relay System would have the report to him in sixteen days. Next, he accessed the invoice Molly had transmitted to him last night.

"Oh wow!" He cross referenced the invoice to the accounting records—*No match*. He cross referenced it to the inventory records—*No match*. "This is getting interesting."

A mischievous smile parted his lips, and he licked them with a worrying tongue. He rubbed his hands together and typed on his virtual keyboard, searching all records for the invoiced items. 1

match. But the cursor sat blinking. He clicked the track ball and touched his iComm link. "Access file."

The cursor remained a blinking red light. His eyebrows rose, and his mouth twisted to the right. "Oh-kay."

He pulled out a drawer to his left and lifted a portable storage drive. It looked like a short, plastic Popsicle stick after all the frozen sweetness had been sucked away. He pushed it into the port on the front of his computer. His fingers flew across his keyboard. He hit enter and stared at the screen. The computer whirred quietly, and the red light blinked. Finally it turned green for a second. Data spilled across the screen. It was in a raw source code, numbers and letters A through F. Gordon smiled, opened another app to convert the hexadecimal data, and read the information.

Before long, Frank entered the office. "Morning, Boss."

Gordon flashed off his screen and turned around. His eyes were still wide with excitement.

"What?" Frank stopped mid-stride.

"Nothing." Gordon swallowed and focused on settling his heartbeat. "Too much coffee."

"O-kay." Frank stared at Gordon as he continued walking toward his work station.

Gordon turned back around and removed his portable storage device. He slipped it into his pocket and rose from his chair. "Listen, I—uh, need to go."

Frank looked up. "Sure."

"Yeah, so…I'll be back." Gordon hurried from the room. He had to find Molly.

He crossed the compound and entered the Security Building. He walked quickly down the hall toward the security work stations. As he passed the room full of desks, he glanced at Molly. Her eyes met his. A slight nod, and he moved directly for the exit door. He struggled to breathe normally as he leaned against the building and waited. Soon the door opened, and Molly peeked out.

"You looking for me?"

"Come here!" he demanded and walked along the side of the building.

"What?"

"Just come here." He had not caught his breath yet.

Molly walked toward him. His eyes swept around the corner and across the back of the area behind the building. Satisfied they were alone, he said, "That invoice you sent me?"

"Yeah."

"Those cryogenics supplies are nowhere in the laboratory's inventory. I don't know what they're for, not yet. But, they are not part of the known practices of this operation. I've suspected something like this was going on. I told your chief on Earth—"

"What are you saying?"

"I'm saying," Gordon swallowed and closed his eyes. He had to get control of his breathing. "Those cryogenic supplies are for something off base and are not part of this organization's inventory. Molly, this is the best evidence we've found to prove they are moving something out of here and to who-knows-where, off base."

"Pirating?" The word barely carried on her breath.

"Strong possibility! Frozen embryos are a marketable commodity out here in the vast reaches of civilization. I'll keep looking into it, you do the same. We'll meet again in a few days. And Molly," he looked around, "be very, very careful."

"Of course." She smiled a wary smile.

"I gotta go." He spun around and jogged around the building.

***

Molly walked back to the door. Gordon's words reverberated in her mind, *off base*. Off base where? To whom? She stopped in her tracks.

The door swung open and Roger stuck his head out. A breeze lifted his hair in an unnatural way. "Molly? What are you doing?"

"I—I thought I heard something. Apparently it was my imagination."

"Okay, so…you wanna come back in now?"

"Sure." Heat flushed her face. She kept her eyes focused on the ground. Did Roger see Gordon? He didn't act like it. Then again…she glanced back at the corner in which Gordon had disappeared. He had been out of sight when Roger opened the door. She looked at her supervisor for any signal. He looked curious but oblivious. She sighed and walked through the door Roger held open. "I thought I'd do a compound sweep."

"On your second day?" Roger's eyebrows squeezed together.

"Why not?" She cognitively grabbed the Bible Cheat Sheet Program and mentally accessed her thought. "'...because of idle hands, the house leaks.' - Ecclesiastes 10:18. Besides, it's not like I don't remember what you showed me yesterday."

Roger stared at her for a moment. "Well, if you feel you're ready to perform a compound sweep, then I suppose you should do a compound sweep."

Molly watched his face but saw nothing of concern. "Okay, then. I'll be back in a few hours."

"If you need any directions or anything, just call on the security iComm link, channel twelve. You received access to it when you received your clearance."

"Channel twelve, gotcha." Molly nodded. "Anything else?"

Roger shook his head. "Nothing I can think of right now."

"Okay, see ya later." Molly nodded once and left the building. To her right was the infirmary. The automated doors opened as she approached the entrance. Inside, she glanced right and then left. The receptionist looked up and returned to her work on the desk. Molly turned right and walked slowly down the hall, glancing into each open door. Nothing looked out of place. She continued down the hall and turned right.

In the middle of the back hall, a large metal door caught her eye. She took hold of the handle and pulled. It was locked. But the door did not have a locking scanner. *Hmm.* Security ought to have access to all areas. Her eyes swept the hall. A nurse's station was ten feet ahead. An older Omicron woman with silver fur-like hair and white-blue eyes looked up as Molly leaned on the counter.

"Hi." Molly flashed her warmest smile. "Just doing a security sweep."

The admin nodded.

"What does that door back there go to?"

The Admin stood up and looked down the hall. She shrugged.

"You've never been through that door?" Molly continued her practiced smile.

"Can't say I ever needed to." Her deep voice had the same gravelly quality to it she had heard at the banquet with the Lupuses. The Admin's eyes glanced back the other way down the hall.

What's she looking for? Or who? The Admin sat back down and continued sorting films.

"Know how I can get in there?" Molly pressed.

Frosty blue eyes rose to meet hers. She held the gaze and waited for an answer.

"No idea." The Admin's tone was slow, deliberate, and chilly.

"What's beside that area?"

"The Pathology Lab is that way." The Admin pointed back to her left. "And...I don't have any idea what's through *that door*. I guess whatever is through *that door* is the space behind *that door*." She shrugged again and sat back down.

"Okay. *Thank you*." Molly imitated the woman's tone and dipped her head as salutation, and turned to walk further down the hall. *Snarky old bat.* She entered the outer Pathology Lab and navigated her way to where she could see what she figured to be a wall of the locked area beyond the laboratory. At the back of the lab, there was another metal door, identical to the one in the infirmary hall. Exactly like the one she had tried, it had no locking scanner, just a handle. So much for her security clearance.

Molly continued her sweep of the laboratory all the while looking for any other entrance into the area behind the lab. The doors exiting onto the compound were a few feet in front of her as she strolled past the glass-walled laboratory. Her dream niggled at her mind as she approached an exit door. If she saw peacocks—

"Miss Jacobsen?" Deuce's voice called to her left. He leaned out of a room and tilted his head toward the interior. Molly hurried to him and entered the file room as he stepped back to allow her entrance. It was large. Rows and rows of file containers. A table stood against the wall to her right. Deuce walked over to the table and pointed at several films lying out.

"What's this?" Molly glared between him and the films.

"I'm trying to make sense of these nonviable births. So far, none of them add up. I can't seem to locate the mothers' either. Seems they've been reassigned, but no one can tell me where. I find that very odd. Just thought you'd like to know."

"Yes, thanks." Molly leaned over the table to look at the films. Were they the same films she had in her room? She strained to read the patient's names. The print was too small.

"There are six missionary surrogates who are prenatal patients. I'm going to follow their progress very closely. I'm not an obstetrician, but the OB here on staff is happy to have someone take some pressure off his overloaded schedule."

"So you're in."

"Yeah, I'm in." An uncertain smile waned from his face.

She straightened and crossed her arms over her chest. "And, what does your father think of this."

Deuce stepped back. "What? I haven't—!" His shoulders rounded as he exhaled a long sigh. "I told you, Molly, I'm not here to—"

"I didn't mean—I'm sorry." Molly looked down at the films. Heat flushed her cheeks.

"Don't worry. My goal is to prove to you that I'm not here to hurt anybody, least of all you." Deuce placed a tender hand on Molly's shoulder.

She fought the urge to flinch. Deuce leaned in to her. This time, Molly stepped away. "Look, what happened last night, it—it was inappropriate. And it won't happen again." Her chin rose slightly.

"Oh, well. I'm sorry to hear that." He ran his hand through his hair. "I suppose it's I who should apologize, then."

"If you figure anything out on these," she pointed at the table, ignoring the uncomfortable tension, "let me know, okay?"

"Of course."

Molly held his gaze a moment longer. A warm sensation pierced her middle. She swallowed hard and turned to leave the file room and the *temptation*.

The Bible cheat sheet sprang to life in her visual range. "For out of the heart come evil thoughts— Matthew 15:19."

"Oh my gosh!" She shook her head as a way of shaking the thought-activating program into submission. Glancing toward the lab, she scanned the area. A technician was busy typing data into her computer station in one of the small offices.

"Excuse me." Molly stuck her head into the lab. The tech startled and whirled around. Her eyes remained wide.

"Oh, I'm sorry. I didn't mean to frighten you." Molly stepped back. "Is Dr. Stork around today?"

"Huh? Oh, I—I didn't hear you walk in." The tech's face glowed pink.

"So, is Dr. Stork here?"

"Um," Ms. Tech leaned to her left to look around Molly and into the glass walled labs. She pointed at a room. "Yes, there he is, in the Cryo-Staging Lab."

Molly followed her point and saw Dr. Stork bent over a microscope. She turned back to the technician. "Thank you."

The tech had already returned to her task. Molly walked over to the Cryo-Staging area and tapped on the glass wall. Dr. Stork lifted his head, his eyes meeting hers. He held up one finger and spoke to his assistant, an Omnicron female. She nodded and returned to the microscope and entered something into an electronic tables to her left.

Stork stepped into a vestibule and removed his outer covering. It looked like yellow plastic wrap, except it held its shape as he hung it on a hook. A blast of white mist washed over him, causing his hair to lift. He blinked swiftly but kept his gaze on Molly. Eventually, he opened the lab door and stepped out.

"Ah, Molly. What may I do for you?" Dr. Stork said in an overly friendly tone.

Molly sensed annoyance. "I'm sorry to bother you, Dr. Stork. I was performing a compound sweep and I found an area of the lab I could not get into." She held his patient gaze. "The door's locked."

Dr. Stork said nothing.

"Do you have a key? I just need to be sure that area is secure."

"There's nothing in that area needing... surveillance. It's just storage, Miss Jacobsen." Dr.

Stork's eyes shifted to his right. He had probably checked the time.

"Well, how can you be sure? I didn't say what area I needed in to."

"There's only one area secured above your pay grade, Miss Jacobsen."

Above my pay grade? "Well, all the more reason for me to scan it, a storage compartment would be the perfect place for someone with mischief on their mind, to do something—harmful." Molly exposed her dazzling white teeth in what she knew was her most brilliant smile.

"I assure you, Miss Jacobsen, that area is mischief free and well protected." Dr. Stork returned her broad smile.

They held each other's eye contact without blinking. Molly broke the stare and glanced behind Dr. Stork. He turned to see what she spied. No one was behind him, but Molly was able to reach out with her senses while he looked away. *Annoyance. Impatience.*

There was something behind that locked door, and it was not some benign storage. "I simply want to make sure everything is as it should be, Dr. Stork. For security purposes."

"I understand, Miss Jacobsen, but I assure you, all is well behind that door. In fact, I personally guarantee you it is securely contained."

"Your personal guarantee isn't good enough for a security hound like me." She forced a chuckle. "I need to see that it's all right with my own eyes. Just once, then I'll let it be." Molly pressed harder, maintaining the brilliant and practiced smile.

"I see." Stork dropped his eyes to the floor. "Well, I'll have to locate the security code and let you know when you can scan the room." His fake smile returned to his face. "I've got some pressing assignments right now." His eyes darted right. "I'll contact you."

Molly knew it was a stall. She breathed a heavy sigh. "Okay, Dr. Stork. I expect you to contact me later today then."

"Of course." He continued to smile although it was waning.

Molly stared at the man a moment longer, she knew he was lying, before she turned and exited the laboratory.

Mentally, she developed a list of what she needed.

1. Nonviable births - live births? Adopted? Anyone decide to keep baby, like Kita, get reassigned? Where?

2. Physical evidence Michael - Kita - Lupuses

3. Locked door behind Infirmary-Laboratory.

She glanced at Stork as he re-entered the decontaminating chamber.

4. Locked area - connected? AF Invoice? Pirating?

She would type this list later and include it in her update for the chief. Should she update Deuce as well? The same warm feeling permeated her as the memory of Deuce kissing her hung in her mind like a kite caught in a tree. He'd be a perfect ally if he wasn't Abraham's son.

The second message from AF flashed in her memory, *Use extreme discretion when choosing allies.* Was Deuce an ally? How about Roger? How could she possibly know who her allies were?

A red light blinked in her peripheral. What now? She touched her iComm link. "Access, Message."

Molly, on your swing back through the infirmary, please see me, no hurry. —D

Molly stopped walking and looked back at the infirmary. What did he want? Or...what had he found? She quickened her step.

CHAPTER TWENTY-TWO

Molly completed the compound sweep with zero incidents. At least where she could cast her eyes had zero incidents. She hurried back to the infirmary and Deuce's curious summoning. As she approached the receptionist's desk, the girl glanced up, looked down, and then darted her eyes back up.

"Oh, Security Officer Jacobsen! Dr. Abraham left strict orders to page him the minute you got here."

"Okay? Thank you." He had said no hurry...

"Molly!" Deuce came up the hall quickly. "Could you come with me?"

"What are you up to?" She spoke softly, hoping only he could hear.

"Just come with me. Please?"

Molly followed him to a room labeled, "Medical Personnel Only." Inside the room were couches, small tables and chairs, a food preservation appliance, two coffee machines, and a food generating box.

"Okay, I'm here. What?"

Deuce smiled that wicked smile. "Look, I just wanted to invite you to have dinner with my dad and me."

"Oh." Molly stared at Deuce, curious concern flipped into alarm. "Are you kidding me?"

"No, I'm quite serious."

"How could you ask me to have dinner with your dad?"

"Because—The Lupuses are going to be there too, and I thought you would like to nonchalantly ask some questions."

"The Lupuses? As in all three?"

"Yes, Michael is coming."

"I don't know…"

"You get to be with your nephew and interrogate the people of interest in your investigation." Deuce looked concerned.

"That would be stellar, but..." Molly stared at the table.

"Of course it would. But what?"

"But it would be really..." How could she explain? Couldn't he understand the depth at which she loathed his father, and the Lupuses? She didn't want to dine with those people! If anything, she wanted to hurt them, severely. The only reason she might, maybe, consider going would be to see Michael. She let that thought linger in her mind. "It's just difficult."

"Oh." Deuce's face dropped as he nodded. "I'm just trying to help."

"I don't know how neutral I could be around them." Molly searched his face. "I-I'll question the Lupuses in my own time. And Deuce—"

"Yes?"

"I don't know about having dinner with your dad, ever again. I'm sorry!" Molly hated telling him the truth, but what else could she do?

"Besides, the last dinner caused me nightmares." She chuckled.

"Molly, I understand." He leaned back. "What nightmares?"

"Nothing." She felt heat flush her face.

"I get that you don't trust my dad, or me for that matter, but this is an opportunity to talk to and ask questions of the very people from whom you need answers. I can help you go straight to the source, and they'll never suspect a thing. They think you're simply..." He cleared his throat. "My date."

Molly's eyes shot up. "Your date!"

"Well! I had to have a reason for you to accompany me to the dinner!" Deuce reached up and touched the side of her face. "And I really would like for you to join me."

Tingling sensations set Molly's nerves on fire. She stared into his eyes, sensing nothing but sincerity. It *was* an amazing opportunity to talk to the Lupuses, casually, and be around her nephew. Talking to Michael would be galactic. So long as she could keep her emotions intact. She had to steel herself and do it. For Kita. For Michael.

"Okay," Molly whispered. "I'll go."

"Prime. I'll come by your quarters around eight o'clock tonight."

"Eight?"

"Well, yes. It seems Omicronian's eat late. And I have infirmary duty until seven anyway."

"I see. Okay. I'll be ready at eight. And Deuce," Molly touched his arm. He looked down at her hand and back up into her eyes. She muttered, "Thank you."

"Of course." That innocently wicked smile returned to his face, and his eyes twinkled.

Molly pressed her lips together and smiled tightly. She did appreciate his efforts. She hoped she was doing the right thing, and he wasn't setting her up for something that would bite her on the backside later.

***

What does one wear to dinner with one's sworn enemy? Molly lifted the t-shirts and shorts she had discarded earlier on her bed. Slacks? None of this would do. She stormed out of her room and rapped on Miriam's door.

"Oh, Molly!" Miriam clearly appeared to be stunned to see her. "Uh, come in."

"I'm having dinner with the Abraham's and the Lupuses tonight and—"

Miriam's eyes sparkled. "And you haven't a thing to wear?"

Molly nodded. Tears stung her eyes, but she fought hard to suppress them.

"Honey, you've come to the right place. Welcome to Miriam's Boutique." She stepped back from the door and gestured her arm in a sweeping motion.

She was right, she had quite an assortment. Molly looked through Miriam's clothes, one by one, sliding the garments across the hanger bar. Nothing looked like what Molly would have chosen on her own. Finally, Miriam pulled out a black linen-silk blend dress pants and a simple, white shirt.

"Oooh, I like that," Molly cooed.

"Yes, that would be perfect for you." A white faux leather jacket hung in Miriam's right hand. She held it back for inspection and laid it across the white shirt. "Now, do you have black shoes?" Miriam looked down at Molly's khaki, lace-up loafers.

Molly's eyes dropped to her feet. "Well, no."

"Don't worry! We look—" Miriam examined Molly's foot "—the same size. Look here." She pulled a large box out from under her bed and flipped the lid back to reveal twenty pairs of shoes. She pulled out a short-healed, black loafer.

Molly's eyes widened. "Perfect!"

"I agree. And here are some earrings too." Miriam held out some black pearl studs.

"Peasy!" Molly shook her head. "Thank you so much, Miriam."

"You are so welcome." Creases deepened in Miriam's eyes as she smiled.

Molly gathered the borrowed clothes, shoes, and earrings and hurried back to her room.

At eight o'clock sharp, hollow tapping on her door halted Molly's pacing. Her heart slammed against her sternum as she spun toward the door. She glanced in the mirror above the tiny dresser. Her experimental French braid was holding. Just breathe! She opened the door.

A swift bolt of shock pierced her. "Roger!"

"Hi Molly, we need to talk." He looked her up and down. "Did I catch you at a bad time?"

"Um, yes and no. I'm waiting for someone to pick me up." Heat rose in her face. She looked past Roger, no Deuce, and stepped back from her door, leaving it open. "Come on in."

Roger walked in and looked around. "Have you not unpacked yet?"

Molly chuckled. "Yeah, I didn't bring much. I'm a simple gal."

"I see." Roger clinched his jaw.

"So...you wanted to talk to me?"

"Yes, well, it seems when you performed your compound sweep today, you tried to access some areas that—don't need to be swept."

"You're kidding, right?"

Roger's eyes rose to meet hers. "Molly, you're new so I don't expect you to know all the protocol. This is a friendly warning, don't bother Dr. Stork with fully secured areas. The sterility integrity in some areas cannot be compromised. Therefore, access is limited to a small number of personnel."

Molly stared at her boss, "Oh-kay." She said slowly, processing his words. "But—if I may, how do we know the area doesn't need surveillance if we haven't witnessed that it is secure? Besides, he said it was storage, why would—"

"Molly!" Roger closed his eyes and drew air into his lungs. "I'm here to help you, not argue with you."

Knuckles rapped on Molly's door frame. Molly shifted her eyes to the still open door. Humiliation shot through her nerves like a sudden static shock. Roger also rotated in response. Molly squeezed her eyes and cringed. How much did he hear?

Roger faced Molly again. "This is your date?"

Her eyes pierced Roger's. "I—he—we're just friends." She glanced past Roger and caught Deuce's expression. His eyebrows rose, and his smile faded like wax on a warm window pane.

"Well, I'll let you get to your evening," Roger maintained his glare with Molly.

She closed her eyes. A sigh escaped her lips. She hated being in trouble with the boss, even though technically *Roger* was not her *real* boss. "Okay, I'll see you tomorrow."

"Sure. Please remember what we talked about." Roger moved toward her door.

"Of course." She resisted the urge to stand at attention, as she always did in the Chief Chisula's office.

Roger nodded as he slipped past Deuce. "Dr. Abraham."

Deuce stepped back to allow the man passage and returned to the doorframe. "What was that about?"

"Nothing." Warm sensations flooded Molly's chest and face. Even her blushing was embarrassing and it made her mad. "Ready?"

"If you are." Deuce placed his hand on her elbow. "You look nice, by the way." He leaned to look at her back. "I like the braid."

The warm sensation washed over her again. Would she ever stop reacting to him this way? She let him lead her out of the residential building but halted when he turned toward the vessel pad. "Where are we going?"

This time it was Deuce who flushed. "I've been commissioned a transport. It's right over here." A small two-seat vessel hovered in its reserved spot. A sign attached to the cement barrier framing the pads read, "Reserved for Dr. A. Abraham."

"What can I say, it comes with the job." He shrugged and opened her side of the vessel.

"Or the lineage." She glared at him then ducked to enter the passenger seat. As the door closed, the safety harness wrapped around her chest and waist. Deuce sat in the driver's seat and turned toward Molly. "Are you sure you're ready for this?"

"As ready as I'll ever be," she confessed.

Deuce reached toward her arm, hesitated, and activated his iComm link instead. "Transport, secure code 982, Abraham Residence." The vessel rose further from the pad, backed out of the parking space, and moved toward the designated location.

Molly's heartbeat increased. She focused her energy on slowing it back down to normal. When the craft slowed to turn into the path leading to the house, her heart took over and beat out a rhythm against her ribs. She closed her eyes and focused on controlling her lungs. Like her heart, she felt she needed to break out of an imperceptible cage.

Deuce said nothing. Thank goodness. Hopefully, he'd learned, in their three months together, to let her deal with her emotions without trying to interfere. Glancing her way before exiting his seat, he slipped out of the vessel, and walked around to her side. She jumped when her door opened and the safety harness released, seemingly on its own. The blaring sunlight hurt her eyes even though she squinted and held her hand over her brow as she stood. He waited patiently two paces from the vehicle, allowing her space and time to find her balance, before he guided her with a gentle grasp at her elbow to the entrance.

An Omicronian dressed in a formal black suit and starched white shirt answered the door, and allowed Deuce into the home. He led them directly to the dining room announcing their arrival. The three adults and Michael were already positioned around a large dining table. Two female servants, dressed in tight black, skirted uniforms stood at the ready in two corners behind Mr. Lupus who held the head-of-the-table position. Mr. Abraham sat to his right and Mrs. Lupus to his left. Michael squirmed in his oversized chair to her left.

As Deuce and Molly entered the dining room, Michael's smile lit up his eyes. Her heart skipped a beat and then pounded double time. She returned his smile and debated whether to run to him and hug him fiercely, or dash to the facilities and throw up. She settled with nodding toward him instead.

"Sorry we're late, Dad." Deuce clung a little too tight to Molly's elbow.

She glanced at him. Was he nervous, too? Rather than jerking away, she managed to ease from his vise grip and stand behind a chair across from Michael.

"Not a problem, Son, not a problem. We know you two are busy with your—duties." Mr. Abraham leaned back in his high-back chair with a broad smile.

Mr. and Mrs. Lupus held a genuine appearance of grace and nodded.

"We are pleased to see you again, Austin, Molly." Argenteus reiterated Abraham's assurance.

Deuce pulled Molly's chair out and pushed her in, then seated himself next to his dad.

Michael's familial frequency, or rather Kita's, strummed her senses. She smiled at him and forced herself to look toward Mr. Abraham when he spoke again.

"Besides, we haven't been served yet. You haven't missed a thing!" Abraham continued, "However, now that you are here, shall we begin?" He turned his head toward the main door to the dining room. "Pelusium! We'll begin dining now."

"As you wish." Pelusium nodded and backed out of the room. When had he re-entered the doorway? A tingle of weirdness skipped across Molly's senses. The two servants who had been standing erect in the corners followed him. Moments later, the two female servants entered and filled soup bowls. The clear broth steamed a mouth-watering aroma. An audible rumble roiled in Molly's stomach. Deuce glanced at her and smiled. She shrugged and lifted her spoon and scooped some broth.

"Well, I do hope you enjoy this meal, shall we bow our heads?" Mr. Abraham reached out and took Mr. Lupus' and Deuce's hand.

Molly fumbled with her spoon and accepted Deuce's proffered hand as Michael reached over and took Mrs. Lupus' hand. The table was too wide for Molly to hold Michael's. Regret washed over her. Abraham prayed, but Molly couldn't hear a word he said. Her blood surged past her ears and drowned out his voice.

She stared at her nephew with his head bowed, and his eyes closed. Her senses reached out to him and returned with happiness, curiosity, and hunger. Molly suppressed a chuckle. Michael raised his head and caught her staring at him. Did he sense her as well? She smiled, waiting for the final Amen, and resumed sipping her soup.

It tasted as good as it smelled. An onion broth, she deduced. Glancing up at Michael, she couldn't help but smile.

He sat up straight with his left hand in his lap. He ate quietly but quickly. Molly imitated his immaculate table manners. Mrs. Lupus looked up at Molly and followed her gaze to Michael. She smiled and continued sipping her soup.

As if cued by a director, the two females entered and removed empty bowls and replaced them with white bone china. On the plate was a slice of meat encircled with a bread crust, a green vegetable that looked like a cross between asparagus and broccoli, and a creamy-cheesy potato-looking side dish. And the most wonderful smelling yeast rolls imaginable. Tall crystal glasses were filled with ice and a brown liquid, probably tea, at least she hoped it was tea.

"Mmm." Molly inhaled the aroma from her plate. "This smells extreme."

"Yes, it does." Deuce breathed in his plate's bouquet.

She intended a quick glance at Michael, but in that moment, time stood still. Her gaze became a stare. The authors of etiquette training would have hung their heads in shame. But she couldn't pull her eyes from the child. If only Kita were here. Forcing her neck to bend forward as if in reverent prayer, she redirected her gaze to her plate as she picked up her knife and fork. Focusing on cutting her meat, she blinked away the tears that threatened to betray her indifferent façade.

Mrs. Lupus cleared her throat. "Do you have children, Miss Jacobsen?"

Molly lifted her eyes to meet Mrs. Lupus'. "Me? No, no kids. I'm not married." Molly glanced awkwardly toward Deuce. He made no eye contact. He was no help.

"Oh." Mrs. Lupus nodded. "Our little AJ here is such a blessing to us. So many obstacles stood in our way—" Her eyes intent on Molly "—but in the end, well, our prayers were answered and we received this *precious* child. It was a glorious day in our home. I hope you will be as blessed someday." She patted the top of his head.

Embarrassed eyes looked up at his mother while a playful smile split his mouth wide open. The canine resemblance became a blatant reminder of his Omicronian lineage.

Molly started, gasping a quick breath of air. Her stomach knotted with anger, and then sadness. She swallowed. "Um, thank you. I—I hope so, too."

Mrs. Lupus had seemed to choose her words carefully. Could it be she had just confessed this was Kita's son? Had Kita's indecision been one of those obstacles or was Molly just hearing what she wanted to hear, for evidence sake? She needed professional objectivity. Glancing at Deuce, who avoided her completely by focusing on his plate, she returned her attention to the Lupuses and ventured a question. "What does AJ stand for?"

Mr. Lupus grinned warmly toward Michael. "Argenteus, Junior of course." Michael returned the smile with sharp little puppy teeth broadly exposed.

"Of course." Molly forced herself to eat, although she was no longer hungry. She watched Michael when she could without others noticing her fixation. When he looked up at her, she smiled and dropped her eyes. The Lupuses were loving parents, and he seemed happy. Molly rolled these thoughts around in her head while she attempted to eat her food. She sipped her iced tea and was surprised to find it had lemon and sugar in it.

"How old are you, —um, AJ?" Molly pursed her lips.

Mrs. Lupus' eyes fluttered a glance at Molly before returning to her meal. Her eyebrows remained pulled together.

"I have seven years." His voice had the Omicron deepness but lacked the gravelly quality of the other locals. Was this common in the children or just the cross-bread ones?

Molly closed her eyes and held her breath a second. She smiled at him. "So you're in, what, second year grammar school?"

He looked at her oddly, and then looked at his mother.

Mrs. Lupus tilted her head. "Well, yes and no."

Molly stared at her. "I beg your pardon?"

"I school him myself. He's very intelligent and reads on a ten-year level and is working arithmetic problems at a twelve year level."

"Oh. I see." Molly looked back at Michael. "Of course you are—very intelligent that is—my sister was like that. Way advanced in school." Molly returned her eye contact to Mrs. Lupus'. She reflected no recognition or guilt or anything other than pride in the child she considered her son.

"It's quite a challenge to keep ahead of him, but my husband is able to acquire studies that interest AJ so that's helpful."

"I'm sure that *is* helpful." Molly glared at Mr. Lupus. He too did not register any guilt. Molly discretely reached out with her senses but reeled back immediately. A sensation similar to a cold, hard slap across her face retracted her stretch. Did

Lupus do that? She stared at him. He grinned warmly, but she felt a cold chill shimmer down her spine.

"So, Molly, how are you enjoying your assignment?" Mr. Abraham broke the silence that hung between everyone.

"Huh?" She turned to stare at Abraham. "Oh, so far so good, I guess." She glanced at Deuce. "How long have you been here, Mr. Abraham?"

"Austin! Please. And I've been here twelve years." He smiled broadly at the Lupuses. "Twelve *amazing* years."

The Lupuses nodded a side-ways sort of tilt to their heads. Reverence? Acknowledgement? Molly struggled to decipher the gesture. She glanced at Deuce again, something flashed across his eyes. Pain? Insult?

"And"—her eyes returned to Mr. Abraham —"what keeps you here?"

His smile faded. "I'm sorry?"

"I mean, The Abraham Project seems to be well established, I'm just wondering what keeps you here. Aren't there other planets in need of assistance?"

"Oh, I see. Well, I have to say I have settled here. It feels like home for me, and I don't feel *called* to go to another planet. You know what I mean?"

"No, I'm not sure I do."

"I'm here doing Gawd's will, and I do not feel He has called me to move beyond this beautiful place. When He does, then I will do as He wishes." The broad smile returned to his face.

Molly thought about the sensory slap from Lupus earlier and wished she could reach out to him now. See how he felt about Abraham's professing to being *called by God to stay here*. Her gut told her Abraham was lying through his bleached white teeth. "Well, it certainly looks like you are—at home here."

Pain shot up from Molly's ankle, and she caught her breath. She turned to look at Deuce. His eyes widened. She got his message, *Hush up*.

Mr. Abraham looked around the dining room. "Oh this? This house was actually a gift from the Lupuses. They insisted on expressing their appreciation for what TAP has done for their future existence by gifting me with their home and built themselves another, the one you went to the first night you were here."

Molly nodded and pursed her lips, while resisting the need to rub her sore ankle.

The two female attendants entered the room pushing a cart of desserts. One removed the empty plates while the other distracted everybody at the table with an artful display of choices from the cart. There were slices of fruity cake with fluffy white icing, golden fruit-filled pies topped with speckled vanilla ice cream, powdered sugar dusted cream puffs, deep creamy cheese cake topped with a colorful assortment of fresh berries.

Molly declined. Her gut was reeling from overloaded sensory information. Even though she had not been able to stretch her *gift* to Mr. Lupus, the non-contact had told her enough. He was guarded and probably *gifted* as well.

Tonight's experience lit a fire in her chest which was not heartburn from the unfamiliar food. Watching them interact so comfortably with her nephew, Mrs. Lupus practically confessing he was her sister's child, and Mr. Abraham's flamboyant personae. Her eyes remained on Michael.

A sharp pain stabbed her in the rib. Deuce's elbow brought her attention back to the adults. "I said, 'Isn't that right, Molly?'"

Her palms ached from clinched fists and a headache brewed above her tightly held jaw. "Uh, what?"

Deuce pursed his lips. "I couldn't thank you enough for staying awake with me while my ankle healed. We enjoyed getting to know each other."

"Oh...oh yeah. It was stellar."

Coffee was served immediately after dessert selections from elaborate silver urns, and Michael was served warmed chocolate milk. Molly uncomfortably sipped her coffee and watched the time in her peripheral, while the others enjoyed their selection of sweet endings. Would this night ever be over?

When the servers returned to take away the empty dessert dishes, Mr. Abraham invited everyone to move to the den. Michael yawned widely. His canine gaping maw fascinated Molly.

Lily turned and whispered something to her husband. Molly's heart sank. Did that mean they would decline staying any later? She was torn between wanting to leave, and wanting to stay to talk to Michael. His voice thrilled her and watching Kita's gestures in his movements made her long to remain. She'd give anything to set him in her lap and read to him or have him read to her.

"Thank you, Austin, for a wonderful dinner and wonderful company," Lupus' eyes swept from Abraham to Deuce to Molly. "But we need to put our son to bed and decline your invitation for what I am sure would have been some delightful camaraderie in *your* den."

Tack! Molly cursed in her mind.

Abraham, Senior wiped his mouth unnecessarily before wadding his napkin and tucking it next to his cup and saucer. "Of course, Argenteus, of course."

Molly pushed her foot into Deuce's ankle and chuckled when he winced. Her eyes widened when he looked at her.

"We need to be going, too, Dad. It's been a long day for both of us."

Molly added, "Yes, but thank you for a delightful dinner."

Deuce and Molly followed the Lupus family toward the front door.

Molly intentionally walked close behind Michael who was lagging behind. His weary legs moved forward, but his feet shuffled. Molly mused at his sluggish movements. He'd be asleep before they left the transportation path. She reached out to ruffle his head but thought better of it. Her eyes lifted to the Lupuses.

They seemed focused on crossing the threshold and didn't appear to be concerned with her proximity to their son. She gnawed on her lip. Could she chance an opportunity to touch Michael's soft fur-covered head? A slight tremble betrayed her bold out-stretched hand. Gently she lowered her palm on to his head. The shock of his silky feel caused her to retract her hand slightly, but then she sunk her fingers into his silver pelt and rubbed the top of his head like one would praise a well behaved dog.

He smiled a sleepy smile and nuzzled against her palm. She returned his smile and dropped her hand to her side. The sensation stayed in her heart like a glowing candle through a moonless night.

Disappointment darkened Abraham's face as everyone shuffled toward the front doors. Good nights were exchanged, and the two couples exited the home. Abraham stood on the rounded porch and waved as the two vessels drifted down the driveway.

CHAPTER TWENTY-THREE

Molly rode in silence until their residential quarters came into view. Deuce landed the vessel on his reserved pad and turned to Molly. "You all right?"

"Yeah. I told you this would be really hard for me. It hurts to be around him and yet not be able to speak to him…like…I would if…he knew I was his aunt." *Aunt Molly.* She mulled that over in her mouth like an unfamiliar hard candy.

"I know, but did you learn anything?"

"Yes." She glanced up at Deuce and back down at her lap. "Your dad is hiding something. Mr. Lupus is very guarded, and I think Mrs Lupus as much as admitted she knows Mich—I mean, AJ is my sister's child."

"Huh. Well, there you go. You're closer than you were. Right?"

"And that doesn't bother you?" she asked. "That I suspect your father?"

"Molly, I told you I don't trust him, either. Something is not right here. Your sister, other women, these medical records do not add up. I want to know what's going on here just like you do. Granted, it's not my sister, but as a healer, I have my Hippocratic Oath, and I don't want any harm to come to any of these women."

A red light blinked in her peripheral. Her eyes darted to it and back to Deuce's sympathetic face. Could she trust him? When she reached out with her senses to Mr. Lupus, she was slapped back. Deuce's father seemed to block her too. But when she reached out to Deuce, she always received sincerity, concern, and dedication. Was he masking his feelings? Was that even possible?

Still, having the opportunity to interact with Michael was galactic. He was an amazing kid. Pain gripped her heart. How she wished he had not been stolen from Kita. How she wished Kita knew him. A thought popped into her head, if Kita had brought him home, he'd be four now. But, because he stayed here, he was seven.

Here, he was reading on a third year level and doing math at a fifth. On Earth, he wouldn't have entered school yet. What an odd perspective.

"What are you thinking?" Deuce interrupted Molly's reverie.

Her head jerked up, "Nothing. I've gotta mes— I've gotta go." Goodness, she did not want to tell him she had a message waiting. What was she thinking! It could be Gordon, or AF or anybody, but she didn't want to share that with him. Not yet. And she would heed AF's advice to use extreme discretion in choosing her allies.

"I really wish you would trust me, Molly." Deuce touched her hand.

She stared at his hand over hers. The red blinking beckoned her attention. Mentally, she accessed it just to see who had sent the message but kept her gaze on Deuce's hand. He had masculine hands although they were soft. Doctor's hands, unaccustomed to hard laborious work. Healing hands. Could he heal her pain? Kita's?

Michael's? White letters appeared in her lower peripheral.

Be very, very careful when you dine with the enemy. People have disappeared and never raised a manicured eyebrow from security. Explanations are given, of course, but it's as if you were six-hundred lightyears from the truth. — AF.

Molly gasped. "I gotta go!"

"What's wrong?" Deuce squeezed her hand.

She yanked her hand out from under his. Why did she feel like his touch burned? Or was it the message from AF? The mystery person knew who she'd had dinner with, and it wasn't piggybacked this time. He referred to the dining companions as the enemy. But who was the enemy? Mr. Abraham, Deuce, the Lupuses, or all of them? "Nothing, I gotta go. I'm all right. I just need to go to my room, okay? Thank you for letting me spend time with— AJ."

Deuce tilted his head. "You're calling him AJ now?"

"Well, for now." She dipped her head and reached for an exit handle, but there was nothing to release her door. "Deuce, please."

"Of course." He touched his iComm link and released the doors. Both opened. Molly slid out. Deuce hurried around the vessel and walked with her to the residential building. Outside her room, she spun around to face him.

"This is so awkward." She glanced up at him. "I feel like I should tell you how much I enjoyed dinner and thank you for taking me, but this isn't really a date, it's an investigation. And yet...I feel... confused."

"About what?" Deuce lowered his head to level his eyes with hers.

"Us."

Deuce smiled. "So there is an us?"

"No. Of course not. I mean—"

"It's all right. You need time. No pressure, okay?" Deuce placed his hand on her shoulder. "I had a good time, too." He bent and kissed her cheek and walked away.

Molly stared at his back. She touched her cheek where the warmth of his kiss lingered. "Why are you such an enigma, Dr. Abraham?" *Lord, help me discern my enemies from my allies.*

A small voice resonated in her mind, *Let those who have ears, hear*.

Molly's eyes darted left and right, but her head stayed straight. What was that? Who was she perceiving? No one was within visual range. She reached out with her senses. No one registered out of the ordinary. Most of the residential dwellers were either asleep or quietly occupied in their rooms. *Who was that?*

I Am with you.

Molly froze. Who? She fumbled to unlock her door. Seriously? Trembling hands gently closed the door and secured the bolt. The fine hairs on the nape of her neck rose. She shivered and lowered herself down onto her bed. Tears pooled in her eyes. She blinked, and they spilled over her lashes. Was Gordon straight-shooting messages to her now? Or was this some sort of psychic connection? But with who?

Molly wiped her tears. She pulled off the borrowed clothes, gently draped them over the desk chair, slipped on her usual sleeping attire, a t-shirt and boxers, and glided into bed. Her father, preaching in earnest, floated to the surface of her mind like a message in a child's 8-ball toy.

Could it be...that still small voice she knew as a child, way out here, six hundred lightyears from...the truth? AF's message surfaced too. After all these years, could God actually be reaching out to her?

She swung her legs out from under her covers but hesitated. *Don't be ridiculous!* She pulled back under her covers and stared at the ceiling. Somebody had contacted her. Technology was different here, more advanced in a lot of areas. She was letting her childhood superstitions get the best of her. She knew better. God no longer heard her prayers. And she couldn't hear Him.

She curled up on her side and hugged her pillow. A shiver rippled over her arms, so she tucked them under the blanket and drew her limbs closer to her torso. She hadn't felt like this since she was a young girl, afraid of the dark. But she had Kita then. They would curl up together in one bed like kittens and sleep would overtake her. A tear fell from her eye. She missed home. She missed her twin. She didn't want to be here. Tears soaked her pillow. Eventually, she slipped into a fitful sleep.

***

Burrrpp, Burrrpp, Burrrpp.

Deuce's iComm link alarm sounded. He forced his sluggish eyes open. Sleep had not been easy for him. His mind had been filled with Molly, her unresolved issues with her sister, Michael, the senseless records, the current pregnancies, and to be honest, the project that bore his name. He touched behind his ear and dismissed the alarm. His gut instincts were never wrong, and his gut told him a piece of the puzzle was locked away behind that door in the infirmary. But how could he get in there?

He had tried to find out through the staff. Lips were tight about that subject. Either people did not know, or they were part of the cover up, or whatever it was that kept that door locked. His father was the way through that door. He had to convince his father he wanted in on the project.

How could he overcome all the years they have been apart, physically and emotionally, and win his dad's trust enough to share what could possibly be the darkest secret of The Abraham Project?

Then again, he was the son. The only son. Getting Dad's trust shouldn't be that hard. Perseverance should prove fruitful. He would continue to have dinner with him, feel him out. Even if that meant making his father believe he was not interested in Molly. He could say he had simply been determining her intentions. Keep your friends close and your enemies even closer. Now he was thinking like his dad. Deuce touched his iComm link. *Call, Infirmary.*

The red-headed receptionist answered. What was her name? "Libby?"

"Yes, this is Libby."

"This is Dr. Abraham."

"Oh hi, Doctor, what can I do for you?"

"Who's on staff today?"

"Um…let's see." Deuce could hear her long fingernails tapping a virtual keyboard. "Dr. Stork, of course—" she snorted a giggle "—Dr. Lenard…

and Dr. Rotcod. You want me to page one of them?"

"Yes, let me speak to Dr. Stork."

"Sure. I mean, one moment please while I connect you." She giggled.

Deuce listened to clicking and a buzzing sound. "Dr. Stork."

"Yeah, Stork, this is Abraham. Listen, if it's not too busy up there today, I'd like to take some time and see my dad."

"Ah, yes. This was expected. I think we can handle it here. You go be with the old man."

Expected? What did that mean? "Great. Listen, if anything happens just contact me, and I'll return on the double."

"Of course. Have a swell day with Austin."

"Uh, thank you." *Swell day? Okay?*

Deuce touched his link to disconnect the call. "Call, Dad." Deuce listened as the connection buzzed then clicked. "You have reached Austin Abraham. I am not available at this time. Please leave a message, and I'll get back to you as soon as I can. May Gawd bless you and keep you." His southern twang grated Deuce's nerves.

"Hey Dad, Deuce here, I've got the day off and thought we'd spend some time together. So…" a blue light flashed in his peripheral. He disconnected. "Answer, call."

"Deuce, sorry I missed your call," his dad said between gasps of air.

"It's okay. Are you all right?"

"Sure. Just rushed to get the phone."

That winded from answering a iComm link? His dad looked to be in better shape than that. "Well, I have the day off and wondered if you were available."

"Sure, sure. Oh wonderful! Or, what is it you say, galactic? I've got a couple of meetings scheduled, but I can postpone them—"

"No, go ahead and keep them. I'll just hang out with you and see what it is you do all day." Deuce hated the chuckle that slipped from his throat.

"Well, sure, why not? That sounds like a plan. Have you had breakfast?"

"No. I'll have it with you. So, stellar, I'll be there in a few."

"See you then."

Deuce disconnected. He took a quick shower and jogged over to his dad's office.

***

"Austin!" Mr. Abraham greeted Deuce as he entered the TAP headquarters.

"It's Deuce, Dad." He suppressed the child-reflexed eye roll.

"Oh, of course, forgive me—I thought you might have outgrown that." Abraham led him to a portable table that had a carafe of coffee, sweet rolls and fruit. "So, what are you interested in doing today?

Deuce poured himself a mug and picked up a cinnamon roll. "Just whatever you have scheduled to do." He spoke past the bread in his mouth. "I want to see what my old man is up to here."

A poker perfect grin, hopefully, masked his trepidation. He had to pull this off and, for heaven's sake, he could not reveal the cards he hoped he held close enough to his chest to fool the toughest player he had ever dealt a hand.

Abraham's smile dropped into a straight-face-expression. "What do you mean?"

"I simply mean, I haven't seen or heard from you in over twenty years. So now I'm here on this planet, with you, and I want to know more about you. Be part of your life. Work with you in whatever it is you're doing. For the good of these people, right?"

"Well, sure, son. But, what about your medical practice?" Abraham glared at him.

"You don't honestly think I traveled six hundred lightyears *just* to be a doctor, do you? I could do that back on Earth. I mean, I certainly can, and will, establish a practice, but I know there's more for me here—with you, than I could ever have back home." Deuce broadened his smile to punctuate his gambler's façade.

Abraham hesitated, then reached for the carafe and poured himself more coffee. "Really?"

"Yes, of course." Deuce sat down in the chair facing his dad's desk. "So you think there's a chance of giving me an office or a desk?"

Abraham lifted his coffee but stopped half way to his mouth. "Oh. Uh, sure, sure. I'll see to it today." He set the cup down and stared at its contents. Deuce couldn't discern what he might be thinking? Suddenly, he looked up and smiled.

"In fact, I can do better than that, if you'll let me." He raised one eyebrow and stared at Deuce.

It was Deuce's play, but what could he say? He had no idea where his father was going with this, or if he was simply calling Deuce's bluff. He remained quiet and let his dad play out his hand.

"Son, the Lupuses have been very generous with me, as you know. They've provided me with a luxurious home, which has an amazing servants' quarters that's not being used. I'd like to offer it to you as an apartment. It's fully furnished, and I can have it ready for you to move into—oh, say, by this evening."

Deuce nodded with a hesitant smile. Did he want to be *that* close to his dad?

"I'm supposed to be here with the missionaries." He considered the possibilities. "But surely they'd understand me wanting to live near you."

"Of course. I'm sure they would. Besides, most of the missionaries eventually get their own homes.

But, if you think it will cause you disgruntled relations…"

Deuce stared at the steaming, black liquid in his cup. He could agree to this apartment and keep his room at the village. Keep an eye on his dad's affairs and have a place for a quick rest when he worked long hours at the infirmary. He couldn't see a down-side to this idea. "I accept. And I thank you…Dad." He swallowed.

"Wonderful." Abraham clapped his hands. "What sort of work are you wanting to do here, son?"

"Well, you know, I'll have to continue to work at the infirmary in order to establish a practice. But I'd like to shadow you on my days off. I'll be your junior man." Deuce threw back his head and laughed. "Get it? Junior is your junior man!" He continued to laugh and prayed it didn't sound as fake to his dad as it did to himself.

Abraham chuckled. "Yeah, I get it. Actually, son, I've dreamed of the day when you would join me."

The laugh caught in Deuce's throat. He stared at his dad. "Really?"

"Of course! We've been apart too long. But that's water under the aqueduct. This is going to be great."

"Yes. Yes, it is. So..." Deuce stood and rubbed his hands together. "What's the first order of business?"

"Okay." Abraham listed his day's agenda.

Deuce picked up another roll and tore out a bite. Was his dad buying any of this?

CHAPTER TWENTY-FOUR

Molly woke before her alarm. She dressed in her new uniform shirt and shorts, pulled her hair out of last night's braid and into the usual ponytail, and walked to the common kitchen. After a solitary cup of coffee and toast, she headed to her office.

"Hey, Boss." She lifted a green, transparent clipboard from her desk. "Compound sweep?"

"Okay, but don't make anybody mad today. Please?"

"Who, me?" Molly tucked the clip board under her arm and headed out the door.

In the infirmary, she approached the strawberry-blond receptionist, "It's...Libby, right?"

Libby nodded. "Dr. Abraham isn't here, Security Officer Jacobsen."

"Oh really?" Molly cringed, resisted saying, *We're just friends*, but looked down the hall as if she might see him anyway. "Please, call me Molly. I'm just here for a compound sweep. Know of any trouble in the infirmary last night or this morning?"

Libby shook her head, "None that I know of. Been pretty quiet all week—Molly. " She said her name as if she were trying it on for a fit.

"That's good news, isn't it?"

Libby nodded.

"Since you mentioned it, do you know where Dr. Abraham is?"

"Oh, I assumed you...I heard he took the day off. Wanted time with his father, I suppose. Can't blame him, you know, all those years apart—"

"Seriously? I mean..." A knot twisted in Molly's stomach. What was he doing spending the entire day with Abraham? Just when she leaned toward trusting him. She sensed Libby's curious stare and returned her gaze on the girl. "Well, I'll see you around, then."

"Okay, have a good one." Libby lowered her eyes to her work.

Molly walked the halls of the infirmary, mulling over what Libby had said. She entered the Lab's corridor. Dr. Stork looked up as she walked past the glass wall. He tipped his head back and widened his eyes in greeting, a tray of vials, half full with a pale pink liquid, sat to his right, at his ready.

What a fool I have been. Of course Deuce would seek out his father. It's his *father* after all. How could she believe he would forsake blood kin and help her investigate the cruel hoax played on Kita and her baby? Only he's not a baby. He's a big boy, smart too.

Wham! Molly smashed into an opened door. Dr. Stork gasped. "Oh Molly, I'm sorry. I wasn't looking where you were going."

"That's all right, Dr. Stork..." Molly realized the backhanded way he apologized. "I suppose I wasn't watching where *you* were going, either." She chuckled. But he did not laugh, or smile. He continued on his path toward his office.

Molly quickly turned to exit the glass corridor, but a solid wall of white lab coat blocked her egress.

"You really don't look like your sister." An Omicron lab technician glared down at her. Molly glanced around to see if anyone had heard him. His name tag read, Levi Branson. His eyes narrowed.

She swallowed to regain her composure. "What? Why would you say that?"

Levi took hold of her elbow and lifted it into her shoulder, causing her to rise up on her tip toes. He walked her toward the door or rather *dragged* her to the door. "You don't belong in here, Miss Jacobsen. For Kita's sake, as well as your own, leave things alone."

"Wha—" She stumbled into the hall. Heat flushed her face. She glanced both directions, hoping her humiliation was not witnessed. Nurses and Environmental Sanitation personnel scurried past the lab, eyes aimed toward the floor. How much of this Lab activity is ignored?

She found the first door out of the infirmary and continued her compound sweep, pondering Stork's encounter, the lab technician man-handling her, and Deuce's absence. Was there anybody on this planet she could trust?

Outside, she still scanned for the possibility of peacocks…or bees, and shook her head at the ridiculous thought. Her eyes swept to the left. Twelve women stacked grapefruit-sized stones along the length of a ditch. Five men were standing in the culvert, taking the stones from the women and placing them in precise alignment inside the watercourse. Molly approached them, shielding her eyes from the bright mid-morning suns.

"Hello. I'm Secur—I'm Molly." Her gut tightened.

Most of the women responded with "Hi," or "Hey," but no one looked directly at her.

"Is this the aquifer?" Molly looked at the length of the trough behind them. In the distance, she noticed Julio walking beside another man. They both wore dark-grey hard-hats and Julio carried a large scroll, blueprints perhaps. She returned her gaze to the women.

"Is there something you need—Molly." A tall blonde who looked to be in her early thirties spoke while the other eleven continued working. She had a killer tan, probably an advantage to working outdoors.

"No, just curious. Where will the water come from?" Molly held her hand over her eyes and followed the ditch out past where the people were working but could not see the source of water. Julio and the other man had stopped walking. Both seemed to be watching Molly's interaction with the stone stackers. Or was she just paranoid?

"There's a well five hundred meters that way." The woman shoved a gloved thumb over her shoulder.

"Oh, I see. And are you all with the missionary pilgrims? The Abraham Project?" Molly scanned their sweaty faces.

Four of the women stopped working and looked at the woman Molly talked to. She exchanged a glance with them and licked her lips. "How else would we get here?"

"Well, sure. I'm sorry, I didn't catch your name."

The woman glared at Molly. Her eyes ran up and down her frame. Eventually she uttered, "Name's Carol."

"I'm Molly."

Carol's glare hardened. "So you said."

"I'm just trying to figure things out. I don't mean to intrude." Molly stood her ground.

Two more women stopped working, shielding their eyes, and stared at Molly. "Carol, just introduce everybody, so we can get back to work." A petite dark haired gal blurted, sweat clinging to her face like dew drops.

"Okay—" Carol tilted her head and shot an angry look toward the petite woman "—me and these four, Rita, Wanda, LaTrell, and Talitha, have been here seven years. Earla, Luz, and Margaret there"—she pointed at three other women—"have been here ten years. Those other four over there, Frances, Cyndi, Nadine, and Adelia, have been here three years. Right, Franny?"

Frances nodded but did not look up from her stone stacking. Adelia, the petite woman, resumed her work.

Molly looked Carol square in the eyes. "...and you volunteered to work on this aquifer?"

Carol scowled. Her eyes flickered down to Molly's embroidered name. An odd smile formed on her dry lips. "Well, we do what we have to do to help the community."

"That doesn't sound like an answer to me, if you don't mind me saying so." Molly repositioned her stance. Her right knee bent slightly, her foot propped up on a stone, she looked every bit the legal enforcer making an inquiry at a crime scene. Sensing the women's discomfort, she stepped back and forced herself into a more casual stance. Glancing down the way, Julio had continued his walk with the other man.

"It's really hot already. Can I bring you anything?" Another approach might help. Was it too late to get on their good side?

"We have water, and we'll break soon. We don't work in the mid-day suns. No one does."

"Oh, well that's good to know. I was about to go find you umbrellas." Molly chuckled, the women did not. "Hey, you've been here seven years, you say?"

Carol sighed, and then nodded.

"A friend of mind was here then. She's back on Earth now." Molly felt the sudden lifting of heads, but kept her eyes on Carol. "It didn't work out for her. I sure admire you gals for staying and working so hard. These Omicronians seem like nice people, interesting hair, huh?"

Carol stared from under a gloved hand which shielded her eyes. "How do you know Kita?"

"Huh? How did you know I meant Kita?" Molly looked down at the men in the ditch who had stopped working as well. "I—I've known her all my life. We—we went to the same church."

The men turned their backs and continued lining the waterway. The women exchanged nervous glances. Carol stepped closer to Molly. "Listen, keep that to yourself. She did not work out here, like you said, but it's not something people talk about."

"Really, why?" Molly moved closer to Carol.

"Let's just say, Kita seemed like a really sweet girl, but—well, somehow she was granted privileges nobody else gets. Not to gossip, but her and Pastor O—well, we're just not sure what happened. She wasn't held to the commitment, that's all, and Pastor O hasn't been seen since."

"The commitment? Oh! You mean the lifetime commitment to stay here."

"Yeah—" Carol's eyes flickered down to Molly's name on her uniform shirt. "—we all know how hard it is."

Molly reached out with her senses, *anger*, *mistrust* returned to her and something else. Molly let the sensation return fully before she was able to decide what emotion she had picked up. Then she knew.

Fear.

No, it was deeper than that, something life threatening, yet protective. A vision flashed in her mind, a ferocious mother bear, protecting her cub with every ounce of strength left in her body. A bloody paw swiped at the predator. Saliva dripped from her gaping maw, and sharp white teeth snapped as a fierce growl ripped from her throat, echoing across an open field. "Yeah—" Molly cleared her throat "—we were told Pastor O was off somewhere, a-uh, Jacques Breneé filled in for him at our orientation."

Molly forced a smile. She reached out to touch Carol's shoulder to say, *take care,* and then leave. But when she touched Carol, the vision of the mother bear morphed into a woman placing a child in an opaque container, and watching it float away on a hover-gurney into utter darkness. The protective sensation she had sensed was for her child. Had Carol sacrificed her child in order to protect him? Molly closed her eyes and bit her lip. A tear squeezed through her lids. She quickly opened her eyes and stared at Carol, fighting the urge to console her, tell her she understood. Her sister was suffering this same loss.

Carol stared back. "You all right?"

"Sure." Molly cleared the lump in her throat. "Sure, I—if there's nothing you need, I'll let you get back to work. Don't stay out in the heat too long. I'll be worrying about you if you do." Molly forced a weak smile and turned to walk back to the compound.

Tomorrow she'd bring something out to them and try talking again. They knew something about Kita, and she needed to find out what. How hard would it be to get a canopy? Maybe some fruit would be easier. Wonder if there's watermelon on this planet? Molly smiled. If nothing else, maybe the food prep box could make some watermelon for her.

Need an ice chest. Molly planned as she walked. She glanced across the compound toward the transport pads near the residential building. Deuce's vessel sat on his designated pad. She frowned and stepped heavier as she continued the security sweep.

CHAPTER TWENTY-FIVE

Dr. Stork glanced up from his microscope. That pesky new pilgrim, assigned to security, approached the Lab's glass barrier. Even at a thirty foot distance he saw the determined stride indicating her current mission included interfering with his time, again. He had granulosa cell data to document today, and the last thing he needed was a novice security rat poking her nose in where it did not belong.

He detested newly disembarked pilgrims, because of their *I'm-here-to-save-your-world* mentality. Why doesn't Abraham simply cut off any additional pilgrimages? There were plenty of specimens available with the present number of recruits. His Cloning Reproduction Process had been more successful than he anticipated. It wasn't as if they needed new blood, so to speak, to resupply their patho-stock. Besides, Stork had volumes of excellent material for many medical papers once he had time to write them.

Honestly, after that one nearly escaped with an omicron child—there was no telling, really, what repercussions had resulted from that female going back to Earth, sans the child. Surely, her return merited one of two things, either they deemed her insane, in which case they would ignore her claims of fertility malpractice, or an investigation would be triggered, in which case Stork's ground-breaking discoveries would be recognized as tenure-material successes. Even though everything he had developed here was categorized as experimental, his effective rate had been dissertation worthy.

What he had done here could be considered desperate measures beyond established Earth practices, merited by these wolf-people's genealogy which was worlds apart from any precedence back home. Proper protocol would have required a twenty- or even forty-year study, but that had been impossible in this case. These people had become epidemiologically infertile. He suspected some source of radiation on initial assessment, which turned out to be accurate. But, there had been no time to study the source or their pathological history before developing a fertility plan for their reproductive regeneration. He had to dive in and develop DNA splicing and other creative procedures using the Earth recruits donations immediately or there wasn't going to be any people to help. They'd all be dead from old age without any new generations to continue their species.

Thank God, he had intervened and altered that escapees' files. Rabble-rousers like her didn't need to stay on planet anyway. Realistically, odds were, she'd probably be transferred to a psych-unit as soon as the healers on Earth reviewed her transformed medical history. No one would seriously consider her rambled story—what was her name? He looked up at the security officer who now stood glaring at him.

Jacobsen! His head leaned back slightly, anger widened his eyes. I've got to talk to Abraham. Does he realize who she is? He set down the tray of vials and stomped out the lab door.

Wham! Molly Jacobsen ran right into the door he was exiting. Would she ever get out of his business? He sucked in air. "Oh Molly, I'm sorry. I wasn't looking where you were going."

"That's all right, Dr. Stork..." She looked at him curiously. "I suppose I wasn't watching where *you* were going either." She had the audacity to laugh at him.

He cursed under his breath. His eyes stung red hot with rage. He shot past her, stormed into his office, locked the door, and steadied his breathing. Pugh had been reassigned to get him out of Stork's way, did he need to do the same with this new recruit, before everything went south.

He sat behind his hand-carved desk, with an exasperated sigh, and pushed his iComm link. "Call, Abraham." He waited while connecting sounds reverberated. Finally Abraham's recording answered. Stork's jaw ached as his back teeth pressed together tighter and tighter while he listened to Abraham's long winded, self-righteous message play out. When the tone sounded, he barked, "Abraham, this security officer of yours is going to blow everything. Do you have any idea who she is? Get her off my back."

He leaned into his high-back chair and laced his fingers over his belly. Staring at his desktop, he visualized locking Molly in an air-tight chamber and walking away. He could envision her screaming and slipping into unconsciousness. He snickered and slapped his hands on the desk as he pushed himself up and returned to his lab. He had far more important work to accomplish today.

***

Abraham disconnected his iComm link to Deuce. What was he up to? Seriously, who did he think he was fooling?

On the other hand, Abraham reconsidered as he stood up and paced behind his chair, his wife had passed nearly four years ago. What were the odds his son knew about the one little mis-deal that had slipped back to Earth? This had to be a legitimate desire on Deuce's part to connect with him. Why else would Deuce have joined this particular missionary project? There were plenty of others available to him on and near Earth.

Well, time would tell. Abraham sat back down in his luxurious leather chair. Besides, he had leeway with the laws available to him here that he could never have on Earth. As long as Argenteus reigned, his extracurricular activities were at a limitless proportion. Like a double or even triple bookie, Abraham couldn't lose no matter what outcome resulted, he always had the winning ticket. Perhaps he could, eventually, share these lucrative ventures with his only son.

Lupus' only concern had been the local's fertility problems, but that was being handled nicely with Stork's unprincipled tactics in the lab. Lupus' people were reproducing at an astounding rate. Argenteus was as happy as a high-roller who couldn't lose with The Abraham Project's results, especially since he and Lily received that surrogate's kid.

Even the best gamblers drop a card now and then. That one-who-slipped-through wouldn't derail all he had built here. The six-hundred-lightyear's distance was his strongest benefit. No legal enforcer from Earth would make the financial investment necessary to investigate far-fetched claims based on one crazy, whacked out female. Besides, he still had a few of those LEPs in his back pocket. They wouldn't double cross him, even now.

Until he could get a better feel for Deuce's interests, though, he'd use caution when, and if, he exposed his son to his extra dealings. The last thing he needed was a self-righteous son interfering. He had his mother's blood after all. Abraham smiled and touched his iComm link. "Marcos, I'm going to need a fresh breakfast cart in here. Thank you."

Abraham watched Marcos struggle with a new cart and pull the previous one out of the room. "Thank you, Marcos. That will be all. Oh! And when my son arrives, show him in."

Marcos nodded and exited, pushing the cart in front of him.

***

Abraham greeted his son, as he entered his office. His heart swelled with pride when he corrected calling him by his Christian name. He had retained the nickname, Deuce. If only he knew how much that meant to a father who had left little else behind.

Deuce truly surprised him with, "I want to work with you, Dad." How long had it been since he'd heard himself called "Dad." He watched as his son chewed a second sweet roll. Something flashed across Deuce's face, but Abraham wasn't sure if it exposed insecurity or just unfamiliarity.

A red light flashed, distracting his thoughts. Who had called? Mentally he checked the call data. *Ah, Stork. Better check that soon.*

So far, Deuce presented a reasonable yet benign interest. This might work out better than Abraham could have imagined.

"What's the first order of business today?" Deuce inquired.

Abraham hesitated. *Okay, we'll see how far he's really willing to go.* "I've got a meeting with the church leaders and then an accounting department update. We'll break for lunch and get some paper work done, then we have a Department Heads meeting at three o'clock. It's not glamorous, but necessary."

Abraham saw Deuce's grimace behind his sweet roll even though he voiced his agreement.

What Abraham wouldn't give to be able to read Deuce's thoughts. The boy had a good poker face and that could be an asset later on, eventually he would tip his hand. Abraham would watch for his son's tell. Every poker player had one, and it was just a matter of figuring out what Deuce's was. All would be revealed in due time.

"Well, let's get to it then!" Abraham stood and led Deuce to the conference room.

"Go ahead and have a seat. I'll just be a minute." He directed his son to a chair.

"Where are you going?"

"Son, even project managers have to go to the little boy's room from time to time." Abraham smiled and closed the conference room door.

He touched his iComm link and played the message. *Oh great, Stork's got his shorts in a knot again.* Abraham had an easy solution. He touched his iComm link again as he entered his office. "Call, Security Office."

"Roger Dunn," the supervisor answered.

"Dunn, Abraham, here. We've gotta problem…"

***

Abraham disconnected the communication with Dunn. He leaned back in his chair, drumming his fingers on the desk and staring blankly at the wall. This could escalate into a real fiasco. He needed to snip this bud before it had a chance… before Deuce got too deeply intertwined.

He activated his iComm and placed another call.

***

Molly entered the Security office and sat down at her station. She transferred the written data from her clipboard into the security daily log.

"Jacobsen!" Roger hollered from his walled-off station.

Molly jerked, closing her eyes. "Yessir?" She hurried to his office.

"You wanna close that door?"

"Sure. What's up?" Molly tried to sound casual. She had heard those words, that tone, too many times on Earth to not know what was coming.

"I asked you nicely. I even said please." His face grew redder as he spoke. "I thought we had an understanding—"

"What?" Molly's heart dropped to her knees. Why was she always in trouble? Then again, she wasn't here to make friends. Roger could be as likely involved in the heresy as anybody. She stood straighter.

"Molly you managed to peeve Dr. Stork off *again*. That's two days in a row. He wants you reassigned! That's what!"

"Reassigned? I volunteered for this assignment! How can he ask for me to be reassigned?"

"He can, and he has." Roger's face was moving on to purple now.

"I don't understand! I didn't say anything to him. I—I ran into a door he opened, and I think he opened it on purpose to hit me, now that I think about it. Then he said something rude to me, and I made a joke of it…and—"

"And you annoyed one of the most important people in The Abraham Project who now wants you reassigned. Unfortunately, that's how things work around here."

"Is it a temporary reassignment?" Molly tried to keep the octave of her voice level.

"That will be up to you," Roger said in a defeated tone.

"Where am I going?"

"Where everyone goes—to the aquifer. You'll help over there for a few days, and I'll see what I can do to get you back here." He touched his hair, and his face was returning to a normal color. Surely he realized how ridiculous this was. "That will have to do for now. Molly, really, it's the best I can do."

Molly clinched her teeth but nodded. "Do I report now or in the morning?"

"In the morning. No one works on the aquifer after lunch. It's deadly hot under the afternoon suns." Roger flopped down in his chair as if all his energy had been spent.

"In the morning? Well—okay."

"I'll need you to turn in your security credentials and go check in with Gordon or someone in IT to get your clearance changed for now. I've already called and set it up. Go ahead and do that now, and Molly—"

She looked him in the eyes.

"Stay out of trouble! I'd hate to think where you'd end up if you get into trouble out there."

She nodded and left his office.

***

Gordon met Molly at the door of the technology department. "I heard."

He hustled her into a solitary office.

Stealing herself, she resisted the desire to collapse into his arms. She had to be strong. She had not failed. This was a good move. There was purpose in everything she did. At least, she could make a purpose in everything. It was all a matter of attitude. Still…she bit down on her lip to help fight back the tears.

"Listen, don't feel bad. I can see where this will be better."

"Better?" she almost yelled. But hadn't she been having the same thoughts? "Yeah, better."

"Because I don't really have to change your clearance, and the aquifer is where they send all the 'bad' girls and boys. You may likely get more information from those workers than you'll ever get from the infirmary or lab. They're as tight lipped as the Mona Lisa." Gordon smiled.

"You really mean that, don't you?"

He nodded.

Molly let his words settle in her mind. He's right. Reassignment to the aquifer was good, she might be able to convince Carol and the other ladies to share what they know. And she *knew* they knew something.

"Hmm. I think I feel better already." She forced a smile.

Gordon touched her shoulder. "Now, tell me, do you have a report to send home?"

"Actually, I don't. But it looks like I've got some time on my hands this afternoon. I'll go whip something together and send it to you before dinner."

"Good."

"I know the reassignment is good, and all that, but why do I feel like I'm being grounded, or punished, or something really humiliating?"

"Molly, trust me, this is going to work out, because you'll get answers from the people who know what the answers are. See what I mean? I have a good feeling!" Gordon turned her around. "Go. Write your report. Remember why you're here. Shove that demon, Pride, out the window and do what you came here to do. Okay, Jacobsen?"

"Okay." Molly smiled. He was right, dog-gone-it.

"Good." Gordon gently pushed her out of the office.

CHAPTER TWENTY-SIX

The next morning, Molly rose early before the so-called suns-up. Although there were two suns, only one had risen by four. The food preparer machine produced twelve watermelon salads upon demand. She placed them in twelve plastic containers, found a picnic-sized climate controlled food chest, and set it for thirty-seven degrees fahrenheit. She pulled the food chest behind her as she approached the aquifer and the workers. This peace offering had to work.

Carol stepped forward. "What ya got there, newbie?" She eyed the blue and white chest behind Molly.

"I told you I would bring you something. It's watermelon."

Carol's eyebrow shot up. "Really?"

The other women slowly walked up behind Carol to look in the chest.

"Yes. That, and I've been reassigned"—Molly shrugged—"to the aquifer."

"Reeeally?" Carol elongated the word as her mouth split wide with a smile. "You been here, what, three days and you already got reassigned? You must have been a baaad wittle girl!" She snorted a chuckle.

Molly chuckled, too. "It seems I have."

The other ladies didn't laugh, rather, they looked frightened. The men in the ditch snickered and shook their heads. But jovial sensations were not what Molly sensed from their amusement.

Molly pulled on leather gloves and walked over to the pile of stones. "This how it's done?"

She picked up a stone and stacked it alongside the ditch.

Carol opened the food chest and took out a piece of watermelon. The other's stepped around her and reached for their piece. Adelia picked up one of the plastic containers and held it out for the men to share.

"Hey!" Carol hollered toward Molly, "Thanks."

"Sure." Molly turned to get another stone.

They worked without talking for several hours. The second sun had risen and the first burned higher in the sky as if it were nearing eleven o'clock. Molly kept up with the seasoned workers. Good thing she was in prime shape, strong and limber. Luz watched Molly as they passed each other in the bucket-brigade format of stacking the aquifer stones. Molly cocked a brow and tipped her head back as a gesture of understanding. This work was arduous.

"So…" Luz finally spoke. "You knew Kita?"

Carol stopped in her tracks and glared at Luz.

"What?" Luz shrugged. "She's one of us now."

"Yes, I know Kita," Molly said in an attempt to defuse the tension between Carol and Luz. "She came home in bad shape, actually."

"What happened?" Luz asked. The other women stopped working.

"Well, when she got back on Earth, she was confused and claimed she had given birth to a live baby. But, you know, all her medical records indicated her baby hadn't made it." Molly shrugged. "She was clinging to a doll, as if it were the baby. They said she'd attached herself to it here as a way to deal with her grief. We were pretty shocked. It just wasn't like her to go so far off…the deep end.

"But, what I don't understand is, the healers said her medical records showed she was diagnosed as sterile by the clinic here. How could that be?"

The women exchanged a glance.

"Is that what *she* said happened?" Carol stepped closer to Molly.

"No. She said she had been given permission to keep her baby and return home. I don't think she knew about her own fertility issue. Why?" Molly stood still, along with the other women.

"Several of us agreed to be surrogates. It's, like, part of the program. I kind of thought everybody's fertility capabilities were checked before they were accepted into this program."

"Yeah, me too—"

But…" Carol stared off in the distance. "This whole thing is harder than you'd think. When you donate your eggs, it's just a needle in the gut, you know. But when you actually carry their child, your emotions get all tangled up in the…"

Molly fought empathetic tears. "So, you're saying, some of *you*—were surrogates."

They all nodded. "Nearly all of us were. I'm telling you, it's part of the program."

Molly's eyebrows shot up. "What do you mean?"

"Look, I don't know what happened to your friend. We gave up the babies at birth." Carol looked deep into Molly's eyes. A flicker of something glinted there. "That's how it works and nobody's given a choice…you don't back out."

"Really?" Molly considered Carol's answer. "So, as long as you followed through, gave up your babies, everything was fine. But Kita…somehow changed her mind…what happens if you change your mind?"

Tears glistened every woman's eyes. Luz turned away and reached for another stone.

"Nobody changes her mind." Carol said through clinched teeth.

"I'm sorry. I don't mean to be so harsh. I'm just trying to understand." Molly reached out to touch

Luz's shoulder. She jerked away. Molly softened her tone. "What happened to the others—who changed their minds?"

The women exchanged a look that excluded Molly. "It just doesn't happen," Luz muttered and bent to pick up a stone.

A gut feeling told Molly she'd interrogated as much as she was going to for now. "I'm so sorry," she said at last.

Her heart ached for her sister's loss. But her sister's baby didn't die. He was alive and being raised by the very leader of the Omicronians. What happened to the other women? Surely someone bucked the system besides Kita. Gordon had said this aquifer was where they punished people. But these ladies said they followed through. Not willingly, but they did. What was the big cover up? Why did they let Kita keep her baby for two weeks and let her think she was taking him home? And where was Pastor Oliver.

Molly closed her eyes. "May I ask you another question?" Molly picked up a stone and carried it over to the men.

"I suppose," Carol responded.

"If the surrogacy program is so difficult, why —"

"Why would we volunteer to do it?" Carol finished Molly's sentence.

"Yes." Molly waited for the answer.

"We felt it was our destiny"—Carol moved another stone—"to come here and help these women. Pastor Oliver preached many sermons expounding how blessed we would be in return for helping these people in such great need. He encouraged us. And to be honest, these are a kind and loving race of people. Who knew it would be so…hard? We all prayed over the pregnancies and believed with all our hearts that they would fulfill God's plan, but—"

"I understand." Molly touched Carol's shoulder.

One of the men in the ditch cleared his throat. The women turned to look at him. He looked left and right, leaning toward them. "Look, ladies, if you've got your *bonding* done, we need to get some work finished. You know we have a quota and if we don't reach it—"

Carol turned to Molly, an almost feral fear glistened in her eyes. "He's right, let's get moving."

"Of course." Molly hefted another stone. The two suns' heat beat down on them, but while she worked, she replayed their conversation. A pattern was definitely forming, but it wasn't a good one, and it wasn't a Christian one, either. What on Earth —or Omicron—was really going on?

Noon-break sounded, and the aquifer workers grabbed a large container of water. Molly swigged the contents and wiped her mouth with the back of her hand. They had met their quota for the day in spite of the delay Molly had caused. She hurt all over and wanted a cool shower. As she limped to the residential building, she glanced at the transportation pad. Deuce's vessel was gone. She turned and headed to Gordon's office instead. She needed to update him and see what he had found.

Gordon's eyes met Molly's as she entered his area. He tilted his head to the break room. Molly walked past his department and slipped into the designated room. She opened the food preserver and pulled out a water container. She had half of it down when Gordon walked in.

"What's up?"

She gulped and wiped her mouth. "I worked at the aquifer today."

Gordon sniffed and wrinkled his nose. "I can tell."

"Well, sorry, I wanted to give you an update."

He lowered his voice to a whisper. "Really, got some good stuff did ya?

Molly told Gordon what she had learned from the ladies. Gordon accessed his virtual keyboard and cross checked the names of the personnel assigned to the aquifer with the infirmary birth records. He pulled all matches and confirmed they each were documented with live births.

"Are there any records indicating what happened to the women who changed their minds and..." Molly swallowed against a dry mouth. "Am I right? Do all the still-births line up with the women who decided to keep their babies?"

"Hmm." Gordon shook his head. "That's a good question."

He ran his fingers through his dark-brown, coarse curls and closed the virtual keyboard. "But, here's what's interesting. When I cross check recorded information on the"—He paused and glanced down.—"*non-viable* births to the records of babies received by the Omicronian's, they don't all match up. You saw those films I gave you. If the babies were stolen, as we suspect, they should match up, but they don't." Gordon looked up at Molly.

"Yeah, I couldn't connect those dots either. So either," Molly continued the thought, "the babies *really were*…not born alive, or—"

They both looked at each other. Molly thought this through. "Or, they were born alive and… placed somewhere else?"

Molly gasped. "What about the cryogenic inventory I got from AF? Did you ever find it in the records?"

Gordon shook his head. "No, I didn't. What if the babies were born alive, and they were suspended and—"

"And sent off planet! Like, pirated to somewhere else! Man, Gordon. I think we may be onto something! But, I *really* hope we're wrong! And...what about the mothers?" Molly barely breathed the words. They were too disturbing to utter.

They stared at each other. A red light flashed in Molly's peripheral. A tall, thin man walked into the break room. "Boss, you've got an urgent message."

Gordon turned. "I'll be right there." He spun back to Molly.

She gestured a wave, telling him to go. "You go ahead, apparently, I've got a message, too." Molly touched her iComm link as she slipped out of the technology building. "Answer, Message."

Hot potato, cold potato, caution is most dire, even when one thinks she knows what she is doing, ice burns like fire—AF.

"What the—" Molly glanced back at Gordon's building. This message was just plain confusing. What does "ice burns like fire" mean? Molly sighed. She needed time to think. She hurried to the residential building. A cool shower was calling her name.

Under the flow of the water, she ran everything through her head. What does this all add up to?

Pure deception. This artificial *CON*ception looks more like artificial *DE*ception to me. How could she prove the babies were born alive? Other than Kita's word? Frustrated, Molly grabbed the shampoo and lathered her hair.

We know the video-stream was altered. Surely Gordon can decipher the alteration and revive the original data. She rinsed her hair and filled her palm with conditioner. Running the thick liquid through her hair, she turned to face the shower stream.

That would tell us the babies were born alive, but it's not going to tell us where they were taken or to whom they were given. Or what happened to the surrogate mother. She lathered up a netting ball with body wash.

If they are pirating cryogenically suspended babies, then they have to be using a transportation vessel to move them somewhere. That would explain the inventory receipt AF sent me. But who was transporting the cryo-containers? Okay, that's what I've gotta find. The transportation vessels and where they are going. Molly rinsed her head and body, wrapped her hair and torso with towels, and stepped out of the shower.

A sharp pain cracked the back of her head. Stars burst before her eyes. Her knees buckled and slammed into the hard tile. The cool shower room floor slapped her in the face. Out-of-focus, blue pant legs encircled her. The room went black.

CHAPTER TWENTY-SEVEN

Evening didn't exactly fade into dusk on Omicron. One lingering solar sphere faded as the three moons took possession of the sky. This strange purple-grey illumination still fascinated Gordon as he glanced up from his virtual screen. Molly needed to know what he had found. The women whose records indicated a non-viable birth had recorded streams with corrupted overlays and the women were soon reassigned but the assignment had not been the aquifer. In fact, he couldn't find where they had been moved. Record of their existence just disappeared. No food consumption record, no work record, nothing.

He touched his iComm link and then switched to his virtual keyboard. A direct message would be better than speaking. No one could hear, and he could bury the message so that it wasn't traceable. His fingers flew across the keyboard.

"Non-viables' stream deceptive. Reassignment not traceable. Fear the worst. Contact me. –G"

Satisfied with his message, he passed it through an encryptions app and sent it to Molly. His eyes lifted to gaze at the shimmering dull light they called dusk. A low rumble in his stomach reminded him of a need for nourishment. He smiled and turned off his system. As he walked toward the cafeteria, he glanced at the missionary women's wing. Had Molly received his message? Nothing blinked in his peripheral. Why hadn't she responded? Activating his iComm link, he checked out-going messages. Molly had not opened the message. He stopped walking and glanced, again, at the women's wing of the building.

Standing at her door in the long, empty hall, he tapped three times. Where was she? He looked up and down the hall. A petite blond strolled toward him. "Excuse me, do you know Molly Jacobsen."

"Of course." The blond's shiny white teeth glistened as her lips parted in a beauty-queen smile.

"Is she here?"

The blond looked over her shoulder, as if she were verifying Molly's absence.

Gordon smiled. *Why do people do that?*

The woman responded, "I'm not sure. I saw her come in, but I haven't seen her since."

"I'm sorry, you're name…?"

"Oh." She giggled. "I'm Julie."

"Ah, would you do me a favor?"

She nodded.

"Would you check the women's shower room?"

"Sure." She scurried to the showers but returned immediately. "All's empty. Sorry." She shrugged. "The floor's real wet, though. Maybe she took a shower and went out."

"Hmm." Gordon glanced up the hall again. After a day's work at the aquifer, nobody, not even Super Molly'd go out. "Thanks, anyway."

He hurried outside and touched his iComm link. "Call, Dr. Abraham."

The iComm system clicked twice. "Abraham, here."

"Yeah, Dr. Abraham? This is Gordon from IT. Um, I need to give Miss Jacobsen something, and I'm having trouble locating her. You wouldn't happen to know where she is, would you?"

"No, I'm offsite." Deuce sounded concerned, too. "I'll be back within the hour, I'll see if I can locate her. Is there a message I can give her?"

No. I've sent...I mean, just let her know I need to finalize some things with her...for her reassignment—"

"Reassignment?" Abraham spoke louder.

"Yeah. Look, I was just checking to see if you knew where she was. I didn't mean..." Gordon stopped talking. He'd probably said too much. But where could Molly be? A knot cinched in his gut. Hunger no longer plagued him.

"No, really, I'm done here. Let me find you when I get back. I think I know what you've been working on."

"Sure, I'll be in the cafeteria." Where else could he wait and be inconspicuous?

"Good, I'll find you there." Abraham disconnected.

Gordon veered off for the chow line.

***

Mystery-meatloaf and mashed something similar to potatoes cooled, untouched on Gordon's tray. He'd cut the meat into bite size cubes but had no inclination to put any of it in his mouth. Had he tripped up by contacting Dr. Abraham? If the healer knew anything about Molly's whereabouts, it was worth the risk. But if he didn't, then Gordon needed to glide away without revealing anything about her undercover mission. He was a genius with programs, people—not so much. It was easier while he had been the single infil. Now he had to share that duty with Molly. Inadvertently, he lifted a chunk of meat to his mouth. Could he pull this off?

Dr. Abraham crossed the entrance. The disgusting aroma of meat under Gordon's nose reminded him how bad he hated their recipe for meatloaf and halted his movement. He'd soon find out how crafty he could be. Abraham tipped his head back, so Gordon held up his fork full of meat in salutation before shoving it into his mouth. His heart pounded, and his mouth suddenly went dry. He swigged a drink of water and watched the man set a tray with a reuben sandwich and potato chips across from his.

"Gordon." Dr. Abraham held his gaze.

"Yes. Thanks for coming." Gordon winced as he swallowed. "Sorry, if I pulled you away from your work."

"You said something about Molly being reassigned?"

"Yeah, but I haven't been able to find her since noon. Any idea where she might have gone?" Gordon felt a headache forming in his temple. He prayed for the right words.

"You checked the housing quarters, I assume?"

Gordon nodded.

"Where did she get reassigned?"

"Aquifer, I believe." Gordon tried to sound like he didn't know much about the matter.

"Aquifer! Why?" Dr. Abraham ignored his food.

"Um, I'm not sure. I just do the IT end of assignments." Gordon scooped a cube of meat and shoved it in his mouth. It felt like a wad of paper, but he chewed until he could swallow.

"Yeah." Dr. Abraham glared at him. "Which is why you're searching so diligently for her? Look, I know what people think about me. I know, okay! You wouldn't have called me if you weren't really worried. Now, come on. Tell me what you're thinking."

Gordon stared at his tray.

"Look." Abraham lowered his voice and glanced around the commissary. "I know what Molly's trying to do. So cut the crap. If she's missing, something's gone really wrong. And—and we've gotta find her."

Gordon darted his gaze up to meet the doctor's. He couldn't risk Molly's safety. However, there were no odd feelings in his gut, no anomalies. Something about Dr. Abraham felt right. His eyes stayed on the doctor. He had to make a decision. Wiping his hand down his face, he prayed, *Lord help me.*

Gordon's inner spirit recalled Psalms 22:8, "He trusts in the Lord." Why had that verse jumped into his head? He narrowed his eyes and tilted his head. Okay, here goes nothing. Gordon told Dr. Abraham about the deleted portions of birth-video streams, the mainframe deletions, and the reassignments with no further traces.

Abraham sat back and stared at his untouched sandwich. He rubbed his chin. "Okay. Here's what we came here with."

Abraham told Gordon about the concerns he had with Kita Jacobsen's medical file. And the glitch Dwayne Friedman found back on Earth.

The two sat in silence for a moment. "Doc, you wanna see what I've got?"

"Yes."

Deuce followed Gordon to the IT office. Gordon showed him the hidden encrypted file he had recovered from the mainframe partition. They watched the deleted portion of the stream and saw live babies wrapped in blankets and removed from the birthing room. The scene appeared to be as normal of a birth as one would expect with the exception, Deuce noted, the birth mothers were hyper-hysterical, begging to see their child, and the babies had been removed without so much as telling them the gender. This procedure burned in

Deuce's emotions. Something he stored away to be addressed at another time.

"There doesn't seem to be any record of where the babies are taken," Gordon admitted. "And the birth records all indicate non-viable births. Altered streams are in the files. The babies' death certificates are in there too. And! The mother's work records show they are reassigned but I cannot for the life of me figure out where. It's as if they dropped off the planet."

"Did you show this to Molly yet?"

"No. That's why I'm trying to find her." Gordon spun around in his chair.

"Hmm. So, where could she be?" Abraham frowned. "Do you have access to vessels tracking?"

"Of course."

"Let's look at what has come in and gone out in the last few hours."

"You've got it." Gordon's fingers flew across his virtual keyboard. "This may take a few minutes. You want me to contact you when I find something?"

"Yeah, I'll be at the infirmary all evening. Just shoot me a message. Maybe I can search the records over there. Those babies went somewhere…and so did the surrogates."

Deuce shot a message to Molly. "Where R U?"

No reply.

He sent a message to Gordon, asking for a cross reference to medical staff and the date and times of the alleged nonviable births that do not cross reference with any local adoptions.

Gordon replied, "Affirmative."

He contacted Deuce within the hour. "Dr. Timothy Stork signed as Attending Physician on every one of the surrogates' births, including every —" he cleared his throat "—unsuccessful birth."

Deuce stood at an empty admin counter, his eyes on a patient's films, trying to appear as if he were talking to himself. He tucked his chin close to his chest to control his volume. "That's not possible! I was afraid of this. It had to be a rubber stamp signature?"

"Beats me, Doc. But I think we are definitely on to something."

"How so?"

"I cross referenced healers on duty when the… I'm sorry, I just can't say, 'dead babies,' okay, let's call them 'nonviables.'"

"Okay…"

"When the nonviables were born, like you asked—

"And…" Deuce wearied with Gordon's delay.

"Yeah, varies. But, Dr. Rotcod and Dr. Lenard —eighty percent of the time, which makes sense, Rotcod's Pediatrics and Lenard's OB-GYN. And… Stork was always in his lab, at least according to the duty rosters, no matter the hour.

"Oh, and I may have something on vessel activity. What would you say Molly weighs-in at?"

"I—don't know, one-thirty, one-thirty-five? Why?"

"Well, I've got an anomaly with one vessel, it's one-thirty-eight-point-two over its ascribed weight."

Deuce looked up. "Really? Can you put a tracking app on it and, I don't know, maybe forward it to me?"

"Doc! Of course I can. Stand by."

Deuce smiled as he touched his iComm link and activated the tracing app networked to him. Gordon reminded him of Dwayne back on Earth. A green line-map illuminated before him. A blinking blue arrow indicated where the overweight vessel was going. Deuce dropped the film and strode as quickly as possible without running to his own private vessel. He thanked God for IT, and its many devises. Then he prayed he would find Molly, and she'd be safe.

CHAPTER TWENTY-EIGHT

Molly forced her eyes open. A sharp dagger of light penetrated her head. She squeezed her eyes together and dreaded opening them again. When she did, blurred double images slowly moved into one but fanned back out. Her shoulder muscles burned. A sharp pain radiated from her wrists and ankles. She moved to touch a tender spot at the base of her head, but her hands would not come up. They were tied behind her back. A shiver rippled down her body, leaving goose bumps in its wake. In fact, the floor where she laid felt frozen. It appeared to be cement. Was she in a freezer? She tried to focus again.

Where was she last? The shower! Her eyes darted down. A dark blue jump suit covered her body, no shoes. It looked like a workman's suit with a large zipper from her knee to her neck. A dull memory stirred, blue pant legs. Her hair felt so cold and stiff. Would she freeze to death? Her ankles were bound, like her wrists, with zip ties and none too loosely. A nerve caught every movement between her boney ankles. Another shiver rippled through her. But, the cold air was not the only cause.

A red light flashed rhythmically in her right peripheral, indicating several messages. Mentally, she accessed the caller information. Gordon, twice. Deuce, three times.

Her heart sped up, and her breathing was more like a pant.

"Call, Gordon," she mumbled. Static pierced her ears. She cringed from the agony. Somehow her iComm link transmission was blocked. Panic scrambled to engulf her senses.

Metal scraped against concrete. She wasn't alone. She curled her head back to look into the direction of the noise. Three men, dressed in dark blue jumpsuits, sat on metal chairs in the center of the large expanse. Where was she? It looked like a warehouse or garage. Metal canisters stood neatly on pallets to her right. White vapor floated away from the metal skin.

A clacking sound caught her attention. The men threw something on the floor between them. Cheers and groans followed. They were playing some sort of game. She reached out her senses.

Gambling! She pushed out further toward them but yanked back. What she sensed made her feel— dirty, defiled. They were gambling for the right to have her. Biblically *have* her. Terror stabbed her gut. She closed her eyes and forced the sensation down. *Keep fluid, find a way out.* They were distracted by their game of chance, for now. If she could move to where they couldn't see her...

She slowly scooted toward the pallets to her right. The cold penetrated her suit and the pain in her head radiated to her eyeballs. The closer she got to the pallets, the more the cold hurt. It burned. Perhaps there was a sharp edge where she could cut the bindings. She gritted her teeth. This was so painful. Ever so slowly, she inched toward the pallets, suppressing nausea.

"What are you mongrels doing?" A man with a booming voice entered the warehouse. Now she wished she hadn't moved. She could no longer see the men or the man with the booming voice. It sounded familiar, but without the strong southern accent. Her head hurt too bad to figure it out.

"We've got a shipment going out tonight, and you're sitting here playing games. Pugh, I expected more outta you." *Smack.* One of them had been slapped. "Maybe you need more time under the suns."

Chairs scraped on the concrete floor. "Now get those cryo-pads loaded into the reefer-vessels. Be ready to go after dark. The colonies are expecting delivery before suns rise. They know what to do with the *special delivery*, so DO NOT tack this up!"

Footsteps indicated they scrambled to do his bidding. Soon, leather soled shoes walked away, and a door opened and closed. The workers' pace slowed.

"What do we do about...her?" one of them asked. Molly heard footsteps approaching.

"You heard what Abraham said, she's included in the shipment. The poison'll take care of the rest. Leave her alone for now."

Poison! Abraham! Molly pressed herself against the pallets. The cold burned. She stiffened and inch-wormed away.

"Get this vessel loaded, boys!" another man called out. The footsteps faded away from her.

Poison! Her stomach cramped, and she doubled over with it. "Please!" she forced the word. Her throat felt so raw, like it was sore from screaming at a ball game. "Please help me!"

"Oh, we'll help ya all right." Another man called out. "Just as soon as we get this vessel loaded. Then we'll help you *real* good." A thud sounded. Had the one Abraham said he expected more from hit the other one?

A sudden shock flashed through Molly's nerves. He had called him Pugh. Pastor Oliver Pugh? She pushed back against the corner between the pallets and the wall. Her eyes swept the area to her left. The canisters were steaming. No, not steaming.

Ice burns like fire. The message from AF came to her. Did AF have something to do with her kidnapping? She pushed herself up against the wall and moved so that her feet were in front of her. Pushing with trembling legs, she slid up the wall until she was standing, unsteady, but standing. Zinging pain shot through her bound ankles. A short distance to the stacked canister, she maneuvered over to them and pushed her wrist against the metal frame. She jerked away and sucked air. The cold burned.

Focus! She closed her eyes, pressed her teeth together, and pushed her wrist against the metal again. *Augh.* It took everything she had to suppress a scream. If she could hold the plastic tie against the sub-zero cylinder...

The cold encircled her wrists. Plastic cut into her skin as she tried to pull them apart. It held a moment, then, *snap,* the tie broke.

Molly released her breath and panted. *Thank God.* She brought her hands around to her front and pressed her warm tongue to the freezer-burned skin. A traitorous tear slid down her cheek. She looked down at her ankles and over at the canisters. It had to be done.

Her legs were so weak, it was easy to slide back down the wall and roll on to her back. The hard part was lifting her legs to the canisters and pressing her bound ankles against the frigid metal. It took all her strength to pack down a whimper. Soon, it too snapped and broke apart. She breathed a heavy sigh and panted. Her stomach knotted, and she rolled into the pain.

Some poisons you purge, some you dilute. *Dear God, what do I do?*

"Poison," she scanned her First-aid knowledge for an answer. Marti's Bible Cheat Sheet illuminated in her visual range. A long list of verses which included the word, "poison," scrolled up quicker than she could read. Anger roiled in her gut. Through clinched teeth she uttered, "Jesus, just help me!"

The Cheat Sheet blinked and one verse illuminated, "You will vomit up the little you have eaten… - Proverbs 23:8" Could this be her answer? What choice did she really have? With two fingers, she forced herself to retch and then held her breath so she wouldn't inhale any potential vapors until she could move away from the heaved fluids. Again, she pushed her fingers deep against the back of her tongue and continued to move and empty her stomach. The cramps still came, but hopefully she had enough of it out that she wouldn't die.

Please God, I don't want to die.

A wave of guilt washed over her. She'd rejected God for so many years. Now she called out to Him. But this truly was a life or death situation. She was deep in the valley of the shadow...she had lots of wants!

She pushed herself up to stand and peered around the canister stacks. The men were inside the reefer-vessel. Which one was Pugh? She glanced around the warehouse and saw two doors to her left. Her head hurt, her eyes burned, her stomach clamped down with pain and the room spun, but she staggered toward the first door. A final glance to see where the men might be, still in the vessel. She shoved the door open.

Dusk dimmed her view of the surrounding arid land. Her eyes needed to adjust. Instead, she pushed herself out the door and along the side of the warehouse. Her hand trailed along the outer stucco wall to steady her escape. She stumbled and landed hard on her knees. Pain shot up her thighs and into her hip. She forced herself back up and staggered around the corner. Abruptly, she slammed into a man and fell backward.

"No!" she screamed and crab-crawled on her back away from him. She flipped over and propelled herself forward. The gyration made nausea swirl along with her head.

The man grabbed her. His voice was familiar, but she couldn't make out his words.

She gagged with the insistent nausea but fought his hold.

"Molly! It's me!" Deuce clung to her wriggling form.

Wild instincts fought the grip on her arms. "Let go, let go!" she muttered past a restricted throat.

"Molly! It's me, Deuce!" He continued to hold her.

She squinted into his face. Her vision was double, but it was Deuce she saw. She stopped fighting and collapsed into his embrace. "Deuce!"

He held her as she cried. "Come on. We've gotta get you out of here."

"I think it was your dad! And…"

"What?"

Molly tried to look him in the eyes. Which set? "How'd you find me?"

"I'll explain later. Let's go!" Deuce pushed her as he ran toward his individual transportation vessel.

"Deuce!" Molly's knees collapsed. He lifted her in his arms. "I'm...poisoned!" The words escaped barely more than a sigh.

He shoved her into the passenger seat. "We'll go straight to the infirmary." Her door closed and the safety harness fastened around her.

Her head lolled against the high back seat. "I threw up." She scraped her teeth across her lower lip.

"You're gonna be all right." Deuce sounded yards away.

Blackness waxed and waned her consciousness. Vague awareness drifted in and out of her senses. Deuce spoke to her, "Stay with me Molly."

Someone lifted and lowered her onto a stiff bed. A cool cloth covered her as dizzying lights flashed overhead. She tried to force her eyes open, but they would not cooperate. She could hear

Deuce's voice, way off in a tunnel, barking orders. She was in the infirmary. Deuce would save her. She relented to drift toward the peaceful darkness that beckoned her so tenderly.

CHAPTER TWENTY-NINE

"She's poisoned! Lord only knows what type of poison." Deuce yelled at the receiving staff. "I need a tox screen, CBC, and culture, stat!"

He shouted his orders across Molly's limp body as he ran alongside her gurney. "I want one thousand milliliters saline, a hundred percent, wide open, flush her system. Get me twenty-five milliliters Propranolol."

"You want to slow down her heart rate, too, Doctor?" The charge nurse scurried after the gurney.

"Yes, exactly, the less her heart pumps the better chance we have to keep the poison from killing her," he answered. "Get a heart monitor on her, too, we've gotta make sure we haven't suppressed it too much."

He spoke directly to the nurse who had questioned him. She ran to the med closet. "Let's get a cath in. I want her bladder completely drained and flush her bowels. Get a cooling pad under her, too. The cooler the better. Slow her system down."

Deuce lifted his head. "She's been poisoned, people, move it!"

The gurney was brought alongside the infirmary bed.

"One...two...three." Deuce and two nurses lifted a corner of the sheet under Molly's limp body and transferred her to the bed. The blue jump suit was cut away, IV shunts were put in place, and heart monitor wires were attached to her chest and abdomen. A machine beeped to life and continued with each contraction of her heart. An oxygen monitor was clipped to her index finger. One nurse inserted the foley while another prepared the enema solution. Once the IV bags were in place, Deuce injected the Propranolol in the by-pass tube.

Deep down, he was thankful she was unconscious. The procedure to cleanse her body of the poison would not be pleasant if she were awake. He stood back and let the nurses perform the tasks he had ordered. He'd have to wake her soon, but for now, the more she rested, the less her heart would pump the poison through her system. She'd said she had thrown up. Let's hope that gave her a head start. With God's mercy, the tox screen would tell him what poison he was dealing with, and he could antidote it immediately. If he had to, he'd do a dialysis and just clean out her blood.

He looked at the nurse drawing Molly's blood. "I want a cross match for blood type, too." Deuce stepped out of the room and forced himself to breathe. He ran his fingers through his hair and closed his eyes. In his lifetime, he'd passed through many phases of emotions toward his dad. Today, he hated him more than imaginable. This time, he didn't hurt Deuce, but the woman he—

Deuce's eyes shot open.

—loved. He had not considered what he felt for Molly before. But it was true. He loved her. He turned around and looked through the open door. A sheet covered Molly's limp body. The nurses were completing the tasks, and settling down to monitor the patient.

"I want the results of that tox screen!" he demanded. "Now!"

A portly nurse nodded and hurried from the room. Deuce tried to remember her name. *Betty, maybe. Betsy?* He rubbed the deep crevice between his brow.

"Oooh! Sweet Jesus! It hurts!" a woman screamed. Deuce jerked his head toward the sound. The emergency doors slid closed behind two women carrying a third across their arms like a basket seat. Fluid trailed behind the one being carried. She was pregnant. From the looks of things, she wouldn't be pregnant much longer.

Deuce ran toward them. "Get a hover chair over here!" he ordered. "Your water break?"

"Yes. Owww!" She doubled over in the chair. Her knuckles drained to white as she gripped the arm rests.

He rubbed the back of her shoulder, "Breathe, sit up, breathe through the pain."

She obeyed, and blew and sucked air until the contraction eased.

He guessed her contractions were two minutes apart. There hadn't been time to know for sure.

"Hurry, let's get her into an examination room," he told the nurse who had brought the chair.

Deuce glanced down the hall toward Molly's room. He fought to let go of the desperate need to be with her. "Notify me the *second* we get the lab report on Jacobsen!" he barked as he rushed into the pregnant woman's examination room.

"Yes, Doctor," a voice responded. "But, Doctor!" she called after him.

"What?" he turned from the examination room door.

"She's a surrogate." The nurse pointed toward the room.

"Okay, well, she's about to give birth. That procedure is the same no matter what, right?"

"Sure, but—" the nurse hesitated.

Deuce stared at her a moment. A scream resounded in the room, and Deuce rushed in. The nurse's words lingered in his thoughts.

***

"How's everything going?" Dr. Stork entered the examination room. His smile contrasted the glare of hostility in his eyes. He lifted the patient's film, stylus poised to write, but squinted his eyes and returned the stylus to his coat pocket. Anger flushed his face crimson.

Dr. Abraham splashed water on his arms. Antibacterial soap slid off his skin. He turned at the sound of the doctor's voice. "Everything's fine here, Doctor. Can I help you?" He reached for several disposable towels and dried his hands and arms.

"No, no," Dr. Stork glanced at the newborn baby in the woman's arms.

She smiled at the doctor, tears soaked her face.

He did not return her jubilation. Instead he stepped up close to Deuce and spoke quietly, "May I speak with you, Dr. Abraham?" He tilted his head toward the door. "Outside, if you please."

"Of course," Deuce answered serenely and turned to his patient. "We'll just be a moment. You rest." He threw away the moist towels.

The woman smiled, but concern filled her eyes.

Dr. Stork smiled that edgy smile. "What do you think you're doing?"

"What do you mean, Dr. Stork? I helped deliver a baby."

"Yes, and you let the surrogate hold that baby! That's *not* how we do things here. There are *procedures*."

"My studies taught me that letting a surrogate mother hold the baby before she gives it up to the adopting parents is both psychologically and physically beneficial. Besides, she was bleeding and letting her nurse the bab—"

"What!" Stork pressed his face into Deuce's. "You let her nurse the surrogate child!"

Deuce stepped back. "Yes, we needed her body to contract the uterus and clamp down those rogue blood vessels. She's fine now, thanks for asking."

Deuce's eyebrows squeezed together. "We stopped the bleeding without having to interfere medically. And if I may ask, what business is it of yours? You are not an OB, you don't deliver the babies. You're at the other end of this—operation." Deuce let the accusation hang between them.

Stork stared at him a moment. His smile widened. "While that is true, I like to check on the patients when the child is born. Confirm all our research is going well for the resulting viable neonate."

"...The resulting viable neonate? Is that what you call them? Look, Doctor, these are not test-tube samples. These are living, breathing children. And the surrogate mothers are just as alive and needing of emotional counseling to deal with the separation. This infirmary, these *procedures*, as you put them, has not taken *that* into consideration. But I assure you, they will now that I am here."

Stork glared into Deuce's eyes. His mouth opened and then closed. The muscle on the back of his jaw bulged. "We'll see about that, Doctor Abraham." His footsteps pounded down the empty hallway toward his lab.

Deuce did not bother to watch him leave. Instead, he returned to his patient.

"Dr. Abraham," a nurse called from the door. "Miss Jacobsen is awake, and we have the lab results."

"Thank you."

Dr. Denny Rotcod, the Omicronian Pediatric Practitioner, had arrived and was examining the baby. The mother was stable. Deuce excused himself and hurried down to Molly's room.

A weak smile lit up Molly's face when Deuce entered her room. "You did it," she breathed the words. He squeezed her hand and turned to the silver-haired resident at her side. Her name tag read Yelsie.

She handed Deuce the film with the lab results. "The poison was derived from a local plant. We call it "X" because the name is…well, difficult for your kind to pronounce," she said slowly, sadness filled her tone. "And here is the antidote."

She handed him a large syringe.

"We are not sure how the human pathology will react to this antidote, but in Omicronians it generally causes an irritating rash that fades after a few days. It is better than the alternative." She shrugged. "May I assume you will want to administer a large dose of antihistamine to handle the potential rash?"

Deuce glanced at Molly. "Well, let's give it to her and watch very closely to see if she has the same reaction. Have an epinephrine ready, too, just in case."

Yelsie turned to a tray and lifted another syringe. Deuce nodded and injected Molly with the antidote. Her eyes closed as if she were drifting back asleep.

Deuce and Yelsie watched Molly intently. Her monitor beeped rhythmically. Deuce lifted his eyes to the jagged tracers. Her oxygen level remained steady. Her sinus rhythm remained steady. Her heart rate read sixty three. He sighed with relief. The monitor lights blinked off then back on. Molly's heart rate changed to sixty one, fifty nine, fifty six, fifty three.

Molly gasped for air as her chest arched up like a taut bow. She fell back against the bed and vibrated with convulsions. White bubbles trickled from the corner of her mouth.

Deuce reached for the epinephrine. But Yelsie pulled it back from his reach. "Wait," she stated.

"Give me that!" Deuce demanded.

Yelsie held the syringe back, out of his reach.

"Are you trying to kill her?" Deuce yelled. "Doctor, give me that syringe."

"No, Doctor. Wait." The wide wolf-like teeth parted and snapped close as she pulled away from him. "Look!"

Deuce followed her gaze. Molly's seizures abated. His eyes darted to the monitor. Her heart rate flashed, sixty four, sixty eight, seventy, seventy, seventy.

Deuce let out his breath. He ran his hand down his face and drew more air into his lungs. He looked up at Yelsie. "How did you know?"

"I didn't. But, her reaction was the same as my people's. Our physiology isn't so different. Besides, it was a local poison. You needed a local to assist you." She shrugged again.

He leaned over Molly and examined her skin. Red welts began to rise on her neck. He pulled her gown down past her collar bone and confirmed the rash was spreading quickly. "Better administer that antihistamine—"

Yelsie already pushed the plunger on a syringe inserted in the IV bypass shunt. Deuce smiled. "Is there anything else I need to know about this poison?"

"Once the patient recovers from the rash, they are generally good. Periodic liver function tests should be scheduled. Untreated, it is obvious, this is highly lethal. You made all the right orders, getting her system flushed. It gave her a fighting advantage." Yelsie's smile was the wide canine maw, filled with bright white teeth. Would he ever get used to the Omicronian's mouth?

Deuce nodded and lowered himself into a chair. It was going to be a long night, but, at least Molly wasn't in the morgue. He closed his eyes and heard the door open and close. Yelsie had left the room. He placed his elbows on his knees and propped his head on two index fingers, his thumbs supported his jaw. The rhythmic beeping of Molly's heart monitor lulled his mind as he drifted into a shallow sleep.

***

"How's the little patient?" A loud southern drawl startled Deuce awake. He lifted his head and jerked to his feet. "What are you doing here?"

"Son, I heard our Molly was sick, and I came as soon as I could." The sincerity of his tone could have won a red-carpet award back on Earth.

"Our? Molly?" Deuce tried to act calm. He couldn't give away the knowledge of his dad's involvement. "I'm sorry. It—It's been a long night."

Abraham Senior approached Deuce and patted his shoulder. "Sure, sure. It's all right. When we care about somebody or something, we protect it with our lives. Like a lion protects his pride."

Deuce tensed under his father's touch. *Lion? Pride? Was he prowling* like *a lion, as the Bible speaks of the devil, 'looking for those he can devour?'*

"Who found her?" Abraham asked.

"What does it matter?" Deuce glared at his dad.

"Just curious, son."

"I found her, actually."

"You?" His dad flashed a look of surprise, but quickly hid the emotion behind a well-rehearsed façade.

"I had a workmate run a trace on all vessels. We found one overweight and worked from there."

Deuce chose his words carefully. "I rushed her back here."

Abraham glared at Deuce. "Well, thank Gawd for your workmate…and your good instincts."

"It seems we have a traitor among us, Dad." Deuce studied his reaction. "Someone wanted Molly dead. Why do you suppose they would want that?"

Abraham shook his head. His pretense of concern seemed authentic, but Deuce wasn't falling for any of it.

"I can't imagine, son. We are all here to help. Why would anybody want to hurt a single one of us?"

Deuce stared at his father.

The senior Abraham watched Molly sleep. "I'll start an investigation immediately."

"I would hope so." Deuce gritted his teeth. He wasn't sure which hurt more, his heart or his gut. He had come to this planet hoping, deep down, he would find a man who had changed. A father he had hoped would be different from the one who broke his mother's heart and abandoned him as a child.

This proved nothing had changed. Or if it had, it was for the worse. He had become a Lord here six hundred lightyears from Earth. The law was firmly in his control. And so were the mercies of the people who came here to help.

Nausea grabbed Deuce's gut. "I—I need to check on some other patients. And Miss Jacobsen needs to rest."

Abraham nodded and walked with his son into the hall. "You let me know how she's doing, won't ya. And I'll keep you abreast of my investigation. We'll find out who did this, son. Something like this can't go unpunished." Abraham took a step away from Deuce then turned back. "Who'd you say did that vessel trace?"

"Uh, I didn't catch is name."

He watched his father walk down the hall and exit the infirmary. He'd better warn Gordon. The sick feeling washed over him again. He swallowed the emotions and the bitter bile bubbling in the back of his throat.

CHAPTER THIRTY

Gordon's fingers furiously tapped his virtual keyboard. He had eight screens open at once. Every invoice trail hit a dead end. A red light blinked in his peripheral. The pattern indicated it was urgent. He ignored it for now. Accessing a network linking inventory, he copied and pasted the computer address and pinged into the connection. A security wall blocked his first attempt. He chuckled. His fingers moved quickly, accessing another app. He leaned back and sipped his coffee.

The red light blinked. *Hold on!*

He was in. His fingers gyrated across his keyboard. He entered keywords and hit search. A list of viable matches began scrolling down one of the eight screens. He squinted to focus on that screen and selected a potential candidate.

The red light blinked. The number two glowed next to the light. Then three. The messages were piling up.

A packet folder opened and invoices spilled out on his screens. He scanned them.

His eyes widened. "Whoa!"

He leaned back in his chair. Quickly, he copied them into a virtual folder, pounded out the address, and hit send. A door opened and footsteps shuffled through the hall. Gordon glanced over his shoulder as he closed his virtual screens.

Three mangy Omicron guards stood behind Gordon's chair, weapons aimed at his chest. He swiveled his chair and slowly raised his hands. "Is this really necessary?"

Mr. Abraham strolled in, his eyes widened as an evil smile split his mouth, exposing over-whitened teeth. He nodded. "Men, I think we've found our mole."

***

Deuce rubbed the back of his neck. He needed to check on the surrogate mother. Her baby would be transferred soon, and he wanted to be sure she was prepared. He made a mental note to check on the medical staff for Psychology backgrounds. One was needed to properly execute this surrogate practice. There were just too many emotions involved, and a surrogate volunteer couldn't possibly realize from the beginning what an emotional toll such an act of kindness caused.

He entered her room and stopped short.

Her body trembled beneath the pale green linen blanket. She hiccuped and turned onto her back. Tear-soaked eyes peered toward him from behind her limp arm draped across her forehead.

"I didn't know it would be this hard," she whimpered.

Deuce drew his eyebrows together and closed the gap to her bedside. "What? Where's your baby?"

"They took her. It was time." She turned back over and curled up in a tight ball. Her shoulders quivered as she sobbed into her pillow.

"Time? I hadn't released her—or you," he said through his teeth. Her trembling form broke his heart. The method by which this program had been administered was cruel. He reached out to touch her shoulder but drew back. His fists balled at his side. He hated how this program had been set up. He might do away with it all together.

"I'm so sorry." He choked out the words. This had to change!

An Omicronian admin glanced up as he stomped up to her. "Who released the surrogate's baby?" He spoke harsher than he intended.

The admin cringed and stared wild eyed at him. "Who?"

"The surrogate who delivered last night, who released her baby?" He shoved his thumb over his shoulder.

"Uh." She clicked her flat pad keyboard. "Dr. Stork released the baby, Doctor."

"Stork!" Heat filled Deuce's face. He clinched his jaw tight and looked over his shoulder toward the laboratory. "Thank you," he said absently and stormed down the hall. This was too much.

"Stork!" he hollered as he shoved through the Laboratory doors.

White lab-coat-wrapped technicians jerked up to stand and stared at him.

"Where's Stork?" he asked no one in particular.

Several pointed toward Dr. Stork's office.

Deuce pounded great strides toward the office. "What do you mean releasing my patient without my permission?"

Stork looked up from his films. Emotionless serenity masked his face. "Whatever do you mean, Dr. Abraham?"

"The surrogate...last night's delivery...you released her baby...had it taken away from her too soon."

"Too soon?" Stork chuckled. "You exposed her to the baby far too long, Doctor. I told you, we have procedures here for a reason. If your patient is upset, I'm sorry, but it was *you* who allowed her to become emotionally attached."

Deuce ground his teeth. His jaw hurt. He glared at the insane man before him. "This is barbaric, and you know it."

Stork's eyebrows lifted causing his receding hairline to shove back on his head. His mask morphed into innocence. "Our mission here, Doctor"—he slowly removed his reading glasses —"is to assist the local Omicronian's with their reproductive issues. The volunteers know what they are agreeing to. Everything is explained to them in full. They sign affidavits and disclaimers. We have done nothing wrong."

"Nothing wrong?" Spit sprayed from Deuce's mouth. "You're doing everything wrong, Doctor. You shouldn't have *any* involvement in the delivery side of this practice. You shouldn't be involved in surrogate placement, delivery, or anything else. You should be in your lab, perfecting your science, improving conception, and that's it."

His chest heaved for air, his limbs trembled with anger, and his fists clinched in a tight ball. He wanted to smash one of them into that smug face of Stork's. Instead, he struggled to remain still.

Stork steepled his fingers and puckered his lips. A long sigh whistled through his nose. "You, Doctor Abraham, seem to be under the impression that you have a say in how things have been established here. Just because you are who you are doesn't give you authority to take over our conventional practices."

Deuce raised his eyebrows high on his forehead.

"Look, we designed this program the way it is for reasons that are conducive to the needs of the people. The Omicronians. It's not set up to serve the Earth people. They are not the ones who were in trouble. Now, I suggest you *back off* and rethink your high and mighty ideals, Doctor Abraham. Better yet, go have a long talk with your father. Let him explain to you who is in charge and why."

Stork stood. "Now, get out of my lab before I ask the security patrol to escort you. Good day, Doctor Abraham."

Deuce glared at Stork. Heat flushed his face, and his ears burned. Yet, he could think of no rebuttal. Had his father set everything up like this? How could anybody establish procedures that didn't take into account the emotional well-being of the surrogates? This was wrong. His father had to know it was wrong.

Deuce narrowed his glare at Stork. He would leave the lab, but he would find the answers to his questions. Then he'd put an end to it. The people of Omicron deserved a legitimate system to help with their reproductive problems, but not at the expense of the people who thought they came here to help.

"Fine, Stork, but you haven't heard the last of me." He turned to exit the lab and the infirmary. He needed to talk to Gordon. There had to be a way to find out how all this linked together. Those cryo-vessels were going somewhere and delivering something. Deuce knew in his gut it wasn't good. And he also knew his father was at the heart of it, profiting by it. Women like Kita were completely sterilized when they were supposed to be donating a few eggs. Was his father stealing the Earth women's entire supply and…selling them on a black market? Were all the donors from Earth now sterile? Was Molly?

No, not Molly. She was adamant about the women from her group not donating anything right away. Had she been careful enough? Now that she was in the infirmary was she at risk? How invasive were their practices?

Deuce stopped walking and shook his head. He was torn between going to warn Gordon and checking on Molly. His heart sank. What if the women had all been sterilized? How could he ever fix that? He looked back at the infirmary. He'd go check on Molly and then go see Gordon.

CHAPTER THIRTY-ONE

Molly's eyes fluttered open, and the room slowly came into focus. She sat up and gasped. The monitor beeped rhythmically above her head. An IV tube ran the length of her arm, along with a spiral wrapping of gauze.

Poisoned!

No, Deuce had saved her. Brought her here. She scanned the room. Her neck itched. She scratched at it but touched soft gauze instead. *Ahhh*, her skin burned. A yellow ointment oozed through the open weave on her arms. What was this? She rubbed them together, but it only agitated the pain.

A red light blinked in her peripheral. She opened the iComm link.

Timing is crucial. G @ colonies. Path leads from where there is no key. Not all pirates wear black patches, but X still marks the spot. —AF

"I hate puzzles!" she screamed and rubbed the gauze across her collar bone.

Her door swung open. A silver-mane doctor rushed into the room. "Miss Jacobsen! Are you all right?"

"I itch!" She scrubbed her arms together.

"You must not do that. Here, I will give you something for the discomfort." She hurried out and returned with a syringe.

"What is that?" Molly drew away from her.

"Antihistamine with an analgesic for the pain." She sunk the needle in the IV tube and pushed the plunger down.

"Where's Doctor Abraham?" Molly watched the syringe empty.

"I am not sure. I can check if you like." She smiled that startling canine smile.

Molly glanced at her name tag. "I'd appreciate that, Dr. Yelsie." She returned her smile and forced her arms down to her side. "Can I ask you something?"

Dr. Yelsie capped the syringe and slipped it into a sharps container. "Sure."

"Do you know what 'the colonies' is?"

Dr. Yelsie stiffened. Her eyes darted to the door. "Never heard of it. Why?"

"Never mind. I think I had a weird dream."

"Poison will do that to you." Dr. Yelsie smiled, but it wasn't the usual gaping canine grin. She checked Molly's monitor and IV lines and updated her film. "Try to get some rest. The antihistamine should help you sleep. You have a couple more days of this." She pointed at the gauze covered hives on Molly's arms. "Then you can go home."

"What is it?"

"This is an after-effect of the antidote. It is a local remedy. We were not sure how you might react."

"I feel fine, otherwise. Can't I go home and take the antihistamine there?"

"This is up to Dr. Abraham, Miss Jacobsen, not me" A coy grin split her mouth as she adjusted Molly's covers. "Now, rest. I will locate Doctor Abraham."

Dr. Yelsie knew something about the colonies. Molly sensed fear the minute she mentioned it. Whatever the colonies were, the Omicronians were terrified. At least this one was. Did all the locals know about them? Did Gordon know?

Gordon!

G in colonies. Oh, no! *X still marks the spot*? She threw off her covers, but the IV pulled her back into the bed. She clawed at the tape and yanked the needle out of her arm. If "Path leads from where there is no key" meant what she thought it did, she knew where to start.

Where were her clothes?

"What are you doing?" Deuce shoved through the door.

Molly spun around. "Deuce! They've got Gordon! We've gotta get into those locked areas." She opened a cabinet door. Empty! She spun around to face Deuce. "I need clothes!"

"You weren't—Wait." He exited the room.

She leaned against the bed and waited, her heart pounding in her chest. She stared at the floor, one gauze covered hand over her heart, trying to focus on calming herself. Soon he re-entered and pushed a bundle into her hands. She tore the tape and dumped the contents onto the bed. Green surgical scrubs spilled out along with faux leather booties.

"Turn around or…or close your eyes."

Deuce stared for a moment. His mouth moved but no words came out. A half smile curled at his lips as he turned his back to her. "How do you know about Gordon?"

"I got another message from AF, he told me Gordon's in the colonies. What's the colonies?" She pulled off the infirmary gown.

"I have no idea. Who's AF?"

"I don't know but—" she told him what the message said, word for word. "'Where there is no key' has to be those doors near the lab…it's gotta be the way in."

"X still marks the spot?" Deuce ran his fingers through his dark curls. "An Omicronian resident said the poison was from a plant." He glanced over his shoulder but returned his stare to the wall. "She said it was called 'X' because we couldn't pronounce it in their native tongue."

"What plant?" Molly pulled up the green pants and slipped a gauze-covered arm into the matching shirt. She pulled her hair out from inside the shirt and bent to slide on a slipper.

"The plant used to poison you. Does that mean X, the poisonous plant, is at the colonies? Maybe that's what AF meant. Where ever that plant is grown is where these colonies are…"

"And where Gordon is," they said together.

"Okay." Molly stepped up close to Deuce. "So where's this resident?"

"I think she's right outside." Deuce pushed the door open and glanced down the hall.

"You mean Dr. Yelsie?" Molly pushed past him and scanned the hall, too.

"Yes, that's her name."

"Yeah, well, she's not gonna help us. She got stiff as a board when I asked her about the colonies. So what *was* the poison?"

"I'm not sure."

"Was it in my file?"

"I'll check." Deuce lifted Molly's film, tucked it under his arm, and looped his other through hers.

"Let's get you outta here and figure out what to do."

She let him lead her out.

***

Gordon bounced around on a bench attached to the side of the windowless transport vessel. Where were they taking him? He had tried to keep track of the turns, stops, and distance he had traveled. The route had not made sense.

The external sounds indicated they were no longer traversing inner-village roads. The continuous movement now indicated they followed a rural road. He'd never been outside of the residential village. How barren or plush it might be, he had no knowledge.

He myopically scanned his iComm range. Nothing, no numbers, no signaling lights, no data. It was disorienting not having information streaming in his peripheral at all times. He touched the vessel wall for balance. A flame of phobic fear burned deep in his chest.

At least now, perhaps, he'd know where people were being taken when they disappeared. What a way to find out, though. A sardonic chuckle escaped his lips.

Abruptly, the vessel slammed to a halt, and he shifted his feet to keep from tumbling to the floor. Doors opened and closed. Gravelly voices resounded. Boots stomped to and fro. Then nothing.

His eyes darted around the vessel. The cargo doors were not opening. What were they doing? Beads of sweat collected on his upper lip. His hands and arm pits moistened. No one worked in the afternoon suns. Would they leave him here in the heat to die?

He strained to listen. In the distance a mechanism hummed. He stared at the hazy shadow of the opposite bench and focused. What an odd sounding motor. Nothing like the high tech mechanisms Earth had brought to Omicron. This had to be deep rural.

The Colonies! He stiffened and sucked in air. Had they brought him to the colonies? The mines? Radioactive isotopes were toxic here. This whole planet of people had become sterile because of exposure to this energy source. Why would they bring him here?

His breath came with a shallow, labored effort. His eyes darted back and forth. The vessel tilted. No, he was dizzy. There was no oxygen, no he was hyperventilating? He pulled his shirt over his nose and breathed into the cloth. Counting slowly as he breathed, he focused on controlling the panic. Out of habit, he touched his iComm link. Nothing. Darting eyes jumped all over the vessel, the Panic clawed at his conscience.

Wait! The Bible-verse wrist band. There was a chance. He flipped it over and peeled apart the back layer with his thumb nail. He held down a pin-sized nub. A cone shaped screen, the size of an orange, lit up inches above the band. Gordon touched the app icon. A hot-spot iComm link activated. He reattached the back and slipped the band over his wrist. His implanted iComm link lit up.

Boots stomped near the vessel. Gordon scrambled out a message, encrypted its IP address, and hit send.

Lord, let this go through, he prayed.

The stomping halted next to the rear of the vessel. An opening mechanism whined, and a crack of light split between the two doors. An oily stench seeped in with the light.

Gordon stiffened and his heart pounded in his chest. His lungs heaved out of control. Was this it? Two Omicron heathens pointed two dark metal pipes stacked on top of each other with a third smaller tube, possibly a scope, at his chest. Barbaric weapons. The laser light from the top tube warmed his skin beneath his cotton shirt. This weapon was nothing like anything he'd ever seen. He gritted his teeth but refused to flinch.

"Welcome to the colonies, Gordon," The soft spoken Oliver Pugh stood a few strides behind the laser wielding guards. He'd been missing for over three years. A dark gap in his teeth and thinning hair indicated the exposure had affected his body. A bloody bruised eye and lip indicated someone had recently reprimanded him or something. He wore a long, dirt tone tunic and moccasin-like boots.

Gordon glanced over Pastor Pugh's shoulder. A pale yellow wall of crumbling rock stood behind him. Sprigs of spiny-looking red and orange flowers filled linear crevices.

"Pastor Pugh! What happened to you?"

"Me? Oh, I'm the sacrificial lamb. I let a girl escape this hell-hole so people on Earth would know how corrupt this mission had become. Only instead of killing me, they 'reassigned' me—" he wiggled fingers in the air "—It was this or death. At the time, I had hope of escaping anywhere they might put me. Now, I pray every day the Good Lord will take me home, but like Jesus, I'm afraid I have been forsaken." He made a quick gesture to look up toward heaven, but the two suns' harshness caused his eyes to squint closed. He returned his gaze to Gordon.

"Where are we, Pastor?"

"Oh, I'm no Pastor. Not any more." Sadness consumed his expression.

"But, this?" Pugh gestured toward something Gordon could not see from inside the vessel and staggered backward slightly. He spoke loudly, as if he wanted someone far away to hear as well. "This is what keeps this planet supplied in an energy source, without which no one could function at all."

He bent at the waste and hacked something up, spitting it on the ground. He continued in a softer voice, "*This*, my friend, is the Colonies. And another branch of The Abraham Project's prolific endeavors of which I have the privilege, God help me, to oversee."

He wiped his mouth with the back of a dirty hand and nodded at the guards. They leaped into the vessel and grabbed Gordon by the shoulders. He stumbled as they shoved him out. The scene blanched from the harsh two suns. He squinted against the pain in his eyes and his head, and tried to look around.

An entrance, similar to a large cavern back on Earth, was to his right. The humming mechanism he had heard belonged to a railway system leading into the mouth of the cavern. Guards paced the perimeter. Cargo vessels lined up beyond the railway tracks. Large shoveling machines belched black exhaust as they dug into a mound of purple crystalized stones and dumped a payload into the vessels. A line of small, pale people, all dressed identically in dirt-tone tunics and knee-high moccasin-styled boots, marched toward a smaller pile of purple rock, dumped the contents of their baskets, and then returned into the cavern.

A yellow warning light blinked in Gordon's left peripheral. The radiation exposure registered immediately. Gordon cringed.

God protect me.

CHAPTER THIRTY-TWO

Molly slumped in the passenger seat. Her heavy eyelids would not reopen without great effort when she blinked. Side effects of antihistamine weighed down her limbs. She forced her eyes open and tried to focus on the passing landscape.

"Where are we going?" She blinked slowly.

"The only place I can hide you in plain sight." Deuce glanced at her but returned his eyes to the road.

She let her head fall back against the head rest. "What does that mean?"

"Dad gave me an apartment out behind his place. We're going there."

"What! Deuce, no!" Molly nearly crawled out of her seat.

"Look, you're not safe in the village. We need to find Gordon. To do that, we need a plan." He ran his hand through his thick hair. "I don't know what else to do."

"What if somebody sees me," she whispered. "Like your father."

"Not if I can help it." Deuce touched her arm. "I've transitioned the windows on this ITV. Nobody can see in. There's a private entrance at the apartment. Plus—"

She licked her dry lips and stared into his forward facing eyes.

"—Gordon linked my system so he could discretely answer some questions I had." A nervous smile bowed Deuce's mouth, and then he swallowed.

Molly chewed the inside of her cheek as she stared at him. Her antihistamine-ladened mind gradually processed her thoughts. Somebody tried to poison her. Obviously, she wasn't safe in the missionary quarters. What choice did she have, really? She eased herself back against the seat. Her eyes darted about the floor board and dash. She drew in a long sigh and focused on calming her racing heartbeat. *God help me if I'm wrong about this man.*

Deuce pulled as close to the detached apartment as possible so his ITV wouldn't be seen from the big house. Large foliage, similar to palm bushes and banana trees, blocked most of the view of the pink stucco covered servant's quarters. Molly's knees gave way as she exited the ITV. She held herself upright by leaning on the vessel and glanced around. Confirming they were undetected, she forced herself to step out and move to the deck. A red light flashed a pattern of two flashes then three. Priority One message.

Deuce reached up to his iComm link at the same time she did. Their eyes met. The message opened. "Gordon!" they whispered simultaneously. She paused on the teak wood deck and read the message.

Location unknown. Colonies=Mines! Proof sent slaves farmed.

"What does that mean?" Molly adjusted her vision to include Deuce.

"No idea. Let's get inside."

Molly forced her rebellious muscles forward through the vertically sliding door. Stucco white walls, ceiling beams, and windows flowed smoothly as if sculpted from one large piece of clay. There wasn't a ninety degree angle anywhere except where the wall met the dark teak wood floor. The furniture was made of a native jointed wood similar to bamboo from Earth. Cushions softened seating in the dining room chairs and living room set. Woven baskets of dried plants adorned the walls. Fresh flowers, a cross between birds-of-paradise and gladiolas, stood in vases on side tables and a dining hutch. The place was immaculate.

"You live here?" Molly leaned against a dining room chair.

"Well, I still have my room at the missionary quarters. I figured this would let me keep an eye on him. You know?" He dropped his ITV device in a brown ceramic dish the shape of a large leaf.

"First things first, Molly. You need rest." Deuce gently guided her down a hall and into a bedroom. A four-poster, dark wood bed centered a wall. Mosquito netting draped from each post. A white billowy coverlet and large oval pillows dressed the mattress.

Molly sighed. How could she sleep? Yet, that bed beckoned her. "Okay, just a nap."

She crawled onto the covers and sank down into the down-filled bedspread. Deuce draped a silky linen throw over her shoulder, and she turned onto her side. A familiar fragrance drifted from the linen. If she were back home, she'd swear it was Egyptian cotton, scented with lavender oil.

The door closed. Tension waned in the softness on which she lay. Deuce would protect her. She was safe, even though she was mere yards from his father, the man she feared the most. The irony made her frown. But that expression slid away with a heavy sigh. Her body sunk deeper in the cloud-soft covers. Consciousness ebbed from her mind.

***

A golden-black cloud grew bigger in the distance, as Molly paused on her patrol to watch its movements. It darted about in the air, ebbing closer to where she stood.

The swarm of bees whizzed past her. She couldn't move. She stared at the cloud as it swirled around her like a dust funnel. Their eerie buzz seemed amplified. She tilted her head and concentrated on the noise they made. Once again, words formed in the buzz. She closed her eyes to listen.

"Esssther dared to go before the King."

Her eyes shot open. "What?"

The trail of bees darted away, disappearing in the woods.

A red illumination filled the compound. The weird sensation of déjà vu filled her senses. She held her hand up in front of her face, it glowed with the crimson brilliance. Something clicked on the ground. A lobster crawled up to her foot and clicked its pinchers. It curled up in a ball and morphed into a bulbous vernix-encrusted embryo.

Molly stared at it with disgust. The embryo swelled and morphed slowly from an infant, into a child, a teen, and, finally, a slime-covered adult. Fine hair covered its entire body, like the ice-man Neanderthal found long ago.

She stared at the spectacle. The adult uncurled and stood. It seemed blind to her presence. The ground rumbled, and a mound pushed up in the grassy meadow of the compound, breaking open like an infected wound erupting. A rustic wood and iron pin door filled an arched opening, cast iron bolt hinges moaned from rust and humidity as the door slowly creaked open. A cavernous mouth, dark and damp, lay beyond. The adult walked into the gaping chasm. He was gone.

To her right, a muster of peacocks gathered around two men. She focused to recognize who stood between the birds. Austin Abraham, Senior and His High Exalted Argenteus Lupus gazed upon the proud birds as they strutted and pranced around them. They lifted their hands and applauded. The birds responded by holding their heads high and fanned out their magnificent tail feathers. A dance ensued among the male birds as they displayed their stunning plumage.

The cloud of bees darted back and spun around her again. They encircled her several times. This time they brushed against her body. She moved away from the pelting impact. They responded by adjusting their flight. They were guiding her off the compound. She let them direct her to an open field. It was barren and rock-strewn. Deuce leaned against a large bolder. He straightened as she approached him. The bees swirled around them both and funneled up into the bright steel-blue sky, leaving them in one another's embrace. He lowered his head and his lips toward hers. She leaned her head over and back to receive the impending kiss. The suns' heat beat down on her, and sweat formed on her face and under her shirt. The anticipation of his kiss burned in her soul.

"You need to see this." Deuce uttered against her wanting lips.

She stared at him.

***

"Molly! You need to see this," Deuce's voice was near. Someone shook her shoulder. She opened her eyes. He perched on the side of the bed. "Molly? Wake up. I've found something."

"Found something?" She touched her lips. The expectancy of the near kiss lingered in her nerves.

"Come on, I need to show you something." He stood and extended his hand.

She took it as he pulled her from the bed and guided her through the living room to an alcove. An iComm system sat nestled into a protrusion, like a built-in desk, molded with the wall. Deuce activated the system and sat down.

Molly stood behind him. She absently rubbed the heel of her palm against her collar bone.

He turned to glance at her and jumped up. "Here."

Gesturing for her to sit down, he pulled a wicker-back dining chair over to the alcove. "Gordon partitioned the hard drive. He said the information would be encrypted, but I ran this program he gave me and…"

She glanced at the system unit. Deuce's ITV device dangled from a port.

Following her gaze, Deuce commented, "Gordon loaded all kinds of stuff on this." He pointed at the vessel key.

An icon of a wolf running in place appeared on the virtual screen as they waited and watched.

Molly bit her lip as she leaned her chin against her fists, elbows on the sculpted desk, to watch the wolf in motion. Her eyelids were heavy, but she forced them open. The itching sensation beckoned her attention, she gingerly rubbed her forearms together, but forced herself to stop. Eventually, the icon sat down and exploded as simulated papers floated into a fanned configuration across the screen. She blinked to focus her rebellious vision and scanned the documents as they appeared. Her eyes widened as she read. The itching faded from her awareness. "Oh no!" she murmured.

Deuce nodded. "What are they doing?"

Molly slapped her hand over her mouth. "We need to get into that lab."

"And we need to find Gordon," Deuce whispered. "I think they're in the same place."

Molly looked down the hall. "I think you're right. How many bedrooms you got here?"

"Three."

"Good. We'll bring him here."

Deuce turned around. "How can we get through without being noticed?"

"I've got a plan."

***

Molly told Deuce about her dream. The story of Esther was so clear in her mind. "Esther boldly entered the Kings court and invited him to a banquet. She exposed her uncle's traitor, Haman, and his devious plan against the Israelites, during the banquet." She searched his eyes for understanding.

He looked lost.

"Well, actually she held several banquets, but we don't have time for that. But, that's what we'll do. I'll contact Davidette and Julie. If anybody can pull together a banquet with short notice, those two can." She giggled. And to think, they always drove her crazy with their fancy pinafore cakes and perfect party dresses. Now, she thanked God they were here on this planet.

"We'll have a parade to honor the families that have been blessed by our missionary efforts. Make it a celebration of the abundant life restored. Your dad, Stork, and Lupus won't be able to refuse attendance. Everybody will be there."

"Except us," Deuce said slowly.

"Right." He was catching on. "We'll be figuring out how to get through those locked doors." She bit her lip. "Somehow."

Deuce smiled. "Ah, Gordon's link…" He turned back to his system. "There's a security protocol app. Let me see if I can—"

Molly glanced through the large windows facing the senior Abraham's home. Large leafed plants obscured her view. Wrought iron furnishings dotted an expansive veranda. A linen pant leg and loafer swung from a crossed leg. Molly gasped and slid back into the hall.

Deuce looked up from his task.

She pointed at the window and mouthed, "Your dad."

Deuce put an index finger to his mouth. He whispered, "It's all right. He can't see us."

He returned to the keyboard and continued to scan for the program.

Her heart pounded, and her breath came too fast. The cool clay wall seeped comfort into her startled nerves. She closed her eyes and waited. Once he had the security key, she'd call the girls.

"Ah!" Deuce glanced at her. "I've got it." A few more clicks, and he touched his iComm link. "There."

"What did you do?" Molly stepped up to his virtual screen. She didn't recognize anything.

"I've transferred the program link to my iComm. We can unlock those doors now."

A smile parted her lips as she touched her iComm link. "Conference call, Davidette, add Julie."

CHAPTER THIRTY-THREE

"Okay, Molly…Yeah, I understand," Davidette spoke for the two. "…Of course we can do this! Remember who you're talking to?…No, I think it's a prime idea. Leave everything to us." A wicked, large smile drew taut across Davidette's face and her eyes sparkled. Julie returned the jubilant grin.

Activating her iComm link Davidette stated, "Message, MissionaryGroup3." Her recruits would meet in thirty minutes in the common room of the quarters. Julie pulled out a pad of film and started sketching out some designs. A giggle escaped her lips. This was higher-learning school prom all over, only this time, it included a parade. What could possibly be more fun?

Davidette ran to the kitchen and started barking commands at the food generator. One can't have a meeting without eats and drinks.

***

Davidette gestured with flat palms to quiet the eleven gathered in the common room. "Let's open with a word of prayer."

Everybody bowed their heads, and Davidette prayed.

"Molly and Deuce are on an important and exciting mission, and they need our help. Evil is among the flocks."

"Evil?" Reah blinked, her face blanched with fear. Murmurs rippled across the eleven onlookers. Davidette gestured again with flat palms.

"It's all right. We've got a plan. Remember how Esther rooted out her Uncle Mordecai's enemy for plotting against their people?"

"Didn't he try to destroy the entire Jewish population in the region?" Hayden thumbed through his Bible app.

"Yes, exactly." Davidette nodded. "Well, we're going to follow her example. We are throwing a banquet. Everybody in the village will be invited. We will honor those who have benefited from The Abraham Project. And no one will be the wiser as to who we are ferreting out as the enemy. We are calling it 'A Celebration of Abundant Life Restored,' ...or something like that." She furrowed her brow, considering the length of that title.

"A banquet? When?" Jody's delicate brows pressed together.

"Tonight. And we need a parade this afternoon."

"What?" Alyce and Miriam said at once and turned to look at the other.

"Yes. The parade will get everybody in a festive mood and pull them away from their work. We can do this. It'll just take some coordination."

"Miriam, you and Roma go gather all the children. Daniel, will you please procure two flat-bed vessels and take it to the school pad. The children and you two gals will decorate it for a float. Be thinking of a theme for each. Abundant Life...you know." She motioned toward Miriam.

"Julie, I'm putting you in charge of decorating the big hall, and Pam, and Julio. "We want festive but formal."

"Like a prom," Julie added.

Davidette nodded. "Yes, exactly!"

"Hayden, I need you to send an iComm invite to everybody in this village. Do you have access to the mass address list?"

"Yes, we have that." Hayden nodded.

"Prime. I'll design an invitation and forward it to you shortly."

"Sonya, Alyce and I will prepare a banquet meal fit for a king." Davidette laughed. "I'll contact Mrs. Lupus personally. She'll know how we can roast a pig, or something, on short notice, I'll bet."

She nodded confidence and stared at the eleven. Were they on the same filament with her? "Remember this is a diversion for Molly and Deuce, we've gotta really make this happen." She clapped her hands. "Go. Let's get this party happening."

Hayden stepped up to her and waited. Davidette touched her iComm link and held up one finger, indicating for him to wait. Mrs. Lupus's servant answered, and Davidette waited for the matriarch. She smiled at Hayden. Mrs. Lupus answered, and Davidette explained their desire to honor the leaders and inquired how she should go about getting roasted meat for the evening. As expected, Mrs. Lupus had a way and offered to have the prepared meat delivered to the Great Hall by the designated time. She blessed Davidette and disconnected.

Davidette sighed. "I like that lady..." *and I hope she's not our target ferretee.*

She sat down and sketched out a design for the invitation. Making a digital copy with her iComm link, she uplinked it to Hayden. "You should have it now. Please be sure it is sent 'Urgent, Top Priority."

"Will do." Hayden made his way down the men's hall.

"Okay. Now for side dishes." Sonya and Alyce followed her to the Commissary. They needed bigger food generating machines.

***

"What is this nonsense?" Stork barked into Abraham's iComm.

"The new recruits wish to honor us, and the work *you* have accomplished, Doctor, is that such a bad thing?" Austin Abraham leaned back in his oversized office chair.

"I don't have time for this."

"Well, you need to make time for it. It's not going to hurt any of your work to be away for one evening. The consequences of you not being there could prove to be more detrimental. You do not want to disappoint His High Exalted, now do you? Besides, the meal promises to be excellent—uh, *prime* as the kids say now-a-days." Abraham chuckled.

Stork growled an agreement. "Fine, I'll be there."

What choice did he have? This was ridiculous. A waste of time, nothing but fluff and circumstance. He had serious work to do. Still. Just like back on Earth, he had to appease the hands that funded his work. He knew that ritual all too well. He simply thought he'd left that degrading task six hundred lightyears behind.

"Very good, old man." Abraham continued to prod him. "His High Exalted and I will see you this evening,"

"Right." Stork disconnected. He glanced around the lab. He hadn't worn a tuxedo in a decade. Did the thing still fit?

The atmosphere in the lab accelerated with jubilation. Apparently everyone was excited about this ridiculous banquet. Their exuberance only increased his foul mood. However, he had to admit, perhaps it was good to celebrate, it added to the legitimacy of his unorthodox methods. He set to finalize the open projects and shut down.

***

A large kettle drum resounded as the parade began at the far end of the compound. The route would encircle the entire campus and end where it began. Omicron children filled one flat-bed vessel, and twelve of the fourteen newest recruits plus several veteran missionaries filled the other. Missionaries and some locals, dressed as clowns, walked in front of the children's vessels. A brass and woodwind band marched behind the adult's vessel, a snare and bass drum kept their beat. A twirlers' group walked behind the band. And a dance troupe pranced behind them. Beaded necklaces, candy, and little toys flew from the two floats and were caught by the eager villagers. Streamers floated through the air and brightly colored confetti littered the hard-top.

Two figures swallowed up by the crowd stayed back and blended in until the festivities were well underway. Only Davidette noticed their movement.

The children sang songs along the route, alternating with the missionaries' float singing Hymns.

The two discrete shadows slipped into the darker edges and slid along the walls toward the laboratory.

Two vessels stopped in front of the risers seating the honored guests, Austin Abraham, the Lupuses, and Doctor Stork. Lucy Pugh, Oliver Pugh's wife, sat among them although she clearly did not fit in. Her red swollen eyes told another story.

Other officials of the village and compound filled the risers as well. Together, the children and the missionaries performed a slow, melodic tune with beautiful harmony and interlacing choruses. The risers shook as the spectators leaped to their feet, clapping fervently. Lucy stood when the other stood, politely clapping. Stork reluctantly stood and clapped enough to appease his funders.

The vessels moved forward again. The next group stopped and performed their specialty. The performers did their best and were rewarded with enthusiasm and cheers.

As the applause died down for the final dance group, Davidette stepped out onto the hard-top. Her iComm link amplified her voice. "We of the latest recruits, thank you." She bowed her head in homage.

"This mission has blessed us beyond words. We pray our humble work honors you and blesses you, as well. As a small token of our esteem, we invite you now to come to the Great Hall and enjoy a feast prepared by your own, Her High Exalted Lily Lupus—"

The roar of applause interrupted her speech, but she smiled. She, too, held clapping hands toward Mrs. Lupus. When the adulation waned she continued, "—and we, your humble servants. The work here, through The Abraham Project, is amazing. We are so proud to be a small part. So, tonight, we honor you, the founders, the visionaries, the leaders of a Godly ordained project to help a people who once had no hope." Her voice cracked. She paused for control. "Tonight we express our admiration by preparing this feast. We pray you enjoy the food, the entertainment, and the camaraderie. So, without further ado—"

She gestured toward the Great Hall. The people gingerly filed out of the risers. The missionaries followed, and the children followed them. The remainder of the spectators fell in behind the children, and the building filled with joyful celebration.

Fresh flowers floated in glass bowls every four paces along long tables placed end to end. A larger arrangement centered the Honoree's table. Black cloth covered every horizontal surface, and elegant crystal icicles hung from filaments attached to the ceiling. The contrast was stunning, a black and crystal ice scape.

A two-sided serve-yourself buffet line had been set up on one end of the room. Several small, roasted pig-beasts started the line of dishes. The golden brown skins glistened on a bed of long, green leaves. Its meat, pulled and cut into bite size pieces, mounded on ceramic platters along both sides of the animals' torso. Beyond the pig-beasts were bright colored bowls of red potatoes, green beans, macaroni salads, English peas, kernel corn, sugar beets, asparagus, and steamed broccoli.

Among these familiar Earthly vegetables, were many more local vegetables unfamiliar to the pilgrims' palates, yet colorful and tempting in aroma. The host cooks were not certain how to pronounce the names but prepared them with help from the commissary staff. Fruits of all kinds, elegantly displayed in a flowing tower, were the last to select at the end of the buffet line.

Davidette sidled up next to Mr. Abraham and whispered in his ear. He gave a call to bow heads and said grace in his elongated southern drawl. Everyone moved up the line slowly to prepare their abundant helping of food and then found seating at the long rows of elegantly decorated tables. The honored guests, of course, were seated at a head table.

CHAPTER THIRTY-FOUR

An uncanny silence amplified their otherwise indiscernible scampering. The parade had worked beautifully. The lab was completely empty, except for Molly and Deuce. She lurked behind him, scanning the empty hallway as he accessed his iComm link. A heavy metal door blocked their path to finding Gordon and the secrets he had unveiled. This strange door, with a locked handle but no lock mechanism, looked impenetrable. Hopefully Gordon's program would work. So long as Deuce could figure out how to access it and run the program.

He was a brilliant doctor, but she had no idea what kind of computer operator he might be. Let alone a hacker. *Lord, please help him figure it out.* Her throat was dry, but moisture dampened her underarms. She licked her lips and shook the front of her surgical scrub shirt. The wait was excruciating. The sooner they got through this door, the calmer she'd be. Hopefully.

A click echoed off the stark walls, and the door started humming.

"Ha!" Deuce whispered and glanced at her with an accomplished smile.

Molly jumped back and stared at the seal. A vacuum of air swooshed as the crack widened, and the door sluggishly swung open. Resisting the urge to try and slide through the crevice before the door fully opened, she shifted her weight back and forth. Her eyes darted one last time down the hall. Still empty.

She glared at the ever widening gap. *Come on, come on, come on.*

Immediately, inside the door, a set a stairs descended into darkness. Deuce looked at Molly with a raised eyebrow. She returned his inquisition, and the two flipped on their flashlights. An odd smell rose from the dank darkness along with a chill. Each step they took resounded in the black silence like a paddle slapping the surface of water.

The muscles in her back drew tight toward her shoulders, but she kept moving. The door closed behind them, sealing the infirmary light out and the pitch black in.

A straight set of stairs, visible only within the cone of light, led them into the bowel of who knew what. Would they find their answers down here? Or would it only lead them to benign storage as Stork had said? A chill swept over her as she stepped onto the basement floor. Rubbing her arms, criss-crossed around her waist, she glanced at Deuce. "Brrr."

At the last step, Molly touched the wall and found a flat switch. Harsh tubed lights illuminated a rough walled, concrete room. "Is this some kind of freezer storage?"

Rows and rows of cabinets filled the twenty-five foot by twenty foot rectangular room. Nine-digit numbers labeled each cabinet door. Molly walked one way, Deuce the other. Each scanned the labels. Nothing but numbers.

Her eyes roved over the digits. Then she saw it. Her heart slammed against her chest. She gasped and whispered, "Deuce."

He looked over his row of cabinets, and their eyes met.

"It's Kita's." She could barely breathe. "They used our Social IDs from Earth. This is hers. It's one number ahead of mine." She swallowed. Trembling hands reached up and pulled the handle. Frozen mist swirled from the cabinet as the drawer slid on its track. Molly swept it away. Multiple sets of cubes holding sixteen small cylinders, rested inside. She reached in, but Deuce blocked her arm. When had he stepped up behind her?

"Don't. You'll get freeze burn." Deuce pulled her back.

Molly's eyes stung as tears filled them. "Are these…Kita's…eggs?"

"Possibly, or embryos…or both." Deuce nodded.

Molly scanned the number identifications. There were hundreds, maybe thousands. "Are all these the same thing?"

"Probably." Deuce randomly opened another drawer. "Looks that way."

Molly tenderly closed Kita's drawer as if she were closing a morgue locker. She pressed her lips together and bit over them.

"Come on. Let's see what's in here." He motioned toward a single door at the back of the room. Stunned silence hung between them as they approached the metal door. Would it be locked? Deuce pushed the horizontal bar, and the door gave way. Another tomb-black room lay beyond. Sultry humidity wafted through the open door. A fog filled the space between the two contrasting rooms. He felt the wall and pressed the switch. Soft orange-pink recessed lights flickered to life like a marquee toward the vast opposite end of the room. This light was nothing more than a diffused night light.

Deuce stood stoic, staring, his jaw slack.

Molly stepped up behind him. "What?"

Her gaze followed his, and her mouth dropped open. She couldn't move. She couldn't speak. She just stared.

Hundreds of transparent tubes, about three feet in diameter, lined four rows. Each perched on a dark opaque square column. Bubbles ascended a bluish liquid that surrounded nearly fully developed fetuses. Molly walked between two rows, staring at each baby. They were not cross bred with the Omicronians. These looked fully human.

No, wait. They seemed to have a fine coat of fur all over their body. Otherwise they *did* look human. Missing was the full mane prevalent to all the Omicrons. Perhaps this was a hybrid, but why? As she walked the length of the row, the babies were bigger. A one-year-old size, then two. The tubes went down the row as far as she could see.

How big was this room?

A yellow warning light began flashing to her left peripheral. Radioactive readings scrolled across the bottom of her visual range. She ignored it.

Farther down, the bodies filled the length of the tubes. Were there full grown species at the other end?

"What in God's name are they doing in here?" Deuce's whisper split the silence.

Her eyes darted to his. "I. Have. No. Idea."

Next to her, a body jerked. The approximately four-year-old child stared at her through the murky blue fluid. He blinked...and frowned. She jumped away from it. Her heart pounded, and she gasped for air.

"Oh!" She slammed into the opposite wall of tubes. Those three specimens jerked and turned. Startled eyes met hers. A scream, stifled by fear, caught in her throat. She covered her mouth with her hand and tried to stand still. She squeezed her eyes closed.

Deuce touched her shoulder. She gasped. He pulled her into his arms, and she dissolved into sobs against his chest.

"It's radioactive in here," Deuce said in a small quiet voice.

"I know." Her voice muffled into his shirt.

He tilted his head and stared at another child. "You...you don't suppose these are the 'slaves' Gordon referred to? ...for the mines?"

Molly's eyes jerked up to his. "Gradual radiation exposure to create tolerance?"

"That's my guess. But—how is that possible?" The atmosphere of a nursery forced him to speak with a soft voice. He didn't want to wake the sleeping babies—he looked down the long row—or children.

"Is this what Stork is really working on in his labs? Radiation tolerance? For—for cloned slaves in the colonies?" She swallowed hard. "To mine the ore?"

Deuce raised his brows and nodded. "That's my guess. Goodness, think of the lives that could be saved from cancer with this research. They must have developed some sort of cell regeneration, or restoration, to overcome the effects of radiation, you know, tumors and such. If—if it were used properly."

"How far back does this go?" She stepped around him and began walking the length. A creepy sensation clung to her like a spider web.

"I don't know, but we need to record this." He touched his iComm link and began recording as he walked.

Molly touched numerical markings at the base of one tube. Similar markings were on every container. She stared closely. "You don't suppose these are dates?"

She moved to the next tube. Then the next. "Deuce, if these are dates, like inception dates, they are growing these people with some sort of unnatural accelerant."

Deuce looked at the tubes next to him. "I see what you mean."

She followed him down the line. The room seemed endless. Finally, they came to the last tubes. The encased children appeared to be right at puberty, maybe twelve to fourteen years old. She touched the markings. "If these are dates, these children were grown in less than four years."

Deuce looked over her shoulder. "I think you're right. But how?"

The room ended in a moist rock wall. A rustic wood and iron pin door filled the arched opening. He stopped recording and lifted the cast iron bolt and shoved his weight against the door. The hinges moaned from rust and humidity. A dark, cavernous tunnel extended before them.

Déjà vu washed over Molly. She had seen this before, in her dream.

An open-seat train sat on tracks to their left. It looked like a tourist ride. Folded clothing filled the wall to their right. A neat pile of woven linen blankets stacked next to the clothing. Soft leather boots, like deer-hide moccasins, filled square cubby holes which covered the remainder of the wall from ceiling to floor.

Molly scanned every detail. Words slowly spilled from her thoughts. "You suppose, they come out of there...dress them in these...wrap them in those...and fit them with the boots? Then load them into this train and carry them down to —"

She couldn't finish. But she knew where this tunnel went. AF's last message had said, "Path leads from where there is no key." Those doors Deuce had opened had no key. This was that path to where they would find Gordon and God only knew what else.

Deuce swept the train with a discerning eye and aimed his flashlight across the wall. A box protruded from the rock. He walked over to it and opened the metal door. With great effort, he pushed up on a lever, and the train hummed to life. "Wanna ride?"

Molly stared at him.

"Or do you think we should walk?"

"There's no telling how far this goes." She shrugged. "Gordon said 'location unknown.' It couldn't be very close to the village, or he would have known where he was. And—and I'd think we'd have seen something if it weren't a long ways away. What I do know is we better take a couple of those outfits."

She gathered two tunics and two moccasin pairs, walked over to the train, and sat on a bench.

Deuce examined the box and pushed a large button. The train jerked and began to move forward.

Her eyebrows rose as she watched him fade away.

He ran and jumped onto a seat. Crouching, he stepped from bench to bench until he reached the front. "There're mechanisms up here," he called back to her. She stepped from seat to seat, lowering herself into the bench behind him, she asked, "Should we record this too?"

"Hmm. If the scenery changes I will. For now, let's just see where this leads."

She nodded and sat back, holding the clothes tight against her chest.

Little glowing mounds dotted the railway. Eventually, the mounds became sufficient lighting. They watched the crumbling rock wall in silence as the train hummed down the tunnel. Cold, saturating moisture cooled Molly's face, and her hair began to swell into a frizzed mess. She gathered it into her hand and slipped an ever present elastic tie over the aggressive mop. She flexed her stiffening fingers. This cool humidity made her bones ache. Or was it the underground pressure of the cavern? Or the radiation? She checked the scrolling readings.

"Are these levels dangerous?"

Deuce turned to look at her. He scanned his lower peripheral. "They're high, but not lethal with limited exposure."

"Okay, just checking." She stared at the crumbly wall sweeping by. What would they find at the end of this track? Was Gordon still alive? She drew in a slow, deep breath.

The hum of the train lulled Molly into a tranquil state. Time became obscure. Deuce reached down and pulled a lever. The train began to slow. A glow in the distance exposed a wide opening as if the tunnel simply opened like a vessel highway. The air seemed arid and crusty, and dried sweat tightened Molly's face. Beyond the tunnel's end appeared to be nothing but a blanched white space. Molly's gut told her there was a lot more. Should they walk, or more accurately, sneak out from here?

CHAPTER THIRTY-FIVE

Deuce squatted against the desiccated wall, mere yards from the tunnel's opening. Molly crouched behind him. They had to let their pupils adjust to the harsh double suns' light. Voices mumbled beyond the cavern. Mechanisms hummed and occasionally metal hit against metal. The sound of rocks or dirt sliding, then more mechanical humming indicated some sort of raw material was being transferred.

A harsh gravelly voice snarled, "Has this rat had water?"

"How would I know?" another snarled back.

"Well?" A thud, like something solid being kicked. "You need water or what?"

"Y-Yes. Please." A weak voice croaked.

Gordon! Deuce spun to see Molly's confirming expression. He motioned for her to follow. As one, they inched along the flaky wall. Molly strained to see into the bleached-out expanse beyond the tunnel.

Amazing how different this terrain looked compared to the plush tropical village. A chalky desert, dry and hazy with dust, extended as far as she could see. The two suns' heat scorched everything. She squinted, but it did little good. Uber dark glasses were required out here. She had none.

Cognitive thought keyed up the Bible cheat sheet. "'The fourth angel poured out his bowl on the sun, and the sun was allowed to scorch people with fire.' Revelations 16:8."

A reflective smile creased her lips, if only Marti knew how responsive her program had been to Molly's thoughts. Certainly this planet's two suns' scorching heat exemplified God's wrath in end times. A shiver raised her head. "Not now, Lord," she prayed.

A figure crouched to the right of the tunnel's opening. He appeared to be attached to a desert vessel. His dark skin covered in the chalky dirt made him look like the reverse image of a coal miner back on Earth. A tunic covered figure bent toward him, perhaps he was being given water.

Deuce looked down at his feet, and then picked up a small rock. He glanced at the workers. The guards had moved on to other duties or interests. The man had walked away. Deuce tossed the stone toward Gordon.

Gordon's eyes moved first, then his head. His face lit up and his eyes widened in a nonverbal communication but stayed silent.

Deuce gestured, "Stay there."

Gordon shrugged one shoulder.

Molly ducked out from behind Deuce for a quick smile and wave, and darted over to the train bench where she'd laid the tunics. She slipped one over her head and pulled the scrub shirt out from under it, leaving the green scrub pants on underneath. The exchange of fabrics irritated her rash, but she suppressed the desire to rub the red bumps. Tossing a tunic to Deuce, she leaned over to pull off her scrub shoes and replaced them with the soft leather boots. She scraped her unruly hair back into a baggy bun and pulled the hair tie around to hold it in place.

Deuce had changed clothes, too. His garment hugged his adult-size chest. The knees of his pants could be seen between the tunic and the boots. Thank goodness the garments were meant to be worn loose. An unfamiliar sensation zinged through her nerves. She shook her head to focus her thoughts. He had piled his clothes on the train bench next to her scrub top. Together they crowded next to the entrance and scanned the scene. A pale yellow wall of crumbling rock was to their left. A raw opening to another cavern tunnel split a wide maw in the wall. Spindly red-orange flowers covered the mound and trailed off into the distance.

X still marks the spot, AF had messaged. Could the innocuous beauty of these flowers be the source of Molly's poison?

A huge dirt-hauling vessel hovered next to the cavern, and a front-end loader scooped from a mountainous pile of pinkish-purple rocks.

Deuce pointed at the rock. "The ore?"

Molly shrugged and nodded.

Voices echoed from the cavern's mouth. Two guards led a procession of tunic covered youth, a short pelt of fur covered their otherwise exposed skin. Each pushed a cart, or carried a basket, filled with the purple rock. Their expressionless faces, neither happy nor sad, seemed focused on their task, and their shuffling feet continuously moved them forward.

The guards parted at the opening and stationed themselves on either side, flanking the workers egress. The teens dumped their carts and baskets onto the existing pile, filed over to a large vessel, where the same tunic clad man who had given Gordon water, stood. Several women stood with him, wearing the same earth tone tunics.

He poured a clear liquid into a metallic cylinder, held out by the youth and tethered to the child's waste. The man spoke softly to each one and they responded with an affirmative nod. His right eye was nearly swollen shut and surrounded by purple and green bruising. Some of the women handed the children a bulbous biscuit, food perhaps, while others filled their cylinders with the clear liquid. The procession pivoted to reenter the cavern, led by the two guards.

Deuce turned to Molly, his eyes wide with alarm. "I get it now." He barely breathed the words.

"What?" she mouthed.

"You said the ladies at the aquifer said no one worked in the mid-day suns."

"Right?"

"These clones are a hybrid of the Omicron-human DNA splice. They had just enough of the wolf-fur to protect their skin from the harsh suns."

Molly nodded and watched the procession.

"That man!" he mouthed the words. "Those women…"

She stared at them. Was this the missing Pastor Oliver Pugh? And the missing women? Was this what happened to the ones who went against the system? How had Kita escaped this?

Deuce motioned toward the water line. She nodded and crouched low. They scurried over to approach the man without notice. Deuce slipped up behind the man and clasped one hand over his mouth, the other around his arms and chest, immobilizing him. The man struggled, dropping his bladder full of water. Mud splattered on their boots as water blended with dirt. The women huddled together, but didn't make a sound.

Deuce held tight. The man leaned forward and reared backward, unable to loosen Deuce's hold. Finally, he stopped and lifted his hand, bent only at the elbows because of Deuce's hold.

Deuce held on a moment longer, slowly releasing the man. He didn't flinch. He didn't holler out. Deuce spun the man around and stared into his eyes. The man glanced at Molly and returned his startled eyes back to meet Deuce's.

Deuce put an index finger to his mouth and lifted the nearly empty bladder to the man's hands. He received it and stood still. Deuce slid up next to the vessel. Molly followed close behind him. They inched their way down the length of the carrier. One last glance at the man. He continued to fill cylinders but kept a weary watch on them. Deuce darted over to Gordon, closely followed by Molly.

He was bound by plastic ties looped together to form a chain, ending in a final loop through a D-ring welded to the cargo vessel. Deuce yanked on the plastic chain. It held strong. He looked around. The guards were busy in a zealous argument over something held between them. They threw it down and all but one cheered. The one cursed, which sounded like a cross between a dog growling and a human speaking an ancient old-world language. They were gambling.

"You gotta nail file, something?" Deuce whispered to Molly.

She tilted her head and glared at him. "A nail file? Seriously?"

He shrugged.

Gordon struggled to reach into his pocket and handed Deuce a Swiss-region multi-tooled knife. "Here!"

Deuce leaned back and whispered. "And why do you need us?"

"Where would I go?" Gordon shrugged.

Deuce cut the plastic from Gordon's wrists. The three ran the length of the cargo vessel, and returned to the mouth of the cavern. The man with water slipped out of the shadows, startling the three.

"What are you doing here?" the man whispered.

Up close Molly could see his lip was slit and swollen. "Pastor Oliver?"

"Yes, I'm…Oliver Pugh. But what are you doing here? One word and those guards will kill you."

"Not if we can help it." Deuce reassured him, glancing at the blanched-out entrance.

"If you were going to sound an alarm, you'd already done it." Deuce waited for his reaction. The two men stared at each other. "I'm Deuce Abraham, and this is—"

"I know who she is," His dirty face flushed. "You came because of your sister."

"Yes."

"So, it worked." Redness rimmed his open watery eye. The nearly closed one seeped.

"I suppose." Molly glanced toward the guards.

"This isn't how it looks." Pastor Oliver licked dry lips. "I-I'm here because it's the only way I'm allowed to stay alive."

"But why *are* you out here?" This man may very well have saved her sister's life, but could he be trusted now?

"This was Abraham's idea of a compromise. He banished me from the village and put me here to minister to the cloned children of the mines. Occasionally, I'm utilized on transportation vessels to deliver their goods. You, unfortunately, were once one of those goods. I thanked God when you escaped."

Deuce gestured toward the man's face. "That how you got those?"

Pastor Oliver ducked his head and nodded.

"Come with us!" Molly whispered.

"I can't." Pugh stepped toward the entrance. "I'd be killed. Besides, the children need food and water."

"We'll be back for you...all of you," Deuce assured him.

"Does Lucy know you're here?" Molly again stepped up closer to the Pastor.

Cheers wafted from the guards in the gambling circle.

"I don't know what Lucy knows. We—we haven't been allowed any communication since…"

"HEY!" One of the three guards shouted at Pastor Oliver.

Gordon touched Deuce's shoulder. "We need to go."

Deuce glanced back at Pugh, but he was gone. "Okay. The sooner we get back, the sooner we can get all of them outta here."

Pugh had approached the guards and appeared to be vehemently arguing with them.

Gordon pushed Molly toward the train, followed by Deuce.

"Wait!" Deuce turned suddenly. He stood at the tunnel entrance, touched his iComm link, and scanned the scene they were leaving. Finally, Deuce touched his iComm link and whispered, "Okay, let's go."

A gunfire exploded, the echo reverberating through the cavern. Molly and the men ducked low in their train seats. Gordon pushed the train's mechanism to maximum speed. Bullets zinged off the crumbling walls, ricocheting down the tunnel.

"Deuce!" she cried out. "Pastor Oliver?"

"Stay low," Deuce shoved her down, leaving a protective arm around her shoulders.

***

Davidette gathered her singers together, and they filled the risers at the end of the Great Hall. She blew a tuning whistle, and the group hummed a perfect C. She lifted her arms, her index fingers pointing as she brought her arms down.

Jody led in soprano, harmonized by Miriam, Pam, and Alyce. Hayden and Julio added a third low-alto harmony, and Daniel added a fourth tenor. Reah, Sonya and Roma joined in with harmonizing soprano.

The song was lovely. The guests of honor passively listened, lulled by the melodic seduction of song and a full stomach. Four amazing hymns later, the pilgrims exited the risers.

A team of gymnasts tumbled, ran, and skipped to the stage area. The group of twelve, seven Omicronians and five missionary recruits, delighted their audience with gravity-defying rolls, spins, somersaults, and balancing acts.

Next, a dance team, consisting of a variety of members from a three-year-old blended Omicron child to a twenty-five-year-old missionary recruit, gracefully entered the stage area. They danced an expressionist interpretation of a local favorite, "I Believe in God." An enthusiastic round of applause rewarded their performance.

Following the dance team, a group of Omicron children, including AJ Lupus, filled the risers. The children's Music Director, an adult Omicron woman, squatted four feet in front of them and began the performance of a medley from the movie, "A Summer Bunny," a family favorite, it had cutesy expressions and a catchy tune that entertained the audience, parents and the like. Even Mr. Abraham appeared to be amused by the children's associated gestures and antics. Only Dr. Stork sat with a sour face and heaved bored sighs. Lucy Pugh, as had become her new normal, sat in silence and stared at some distant spot on the ground.

As the children jumped and clambered from the risers, another choir waited to enter the multi-leveled structure. They halted when virtual screens appeared on both sides of the stand. Davidette motioned for the waiting choir to return to their seats. Static filled the Great Hall along with murmuring and excited chatter.

Davidette scanned her group as anxious eyes stared at the illuminating screens. She couldn't help but smile as her gaze returned to the screens. *This oughta be good.*

***

"Hi, everyone." Deuce glanced behind himself and returned his gritty, sweat-glazed face to fill the huge screens and swallowed hard. A blurred, dark-rock wall shifted away behind him as if he were moving down a long tunnel at a tremendous speed. He half squatted, half stood and appeared to be quite off balance.

Chatter rose in the Great Hall, and a passive applause expressed the audience's confusion.

"Dr. Deuce Abraham here, we're coming to you live from a place outside the village. But first, I want to thank Davidette, Julie, and everyone on my missionary team for making this possible." His voice shook with the roughness on which he traveled. "This banquet has been held to honor you, Dad, and The Highly Exalted Lupuses, and Dr. Stork, for all that you do for The Abraham Project."

Davidette scanned the table of honor. Austin Abraham's chin rose slightly, a wary look washed over the Lupuses, and Dr. Stork appeared alarmed. Lucy Pugh's face drained of all color but she sat statue still. A smug sensation washed over Davidette. She returned her attention to Deuce's image.

"I'd like to say that I'm amazed by the work you have done here over the past twelve years. And in all honesty, I *am* impressed with the breakthroughs you have accomplished with fertility research, perfecting the interspecies DNA splicing, and bringing populace back to these people. But—" Deuce lost his balance, and fell forward. Whoever held the camera seemed to be affected by the same rough course.

He stiffened and returned to an upright position. "But you have been far too humble." He wagged his finger at his perceived audience. "You have done so much more through this project. Your science has extended far beyond just restoring reproduction. You have found an *ingenious* solution to the problem of mining the planet's key resource for power in spite of the radiation hazards, which caused the fertility problems in the first place."

"I applaud you and your talents." Deuce clapped his hands. "Come on, everyone, let's give a standing ovation for the brilliance of this team of leaders."

Deuce clapped with enthusiasm as if he was in the room. The audience in the Great Hall stood to join him with jubilation toward the honorees. Davidette and her team stood, so as not to stand out, but their claps were less passionate. Their faces tightened with curiosity. What did Deuce know?

The Great Hall's doors opened, and with keen purpose, security personnel began to file into the room. Black Kevlar body armor covered their Khaki uniforms. Roger Dunn led a group who went left, another officer led a group who went right. Davidette watched the men and women, Omicronians and humans, line up along the walls on both sides of the celebrators, guns held vertical to their chests, but ready. They made no effort to do anything other than watch the screens. She turned her see Abraham's reaction. His face glazed with moisture, and his eyes darted about the large room. All exits were blocked.

Mrs. Lupus gracefully floated over to the children's Choir Director and leaned into her. The director nodded and began gathering the children, dancers, gymnasts and singers into a huddled mass. Mrs. Lupus smiled warmly at her son and several other children as they followed the director to the farthest end of the room. The security personnel observed their progress. As the cluster neared the doors, a security person stepped into their path. The director halted, and the children bumped into one another behind her. Fearful concern washed over Mrs. Lupus's face. The Security person solemnly pushed the door open. The Director and the children scurried out the door.

Worry slid from Mrs. Lupus's face as the children exited the Great Hall. Her eyes met Davidette's, and a slight tilt of her head acknowledged approval between the two. She returned to her place next to her husband and sat with an air of regal expectancy.

Deuce began speaking again. Davidette's glare stayed on Mr. Abraham and his honorees. He and Stork looked like rabbits in a snare.

"Let me show you what these amazing leaders have done for this planet." Deuce looked away from the camera. He spoke to someone to the left. "Do you have that recording…Okay. Yeah…"

A moment of static and a shaky picture of the specimen-growing room soon appeared. "Ah, here we have what I like to call 'the Farm.' It seems you have been growing your own workers."

Tube after tube panned past the screen in a jerky motion as if the bearer of the camera were walking along the long line from infants to teens.

A single gasp escaped the entire audience as many collapsed into their seats. A soft murmur filled the air.

"You can see, at least I think you can see, these specimens are from the Earth recruits' selfless and graciously volunteered donations, but with a hybrid wolf-like trait that covers them with a solar-protecting layer of fur. These specimens look like clones to me. And, trouble is, Dad, I don't think this is what the recruits agreed to when they signed the affidavits. In fact, I suspect you took more from their pathological donations than they realized. I know for a fact that at least one recruit went back to Earth completely sterile."

Abraham jerked to his feet, and Lupus followed. Stork glanced around but made no effort to join the other two. The audience's murmurs rose to an audible chatter. Fear and shock filled the recruits' eyes. Davidette immediately reassured her group. "We haven't submitted to anything yet. We're all right."

The security people moved closer to the head table, but still made no effort to stop the movements of the two who had been honored. Mrs. Lupus remained seated beside Dr. Stork. Grave resolution filled her face and Stork's, although neither glanced at the other. Lucy sat as if she were in an executioner's chair, hands flat on the table, back pressed against the seat, eyes straight ahead fixated on something.

"Now, why would anybody need to grow these clones? You all may be wondering. Well, we think we've found the answer to that question. You cannot see my personal data output... What? Oh, you can link it. Okay, look at the bottom of the screen. You will see a yellow flashing light and data scrolling across the bottom."

The specimen tubes footage froze in a blurred view of a ten or twelve year old child with suspended bubbles and blue liquid, and the data began to scroll. "If you are not familiar with these output readings, these are the radiation warnings in my personal iComm link. These numbers indicate there is an impressive level of radiation exposure in this incubation room. My guess is you are developing cell regeneration in these cloned children so that, as they develop, they will be able to work in an area high in radioactivity and not be inhibited by the exposure." Deuce's face filled the screens as if he had leaned into the camera. "How close am I on this, Dad? Stork?"

His mouth split in a sardonic smile. "Now, ladies and gentlemen, let us show you why these clones have been grown in this lab."

Static blanched the screens for a moment. Youth, in dirty tunics and knee-high moccasins, pushed carts and carried baskets into a cavern. The view panned over to a pile of purple crystals, and then over to a large scooping mechanism digging into the other side of the pile and dumping purple gravel into a large vessel.

"But wait!" Deuce's voice spoke as the scene panned to a dozen or so women huddled against a large vessel, and then to Pastor Oliver speaking animatedly with three Omicron guards.

Lucy Pugh gasped, covering her mouth with a trembling hand and seemed to go limp in her chair.

"Good news! We found Pastor Oliver Pugh! And several women who had been presumed missing. Seems they had been *reassigned* to work out here at the Colonies, providing food and water for the cloned workers. In fact, if it weren't for Pastor Oliver, we wouldn't be coming to you now." Deuce's eyes reddened and he cleared his throat.

"Oh, and there's a store-house outside of the village that has a large supply of cryogenic tubes. These tubes have been loaded on cargo vessels and taken somewhere else, I'm not sure where, but I suspect my dear Father has been pirating the very thing he had been sent here to restore."

CHAPTER THIRTY-SIX

The audience's chatter escalated to a loud roar. Abraham inched out from behind the table. His hand covertly slipped under his suit jacket. Lupus slipped out the opposite direction. Abraham yanked out a hand gun, and Lupus did the same.

The security team jerked their weapons into a lethal position, a multitude of clicks filled the air, and red dots covered Abraham's and Lupus' chests. Both froze in place.

A stunned hush fell over the audience. The screens froze on a scoop of purple ore falling into the large transportation vessel.

Stork stood, pressed himself against the back wall, and raised his hands in surrender. Abraham glanced at Dr. Stork, licked his lips, and slowly lifted his hands. The gun held loosely in his right fist. Lupus growled fiercely and leaped onto the lead security team member closest to him.

"NO!" Mrs. Lupus jerked to her feet. Lucy sat catatonic staring straight ahead. She didn't even flinch with the gun fire.

Mr. Lupus' body fell limp at the security line's feet. Dark red blood pooled beneath his riveted body. Abraham's eyes darted between the two lines. He slowly moved back toward the table to stand next to Mrs. Lupus. The red dots stayed on his chest as he moved.

In one smooth motion, he grabbed Lily Lupus, yanked her in front of him like a shield, and pressed his weapon into her side. She gasped. Fear radiated from her eyes as she scanned the security team. No shots were fired. Lily glared at Roger Dunn who led the security line to her right. His eyes met hers as she tipped her chin ever so slightly. She drew in a large gulp of air, slammed her elbow into Abraham's ribs, and dropped to the ground.

Guns fired, and Abraham's body ricocheted back against the wall. A trail of blood streaked above his head as he slid down and sprawled against the floor. Lily crawled to Lucy's chair, pulled her down under the table, and the two crawled to the end of the banquet table to slowly stand with their hands in the air. Lily's face was stained with tears and blood, but she held her chin aloft in a regal, graceful demeanor. Roger Dunn grasped her and Lucy's bicep and pulled them away from the remaining honoree. Another officer relieved Roger and took the women down behind the security line. They exited the Great Hall. Roger pulled Stork, bound his hands behind his back, and escorted him out of the Hall.

The doors banged open, and the audience turned as one to see who entered.

Deuce, Molly, and Gordon ran into the Great Hall. Davidette and the recruits hurried to their friends, hugging them and commending them with accolades.

Molly glanced around. Two blood splattered walls, evidence of the horrible exchange, led her gaze to the two who lay in the pools of their own blood. She touched Deuce's arm.

He followed her fixed gaze to the same two mounds. His euphoric smile melted from his face, like wax sliding off a hot window pane. He walked slowly to his father's body and knelt beside him. His shoulders quivered as he covered his eyes with his hand and wept.

Molly and Davidette exchanged a look, and Molly walked over to Deuce. She knelt down behind him to touch his back.

He reached around, took her wrist, spun around as he stood, pulling her up with him. He buried his face into her shoulder and sobbed. She held him tight. Tears stung her eyes as his grief penetrated her soul.

"I'm so sorry," she sobbed.

"I can't believe how far this went. My dad... my own father robbed his own kind, exploited these people. He...stole those babies. God only knows where those children were sent."

A red light blinked in Molly's peripheral. Beyond it, Gordon stood among the recruits. His animated gestures indicated he was regaling them with his kidnapping and release. Molly's eyebrows pulled together. She touched her iComm link. "Access, message."

Well done, my dear -AF.

"Well done in deed." A deep gravelly voice spoke behind her. Molly turned around. Mrs. Lupus stood mere feet from her. A dark trail of tears stained the matriarch's mottled face. She held out her arms.

"Mrs. Lupus? You're AF?" Molly stared at the woman.

"Yes."

Molly walked into her embrace. Lily Lupus wrapped strong arms around Molly and whispered, "You have been so brave."

"You...are the one who sent me those messages?"

"Yes, my dear. It was I." Mrs. Lupus dabbed a handkerchief against her tear soaked eyes. "I have not agreed with my husband on many things. My heart is broken that it took his life to bring a halt to this madness. You are"—she swallowed hard—"of my son's birth-pack?"

Molly pulled back. How did she know?

"Yes, I know." Lily continued. "Your litter-mate...um, sis—ter, was treated harshly. It was Pastor Oliver's conviction to return her to Earth... but it was Dr. Stork who realized she must return alone. If she had returned with her babe, suspicions would not have been alerted. Pastor Oliver's efforts saved Kita from the fate that enslaved the women before her, and Dr. Stork's scheme brought you here to unravel this exploitation."

Lily lifted her chin nobly. "Miss Jacobsen's cross-bred child was given to me. There was nothing else for me to do but care for him as my own. I love AJ, and there is *nothing* I would not do for him."

Tears stung Molly's eyes. Michael was deeply loved by this woman. She had observed and sensed this many times. "You know I came here to retrieve him for my sister?"

"Yes, I know. But I wonder..." Lily glanced at her husband's body. "What is best? Your sister has had an empty cradle for over seven years, this must cloud her judgement. She is not aware it was the price of her freedom. Still a mother's heart longs for her child, not her liberty. Should you return her child to her, I wonder...

"I suppose someday he might fully understand the love that sought to right this wrong. I fear he will not see this...*reunion* from such a perspective. This life is all he has known, Miss Jacobsen. He is an intelligent child, but I cannot imagine he will comprehend..." Tears choked Lily's words. "Certainly, I empathize with a mother's broken heart. You have a difficult task before you, Miss Jacobsen. I do not relish the position you are in. In fact, I grieve, even now, anticipating the outcome. I suppose I have always feared this day when my joy would be removed from my heart."

Molly followed Lily's gaze, scanning the tragedy and stunned faces. Lily made a valid point. Michael had no idea the controversy his birth and adoption had caused. He was an innocent.

What was best for Michael? How could Molly take him away from the only mother he had ever known? And how could she make Kita understand? As horrible as the thought was, could it be true? He *was* where he belonged? She bit her lip and returned her gaze to Lily.

"I—I don't know what to do," she murmured.

A subtle smile curled at the ends of Lily's mouth. She touched Molly's arm. "I am confident you will make the right decision. One thing I have learned from your people, you have a mighty deity to whom you turn in times such as this. I have witnessed impressive results from your connection. I, too, shall be praying as I have been taught for wisdom in your decision. Although I must confess my prayers shall be slanted. For my desires are strong in the outcome of this matter. Now, if you will excuse me, I must tend to my husband's tragic demise. This, too, will be difficult for little AJ."

Molly stared at Lily as she floated away. The matriarch knelt beside her husband's body. Leaning across him, she began to tremble and whimper. Other Omicronian's gathered around her. As if they had been cued by an invisible orchestral leader, they lifted their heads and cried out a mournful wail.

Molly jerked, her gut clinched, and her heart broke. Their pain penetrated her senses. She turned to leave the Great Hall. Her victory here was now muddled by consequential repercussions, and all she wanted to do was be alone…and cry.

***

Deuce stepped back from Molly. Something had caught her attention. He turned to Gordon and scraped the tears from his face. "What a mess."

Gordon looked around. "Yeah, but you're gonna fix it, right?"

"What? Fix it?" Deuce stared at Gordon's dust covered face.

"Sure. It's the logical next step. You're Abraham's son. It's The Abraham Project. Who better than you?"

"Man, I don't know the first thing about all this."

"That's why you're perfect for the job." Gordon grasped Deuce's shoulder. "Besides, why not start with asking the people who are here what they want?"

"That makes sense." Deuce rubbed the back of his head. He had a lot to think about. He scanned the room. Where was Molly?

The Great Hall's doors opened wide as two gurneys were shoved through. Deuce joined the paramedics and helped gather his father's body into the body bag. Mr. Lupus was loaded up as well, and the two gurneys exited through the same two doors. Deuce rode shotgun in the emergency vessel. No sirens were needed. Nor was an autopsy.

Despite decorum, he would clean his father's body and prepare him for…whatever. The morgue staff would have to understand. This was the least he could do for his father now. Only one question remained. Send him back to Earth, or bury him here on Omicron? He'd have to think that one through. Maybe counsel with Pastor Oliver.

Would his mother want him buried next to her? He had no idea. Would the Omicronians be against his burial here? What he did was appalling, yet there was good that came of it. The future had been restored to many. Children were thriving on this planet again. Another generation was present, where there had been no chance for one. And if he could send Stork's findings to the Cancer Research Institute back on Earth—

Deuce sighed. He just needed to think.

The morgue had a large central room, flanged by four individual rooms. Lupus had been placed in room number one, and Abraham had been placed in room number two. Deuce stood in the second room, alone.

The staff had entered, but he waved them away. Silent understanding seemed to pass between their eyes as they slipped out of the small room.

Sliding on thick purple gloves and a dark-green apron, he picked up clear protective glasses but put them back down. The thick opaque bag encasing his father's body exemplified the barricade between him and the man he had never really known. Staring at the large tabbed zipper, he took a deep breath and pulled the tab down. The zipping sound reverberated in his heart. If only it could have been this simple to connect with his dad.

Why did it have to come to this? What was his father after, really? Was it just the money? He gently pulled the open bag apart and pushed it down on either side of his father's lifeless form. Death had already begun to affect his father's features. Deuce cupped a gloved hand to stroke his father's hair. *Did you have to go so far away from mom and me to find happiness?*

Deuce closed his eyes and clinched his teeth. His mother's loving, sweet face floated into his thoughts. There was always an air of worry. Had this man caused that worry? All those Christmases and birthdays, a gift was always there from Dad. But was it really? Did he ever really love either of them? Deuce cut through the luxurious tuxedo and pulled the ruined fabric away.

He turned to the cabinet, pulled out supplies, and prepared them for cleaning his father's body. Soon, he was ready and turned back to the table. He again pulled the body bag back away from his father's flesh. Squeezing gauze squares, he began cleaning the dried blood. Long, gentle strokes loosened and removed all traces of today's horrible end.

Tears stung his eyes as he gritted his teeth and continued to perform this most sacred ritual of cleaning the dead. It would be his last loving act for his father. The thought came to his mind again. He couldn't help but wonder. *Did you love me, Dad? Did you love Mom?*

With great care, he cleaned each laser-burned intrusion on his chest. Doing all he could on the front, Deuce rolled his dad over and returned to the cabinet. He poured out the crimson water and rinsed out the pan. Adding fresh water, gauze and soap, he turned back to the metal table.

That's when he saw it. He froze in place. His knuckles blanched in his grip on the bath pan. Abraham had a tattoo on the back of his right arm. Two cards—the Queen of Hearts and the Deuce of Hearts, fanned out like a hand in poker. His dad had always referred to him and his mother as these two cards. They were his wild cards.

The weight of the pan became too much. Deuce set it down on the table with a loud thud. He'd read about these permanent markings in medical school. For numerous political reasons, they had been outlawed on Earth over a century ago. Had he gotten it made here?

Deuce yanked off his glove and touched the tattoo with two fingers. Tears streaked his face. Somewhere, somehow, deep down as it may have been, this man loved his wife and only son. He couldn't express it as other's would. But he did make a permanent declaration of it by having this ink put on his body. He had never said it, but it was there for Deuce to find. Maybe he knew something like this would be his final opportunity to reach out and tell his son, "You were important to me."

Deuce shook his head. He picked up the soapy gauze as tears streamed down his face, and continued to clean his father's body. Perhaps it would be best to send him home and bury him beside his mother. Maybe in death the two could lie in peace, side by side. Deuce lifted his head. A bolt of fear shot through his gut.

Had his dad sought salvation? What was his eternal fate? That thought smashed into his gut like a sudden, unexpected rabbit punch. He felt ill. He stepped back from the table and collapsed into a chair and prayed for his father's soul. Only time would answer that question.

CHAPTER THIRTY-SEVEN

Molly sat cross legged on her bed staring at nothing, processing what had happened. All forty-eight recruits gathered in the living quarter's common room. No one wanted to go to bed or be alone, except Molly. Their muffled voices wafted into her solitary room. It was enough knowing they were out there.

Had she accomplished what she set out to do? Had she avenged her sister's loss? Should she now go back to Earth? Why did that thought make her want to cry? What was it about this place? Was this from God? Had this all been predestined?

Her eyes fell upon the tattered, leather covered book. Her father's Bible. She pulled it onto her lap. The book fell open, and she stared at the highlighted words. "Jeremiah 29:11, 'For I know the plans I have for you,' declares the Lord, 'plans to prosper you and not to harm you, plans to give you hope and a future.'"

Her father had underlined key words.

Not to harm you. Kita was heartbroken, Molly had been terrified, Lily would be heartbroken, and what about Michael? Yet, the Word said God did not intend harm. Could this mean these painful things were happening to…*prosper* them? Molly shook her head.

Hope and a future. Did she have a future here? Would it be fair to her family? That was what Kita had planned to do. Kita! Thank God Pastor Oliver had intervened and sent her off planet. But, was it fair for Molly to be the one who stayed and interact with Kita's son while her sister stayed on Earth and did not?

Pastor Oliver probably saved Molly and Deuce's lives today…and Gordon's. She closed her eyes against the memory of the bullets ricocheting in the tunnel. Was Pastor Oliver all right? Or was he martyred for their cause?

A rumble of laughter echoed from the common room. These people had saved her life. In this short time, she had grown to…love them. And Deuce. What did she feel for Deuce?

A warm peaceful sensation washed over her. The thought of Deuce, the too-tight tunic revealing his sculpted muscles, caused a warm feeling to percolate in her mid-section. A smile forced itself onto her lips. He certainly went out of his way to rescue her and keep her safe. Those weeks on the ship, they had grown close. Did she love him? Did he love her?

Molly walked out to the common room. Weary smiles greeted her. She pulled up a chair, turned it around, and sat backward on it. Leaning her arms across the back she rested her chin on her wrists. "So. What now?"

The door opened, and all eyes swung to the entrant. Deuce crossed the threshold. An exhausted smile creased Molly's lips. His eyes met hers. Tears filled his fatigued eyes, and his lip began to quiver. He stretched out his arms, and she rose and stumbled into his embrace. Davidette stood. The others joined her and applauded the two who had become their heroes.

"I'm so sorry." Molly whispered into Deuce's ear.

"I know." He held her tight. "It's all right."

She leaned back to look into his eyes and knitted her brow.

"You'll never believe what I found." He shook his head.

She tilted hers.

"I'll tell you later." He patted her back, and they released their embrace. The pilgrims ran to them, and everyone hugged and cried.

"We need to talk. But surely we need to get some rest." Deuce spoke above the chatter.

"We're all too wound up, Deuce," Hayden said.

Deuce nodded. He pulled up a chair and sat backward. "Well. We need to talk about what you want to do? Stay here or go back to Earth. I've already sent a security team to rescue Pastor Oliver." He paused and glanced at Molly. "I hope he'll be in the infirmary before morning. And we need to figure out what to do about the hybrids, the young people in the mines...and The Abraham Project."

"They're just children, aren't they?" Davidette said. "Those poor kids. They're such innocents."

"Yes, they are about thirteen to twenty years old. Although, I think they were…cultivated in about four years."

"Will they continue to grow at such an accelerated rate?" Miriam asked.

"I have no idea." Deuce shook his head. "If they do, their life span would be about a third of ours."

Davidette stated, "I don't want to leave. I want to stay. And I want to take those children from the mines and see that they are cared for, educated, and…" She sat down. Tears filled her eyes.

"Keep in mind," Deuce added. "These clones are a hybrid, they're a whole other race of species here. Their assimilation may not be such an easy one. Who knows?"

Hayden said, "And I recognize the need for mining that ore. It's a major fuel source. But I don't see why, with all the modern technology we've brought and developed here, we can't convert the mining process to a robotic system." His eyes darted from Deuce to the others.

"Maybe," Daniel said as he scanned the group. "If these children are immune to the radiation, we can educate them and have some of them oversee the robotic operations. Like Engineers or Managers. That might be a prime career choice for those who want to do that. But they need to be given the chance to grow up and make those decisions for themselves."

Deuce swallowed as he nodded. He turned to Gordon. "What do you think?"

Gordon looked up. Surprise flashed in his eyes. "I—I think these are all prime ideas. I think it's doable. I'm sure Stork will be able to give us some answers. Our first priority is to see if Oliver and the other women are all right."

Mumbles rippled through the recruits. "Why? What happened?" Miriam spoke up for the first time.

Deuce, Molly, and Gordon exchanged a glance and Deuce cleared his throat. "We left him arguing with the Guards, and then we heard gun fire. W-We have no idea if they're all right."

The recruits sat in stunned silence.

"We need to pray." Jacque Breneé stood up. He led them in a long and heart-felt prayer for Pugh's and the women's safety, thanksgiving for Deuce, Molly, and Gordon's return, peace and comfort for Mrs. Lupus and her son. He quoted Bible passages related to what he asked of the Lord and ended with, "All these things we ask in your son's holy name, Amen."

The recruits sat silent once again. After some time, Davidette stood up. "I think we should bring the cloned children here."

Julio stood next. "Maybe shut down operations until we can get the robotics in place. But, Deuce… we need to get the Omicronians on board. This takes The Abraham Project in a maximumly different direction. But I think it's the right direction."

"Deuce." Molly bit her lip and fought rebellious tears. "What about the canisters we found? How many women are affected by this?"

She glanced at Gordon. "Can we find where those cryo-tubes were sent? Can any of that be retrieved?"

He shrugged.

Deuce rubbed the back of his head. "Well. They can't be put back, but we have them in the lab basement, and we know who they belong to. I suppose we can just maintain that system, and when the time comes, we can inseminate."

"But..." Molly choked on tears. "What about Kita?"

Deuce sighed. "I don't know."

"So..." Davidette's lip trembled. "We all might have been...robbed?"

"Molly and I were there when you nine were suspended. Molly told you all to hold off on volunteering any pathologicals, remember." Deuce cleared his throat. "I'm positive you are fine. But to be safe, let's schedule every female and have you tested. But the previous recruits—" He glanced at the other thirty-three fearful faces. Several of the men turned to comfort the women. They had been here for years. How many of them had already joined in union? This was already a real issue.

Silence hung between them, like a thick cloud of cold vapor.

"Okay." Davidette reached out and squeezed Miriam's hand.

"Ladies, why don't we organize some of you to help with that? Personnel will be overtaxed at the infirmary if we don't."

"Sure," Jody said. "I'll help."

"Me too," Pam said.

All the women nodded.

"Davidette, you start scheduling everybody tomorrow. Get with Deuce and determine a reasonable time span." Molly said.

Davidette nodded as did Deuce.

"What if..." Carol's eyes filled with tears. "They don't want us to stay? What if they send us home, like they did Kita Jacobsen?"

Deuce took in a long breath. "First of all, you need to know, Kita was rescued. Pastor Oliver risked his own life to be sure she was sent home. Stork too, they knew it would start an investigation, and... well it did. But to answer your question, if the Omicronians want us to leave, well, then I suppose we go home. It *is* their planet after all."

Carol blinked, and tears trailed down her cheeks. "I-I don't want to leave. At least here I can watch my daughter grow up, even if I can't claim her as my own."

Others nodded as tears rolled down their cheeks.

Molly scanned the anxious faces. "We'll talk to the leaders tomorrow."

"Who is that?" Daniel gestured with his hands. "His High Exalted was killed tonight."

Molly smiled. "I have a feeling his wife will be taking his place."

"What?" Several people gasped.

"It turns out she is the one who has been sending me clues to this whole piracy."

"Wow. Really?" Sonya's eyes widened.

Molly sighed. "We really need to stop that mining and get our people back here immediately…and the hybrids."

Gordon nodded. "Agreed."

Fatigue weighed Molly's limbs. She lifted her eyes to Deuce. "I really think we all need to go to bed."

Deuce nodded. "We have a lot to do, and none of it can be done until in the morning. So, Molly's right. Let's try to get a decent night's sleep. It's already after midnight."

He glanced at his peripheral clock. "Let's regroup at oh-nine-hundred."

Davidette frowned. "What is that? Nine o'clock?"

A giggle rippled among the recruits. Miriam nodded. Davidette mumbled, "Why can't we just use normal time?" Everyone stood.

"Wait!" Hayden blocked Daniel from walking away. "Haven't we forgotten something?"

Blank stares answered his question. "We need to ask God for guidance in all this...tomorrow and —"

"You're right." Miriam bowed her head and waited a moment. Everybody clasped hands with the one standing next to them. She gave thanks and asked for the Lord's guidance, acknowledging the huge task ahead of them. She prayed for God to give Deuce wisdom. "Lord, we claim your words for Deuce, guide him as Second Chronicles one, verse ten says, 'Give him wisdom and knowledge, that he may lead this people, for who is able to govern this great people of yours?' and Lord help us turn this evil around for your good as Proverbs two, verse twelve tell us, 'Wisdom will save you from the ways of wicked men, from men whose words are perverse.'"

Miriam went on, pouring out her soul to the Lord. Every eye remained close. "Yes Lord" and "Hallelujah" resounded among the forty-seven. Eventually, she closed with, "In Jesus's name, Amen," and the others repeated it.

Knuckles wiped eyes as everybody turned to seek their solitude. Hopefully, sleep would come easily. Molly stepped closer to Deuce. "What about Michael?"

"I don't know. This is so complicated."

Molly's shoulders rounded. "I agree."

"Sleep on it. Let's talk about it tomorrow." Deuce caught her arm. She turned to him. "You might...want to pray about it."

She shrugged.

***

Molly sat on top of her covers. Sleep evaded her grasp. A tempest of images spun in her head.

Kita's desperate hold on a doll she claimed was her child. Michael singing with the children's choir. The joy between him and the only mother he has ever known. The long row of various sized, fur covered children floating in bubbling tubes of blue life fluids. Dirty, tunic clad teenagers marching from the mouth of the mines. Their lack of expression haunted her more than their existence. The blood splattered wall above Abraham's body. The dark pool beneath Lupus'. Mrs. Lupus' outstretched arms.

Her stomach knotted. Nausea tightened her throat. She closed her eyes and rocked back and forth. Tears spilled down her face, and a moan escaped her lips. Her eyes popped open, and her father's Bible centered in her view. She pulled it to her chest and hugged the leather binding as if she were hugging her own father.

"Oh God, please," she whimpered. "Please help me do what's right. Kita deserves to have her son. But Michael doesn't deserve to be ripped away from Lily. Why does it have to be so complicated? Jesus, Jesus, I don't know what to do."

Molly rocked, clinging to the Bible. It slipped from her hands and fell into her lap. She glanced down and wiped her eyes. Job 38 lay before her. Highlighted in blue by her dad's hand.

"Where were you when I laid the Earth's foundation? Tell me, if you understand. Who marked off its dimensions? Surely you know! Who stretched a measuring line across it? On what were its footings set, or who laid its cornerstone—while the morning stars sang together and all the angels shouted for joy?"

She lay back against her pillow and pressed the open Bible against her chest. Her hands resting on the soft leather cover. Silence engulfed her as she closed her eyes.

***

Troublesome images swirled in her mind, concentrating into a single column. The pillar morphed into a single figure of a man, dressed in long white robes, knelt in prayer. Dark beads of blood dripped from his brow. His lips moved, but she couldn't hear his words. She strained to listen. As if he realized she was near, he lifted his head. His tear-filled eyes looked deep into hers. He muttered, "Yet, not as I will, but as you will."

He approached her and stretched out his hand toward her. She reached for him. "Let God's will be done, Molly—"

Molly sat straight up in bed. When had she fallen asleep? She glanced at her peripheral clock. Eight o'clock. She had an hour.

Let God's will be done. What was that exactly? Molly stretched and pulled herself from the bed. She had promised her sister she'd bring Michael home. She'd promised their mother she would return, as well. Now she didn't know what to do. She glanced at her father's Bible. "A little help here?"

CHAPTER THIRTY-EIGHT

"Our meeting with the Omicronians won't happen today." Deuce pulled two cups of coffee from the dispenser. He looked tired.

Molly accepted one from him. "Why?"

"Today has been set aside to memorialize their fallen leader. Seems regardless of what he has done, he is revered and sovereign."

Molly nodded. "What about the mines? The children, the other women?"

"They are being transported to the infirmary as we speak."

Molly opened her mouth but then shut it. She stared at her coffee. Her eyes met Deuce's. "Pastor Oliver?"

Deuce's jaw muscles bulged. "He—Lucy's with him now. He was shot, but the security team we sent got to him in time. He's in bad shape, Molly. The radiation at the mines did a number on his system, and...I just don't know—"

Molly nodded and touched Deuce's arm. "What about your dad?"

Deuce swallowed hard. "Gordon is contacting the transportation system to see when we can get a vessel heading to Earth. He seems to think we can get in on a loop going that way. Perhaps the same one that brought us here."

A lead weight yanked her stomach to the floor. "So, you're taking him back to Earth?"

Steam rose from his cup. He stared at her. "I'm sending him home, yes. Whether I'm accompanying him there—I haven't decided."

She nodded. "I think...I might be on that vessel, so..." She skewed her jaw. "I could see to his departure for you."

"I—" He glanced around the galley. "I wasn't aware you'd made any decisions."

"I promised Kita...and Mom." She sipped her coffee, centering her eyes on the black liquid.

"What about Michael?" Deuce held his cup in a tight grip but did not sip.

She looked into his eyes. Tears swelled and stung her own. "I—just don't know what to do about him."

Deuce nodded. "Well, there's time."

They sat at a small table, holding their cups, but not drinking. A comfortable silence permeated the galley. At last, Molly said, "I suppose if today is dedicated to Lupus's memorial, I should change."

"Aw, don't change." He smiled. "I like you the way you are."

She wrinkled her nose. "Hardy-ho-ho."

"Go on, I'll let everybody know at the nine o'clock meeting."

Molly nodded, but her mind was on other things.

***

Omicronians of different hued pelts poured into the small village. Bright red, orange, yellow, green and blue hand-woven material with strips and florals adorned their torsos.

"It reminds me of a National Geographic spread." Gordon leaned into Molly so she could hear him speak over the mayhem.

"It reminds me of a carnival," Molly yelled back.

Percussion bands marched the same streets the recruits had paraded just the day before. It was the same music that greeted the new recruits when they first arrived. A multitude of children, appearing to range in age from eleven or twelve years old down to three or four, in gold and red costumes clumped together following the bands. Group after group of various performers followed the procession.

A large water-buffalo-like animal pulled an onyx wagon trimmed in ornate gold. Open windows on both sides revealed a black and gold banded cloth covering the sacred remains of their leader. Behind this, four Omicron men, scantily clad in a red-orange loin cloth and an elaborate neck garland of gold, carried an ornate golden chair on which Mrs. Lupus sat in all her grace and dignity. Her bright red wrap, held together with a gold rope at her waist, was accentuated by a golden garland hung around her neck. Michael clung to her side, and she embraced him with a comforting arm. He, too, wore red and gold.

"This must be their black for mourning." Davidette cupped her hand around her mouth, as she shouted to Molly.

Molly shrugged.

As Mrs. Lupus' carriage passed, the people along the parade path began to fall in behind. Eventually, the street emptied as the crowd followed the funeral procession down the transportation path out of the village. Percussion instruments continued to resound as the long line walked the several kilometers and gathered to the right of the road. A tall tower stood at the apex of the growing throng. The onyx wagon pulled up next to the pyre, and the four servants sat Mrs. Lupus' cart on the ground behind the wagon. With great ceremony and pomp, the servants opened the wagon and pulled out two long golden poles, between which Argenteus' body was suspended on a luxurious golden silk fabric.

The crowd stood silent.

The body was lifted high overhead and carried to the pyre. With great care and exact movement, the poles were slid into place. Mrs. Lupus and Michael gingerly walked up next to the tower. She began to hum. Michael tucked his face into her side, and she comforted him with one arm.

The sight of Michael, clinging to this woman's side, broke Molly's heart. She fought the urge to run to him and hold him.

The Omicronian's joined their matriarch in the song that seemed to be a softer version of a growl and yet, there was a rhythm to the melody. A tall, lanky male stepped forward. He wore an elaborate headdress of feathers and fur. His cape, adorned with many colored patches of fur, or maybe feathers, included wide-open sleeves and flowed to his feet. He spoke in a language native to the planet as he crawled up a narrow ladder and stood above Mr. Lupus' body. Reaching into the sleeves, he pulled out handfuls of powder and casted it upon the deceased, chanting in a sing-song manner as he dashed the powder across His High Exalted's body. Omicronians approached the death bed and tossed flowers as the priest continued his elaborate ceremony. This continued for hours.

At last, this part of the ceremony ended. Long strips of wood and bark were stacked over Mr. Lupus but not touching his body. It was as if the people were building a cocoon over him. This was meticulously supervised by the priest, and if the placement appeared to be incorrect, he would pull it out and throw it to the ground. Others would scurry to retrieve the wood and once again, place it over the body.

Molly stared at the unyielding process. Birds, or more appropriately, wolves building a nest, one accepting or rejecting the other's placement of each individual piece came to her mind. These people were not far removed from their feral lineage.

Eventually, the priest seemed to be satisfied with the arrangement of kindling, and he climbed down from the pyre. Another round of flower throwing began, accompanied by singing. This whole time, Mrs. Lupus and Michael stood stoic-still, observing but not participating in any of the preparations.

As this came to an end, Mrs. Lupus turned away from the funeral tower and walked over to a mound of dirt. The four men who had carried her cart followed her. She stood at one end and chanted something over the mound. The four men passed her and began digging with carved wooden paddles. Before long a mass, covered in leaves and encased in stiff netting, was lifted and carried to a large log that had been downed and halved. The outer encasings were pulled back. Large knives were raised into the air and brought down upon the roasted beast that lay beneath.

Mrs. Lupus stepped up to the side and held out a large green leaf with both hands. The chopped substance was scooped onto her leaf until it was deemed full. She gathered a small handful into her fingers and placed it in her mouth. She then fed some to AJ. Turning, she handed the leaf to the person next to her. They, in turn, ate a small amount, held by two fingers and a thumb, and passed the leaf along. This continued until everybody had eaten from the leaf. The four servants saw to it that the leaf remained filled with meat.

When the leaf reached the recruits, they glanced at one another. It looked and smelled like roasted beef. Davidette shrugged and scooped some into her mouth. She nodded approval and handed the leaf off to Hayden. They all participated.

The odd lighting of the Omicron dusk began to transition to a hazy grey-indigo. The priest approached Mrs. Lupus and sprinkled powder over her while he sang in the Omicronian's characteristic cross between a growl and whimper. The sky dulled, replacing the two suns' bleached out light, as the priest concluded his ceremony, he stepped away from the widow, never turning his back on her.

She and Michael walked over to the pyre and lifted a long stick covered in cloth on one end. A servant lit the cloth on fire, and she held the fire high above her head and made circles with the fiery light. Her lips moved. Was she praying...or chanting?

Ultimately, she touched the wooden cocoon with the torch, and it consumed the structure with hungry orange flames. She threw her torch onto the fire and pulled Michael away from the growing heat. All the Omicronians backed away several yards and watched in silence as the inferno rose.

Sparks popped, and red embers floated into the evening sky. Shouts of joy and exaltation rose from the Omicronians. Even Mrs. Lupus seemed to be rejoicing. Perhaps they believed the fire had taken Mr. Lupus's soul to heaven.

Molly privately wondered about the ceremony. The servants who had carried her chair stood at the ready on the four corners as she and Michael returned to their seat. They were lifted and carried back toward the Village. The locals knelt down on one knee as she passed through their multitudes and followed her away from the funeral fire. Only the ornately crowned priest remained with the burning pyre.

***

Hardly a word was spoken among the recruits. Exhaustion had taken its toll. All Molly wanted was to go to bed. By the looks of everyone else, so did they. Good nights and God's blessings were mumbled, and everyone separated as soon as they entered the quarters. Molly showered and dressed for bed, yet she couldn't fall asleep. She stared at her ceiling. Images of Kita, her parents, Michael, Lily Lupus, the frozen canisters, bubbling tubes, and growing embryos remained active in her mind. Would those visions ever stop haunting her?

She drew in a deep breath and let it out slowly. Deuce's words echoed in her thoughts.

You might want to pray about it.

She drew her father's Bible to her chest and slid off her bed. Kneeling like a child saying her Now-I-Lay-Mes, she squeezed her eyes closed, searching her mind for the right words. Tears oozed past her lashes in the oppressive silence. Words would not come. In this most humble position, she sobbed, "Jesus...Jesus...Jesus...I don't know what to do. I don't know what is best for Kita, for Michael, for me. I'm...terrified I'll flub up everybody's lives. I dreamed Jesus told me to let Your will be done...but I don't know what that is."

Molly crumpled to the floor, doubled over into a ball, and continued, "Please, God, hear me. Please help me. Please!" The desperation lifted from her heart and peace took its place. She flattened out on the floor, basking in the tranquility. She had never felt so much calm in her soul. At last, she muttered, "In Jesus's name, Amen."

It took all her willpower to climb back into bed. Serene sleep overtook her before she settled onto her pillow.

***

"Hey! Good news." Gordon turned in his chair as Molly entered the galley. Coffee aroma permeated the room. Deuce and Hayden sat with Gordon, but they pulled over a fourth chair for Molly.

"Huh?" It was all she could utter. Sleep still clung like cobwebs in her mind. She couldn't remember sleeping so soundly. Waking was now her problem.

"A transportation vessel can be here within the week."

A week! Panic shoved drowsiness aside. She sat down hard and stared at him. "Define 'within the week.'"

"Like five days."

"FIVE DAYS!" Molly jumped up and paced. *Five days.*

"I thought this was what you wanted." Gordon's pleading eyes met Deuce's. Deuce shrugged.

"I—I don't know what I want." Molly stopped and stared at the three men. "I've prayed about this, honest I have. I—God's will be done, was my answer." She pushed her hand through her hair, pulling it back from her forehead. "I just don't know what that means."

"You don't have to figure it out this minute." Deuce took ahold of her shoulders and guided her back into a chair. He filled a cup with coffee and handed it to her. "Besides, we don't know what the Omicronians want. We need to start there. All our decisions have to be based on what they say."

Molly nodded. She tried to swallow the coffee, but her throat felt too tight. She slammed the cup down and left the galley.

Immediately, sticking her head back in the door. "When are we meeting with Lily?"

"I'm waiting to hear from her now. I hope today." Deuce glanced at Gordon. Gordon nodded with a shrug, and Molly pursed her lips.

***

The entire population of Earth recruits gathered in the Great Hall. Lily Lupus and several other high ranking Omicronians sat at the head table. Deuce assumed the lead and stood to speak, "Your Highly Exalted, we thank you for meeting with us today."

Lily nodded. "Of course, Dr. Abraham."

"First, we offer our sincere condolences for your loss, and we apologize for intruding on your time of mourning."

She nodded.

"A transportation vessel will arrive, we believe, in five days, Mrs. Lupus. We need to know what you want from us. We could board it and leave you and your people, or we can stay and continue to help as you deem fit."

A surprised look washed over Lily's face but was replaced by her regal air of confidence. "What do you have in mind, if you were to stay?"

Deuce explained Davidette's desire to educate and incorporate the cloned children. He detailed the concerns for the Earth women and their potential loss of reproduction. He outlined the plan to test them and maintain the cellular storage for their future use. Last, he described their desire to convert all mining to robotics and offered continued support from the recruits to implement and program the machinery. "It would be a different direction for The Abraham Project, but if you were to allow us to stay, I feel it is the right direction, and I'm willing to do what I can to see that the Project serves your people in the way it was intended."

"And," Mrs. Lupus stated, "what would be your plans should we decide to evacuate the Project from our planet?"

Deuce stared at her. "We—we would need more than five days, I think. There is the issue with our people's stored cells. There is a whole lab of incomplete fetuses. And there is the population from the mines that would need to be assimilated into your cultures. There is also an issue with finding other...stolen...pathological..." Deuce ran his fingers through his hair. "But, yes, Lily, if you no longer want us here, we will leave."

"I see—"

A buzz of chatter rose.

Molly took hold of Deuce's hand and tried to pull him down. He pulled away. "We need time to sort this whole mess out. My—my dad caused this, but I'm the one who is now responsible for what has happened."

The officials leaned in toward Mrs. Lupus and spoke with animated gestures. She stood slowly and motioned for quiet.

"I can see that further discussions are needed to make appropriate decisions." The crowd quieted down. She remained standing but spoke in a softer tone. "We have grown quite fond of your presence. Now that we know who violated our trust, I feel confident that we can continue to have a symmm-biotic relationship with your people. However, I do not feel obliged to give you...your language would speak it as 'carte blanche,' as my husband did your father. I believe a closely monitored channel of communication is necessary, Dr. Abraham. That being said, I wish to extend to you a—" She smiled her canine grin. "—gesture of new peace and understanding, I grant you permission for proper funeral rites for your father." She bowed her head slightly.

Deuce stared at her. "Thank you, Your Highly Exalted, but I wish to send my father's remains back to Earth. However, if you are saying you are allowed to continue our work here, I do wish to stay."

Molly stared at him.

"As you wish." Mrs. Lupus dipped her head with great formality. "Yes, this is what I am saying. You and your recruits are welcome to stay and develop this new plan you discussed." Her court began to lean into one another and whisper. She held up a hand to silence them. "With closely monitored communication with myself, as I said before."

Deuce smiled. Mrs. Lupus had taken the reins and was already proving to be a noble leader for her people. He lowered his head. "Thank you, Your Highly Exalted."

CHAPTER THIRTY-NINE

Six days later, the transportation vessel arrived, and the shuttle was docked on the planet. Eight recruits chose to return to Earth. The four women were tested for fertility and found to be void. Their frozen specimens were located and carefully prepared for them to take home. Deuce, along with Dr. Stork, documented their medical records for the receiving healers and explained everything to them as well.

It was decided by the Omicron counsel that Dr. Stork may not have been directly involved with the deceptions and would be placed on a probationary status. He would be given, essentially, a two-strikes-and-you-are-out do over. The requirements of his reprieve included at least one documented thesis to be shared with Earth for his cellular regeneration and potential cancer treatment. Other papers would be expected at given intervals, which should keep him busy and out of mischief.

Tears were shed, hugs were shared, and blessings given. It was a grieving process but one that had a remedy. Deuce was grateful for that.

Molly was listed on the manifest for departure, but no one had seen her all day. Deuce activated his iComm link to message her. Gordon and Davidette messaged her as well. None heard back. Deuce had personally prepared Kita's specimen and had it ready to hand to Molly for safe keeping. He intended to oversee all the hibernation suspensions before he allowed the vessel to leave the orbit. He would return on a shuttle.

*****

"Thank you for the tea, Mrs. Lupus." Molly sat ill-at-ease on the Lupus' veranda.

"You may call me Lily. We share one heart for the boy."

The two suns were still low, but the light was bright for morning. Michael had eaten an assortment of fruit and some sort of cereal similar to oatmeal before running off to play with a blue and white ball.

"Do you call that soccer?" Molly glanced toward Lily.

"Soccer? The game of ball? No, we have another name for it. I'm afraid your tongue would not be able to repeat it. We've tried to teach the recruits our language. I suppose you have to have the wolf lineage to pronounce our words." A gracious smile parted her lips.

"Perhaps." Molly stared at Michael as he manipulated the ball with ease. "He seems to be a natural. His moth—my sister was never good at sports. I was the athlete. Funny how twins can be so different." She gazed into her tea cup.

Lily's eyes remained on Molly. "What are you going to do, Miss Jacobsen?"

She lifted her eyes to meet Lily's. Tears stung, but she fought them back. "Molly."

Lily dipped her head. "Molly."

"I love my sister. When she came back to Earth, she was hysterical. She missed her child with every fiber of her being. We had no idea what she had narrowly escaped. I felt so angry. I wanted to bulldoze my way in here, rescue my nephew, and deliver him back into her arms." She swallowed.

Michael stopped the ball then slipped it on top of his foot, bouncing it gracefully while he stood balanced on the other foot. His arms held out at his side to aid in his stable gyrations. He then flipped the ball high in the air and kicked it deep into the garden, disappearing through a thick bush.

Molly returned her gaze to Lily. "I've prayed about this, Lily."

"I'm sure you have." Lily lowered her eyes to her tea. "As have I."

"I think we can come to an agreement." Molly searched the yard for Michael. He emerged from another group of trees. He waved at her and continued to kick and follow his toy.

Lily looked deep into Molly's eyes. "I'm willing to listen."

***

Three years later…

"Oh Mom." Kita paced in front of her mother.

Her father patted the seat next to him. "Honey, come sit down."

"I can't. I just can't sit down."

"Kita, sweetheart, we're lucky they have allowed us to come to the wait station, rather than making us wait on Earth. Now, please, sit down."

"I know, I know." She collapsed in a chair next to her mother.

A uniformed attendant of nondescript gender stood behind a metal and glass pedestal. It stared ahead, expressionless. Suddenly, the attendant looked up.

A green light flashed in Kita's peripheral. Her father and mother reached up to their iComm link at the same time. Apparently they had all been contacted.

"Levi Jacobsen, Sarah Jacobsen, Kita Jacobsen," the attendant announced.

"Yes?" Kita and her parents rushed to the *WAIT HERE* line.

The attendant scanned each. "Come with me, please."

"What's wrong?" Kita murmured.

The attendant led the way. They entered the exit doors and followed a long corridor to the transportation vessel. The door to the vessel swooshed open as they approached. A mechanical attendant greeted them inside the plush lounge of the interplanetary ship. Eight people gingerly walked around the lounge, recovering from stasis. Kita recognized them despite the six years that had passed. She hugged the four women and turned to her parents to introduce each by name.

The attendants stood by until the Jacobsen's indicated they were ready and continued to lead them down a flight a stairs. Icy cool air chilled Kita's skin, and goose bumps rose on her legs. Her knees grew weaker with every step.

Icy smoke billowed from the gaping lid of eight hibernation pods. Twelve remained closed, frosted over. The passengers could not be seen through the white mist. Kita hurried toward the closest capsules. She eagerly inspected the opaque whiteness. Which was Molly and which was Michael?

The escorting attendant stepped up next to the pod and turned as if presenting a display. "Our instructions were to open this pod once you three were on board."

Kita stared at the icy window. Why open only one?

A vacuum sucked air as the locks were released. The pod slowly opened and cold, white smoke slithered over the sides. The attendant stood back and waited.

As the cryo-smoke dissipated, two thick, insulated boxes appeared. Black letters, Molly's handwriting, labeled them both. One read, *Kita Jacobsen, Do Not Open*. The other, *This will explain everything*.

The attendant lifted both boxes and handed them to the Jacobsens. Kita received the one labeled for her, and Levi received the other. "Can we open this here?"

"Yes." The attendant handed him the equivalent of a box cutter, then appeared to go into a stand-by mode.

Levi cut the seal and pulled the box apart. Cradled inside was an iComm-link device. He lifted the device and pushed a red button. A virtual screen illuminated from Kita's implanted link. Her parent's seemed to be receiving the same signal.

Molly appeared on the shared video-stream.

"Hi Mom, Dad, Kita. A lot has happened in the short time I have been here. Of course, I realize for you it's been like six years since we last talked. First of all, Dad, thank you for insisting I take your Bible. You were right. It proved to be invaluable. If it were not for this"—she held the Bible up next to her face—"I don't think I would have been able to come to terms with what I am about to explain to you. Let alone make this decision."

She swallowed. "Okay, in pod number two over there is the remains of Mr. Austin Abraham, Senior. Dad, I need you to see to it that he is property escorted to the cemetery and given a respectable burial next to his wife. The instructions and directions are on an iComm device accompanying his remains. Funding information is in there, also.

"Second, the box in Kita's hands is extremely important. It contains what was stolen from her. This will insure you have an opportunity for more children, Kita. Medical instructions are inside for your healer. Deuce...um, Dr. Abraham, has made sure a thorough explanation is in the medical file enclosed with the canisters. Be careful, though, it has to remain cryogenically frozen."

Molly licked her lips. "Now. About me and about Michael. I'm staying here. I know I swore I would not do that. But things have changed. I am in love with a wonderful doctor. Yes, Dr. Deuce Abraham has stolen my heart, and I'm going to stay here and help him clean up this mess. You were right, Kita, these people are amazing and I believe my purpose, my predestined purpose, is to help them."

Her smile lit up in her tear soaked eyes. "I hope you understand, Mom and Dad. After all, it was you who groomed us to be missionaries. Who knew it would ever end up being me? But here I am and here I'll stay until the Lord tells me otherwise." A blush washed over her face as she continued to smile. "Yes, Dad, I've returned to Him. I'm not saying I've rededicated my life, but I'm working on it."

Sarah took Levi's hand and snuggled against his arm.

Kita stared at the virtual image of her twin sister. Panic rose in her throat like a volcanic eruption. What about Michael?

"Last. We need to talk about Michael, or AJ as he is known here."

Kita's eyes widened. She'd found him!

"He was adopted by the leaders of this planet, Mr. and Mrs. Argenteus Lupus. Through extraordinary circumstances, Mr. Lupus was killed, and Lily Lupus is now the leader. She's an amazing woman and an even more incredible mother. Now, I know this isn't what I came here to do, but Kita, I'm telling you this is what is best for Michael. This is the only life he has ever known. He's only seven years old. Well, by the time you hear this, he'll be ten. Know that he is smart, athletic, and deeply loved. Lily has revealed to him that I am his aunt, and I am allowed to see him whenever I want."

Tears began to slip down Kita's face. She shook her head.

"Now, Mom and Dad, I need to communicate directly with my sister. So I'm disconnecting your link. It's a twin thing—you know."

***

Levi blinked as the virtual screen folded and closed. He rubbed Sarah's arm which was intertwined with his as he considered his daughter who continued to watch her twin's message. She bit her lip, and tears swelled in her eyes. Occasionally, she shook her head. Other times she nodded and sniffed. Molly was getting through, the way only a twin can. He'd observed, in awe, their connection all their life. He smiled at Sarah, and she smiled back. Eventually, his virtual screen lit up, and Molly appeared before them again.

"So. Mom and Dad. I'm counting on you to help Kita get through this. Please know that I am very happy. I've found where I belong. And I'm counting on technology improving to the point that we can communicate in a more timely manner. Oh, and explain to Sal for me, will ya?

LYNN DONOVAN

"Hug each other for me. I love you. This is me,"—a stiff hand snapped to her brow—"Officer Molly Nicole Jacobsen, signing off." She broke off the salute, and the virtual screens closed.

One tear trailed the other on Kita's face. She turned to her mother. "Mom, I have to go."

Sarah met Levi's loving eyes. She turned to her daughter. "We know."

Levi turned to the attendant. "Excuse me."

It revived. "How may I help you, Levi Jacobsen?"

"Is this vessel scheduled to return to Omicron?"

"Yes. Twelve Earth passengers are scheduled to leave in seven days, eighteen hours and thirty-five minutes. And a tentative manifest has been reserved for one to three passengers of your choosing."

Molly had anticipated every possibility. He smiled at his wife. She nodded.

Levi turned back to the attendant. "Well, consider all three of those reservations filled."

THE END

Dear Reader,

Remember, the highest compliment you can give an author is to tell your friends to read their book. If you enjoyed this story, please post a review on <u>amazon.com</u>, <u>goodreads.com</u>, or wherever you shop online for your reading adventures.

And I thank you from the bottom of my heart! I do what I do for an audience of one, God, but your loyal readership allows me to continue to publish and plant His seeds. Thank you!

~Lynn

About the Author

Lynn Donovan spends her days chasing after her muses, trying to get them to settle down long enough to write down their words and actions. The results have produced short stories published in anthologies, full-length novels and one novella.

Lynn enjoys reading and writing Christian fiction, paranormal, and speculative fiction. But you never know what her muses will come up with for a story, so you could see a novel under any given genre. All that can be said is keep your eyes open, cause these muses are not sitting still for long! Oops, there they go again…

You can learn more about Lynn on her blog, SittingOnThePorchWithLynn.blogspot.com, follow her on Twitter @MLynnDonovan, LinkedIn.com at M Lynn Donovan, Face Book at MLDonovan, her Face Book Author page at LynnDonovanFGG, and her website, http://www.lynndonovanwriter.com

Next in this series:

Cloned Chaos

Kita and her parents, Levi and Sarah Jacobsen, take the next transport to Omicron, each with their own agenda. But what they find is nothing like what they expected. Kita has to sort out the chaos and decide what's best for Michael, herself, and the man she left behind on the distant planet. Her twin sister seems to have the perfect life but Kita doesn't know everything.

Levi and Sarah Jacobsen find themselves in a position of mentoring the emotionally wounded Pastor Oliver Pugh, and the Interim Pastor, Jacques Breneé, isn't obliging to Pugh's trauma. Plus, the Jacobsens are placed in charge of the moral issue pertaining to the hybrid clones. They do not fit easily into either society. What is best for them?

Deuce and Molly have accepted their role as head of The Abraham Project and must define what that means for them and for the locals. Will the Chaos tear her family apart. Or will their faith in God be the glue that binds them all back together in time for the birth of their first child?

Watch for this publication in 2016

Other Publications by this Author

Anthologies
The Clockwork Dragon
Supernatural Colorado
Different Dragons II

Novels
The Spirit of Destiny Series-
The Wishing Well Curse
Thorns of Betrayal
Secret Voices

Rocking Horse Shadows

Novella
Christmas Grace, Signing Seeds

Coming in 2016

Cloned Chaos
Echoes from the Loft